DOG-HEAD
Tales from the Neotropics

Three Fictions
Michael Jarvis

Field of Vision Books
Miami, Florida

Dog-Head
Tales from the Neotropics
Copyright © 2015 by Michael Jarvis
Field of Vision Books
All Rights Reserved
Printed in the United States by Lightning Source,
an Ingram Content Group
ISBN 978-0-9885389-5-5

Illustrations by the author

For invaluable editorial assistance,
the author thanks Justine Tal Goldberg

For Beverly
And for Lt. Col. Edmund Ellis Jarvis

Thus men forgot that All deities reside in the human breast.
—William Blake

The civilized man is a more experienced and wiser savage.
—Henry David Thoreau

How can anyone see straight when he does not even see himself and that darkness which he himself carries unconsciously into all his dealings?
—Carl Jung

• CONTENTS •

DOG-HEAD   1

REMNANTS   53

MOHO BIGHT   173

DOG-HEAD

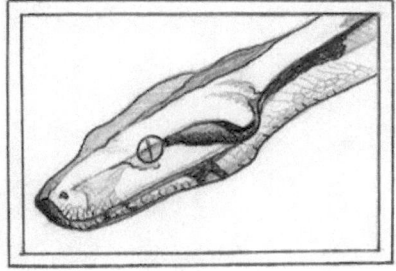

Now the sneaking serpent walks in mild humility,
And the just man rages in the wilds
Where lions roam.
—William Blake

The island, all green mountains and mist, rose out of the crux of two seas. The warm aquamarine of the Caribbean brushed against one side; the darker, rougher Atlantic crashed into the other, spraying the jagged rocks and wind-carved shrubs, constantly sharpening the edges of intricate recesses where small, gray crabs scurried and clung.

Rough cliffs came up to a point overlooking two small bays. On the point, in a clearing behind a dense jumble of short, thorny trees, sat a small wooden house. Large yellow hibiscus flowers stared wide open into the clearing and little green hummingbirds stabbed and poked at them, flitting from one to the other like tiny hyper-surgeons with impossible schedules. Burning pink bougainvillea climbed the house, thick as paint. Out of the sea a double rainbow arched back into the mountains behind the house like the plumes of some monstrous tropical bird.

Harlan Rivers sat in a lawn chair intently following the definition of clouds on the horizon, as if he might see his next move in the slow convolutions. He'd arrived on the island the day before, taking an impulsive vacation to see a girl he hadn't seen for two years. Her name was Patty Roberts. They'd met in England while she was an agriculture student and he was on a European holiday. It had been an instant romance—fast, fun and satisfying. Temporary destiny. They had kept in touch, sporadically, and several months ago she'd gotten a job in the islands with the banana industry. He'd finally taken up the open invitation to visit her—much closer than England now—but arrived during harvest time and immediately regretted the timing.

Patty was an efficiency expert, down on the coast to inspect the fruit and the transfer to ship. At the main depot he'd found her, pale British in khakis and boots, amid black men unloading trucks and stacking boxed bananas. Standing there— straight brown hair falling limply around her neck, hands on hips and sweat stains down the sides of her baggy shirt—she'd seemed surprised to see him, but they had hugged briefly and everyone had stopped working long enough to notice. After that he'd wandered off to look around until she finished.

A huge white freighter was anchored offshore; small wooden boats carried the bananas to it. Beside the jetty a few derelict boats lay sideways in shallow water, sand-stuck and peeling. Chickens with scrawny yellow necks—missing feathers as if they'd already been partly wrung—flipped bits of debris along the shoreline. Farther down the road a black and white goat stretched for a bite of grass, tethered to a monochromatic mass of rust that had once been a Toyota. Several young boys, dark-naked and skinny, played at the shore, trying all at once to swing from a rope tied to a coconut palm that hung out over the water.

At a little restaurant near the water Harlan drank rum punch and watched an old woman, barefoot in a torn, flower-print dress, walking along the beach with a single coconut balanced on her head, her brown, wrinkled arms swinging free at her sides. The sun, a great red ball, sank ever so slowly into the sea and then, as it does, the last half slipped quickly out of sight. The sizzling Harlan heard sounded almost like the faraway hiss of solar steam. He smelled chicken cooking on an open grill; smoke swirled around him. The red-orange light on the water receded, was pulled back to the horizon and sucked over the edge, then rearranged into broad rosy streaks and splayed up into the pale blue of the lower sky. He shut his eyes and slid down in his chair. A radio clicked on; the swaying rhythm of a French-laced dance song crept over him, seemed to gently push his head from side to side. He smiled to himself and relaxed even deeper, thinking he'd be hard to find out here. But sand flies found him, bit into his ankles, piercing his mood and marking the start of night. He finished his drink and left.

By streetlight he took a look at the harbor neighborhood, a sort of wood and tin-roofed amalgamation of shops and dwellings. Strolling casually he stuck to the brighter, busier areas and moved through the people and the traffic, never stopping to linger long.

Back near the depot the line of pickup trucks waiting to off-load was even longer after nightfall. Men stood in groups talking near their vehicles—headlights and radios on, engines off. Every little while they would all move forward a truck length. Near the front Harlan passed a group of young men, dark faces laughing, and suddenly a voice reached out to him. "How you find it, mahn?"

"Find what?"

"Dis little island."

"Fine, so far so good." They were passing a bottle of rum around and offered him some. Strong stuff, it burned going down. He exhaled loudly; a couple of them laughed.

"You a touriss, mahn?"

"Maybe," he said, "but I really came to see that lady," and he pointed into the open building where they could all see Patty holding a clipboard and gesturing to a co-worker.

There was a pause, then someone said, "She a busy woman, dat one."

And Harlan said, "I think she likes her work."

He heard a murmur in the crowd, "Hmmm," then, "She goin to inspec your fruit?" Laughter broke out all around. Another voice added, "An put it in a box?" Fresh laughter. Hand slapping.

Harlan laughed too. "We'll see." He took a long swallow of rum. The truck ahead started up. "Thanks," he said, and handed the bottle back.

"Okay, mahn. Alright."

He walked over to Patty's Land Rover, climbed inside and waited in the passenger seat with a burning throat.

The drive home, to the village where Patty rented a house, took about half an hour. It was late, there was little traffic and she drove fast, blowing the horn automatically before each turn, scanning the next curve for headlights, talking loudly over the engine about bananas and agriculture. Harlan listened for a while, leaning against each turn, watching the road attentively. The car rode roughly, even without hitting the potholes that pitted the twisting road. Rock walls loomed over one side; on the other, the surface dropped off into vine-filled ravines. There was no mention of their first meeting, two years ago. Harlan became uneasy, bouncing along. She seemed consumed with work. Overtired. Finally, when she stopped talking, he thought about the men drinking in line and their fruit inspection joke, but didn't mention it.

When they got to the house Harlan brought in his bag and Patty collapsed in a chair. He stood looking at her with a question on his face. She looked down at her work boots and after a long while said, "I think I'm getting emotionally involved with a man I work with."

He watched bits of dried mud fall to the floor as she scraped one boot with the other. "Thanks for letting me know."

"It just happened recently."

6

"This should be a great vacation," he said.

"We don't have to be lovers for you to enjoy yourself here."

"Really? How do you know that?"

"I just do."

"I'm happy to have your intuition on my side."

And that was it. He wasn't really surprised, not after all this time, just disappointed. Not so much with the woman he saw now but with the loss of the feeling he'd tried to excavate from the past. And with the withering of an expectation that had grown over old memory and into new desire.

She went to bed and after a while Harlan realized that besides feeling disappointed he was also famished. He found half a papaya and some stale coconut cakes in the kitchen and went outside to eat. Afterward he stood listening to the surf bashing down below. The air, full and fragrant, pressed against him and he took it in deeply. Dark mountains stood out clearly against a light sky. The ocean, compressed between the land and the horizon, rippled under a thin layer of moonlight. Eventually he felt sleepy, less hollow, and went inside. He washed his face and sticky hands and brushed his teeth. Quietly he got into the bed beside Patty and lay still, listening to crickets—he couldn't tell if they were inside or out—until he fell asleep. The night passed calmly and when he woke, the sunlight coming through wooden louvers lay in bright stripes on the wall by his head, and Patty was gone.

Harlan sat through the morning watching the landscape, drinking coffee, and wondering if he should leave. By turns he felt unwelcome, unconcerned, anxious and relaxed. Somehow detached. Take it easy, he thought. Look around. Meet some other people. Explore the lush land. The place looks good. More primitive than he imagined.

On the kitchen table he found a note.

Please make yourself at home. If you don't mind, pick up

some fresh bread in the village across the road and up the hill. There is a good beach not too far away. The map below will help you find it. If you have trouble, ask anyone you see for Hidden Bay beach. And if you get lost, my house is in the village of Bonbaie. I shouldn't be too late tonight. Have fun and be careful in the jungle. Don't worry, there are no poisonous snakes here.   Patty

The map showed the road, a series of curves, two villages, an arrow at the start of a trail, and the trail itself winding down to the beach.

Bonbaie seemed to consist of forty or fifty small wooden houses along a red dirt track that gradually wound up a slope and out of sight. On the hillside dense vegetation climbed up and pushed itself upon the village. Here and there flame trees burst blooming out of the green sprawl like fixed fireworks. People greeted Harlan with smiles and upraised hands. Fruit trees and flowers grew between the houses; chickens were everywhere. He passed a field, across which a church and a concrete schoolhouse faced each other like opposing forces. Further up an old lady in a straw hat was baking bread, little loaves the size of bananas, in a smoke-blackened kitchen hut adjacent to her house. Harlan spoke with her through the doorway for several minutes after his purchase. He explained that he was visiting Patty—the old lady smiled—and that he enjoyed the countryside and planned to walk to Hidden Bay. She offered to send her grandson to show him the way and when he declined politely, she jumped outside suddenly, plucked a few grapefruit from a nearby tree and shoved them at Harlan. Surprised, he accepted them, thanking her as he dropped one and picked it up, stuffing them all into his daypack on top of the bread. They said goodbye and he walked away with the elation of a stranger accepted by natives. His former misgivings gave way to serenity and he ambled off down the hill nodding pleasantly to those he encountered.

At the bottom of the hill just off the road, some children

were collecting fallen fruit under a huge breadfruit tree. A little girl about six years old was trying to make a neat pile of those already found, and two boys, a year or two older, were foraging for more, spreading out through the vines and undergrowth where errant fruit might have rolled. As Harlan approached the road the girl looked up at him with big brown eyes and a small mouth that rounded in curiosity; she dropped her task and moved in his direction. She stopped suddenly. Between them, nearly blending into the rocks on the path, a small, thin snake lay motionless. Harlan bent forward to examine it—black and white pattern, sort of checkered and less than two feet long—when the little girl let out a shriek. "Stink snake!" she cried. The two boys came running to the girl, who had already gathered a handful of rocks. She began to throw them at the snake, not very accurately, but forcefully. The slender reptile jerked its head back and started to move away from the children, closer to Harlan, who hadn't moved at all. One of the boys, holding a single weighty breadfruit, a textured green cannonball, stepped forward and raised the weapon over his head.

"Hey!" Harlan yelled. He took a quick step, leaned to scoop up the snake with one hand and raised his other in self-defense. A rock hit his leg and the breadfruit burst heavily on the ground, spotting his tennis shoes with pithy green bits. Straightening, he held the writhing snake high over his head and glared at the children, who stood transfixed.

He thrust his snake-wrapped fist out toward them—the serpent struggled and strained to free itself, stretching outward away from its captor and swinging down closer to the children. In wide-eyed terror they stumbled backward, one boy running onto the road. A horn blared twice. A car coming around the bend swung wide to miss the boy and blew the horn again, angrily, steadily, and Harlan—his arm still outstretched—saw the passengers staring at him as the car curved out of sight. The children cut a wide berth around him and ran up the path on the hill.

Harlan slung the snake—whipping it through the air like cooked spaghetti—across the road where it landed in a bush, bounced once and disappeared from view. He turned quickly to look behind him; the children had stopped halfway up the path and stood together staring at him. Farther up on the side of the hill, a man—shirtless in the sun and motionless as a tree—held a machete and watched Harlan. Standing like some dazed reprobate, Harlan stared back; he could even see the sweat glistening like oil on the man's skin. Then, unexpectedly, a strong smell crawled into his nostrils. Mechanically, he brought his hand to his nose, sniffing, and jerked it away. A pungent odor, thick and musky as a fox, clung to his hand. He examined it closely; there were no marks. The snake had not bitten, but had loosed a peculiar excretion that was not so much a defense as an unpleasant reminder of the encounter. He squatted and wiped his hand vigorously in the roadside weeds, then ripped out a handful and rubbed it between both hands as if he were washing them. Laughter reached him, engulfed him like another scent; he looked up to see the kids howling and pointing. "Little shits," he muttered, wiping his hands on his pants and standing up. He adjusted his pack and moved on down the road, a marked man, trailing the awkward aroma of embarrassment, his previous serenity supplanted by indignation.

He found the trail easily and plunged into the forest, downhill toward the sea. Unseen doves scattered in flurries overhead, breaking the stillness with sudden noises: quick squeaks like rusty wheels and nervous, rapid flappings that seemed to come from all directions at once and receded so fast as to be utterly startling. He scrambled ahead, sliding on leaves, grabbing tall thin saplings for support. Prompting tree lizards to shift quickly on their trunks, revolving out of sight. Finally he had to stop; the path split into several choices. Once his breathing slowed he could hear nothing. It was absolutely still, cool and quiet. Overhead he didn't even see the sky; the canopy of vegetation allowed only rounded fragments of sunlight to dapple the dark forest floor. He proceeded instinctively and soon caught a glimpse of blue sea. The path ended in a sandy stand of coconut palms. There were several piles of husks, wiry brown mounds, but no other signs of people.

Across the mouth of the bay a line of rocks caught the surf and broke it up, releasing only secondary, diluted waves to lap the thin crescent of white sand. The inner periphery, tall palms and bushy sea grapes, came almost to the water; beyond that was swampy jungle. At each end tree-covered cliffs closed the cove from view. Deserted and beautiful. He took off his shoes and walked the length of it, enjoying the solitude, feeling special, select. He dropped his pack in the shade, waded into the surf and swam out to the rocks, over blurry coral heads, wishing he had a mask. He floated, rocking softly, seeing without hearing, looking at the sky. He saw the clouds as great banks of brain coral. Back over sand in shallower water, he dove down and felt the bottom, moving along like a cruising shark, feeling cleansed. Surfacing, he smelled his hand and was surprised to find the snake's scent still present. At the shore he rubbed a handful of sand into his hand and forearm, thinking the rough, salty particles might wear away or absorb the organic odor that clung to his skin. It was the smell of deep earth, fungus-like and raw, and it seemed significant somehow as he stood alone at the edge of the jungle, as if he'd met and now felt the essence of something acutely primordial.

He looked up to see a figure walking toward him from the same direction he'd come. He rinsed his arm and waited, glancing once at his belongings. A boy of about fourteen, clad only in red shorts, approached him walking smoothly and slowly, as if he had all the time in the world. He stopped a few feet from Harlan; a wave fused him to the sand and joined the two of them.

"Snake Mahn," he said.

"Jesus." Harlan laughed. "News travels fast around here."

The boy looked intently at him. "Why you doan kill de snake?"

11

"The thing was this big," Harlan said, holding up his hands for measure. "Harmless. There was no reason to kill it."

"De people here doan like snake."

"People don't seem to like them much anywhere." He wondered if the boy had ever been anywhere else. "Why do you think that is?"

The boy answered without hesitation, "Tet-Chien."

"What's that?"

"Big snake. Very mean."

"Yeah?" He looked past the boy, into the jungle. "How big?"

The boy pointed at the nearest palm tree, one nearly thirty feet tall. "Very big," he said solemnly.

"Oh really?" Harlan smirked. "And where would I find one of these big guys?"

"In de bush."

Harlan looked hard for signs of a joke, but the boy seemed quite serious. "Well I'd sure like to see one." He smiled. "You see, I like snakes."

The boy grinned. "Stay in de bush all night maybe he fine you."

"Perfect! We could drink some rum around the campfire and come back to the village the best of friends."

"Hah hah hah." The boy let out a burst of laughter. "You crazy, mahn."

Harlan rubbed salt off his forehead; it was hot in the sun. "What's your name?"

"Nurius."

"Nurius," Harlan said. "Nurius the curious." He stuck out his hand. "Mine's Harlan."

Nurius shook the hand. "I can show you de snake stone."

"What's the snake stone?"

"Indian place."

Harlan waited for more information but it wasn't forthcoming. "You mean it's a carving or something?"

"De snake, he make de stone by heself."

Harlan ran his hand through his wet hair. "Look, is this a real place? No bullshit."

"Sure, mahn. Very real. True."

He studied the boy's face and looked again at the palm tree. "How far away is this stone?"

"Tirty minute."

"Okay," he said, moving to gather his things. "Let's go."

"Five dollar."

"Ah, Christ!" Harlan turned back to face him. "This isn't a tourist place is it?"

"No way. De stone in de bush."

"Alright. But we'll take a look first. Okay?"

Nurius shrugged and immediately set off. Harlan slung his pack over one shoulder, took a look down the beach, saw no one, grabbed his shoes and fell into step behind his guide.

Inside the treeline another path presented itself, winding into dense foliage, rising toward the road—or at least where Harlan thought the road should be—and cutting back downward. Nurius moved effortlessly through the filtered light, intimate with the ground. Harlan struggled through the steamy air, trying to keep up, telling himself to get in better shape, trying to breathe regularly through his nose. But the ground was uneven and the path frequently disappeared, bush-closed; he would come crashing through to find Nurius standing still, gazing ahead patiently while he waited, before gliding off again. Once, Harlan came over a small rise to find the boy bent over a gurgling stream, drinking from a wild banana leaf he'd fashioned into a cup. He handed it to Harlan, who took great gulps of the clear, cool water and let the rest run down his chin and neck. He was breathing heavily, feeling his sweat surfacing and soaking into his shirt and beading up on his face and hairline. He looked at his watch. "Are we almost there?"

"Not far."

Harlan filled the leaf again and drank more slowly,

watching a small yellow-breasted bananaquit watching him; he dropped the leaf in the stream and the bird disappeared.

They continued. Though still in thick jungle, Harlan thought he could hear the coastline through the trees. Quite suddenly they broke into a small clearing and were standing on a slab of dark-gray rock. The surface was porous and in some places long, thin green stems with angular red flowers grew out and hung over it like the spindly arcs of spiders' legs. The platform of rock resembled a rough stage, supporting at its center a strange vertical protuberance, some growth of itself that rose straight up ten or twelve feet. The stone column was as gnarled as driftwood and stood like some outdoor stalagmite, alone, untouched by hanging limbs or vines. Through the opening in the tree roof, the sun cast light onto the form. Harlan walked up close and moved in a circle around it, amazed, looking for signs of human handiwork or a seam between base and pillar. He saw none. It appeared to be all one piece, a natural creation erupted from the earth—a volcanic rope, thick as an old tree, twisted and piled up on top of itself—in a bizarre occurrence from a far-off instant. A totem of an earlier time.

Then he saw it. Out of the form, the snake. A stone constrictor wrapped upon itself in a pillar of curves. The long body wound upward to the top and came back down, entwined in itself. Midway down was a great square head with hollow sockets, with a jawline tucked into the body and a crease that defined the mouth. Clamped shut. At a certain angle, nearly a smile. Crude yet distinct, it stared out at the viewer dispassionately. Cool, bloodless stone.

Nurius sat at the edge of the rock surface eating a guava; a dozen more lay scattered beside him. Harlan saw the tree nearby heavily laden with the small, round fruit, ripe-yellow and beckoning. He walked over to Nurius and picked one up, held it up and turned it around for inspection. "Beautiful," he said, "just for the picking." He looked slowly around the area and started to smile. "This might have been the Garden of Eden."

Nurius stopped chewing, bits of the sticky fruit clinging to his lips, and stared up at him.

"The original Garden of Eden, man," Harlan continued, pointing at the snake stone with the small fruit. "Only it wasn't an apple. It was a goddamn guava." He bit into the soft fruit with delight, squeezing the skin and sucking the sweet, purplish pulp into his mouth, then laughed and in a dramatic gesture, slung the skin to the center of the clearing. It hit the stone and stuck below the head, leaving a bright yellow spot on the dull gray.

Nurius laughed, picking up a handful of the guavas as he stood. He hurled them one after the other at the target. They smacked loudly, flecking the body with color and giving the stone serpent's skin a random pattern.

Harlan felt a queasy sense of violation welling up in him like bubbles rising underwater. As if he were shoplifting or grave-robbing. "Okay, okay!" he shouted at Nurius. The laughter died away. He held up his hand for silence. Standing perfectly still he listened, straining to hear and staring into the trees beyond the clearing. It was dead quiet and though the area around them still had light, the forest was shifting down toward darkness, beginning to shed its greenness. "It's getting late," he said. "We should get moving."

"Doan worry, mahn. I know de way."

Harlan thought he detected irritation in the boy's voice. As he stepped off the rock onto the ground, he glanced back once more at the vertical stone. That's all he saw. The snake was gone. He squinted hard, not believing his own vision. The stone was there: rock was rock. Everything looked the same but his eyes weren't picking out the particular relief that created the reptilian form. He shook his head, closed his eyes for a second and tried again. Nothing. An optical illusion, the snake somehow camouflaged.

A rapid fluttering of wings broke the stillness too quickly. He jumped, wild-eyed. Across the clearing the shrill, penetrating whistle of a tree frog sounded and was answered in seconds by

15

others. The noise encircled him like a fog. He whirled into the path—Nurius was nowhere in sight—and dove blindly into the shadowland.

He picked up the trail and managed to find his way back without seeing the boy. He followed the boy's footprints across the beach and climbed the trail toward the road. Finally stepping out of the dark trees he found Nurius sitting on a stone at the roadside. He paid the boy and they walked along in silence, then parted with a few words below the village. Harlan got home while it was still twilight.

He showered, had a snack and wandered outside in the darkness. Back inside he tried to read but couldn't. He lay down and fell into a light sleep. The Land Rover, crunching gravel, woke him.

"Ah, the banana republican returns," he said as Patty entered.

She looked tired but smiled nonetheless as she sighed and dropped her bag. "Hi, Harlan. How was your day?"

"Not bad," he said. "A little adventure."

"Oh really?" Her eyebrows rose. "Did you find the beach alright?"

"Yeah, I did. Thanks for the map." He thought back into the day. "And I got some bread." They stood looking at each other, feeling a mutual awkwardness.

"Oh, I brought some fresh fish from town," she said, digging into her bag. "There's a grill outside against the house. Maybe you could start on the fish while I shower and when I get out I'll make a salad."

"Okay, sure. I'm starved."

"Me too."

When everything was nearly ready he toasted some bread on the edge of the grill. Beside the open door they feasted on small, tender redfish, cooked whole with lime, pepper and basil, a salad of tomato and shredded cabbage, salted and limed, with crisp bread and iced rum to fill in the cracks. Harlan recounted

16

the basic events of his day. Patty listened without much comment, seeming to enjoy her visitor's enjoyment and sucking thoughtfully on fish bones. She had never been to the snake stone, but had heard of it. "The Indians that were here said a great snake came out of the sea, created the island and lived in a cave in the mountains. They said when strange men came, the snake went away and left the stone behind. That's the legend, anyway."

"You really should see it," he said.

"One day when I have more time for sightseeing I will."

He asked about the big snake, the real one.

"I haven't seen one but there is some kind of boa constrictor here."

"No kidding." He considered this. "They're not usually all that big."

"I guess they've found a few larger than usual. And when you consider the natives' fear of snakes you can imagine the exaggerations."

Harlan sipped his rum. "Nurius had another name for the boa. Tet— Tet—"

"Tet-Chien."

"That's it. What's that mean?"

"Remember your French?"

"No, I never had any."

"Dog-Head."

"Dog-Head? I don't get it."

"That's what they call it. I don't know, maybe there's some resemblance."

He got up, cut a grapefruit in half and grilled it too. Then he cut out the sections and dripped honey over them for dessert. When he came back to the table he poured two more drinks.

"That's enough for me," she said. They sat without talking for a while, sipping in separate preoccupations. "I have to go over to St. Vincent for a few days," she said. "Maybe a week."

"When?"

17

"In the morning. They're starting to harvest."

"And you'd like me to leave?"

"No, no, you can stay if you want to. I'll show you where to leave the key and you can go when you feel like it."

He thought about it. "I'd like to stay a few more days." A night breeze came up, blew through the house. He watched the coals glowing in the grill. "I didn't think it would be like this," he said. "I didn't know what to expect, really." The thought trailed off. "But I like it here." She said nothing and when he spoke again his tone was more direct. "I'm going into the bush to look for the big snake."

Her eyes narrowed and she leaned forward in her chair. She made a sound like a small cough. "And do what if you find one?"

He shrugged. "I don't know. Maybe just look at it. Maybe catch it—" Then he had another vague idea. "And take it to the village."

"You're joking."

"No, I'm not."

She made a little laugh. "Oh, the great white hunter. What do you want to do, educate these people? You don't know anything about life here." She stood, her chair scraping backward.

He looked up at her. "I'm not interested in lying in the sun and reading Hollywood novels."

"There's a lot of room between those extremes."

"It's just something that appeals to me."

"Since when?"

"Since now."

She laughed again, shaking her head. "Are you trying to prove something to me?"

"Don't take it personally. Why? You think if I was fucking you I wouldn't be doing this?"

"Oh, that's nice. Very nice. So considerate."

"Just blunt."

"More like crude. And aggressive. I know you feel

18

rejected, but I think your reaction is a little strange, that's all."

"It's not a reaction. It's a separate thing altogether."

"It's frivolous. I'm trying to build a relationship with these people."

"And?"

"And credibility is hard to get here. For a foreigner. It can be damaged very easily and now you're going off the bloody deep end."

"Oh, that's it. I see. You're absolutely right. If I catch a snake the entire banana industry will probably just collapse."

"Don't exaggerate."

"Me? You're wrapped up in some old colonial paranoia. You think I'm going to scare people into revolution, or what?"

"This is ridiculous." She started to clear the table.

Harlan went outside, pulled a lounge chair out into the yard and lay down. The crickets conducted themselves loudly, almost obliterating all other sounds, but then behind him he heard the kitchen being cleaned up. Ordinary sounds of small purpose: running water, plates and silverware clinking together, a cabinet door closing. The sounds passed over him like the night air, soothing and tranquil as he lay gazing up into the dark sky. He felt far from home, far from himself. He remembered that people often see animal shapes in cloud formations, and now, out of the cloud banks in his mind, he witnessed graceful serpentine coils, an unknotting mass of self-defining movement. A mound of subtle undulation, it untangled and developed. There it was: a dog's head inside his own. He had fallen asleep.

He awoke in the cool dark of early morning, surprised to see that he was outside. The lounge chair creaked as he got up. He got a blanket and a cushion off the couch and returned outside to the chair, where he slept for a couple more hours until the sky attained the first faint glow of pre-dawn light. He lay still and snug under the blanket, watching the color slowly surface and expand over him. He heard the alarm clock in the house, then the bathroom water, kitchen noise, and a few minutes later, the front door opening. "I'm making tea," Patty said.

He turned his head enough to see her leaning out the door but said nothing.

She brought out two mugs and he took one, sitting up in the chair. She sat down at the other end. The tea steam drifted lazily in the cool stillness. "I have to go," she said. "Just leave the key under that first conch shell." She nodded toward the driveway.

Holding the mug with both hands he drank slowly and deliberately, nurtured by the steam. "Okay," he said, looking at her. "We probably won't see each other again."

Getting up she leaned forward and kissed him lightly on the cheek. "Be careful," she said. She went back inside and came out with two bags. She turned once more at the edge of the driveway and looked back at him sitting on the lounge. She put one bag down and waved, smiling faintly.

"Bon voyage," he said.

She backed the Land Rover out. The sound of the engine receded down the road, around a curve and was gone. He stood and stretched.

He decided to take it easy for the day and returned to Hidden Bay to swim and relax. Again, no one was there when he arrived and he marveled at the solitary beauty of the place. He swam for a long time, then lay back on the sand and watched a blue fishing boat with three men in it pass slowly by the mouth of the bay. He did some exercises in the harder sand near the water and afterwards ate the lunch he'd brought: two mangoes, a peanut butter sandwich and a ginger-flavored soft drink. He made some notes, trying to organize the bush expedition he had in mind. In the early afternoon some young boys arrived to fish from the rocks at the edge of the bay. He watched them from the shade of a palm tree for a while, then left. On the way back through the forest he moved slowly and quietly, searching the branches overhead for the ripple of movement or the stationary pattern, juxtaposed with leaves and limbs, that could reveal the creature he sought. He saw nothing but tree lizards.

Later in the afternoon he went into the village, bought a few items, strolled around talking to people—the old bread lady was happy to see him again—and made casual inquiries about locals who spent time in the bush. He got the name of Johnny Figaro.

That night he went looking for Johnny Figaro on a tour of the local rum shops where the village men met to play dominoes, drink and talk. There were a couple in the village itself and a couple more on the main road between Bonbaie and the next closest village. He found Johnny Figaro at Roger's Goodwill Bar on the main road. There were some cars and small pickup trucks along the road in front of the place and music blared out of the open door. Inside, the ruckus of voices and laughter hummed and jangled and the sharp cracks of dominoes slapping wood split the night.

Johnny Figaro, in jeans and a tee shirt, was playing dominoes, sitting still and quiet, holding all seven pieces in one hand and watching the opening plays. He was dark with high cheekbones and a faint slant to his eyes. He slammed a piece down, breaking the symmetry of the column on the table; the ends of his hair, hanging out wiry and unruly, quivered with the impact. He smiled, his teeth the backsides of dominoes.

Harlan stood at the bar drinking a beer, watching the game. And Johnny, having heard he was wanted, regarded Harlan casually from time to time between his turns. In fact everyone in the place—from the loud boys around the doorway to the grizzled old men in baseball caps playing checkers—noticed Harlan because he was the only outsider and the only white. He sensed no tension though and felt fairly relaxed. Yet he was intent, focused on his plan as he saw it progressing. It wasn't obsession, but the idea had momentum; it excited and lifted him in a way he couldn't explain.

One of the boys next to Harlan at the bar spoke to him. A loud conversation ensued over the music. Harlan bought the next round and then the boys, friendly and eager to talk, reciprocated. They insisted that he wouldn't be sorry if he remained through the weekend. For the action.

"De girls comin out and about."

"Dancing and drinking in the street," Harlan said.

"Dat's right, mahn. An dey love to meet a stranger." They all laughed and the boy closest to Harlan fixed him with a broad grin.

"You like dese island girls?"

"Yeah," Harlan said. "All kinds."

The boy slapped the bar at this and nodding his head vigorously, said, "True, true."

When Harlan turned for his beer he found Johnny Figaro standing next to him. They were the same height; at eye level they checked each other—the face, the look in the eyes, the set of the mouth, the expression, the attitude—for motive and mutual interest. For trust. All this in a second.

"My name's Harlan," he said. "I wanted to talk about the bush." Johnny said nothing and Harlan made a suggestion. "Let's get some rum and go outside."

Johnny beckoned to the barman, speaking rapidly in the island patois. The barman set down a gin bottle that held what appeared to be a bunch of weeds suspended in a clear liquid. Harlan stared at the bottle and made a face. "Cask rum," Johnny said. "De plant cut de taste, make a smooth blend."

Harlan took a sip and gasped, his mouth open wide to get air. It was like grain alcohol with an anisette aftertaste. They got two cups with ice, took the bottle and went out into the street.

Leaning against a car away from the light and activity around the entrance, Harlan slowly worked up to his proposal. He wasn't quite sure how to go about it, how to explain himself, what he was after. He didn't quite know what it was himself. So he talked in wide generalities for a while, just to talk, and they kept drinking, slowly—the only way to drink the stuff—but steadily, developing the bond of strangers that comes quick with drink, conversation, and some degree of curiosity. They talked about the contrast between life in the States and here on the island, between city life and the village life they were living at the moment.

"I mean look at this." Harlan gestured at the darkness, the jungle. "Real rainforest, man. Genuine fucking paradise."

Johnny shrugged. "We got everything, but no money."

"Enjoy it while you can." Harlan pointed at the dark edge of a mountain. "Because when you get money this will be gone. You'll trade it for progress."

Johnny stared at Harlan, whose gaze was fused with the dark and whose voice went on, in a lower tone, almost lost between the bar's music and the night sounds crowding in. "It'll end up wasted, these green mountains, the clean rivers, the parrots and the frogs we're listening to. But then you'll have money, man. Condominiums and pollution and a lot more tourists. What a goddamn shame."

Johnny left to get more ice. When Harlan turned around the bar lights were fuzzy. Johnny came back into view, his plastic sandals scraping the street. He had a Coke to cut the rum further. Harlan sipped the sweeter drink and laughed. "Say goodbye to Roger's," he said. "There's going to be a shopping mall here, right where we're standing."

"What, mahn?"

"Nothing, man." Harlan waved his free hand. "I'm getting off the track here." He was swaying slightly, focusing his thoughts. "I only wanted to ask you about finding Tet-Chien."

Johnny looked a little surprised and Harlan laughed. "I was just thinking, if I'd asked about Tet-Chien in the bar, with the old guys playing checkers—"

"Dey would say dis boy like to quit livin." His eyes sparkled at Harlan.

"No. Really?"

"Dere's a lady in de village will tell you her mahn and his horse get eaten by Tet-Chien."

"She's crazy."

"At least mahn, but she will tell you dis."

"But you're not afraid?"

Johnny laughed. "No, mahn, in de bush I am de master." Harlan took this as fact and neither spoke for a few minutes. Bats flew overhead, over the bar. Johnny held up a joint. "Smoke?" he asked, and lit it, walking away from Roger's Goodwill Bar.

"This should finish me off," Harlan said.

They stopped at the outer edge of the light cast from Roger's. A few figures left the bar and glanced in their direction. The music, filtered through the night air, seemed distant now, the domino cracks muffled and mixed with exclamations and laughter. Overhead a dense starfield pressed close, draped like a cosmic blanket over the black mountains. The frogs and the insect brigades, though almost deafening, were practically unheard, so well meshed were they with the fabric of the night.

"Which work you doin in de States?"

The States? Harlan had been thinking he might be on another planet, or this planet at a much earlier time. "A teacher," he said. "History."

Johnny murmured, full of smoke, and let it out. "An what you want with Tet-Chien?"

It seemed like a long time passed as they finished the joint. Harlan let the smoke escape with his slow, tumbling verbalization. "Everyone has to educate themselves," he said, squinting upward. "Sometimes you just stumble on something."

Johnny stood gazing down the road for a long moment. "True," he said.

A car started in front of Roger's and turned around, shining its lights on them, then passed on the road. They started to walk back to the bar. "I think I need a guide in the bush," Harlan said.

"I too," Johnny said. They walked a few more steps in silence. "Come to my place in de mornin. In Bonbaie, way up de hill. Ask someone for it."

Inside the bar Harlan discovered the price of their drinks was based on what was left in the bottle. "I got it," he said, digging in his pocket.

Johnny waited, then they stepped outside together.

"I'll see you tomorrow then," Harlan said, sticking out his hand.

Johnny tapped the back of Harlan's hand with his fist, turned and went back in.

Harlan stood looking up the road. At the top of the incline two figures were moving down toward the bar. He started walking, trying not to weave too much. He passed the two boys—they nodded and he nodded—and after a few more steps turned to look behind him and saw that the boys had stopped and were looking at him. He kept walking and when he looked again they were gone. After the lights of Roger's were lost behind a curve he was alone in intermittent moonlight. It was a long walk. He passed some roadside houses, quiet and dark, and plodded along, occasionally glancing over his shoulder. There were no cars on the road; his ears strained for any unusual noise. He began to feel a creeping dread as he turned off the road into Patty's long driveway, peering into the cloud-covered darkness. He approached the dark, little house quietly, avoiding the gravel. At the end of the driveway he stopped to listen. The steady rhythm of the surf slowly reached him and had a calming effect. The moon appeared, exposing him and the house. He walked to the door, unlocked it, pulled it open and stood defiantly, backlit by the light outside. There was no one else there. He went in and closed the door, undressed, lay across the bed and quickly slipped into a deep drunken sleep from which dreams were banished.

He woke too early with a hangover and stumbled into the bathroom for aspirin and water, shielding his eyes from the bright sunlight prying in at the windows. Returning to bed he slept soundly for another hour and a half and woke this time feeling much better; his head was still foggy but there remained only traces of the previous night's distrust. He made coffee and walked outside. The day was bright, stark and clear—open, without secrets. The air felt light and he took it in hungrily. As his head cleared, the last mist of apprehension dissipated and by the time he struck out for Johnny's place he felt positively eager. The nebulous vulnerability had gone, or metamorphosed; he was left with a keen sensation of risk, an impersonal, distilled fear, not blended with the scenery or the populace, but distinct and vibrant, like a jewel in sunlight.

Johnny was outside repairing a hammock stretched between the house and a post in the yard. When Harlan appeared they shook hands. Inside the house—a raised wooden box with a door and three windows—Johnny made soft-boiled eggs, which they ate with bread baked that morning, and instant coffee, black. They agreed upon a daily fee for Johnny—he thought they would be gone two or three days—and Harlan wrote down a list of supplies. There was little in the village; he would have to go into town, the capital, that day. It was decided that they would leave for the bush early the next morning.

He tried hitchhiking but finally took a ride on an island bus that was nothing more than a pickup truck with benches. It was fairly crowded and he stood up at the back hanging onto a railing that supported a blue tarp, protection from sun or rain. He enjoyed the ride—up in the breeze swaying with the turns, with an unobstructed view of green hillsides, blue sea and other horn-blowing vehicles flying into sight around blind curves.

In town he purchased clothesline, a flashlight, a sheet of plastic, a machete, a canteen, a cooking pot and some food. Leaving the grocery mart he stepped out into a passing column of school girls: a military unit in black-braided hair, bright blue skirts and white blouses, marching home with satchels and songs. He cut through the line, creating a stir of giggles and glances, and strode up the hot street, passing alongside parked cars and open sidewalk sewers harboring trickles of grayish water, bits of refuse and pecking chickens.

In the evening he walked off his restlessness up and down

the village road, then the main road, stopping here and there for beer and passing conversation. He got home early, checked his provisions once more, and went to bed.

In the cool dark of morning he left the key under the conch shell at the head of the driveway and started walking. He got to Johnny's place before dawn and they drank coffee, not saying much. Johnny lent him a hammock and a pair of rubber boots he had borrowed. Harlan divided the food to be carried. They traveled light; Harlan had his stuffed daypack, rounded and bulky, and Johnny had a cloth bag that with his arms through the handles he carried as a knapsack. They took the trail—a continuation of the village road—when there was enough light to see. But once in the bush the trail was nearly obscured by darkness and the coolness of the wet air was soon negated by the exertion of walking. They descended the Bonbaie ridge—Harlan following Johnny, who with his machete pushed or sliced grasses and branches away—and came down into the relatively flat expanse of a banana farm, accompanied by the shrill chirps of small birds. Walking beneath the broad, drooping leaves in an ethereal gloom of green-filtered light, they stepped softly on shed leaves and heard only the sporadic pattering of ground lizards moving away in bursts of wary speed. Johnny broke off several green bananas and put them in his bag; Harlan looked about uneasily. The place was still as a cemetery. In every direction were more banana trees. They moved through rows of sticky trunks and hard bunches of hanging fruit. Finally they reached the other side and waded into tall grass over their heads. They came out on the bank of a narrow river full of huge rocks and hopped out to one in the middle.

The sun had not yet gotten over the mountains but it was hot now. Harlan's shirt was soaked and covered with grass seeds. Johnny told him they would follow the river upstream for a while; there was no hurry. Harlan took off his shirt and boots and sat down, dangling his feet in the cold water. Johnny crossed the river and disappeared on the other side. He returned minutes later with a green coconut and a shirt-full of guavas; he tossed one to Harlan and dumped the rest on the bank. Harlan was about to bite into the fruit when something underwater touched his foot. He scrambled up onto the rock, cursing and peering into the rush of water and bubbles below.

Crouching in the shallows, Johnny looked over his shoulder and laughed. "Crayfish, mahn," he said. "Keep de spot. Maybe you do de eatin." He suddenly shoved his hands in the water and splashed several minnows onto the grass. He cut them into bits of bait, selected a flexible branch about two feet long and attached a short line and a tiny hook he pulled from a pouch hanging around his neck. He hopped from stone to stone to where Harlan stood, carefully baited the hook and slid it into the water on the downstream side of the rock, where there was no current. Squatting on the rock they both leaned over and stared at the line. Shortly, there was a minute tug; Johnny pulled the stick slightly and the line went taut. He gestured for Harlan's shirt, took it in one hand and with a gentle, steady effort pulled the line up.

"Jesus Christ!" Harlan said. A crayfish nearly a foot long hung by its mouth from the bait, its pincers out to the side, grasping the air. Johnny wrapped the shirt around it, pulled the hook free and went to the bank. From his gear he took a plastic bag, shoved the crayfish inside and weighted it down in the shallows with a fist-sized stone. Within twenty minutes he had caught two more—one nearly as large as the first and one about half its size—and started a small fire between stones on the bank. The sun was out and Harlan lay in a pool in the middle of the stream with only his head showing.

In a pot of boiling water Johnny cooked green bananas and onions, then added a handful of brown, pea-sized river snails for flavor. Last, he dumped in the live crayfish; their dark, mottled shells, the color of river rocks below the surface, quickly became the livid red of cooked crustacean. After adding lime juice and salt they sat on mashed-down grass along the bank and ate the steaming tails and claws, then leisurely sucked out the heads and legs. The bananas were soft and sweet, like the onions, and after they were gone, Johnny drank the juice from the pot and slung the remaining snail shells back into the river. They drank coconut milk, which had cooled slightly in the river, and afterward scooped out the sweet jelly meat. Harlan cleaned the pot with wet sand and lay back in the warm grass and napped for a while. He came out of a mild torpor feeling a little itchy, as though he had become insect terrain. He lay underwater in the swiftest current, arms and legs pressed against rocks, and emerged cool and alert. Sunlight glittered on the surface of the water upstream. Downstream, Johnny was finishing a bath. Harlan scooped water onto the dying coals, raising a small cloud of ash and steam, then rolled the perimeter stones back into the river and splashed more water on the remains of the fire.

Against the current they moved from stone to stone or waded in the shallows, following the river toward the interior, away from the coast. The river was open, sunny, providing space in front and behind; on both sides the bush closed in. Ahead lay higher ground, mountains, rainforest, the wet mists at the top, blue sky. A chicken hawk drifted over them. In the overhanging vegetation along the banks bananaquits and finches twittered in tiny, shrill tones. The air was still and hot; the river kept the two men cool. They stayed with the river until mid-afternoon, combing the banks with their eyes and stopping frequently to submerge in deep spots. Once, they found a small black and white snake like the one the kids had tried to kill, and they studied it for a minute, the slim form so still, delicately poised on a branch, staring back at them. But they sought something bigger, just as quiet and still, perhaps, yet eminently more capable. An invisible creature living on stealth and strength in two worlds—in a dense shadowy world of trees and rain and rotting wood, and in another world of unseen fears and legend.

For some time they had seen the circling of buzzards ahead, near the river, and as they got closer they could tell that some of the birds were descending. They left the river, hacked through a tangle of low vegetation and came upon a neglected field of banana and lime trees that was being reclaimed by the bush. They saw no people, no house. Near the center of the field a group of the large black birds huddled on the ground; several more were in a taller tree at the edge of the field. As the two men approached, the birds spread out, some flapping a few yards away and some lifting off to the tree. There were a few squawking complaints. On the ground, lying on its side in the sun, was a black pig, whole and intact and without any visible wounds except for the nicks and cuts around its face where the vultures had started. Its mouth was open; black flies covered the snout and the edges of the mouth. Johnny turned the pig over with his foot—the flies rose in a buzzing unit and quickly resettled. The pig fell stiffly, flatter side up, bristles matted down but no marks seen.

"He die dis mornin," Johnny said, "but not from a hunter."

Harlan stared down at the pig. "Tet-Chien?"

Johnny shrugged. "Maybe his heart stop."

They walked back to the river and continued upstream through a dazzling light that played off the water, the rocks and the trees along the banks. To Harlan it was a flickering light that unified and balanced everything so that each stone, each ripple, every bend in the course looked the same, in the way that the black flies on the dead pig's face were all alike. His feet were bruised and tired; he kept walking, lulled by the sameness of his surroundings, following Johnny and picking his way through the water and the stones.

They came to the spot where Johnny wanted to leave the river. Harlan sat on a rock and put on socks and boots. They climbed the bank and were in the bush. In a few minutes he realized they were on another trail, though it was barely discernable, winding into the forest and then seeming to continue in the direction they had been traveling with the river.

A hunting trail, Johnny said. And all around them was jungle—palms, tall tree ferns and taller hardwoods with hanging vines that disappeared overhead. Visibility was shallow, determined by the space between trees, by the men's shifting positions, by the illumination strained through the canopy, the filtered sunlight casting indeterminate accents, dim and brighter spots that jumped from tree to ground to vine as the leaves and limbs allowed, wind-stirred way above their heads.

They abruptly began to climb into wetter, steeper terrain where the light was more vague. They went slowly, not going any particular place but only searching, only being in the bush. Walking and plodding upward over rocks, soft ground, slick roots and fallen trunks. In a murky, ground-level closeness, a palpable density of tangle and shadow. Water dripped in slow motion. The dampness absorbed Harlan; he slowly forgot what he was doing there, why he was walking. His determination became unfocused, yet remained to push him onward. He marched without concern or confusion, passing through the forest world almost unaware of it. Thoughts slipped through his head unanchored; he had no past, no future—just the bush. His peripheral vision took in the general atmosphere; his eyes followed the placement of his feet and the position of Johnny Figaro. It seemed as though they could just continue wandering and nothing would happen.

Pulling vines to help himself up an incline, he slipped, reached out instinctively to keep his balance and grabbed the shaft of a thorny palm. It needled into his hand and broke into pieces. Releasing it he slid backwards and crashed against a tree trunk. He sat on the ground breathing heavily and examined his hand. Small black spikes were stuck in his palm. He plucked them out—spots of blood rose—and made a fist, testing the pain and smearing the blood. Somewhat dazed, he looked around slowly. Beside him a heliconia grew, its pointed blossoms—red and orange lobster claws—stabbing out of the greenery. He inhaled deeply and smelled the decay and the leaf rot, the fungus and the earth. Thin, straight seedlings reached timidly upward. Lush

31

bunches of ferns surrounded him. Sitting on the ground he could feel the regeneration, the absolute fecundity. And he smelled rain, already fallen and yet to fall.

As Harlan was getting up Johnny came back and noticed the bloody hand. "Here," he said, tipping a heliconia flower and spilling its cache of held water. And Harlan cleaned his hand this way, rubbing and rinsing with the water from several blossoms.

They trekked onward, Harlan more alert now, walking and watching with concentration, searching the foliage where orchids and bromeliads introduced themselves, where the light was better. They moved beneath giant gommier trees with long, long liana vines trailing down from the sky. At the ground the light was fading, becoming the color of tree trunks.

Moving down a gradual slope, Johnny suddenly stopped. Harlan came up beside him and stood for a minute, wondering. Then he smelled it too—smoke—but he couldn't see it. Cautiously they moved forward. A dog barked. They soon came to an outcrop of large rocks sticking out of the hillside, forming a series of cave-like shelters. The vegetation around the rocks had been cleared away. A fire burned beside one rock, blackened from previous fires. A wisp of smoke rose like a feeble gray vine through the waning light. Beyond the rocks the trail continued and a dog—a mid-sized island mutt, brown and short-haired—came toward them cautiously, barking once every few seconds, announcing their presence. Behind the dog, peering at them from between the trees, was a man. The dog stopped before the crackling fire—Harlan and Johnny stood quite still on the other side—and the man moved slowly toward them carrying a pot of water and a small-gauge shotgun. He was an old man, small and sinewy, black as a forest shadow, wearing a dirty, torn shirt, long pants rolled up at the legs and drawn up at the waist with a piece of rope, and black rubber boots. As he came toward them Johnny spoke in patois and the man listened, glancing at Harlan. The dog remained near the fire, quietly watching the two strangers. Without taking his eyes off them, the old man set the pot on the ground and straightened up again, still holding the gun. He had not yet spoken.

It was beginning to get dark—night noise had started, the volume accumulating—and Harlan grew anxious; they had no campsite yet and the darkness here would be intense. He had also gotten hungry and tired, and the old man's furtive glances were making him nervous.

Harlan took a step. The dog growled and the old man whistled to it. Johnny spoke to the man again, and then, with Harlan, walked around the dog and past the rocks to continue on the trail. The old man called out and they stopped. He reached into the rocks and pulled out a bag from which he took a light, wrinkled bundle. Cradling the gun he walked to Harlan, handed him the frayed end and backed up, unrolling a stiff, crinkling, milky snake skin about twelve feet long. Harlan stared at the skin, down the thousands of joined scales, a length of translucent pattern, to the man squinting at him from the other end. He looked at his own hands; they held the torn remains of the head, just a ragged opening with one opaque eye impression. But still an actual casing, a previous skin of Tet-Chien.

The old man began to reroll the skin, which was flexible but sounded like rustled newspaper. As he got closer to Harlan he looked up into his face and said something Harlan couldn't understand. That close, with his eyes wide and his mouth twisted open, showing the spaces of missing teeth, the odor he carried was noticeable.

Harlan backed away and when Johnny started down the trail again Harlan caught right up to him. "What did he say?"

"He say when you find de suit you will find de beast."

A few seconds later Harlan asked, "Why did he keep that skin?"

And Johnny, not answering right away, finally said, "I doan know."

They came again to the river. The sky was still twilight. The river was wider here, and across the expanse, over the water and its reflected light, the bush on the opposite bank already looked black and impenetrable. Insects screamed across the water and the answers, like echoes, shot back and forth so rapidly that the noise was constant. A bird ripped out of the trees in a flutter and disappeared over the water. Stars appeared between roving clouds, and the darkness settled loudly.

They followed the edge of the river, combing the bank with flashlights, attracting moths and other winged insects, uncovering tiny, golden frogs and large, yellow-fleshed snails clinging to leaves, frozen in the light. Mosquitoes bothered them and they cut back into the bush to find a place to camp. Again they went up, making a path between trees, hacking bush, creating some havoc in the darkness. And moving slowly, probing with light, utilizing this optimum time in the search for the silent beast. For somewhere around them in the same dark forest the beast was on the move too, unwinding its languid coils, stretching its rested muscles and sliding out through the trees in a rippling courtship of the unwary.

Johnny picked the spot, a somewhat level area with a configuration that favored the hanging of hammocks. They strung them, then hung another line above each for its tarp; they foraged for dry wood and kept it under plastic. Their small fire illuminated the immediate area. Harlan boiled water for tea and then started the rice. The night sounds became background as they sipped the hot tea and rested pleasantly after so much walking. Harlan's feet were sore and his right hand throbbed but otherwise he felt calm, and in his tiredness not so far out of place.

"You know that old man?" he asked, cutting onion into the pot.

"He is a hunter from a village over de mountain." Johnny sat in his hammock swaying slightly, dark eyes glowing with reflection. "I see him in de bush before."

"What's he hunt?"

"Possum. In de daytime I think he shoot birds too. Parrots."

34

"He seems a little crazy."

"I can't say, mahn."

"So he's out hunting now?" Harlan squinted into the wall of darkness wrapped around their pale perimeter of light.

"Maybe."

Harlan stirred the pot and watched a column of ants move up a tree next to his hammock. "Doesn't seem like you'd meet too many other people out here."

"True." Johnny cut into a mango he'd taken from his bag; juice ran down his wrist. "Dere's a mahn livin in de bush here an dere. Wildmahn. If you meet dis mahn you could worry." He looked at Harlan.

"It figures." Harlan shook his head. "In the thick of the jungle," he gestured with the spoon he held, "beware the other man."

When the rice was done Harlan mixed in sardines and split the portion. After they'd eaten he washed the pot with canteen water and made more tea, this time with a couple of shots of rum thrown in. Then he was ready to go on with the quest.

"Soon it rains," Johnny said.

"Yeah? Okay, so we stay right in this area."

They put everything in the hammocks, lashed the tarps down over them and left with flashlights and machetes, marking a tree on each of the four sides of the camp.

They could see no moon or stars, feel no wind. Except for the elevation of the terrain there seemed to Harlan to be no directional indicators. Everywhere was bush: trees, leaves, roots, vines, webs, ants, moths. And outside the thin darting light beams, the monstrous darkness. An inexorable force that human eyes could not adjust to.

Harlan marked other trees, hacking sharp sounds into the night, startling the insect world into momentary silence. Bark fell, exposing beetles, worms and larvae. Then drops began to fall, slowly at first, making light taps high overhead. Once they reached ground level the deflected drops had become more of a mist drifting through the light beams.

They turned back and suddenly the rain came hard. They moved quickly—Johnny heading straight to camp with hardly a turn—and scurried under cover to lie wet, each suspended in an isolated darkness. With the rain like drumbeats on the tarps, they could have been miles apart.

Harlan hung nearly motionless in this moist blackness for a long time, tired but not sleepy. The rain went on and on, drumming. Inside the tarp the air got damper and warmer; he lifted the edge and saw nothing, as if a larger tarp covered everything else. He brought the rain from his hand to his face; the cool water relieved the hot closeness for a minute, lessened his claustrophobia.

Unable to move, unable to see, unable to make a sound that would be heard more than a few feet away, he began to feel helpless. His mind wandered and he began to think about men lurking in the bush, wild, barefoot men who didn't care about rain or anything else they stumbled upon. He imagined a machete ripping through the tarp. Where was his? Stuck in the ground near his hammock. He gripped the flashlight in one hand, against his thigh, but he wanted the machete closer, handier.

The rain seemed to be lessening. He listened, alert. Suddenly he heard something, a movement, not rain. Was it Johnny? No. It was from the other side. He lay perfectly still, thumb on the flashlight switch. There it was again. A slow, deliberate movement, a sound like a step in wet leaves. The rain had stopped—now there were just drops rolling off leaves—but each drip that spattered on the tarp jabbed into his ears and interrupted the listening he strained at, the waiting for the next movement. It was a short wait but it seemed very long to him; he was so tired the tension almost put him to sleep, almost made him invisible, lying still inside a black tarp in a black jungle.

A wet twig snapped, barely audible. Harlan threw back the tarp, got one leg out of the hammock as he flicked on the light. The beam jerked around, found the dog—the old man's dog—startled, head down, frozen. The beam kept moving, sweeping the area, erratically searching—there was a rustle—and it flashed on the scampering dog as it vanished between trees.

He stood up, making a full coverage with the light, momentarily stopping on Johnny's quiet hammock, and saw nothing unusual. Heart racing, he finally steadied the beam on his own hammock. A brown grasshopper with a body six inches long hung onto the rope; its antennas matched the body in length and waved slowly in front of it like thin, brittle reeds stirred by separate breezes. He plucked the rope and the insect popped off onto the ground.

He whispered, "Johnny," and the other voice startled him.

"What, mahn?"

"Were you asleep?"

"Before you start jumpin round."

"Sorry. It was the old man's dog."

"Go to sleep, mahn."

But Harlan stayed up for a bit. He brushed his teeth, drank some water and stood doing nothing but allowing his excitement to subside. The episode had left him bare and exposed at some essential level. He wanted to blend into the surrounding bush and be able to sleep. It was elemental—there was only the bush; the darkness was merely a nighttime mask. There was nothing hidden if you knew what was there. He was there also, part of it. He had begun to see its character, the two sides of it: the exotic and the ordinary. The strange and the sublime. There were no shades of darkness, no degrees of the unknown. You belonged and were at home or you were an alien, nervous and afraid. In such an unadorned and unassuming world, could one—an uninitiated witness—pick a side, or was it presented with no choice? Was it dangerous or was it comfortable? Or from a basic approach, wasn't it indispensable? Could anyone really believe it was vital only to the barbarous?

Back in the hammock he rested more easily, suspended as if in nature's womb, and savored the approach of sleep, an exhilarated sleep where dreams couldn't be stopped. Where it might be possible to confront the unknown and grasp it.

Some hours later he saw the black pig in a dream. It lay in the forest with flies swarming around its face. He was some distance away but could clearly see the flies. In the next instant he no longer saw the pig but a dog was trotting toward him. He waited, looking for the pig. He bent down to scratch the dog's head; it licked his hand and followed beside him as he walked. He pulled on vines and searched their upper reaches for snakes. Ahead he saw a hammock with someone lying in it. As he approached with the dog at his feet he saw that it was Johnny in the hammock, still as death. He lay with his eyes open and Harlan noticed with some alarm that he was wrapped up to his neck in a long white snake skin, like a mummy with its head exposed. Harlan stood beside him, feeling that he should look for the old hunter but unable to take his eyes off Johnny. The dog was below the hammock sniffing hesitantly at the snake skin. Johnny spoke, relieving and startling Harlan at the same time; it was his normal voice, calm and unconcerned. "Are you learning?" he said, his eyes staring straight up through the trees.

The question puzzled Harlan. "I can't find Tet-Chien," he said.

Johnny hadn't blinked or moved. "What is the bush then, mahn?"

In the distance Harlan heard a muffled boom, as though a tree had fallen to the forest floor. He lost contact with the dream and struggled up through a light green sleep. When he opened his eyes he knew he had heard a shotgun blast.

He threw back the tarp and saw Johnny huddled over the sticks of a small, sputtering fire. In a minute the hissing flames flickered under the aluminum pot and tossed light on nearby tree trunks as a gray-green luminosity crept down from the high canopy like mist.

38

Harlan sat sleepily on his hammock and waited for the tea. He watched a cricket crawling up his boot and shook it off. Birds trilled and bounced about overhead. Water dripped off the tarps, the leaves. He shook involuntarily and rubbed his arms in the coolness. Grabbing his canteen he flicked a snail off and stood and took a drink, peering above him as he drained it, then walked a few yards away to urinate.

They broke camp and set out on a dawn excursion, moving along the slope above the river as soon as they'd replenished their water supply. They went smoothly, not talking or making much noise of any kind. Sunlight crept in sideways, slipping between leaves and limbs to create new patterns, shadows and shapes. Silent lizards moved into the light. And with the day came a stillness, a quietness after the dark, writhing night. There was only the slight buzzing of diurnal insects as the heat rose.

Johnny stopped and took a drink from his bottle. He smiled as Harlan approached.

"What?" Harlan asked.

"Look," Johnny said, and nodded. Before them stood a huge strangler fig, its interlaced vine-limbs surrounding and climbing but no longer needing its original host. The dead brown trunk of a tree—its remains like a rotten telephone pole—had begun to crumble inside its killer. The fig's thick green leaves reached out to touch other trees; its tentacles twined up out of sight.

"Incredible," Harlan said. He looked at Johnny.

"Look again, mahn."

Scanning the area around the big fig his eyes passed over a sturdy sapling beside it and then darted back to a spot of motion where he focused on a form gliding through a gap in the foliage. Rather than locomotion it appeared to be a shuddering in one spot, like a single muscle flexing steadily. Then the sapling gave it away, bending slowly as the weight poured into its top branches. A pattern of light and dark browns, a finely mottled limb like ripe, supple wood, it flowed and stopped, a thick section of a camouflaged hunter, and then waited, deciding—however it came to make such distinctions—on the course to follow.

Harlan stood awestruck, hardly glancing at Johnny for fear of losing sight of the snake. He couldn't see its head and didn't know if it saw him.

Watching him Johnny laughed and said, "Okay, mahn, now you have Tet-Chien."

"How big is it?"

Johnny looked up again. Patches of its patterned girth showed between leaves. "Maybe three meters."

"I have to get a better look." Harlan put his pack down and began to climb the fig like a ladder, placing his feet between the criss-crossed ridges and strands its tendrilled growth had fashioned into a trunk. Nearly fifteen feet up he stopped to tighten his grip and then leaned out toward the branches of the sapling.

The boa stared directly at him—the space between them, a mere ten feet, seemed charged like the air around a tuning fork—and he saw it clearly for the first time. A fixed, unblinking stare; immobile eyes in a rectangular head the size of a brick, but narrowing at the mouth and flat there, like a dog's muzzle. Below the suspended head the body moved on its own, coiling and rearranging itself for defense. They remained eye to eye for long moments, Harlan mesmerized and the boa completely expressionless, holding itself in a graceful blend of patience and wound energy. The animal endured with such agile beauty and efficient power—such poise under age-old pressure. Harlan felt unable to move, to look down or shift his hands or otherwise disturb this direct confrontation with the legendary beast—the involuntary ruler in the kingdom of invented evil. Except for man here was the most dangerous prowler in this shadowland, an old form, a fundamental creature of earth. And at the moment, a quiet forest dweller at home.

Ants crawled over Harlan's hand. He shook them off.

The snake remained still, solemn; its tongue flicked out, reading the air. Somewhere below, a dog barked. Harlan looked down. Johnny had moved, was moving away into the trees. The dog was coming, the old man's dog. Harlan began to climb down. Only the snake remained still. Waiting to become invisible.

Harlan scrambled down and jumped the last few feet, scattering dead leaves as he fell to his hands and knees. He looked up to see the dog with its nose to the ground, coming toward him. The old man would not be far behind. The hunter.

Harlan stood up looking around frantically. He didn't see Johnny. He glanced up into the tree and saw the snake too easily. It was doomed. The dog stopped under the strangler fig with its eyes on Harlan. Seconds passed; he wanted to run, to disappear into the bush. But he was alone at the edge of a precipice with panic rising in a primal force, pushing him to jump. He looked up again. The snake was moving, gliding in slow motion, bending the smaller tree on its way to a larger one. The dog began to snarl.

Reaching as high as he could Harlan grabbed the sapling with both hands and tried to sway it. The dog barked furiously. Grunting from the effort, Harlan pushed and pulled and the top-heavy tree bent slowly at first and then began to swing faster under its own accelerating momentum, moving back and forth into other trees and through the space above his head.

The boa, extended in a stretch, was caught by surprise and swung loose, its head dangling down and moving with the tree while its tail struggled to find purchase. Harlan worked harder, watching the hanging snake, seeing its full length as it swung over him.

Pulled by its own weight and unable to find a new hold, the big reptile ripped free and fell. Harlan sprang to the side and the snake landed heavily, thudding on the spongy, leaf-covered ground. The dog flinched and crouched lower, watching the snake as it contracted, pulling its ends closer together.

The dog moved forward and sideways very slowly, neck

fur rising; its nose quivered, sniffing. The snake lunged. Its mouth latched onto the dog's neck and its body contracted to pull the dog to the ground and toward it as it rolled, throwing two loops of itself around the dog's body in one motion, and tightening—all in the space of a heartbeat.

This mass, a writhing entanglement of snake and dog, transformed and became another single creature in Harlan's wild eyes. The dog whimpered, one of its hind legs twitching, scratching at the air. Harlan moved closer and saw the thing roll, wide coils covering the victim, the snake's head flattened and buried in fur so that only the canine head extended from the bundle. A strange beast—smooth, wound reptilian body, a spring tightening itself, with a dog's furry, frightened head staring out, eyes bulging, helpless mouth open and working to emit tiny squeaks.

Out of a background that had become inconsequential to Harlan the old man emerged, bearing down upon the forest drama with narrowed eyes and leveled shotgun.

Harlan stood tight as a cello string and followed the man's slow approach—a cautious approach, wary of the missing Johnny—as the struggle continued at his feet.

The old man stopped a few yards away and raised the gun, aiming at the bulk of the snake. In the next moment Harlan was on the split-second verge of screaming out. A limb cracked somewhere near them and the old man spun around, training his gun on trees.

Harlan grabbed the boa's tail and yanked hard, jerking the entire mass over the ground and loosening the lower coil. He pulled again, extending the unwound weight, taking more of the snake's body. He tried to whip it—like he would a garden hose to send a ripple over the lawn—attempting to break the other coil and stumbling back, dragging the boa while the tail pulled against him to hold the coil. The old man stood watching with his shotgun at waist level.

Harlan jerked again and the snake unwound, its jaws still

fastened to the dog's neck. One more pull sharply to the side and they detached, the dog rolling free and the snake swinging around and twisting under its own power, coming back toward its tail and hissing savagely. Harlan moved backward in a circle, pulling the curve out of the body as the head slid around toward him. After a few revolutions the snake slowed and came only part way around, its eyes on its captor and its mouth open slightly, its thick sides heaving from the exertion.

Harlan looked up with sweat dripping off his face; his arms were tense and his stomach felt tight. The dog had gotten to its feet and stood trembling and gasping, front paws widespread, head low. The old man was staring hard at Harlan. He raised the shotgun and motioned with it for Harlan to step away from the snake.

"No," Harlan yelled, "this is my fucking snake!" The sound reverberated off the trees. And the sun's rays, breaking through the canopy, hit the uneven ground like haphazard spotlights. "Tell him, Johnny," he yelled even louder. "This is my Tet-Chien." The old man looked around him, shifting his feet, turning the gun as his head turned. The dog wheezed and tried to take a step. Around them vines rose like heat waves.

Harlan yanked the boa toward him and put one foot on its neck. The head bowed back, biting at his boot as he slid his foot down to the base of the skull and stretched the tail up over his head with both hands. Almost fully extended, with its head twisting in leaves and dirt, the boa hung heavy and dense as dockyard rope. He cupped one arm under the reptile's midsection to cradle it, then bent down as he released the tail, moving his foot just as he grasped the back of its head. He straightened up holding the angry head away from him and supporting the bulk of the body with one arm, then guided its length around him and allowed it to encircle his stomach twice, taking the weight off his arm and distributing it evenly so he could walk. He remained in control of the head, and thus, of the body and its constricting power. It was snug but not uncomfortable; he took some deep breaths, testing the restraint. His free hand rested on a coil the size of his calf. He turned the boa's head toward him to show it the arrangement, as if it would understand their partnership, while their midsections each drew breaths against the other, pressed together as firmly as a tire holding an inflated tube.

He turned to face the old man, who stood stock-still, mouth tight and eyes wide, looking as if a demon had appeared before him. He glanced down at the dog limping toward him, then back up at Harlan; he held the gun level and met Harlan's gaze with strained, unpredictable eyes. At that moment it seemed to Harlan that the man would shoot the snake and him as one animal. Under the weight and the tension his knees trembled and he widened his stance a little, shuffling leaves. The dog raised its head to look at him and he saw that its neck fur was ruffled and spotted with blood. His eyes shifted to the old man's trigger hand and he tried to swallow; when he couldn't, he attempted to concentrate on that one simple act rather than on the barrel pointing at him. He wondered if everyone died with a dry mouth.

A crazy cry came out of the trees, an alarming sound not of the forest. Harlan and the old man both looked, peering into the spaces between trees, and saw nothing. A second later Johnny yelled something, a few words in patois. Then there was silence. Harlan looked at the old man. Nothing happened.

He took a few steps—the boa tensed, adjusted its coils—and stooped to grab the strap of his pack; he slung it over his shoulder, the machete handle sticking out of the top, and kept walking. He didn't know exactly where he was going, but he went downhill toward the river; the walking was easier that way and he longed for the coolness and open space of the water. He thought vaguely of releasing the reptile there. He pictured it flowing downstream to freedom.

He was careful to watch where he stepped, and used his free hand against trees to steady himself. He felt tired and dazed; only when he had reached the high bank and the river spread before him, clear and resplendent, did it occur to him to look behind. Not far back the old man was following.

Looking for the least treacherous spot to descend the bank he carefully changed hands on the boa and slid his other arm into the loose strap of his pack, balancing the weight on his back. He couldn't run but he could move faster and he started through the grass, picking up speed. He was getting used to the snake's tire-like girth, its smooth weight. And for the moment the boa rode as a passenger, its icy stare patient and alert.

At a place where tree roots protruded from the bank he grappled his way down one-handed on slippery red mud to the rocks and shallow water along the shore. He sloshed downstream as fast as he could, venturing away from the bank to go around a dead limb—a jagged, spindly obstacle that forced him into swifter water. He couldn't see the bottom then and stumbled, bringing a knee down on stone and nearly falling into the current. The snake flexed and loosened but Harlan regained his balance against a boulder and craning his neck caught a glimpse of the old man up on the bank, still following, somehow fixed on the spurious hunt.

Harlan let out a small laugh of amazement as the frustration of his predicament set in. He thought the old man must be traveling at the pace of a half-dead dog and still he couldn't lose him. To release the snake here was no good; it had to be where the current was fastest, in the middle of the river. He saw a place downstream that looked promising—boulders and rapids in mid-stream, and not far beyond that the river rounded a bend. He cupped a handful of water, rubbed it down his face and pushed off, trudging sluggishly onward with his boots full of water.

In a clear sky the sun climbed over the rim of trees and came down hard on the river and on Harlan. Tiny water bugs whizzed over the bright surface of the still pools in the shallows and wasps buzzed in monotones at the walls of the bank. Minnows turned away sharply from his heavy, splashing boots. The snake appeared resigned, torpid and heavier, as if it had become waterlogged. At first the river grew wider, flattening itself over a plane of stones before it narrowed again, funneling the current between large rocks and into swift chutes that churned up bubbles and fine mists of juggled sunlight.

He moved out into the river, dragging himself to the rocks in the middle. The surface of the water swirled around the coils of the snake. The current pressed him against the first boulder he reached and he struggled up on top of it. He stepped across a couple more and came to the center channel; the river surged through a gap in the rocks hardly more than a yard wide and spewed a strip of white water into the bend just ahead. This was the spot. All snakes were natural swimmers. After riding through the rapids the reptile would head toward land; he imagined the thing in calm water, easily wriggling to shore. But suppose it went to the wrong side, where the hunter watched and waited with his gun? Or got shot as it floated by? He turned and scanned the bank for the old man; he couldn't see him but he knew he was there. And Harlan stood in plain sight in the middle of the river, ready to release the animal to its death; he might just as well kill it himself right there, smash its head on the rocks. "Goddamn it!" he said, looking back at the river. He should have crossed it upstream in calmer water; now he would have to cross here. He looked over the narrow chasm of roaring water to the next rock. The more he looked the more perilous it became. He glanced down at the dormant snake. Maybe the old man had given up and gone home; Harlan peered again at the wall of trees. No sign. If the man waited he wasn't showing it any more.

Without all the extra weight he could make this jump without a thought. He slipped his pack off and dangled it by one strap. Holding the boa firmly with his left hand he swung the pack back and forth a few times and heaved it over the rocks; it splashed near the shore, rolled over and lay still in the shallow water. He was a bit lighter now but the snake felt like chains around him; he judged the distance again. Don't release the head, he told himself—and jumped.

He got one foot on the rock, knew he would never stand

upright on it, and fell sideways. He hit the water, grasping at the smooth rock with his free hand and holding the boa's head away from him as they went under. The snake came alive, feeling freedom in the river's motion, unwinding underwater, expanding to a loose circle around the man, while the current's rushing force pulled them into its turbulent funnel. Hindered by the reptile's body and unable to swim, Harlan was sucked feet-first into the rapids, slipping further through the loop of coils even as he held the snake's head out behind him. In the churning roar of bubbles—amid a flashing tangle of snake and arms and flowing shirt—he became desperate for air. His feet scraped bottom and he pushed up into the current taking him along. He broke the surface, his neck in a supple noose that tightened as he struggled, and slid back into white water, rolling over and kicking at the bottom. Swept along, he broke the surface again, seeing the other head in his squeezing hand and pulling at the sleek, flexible coil that choked him in return. He saw the sky and water washing over his eyes, then the water slowed. He was able to stand, fighting the grip at his neck as he dragged them both toward shore—a bobbing, lurching mass of gasping animal that fell splashing, wrapped in a stubborn strangulation of itself.

He lay on part of it, breathing raggedly with his hand around its neck, holding its head at the bottom among the stones. The long muscles relaxed and came undone. He slid free and brought its head to the surface; he loosened his hold and gave it air. The serpentine body slowly stretched out in the water. The snake stared hard at him, its head dark; water droplets glinted on the scales of its nose and dripped from the edge of its parted mouth. Its breath came fast and sharp, like his own.

They rested in the shallow water with the sun on them but he felt cool and imagined his body temperature had dropped in the river, as the reptile's had. In the brightness the wet boa showed its colors, its woven pattern of browns and gold; the curves in its flanks flashed with a bluish iridescence, the scales catching the light like miniature, interlocking prisms.

Across the river the old man stood watching with the dog at his feet and Harlan sat watching him. They regarded each other plainly, without open hostility, acknowledging the conflict. Not as much to do with territory or possession as it was a war of wills. Of philosophy. Harlan had taken a stand and he was trapped, a prisoner of his position. And he understood the hunter would stay on the trail. From habit, superstition or monomania. It made no difference.

He rolled back and put his legs in the air; water poured out of his boots. He stood and hoisted the cool, passive snake around his waist but the tired reptile refused to be rewrapped and slid down his legs. He tried again, to the same result, then draped the bulk of the snake across his shoulders. He walked along the shore to where his pack lay soggy and heavy in the water, bent over and slid the machete out and forced it under his belt. The snake hung loose and balanced, its tail nearly touching the ground. Harlan only wanted to detach them both from this senseless pursuit; to do that he would have to be hidden, their separation a secret. He glanced across the river once more. All he needed was a little time, a decent lead. And the old man, studying his actions, still had to cross the river.

Harlan scrambled up the low bank and straight into the bush. With renewed vigor he pushed through a thicket of undergrowth, holding the snake's head against his chest as they were scratched and poked. Once through, he moved easily between the trees, changing his course as he ran. He brushed past long, thick vines into an area where the canopy was complete and the light gloomy even at midday. Selecting a spot beside a giant, rotting log, he stopped and listened, looking back the way he'd come. Then he bent forward and pushed the boa over his head onto the ground, releasing its head as he stepped back. It remained where it had fallen, still, except for the flickering tongue. He tapped it with the flat of the machete and it moved—the head starting out and then dragging the rest behind it like a train—alongside the dead tree.

48

Released from bondage Harlan ran light and unfettered through the forest, riding the power of a second wind and laughing in the strange stillness as he put more distance between himself and the hunted boa. Then the muffled boom of the shotgun swept through the trees and his fleeting feeling was gone. He stopped, listening in shock as the sound receded. Johnny was giving him more time, he thought, hoping it was only that.

He found a thick brown vine and shinnied up about ten feet, spinning one way and then the other as the vine turned. Leaning back he pulled the machete out and hacked like a madman. Sweat ran in his eyes and bits of flying bark stuck to his face. But the vine was old and tough and resilient. It seemed to be taking too long and making too much noise. His leverage was bad and his arms ached. He cursed under his breath, expecting to look down and see the old man at any second. There was a crack; he dropped the machete and kicked his legs out, trying to swing. The vine snapped and he hit the ground and tumbled. Jumping up, he grabbed the cut length and the machete and took off toward the river, angling in a direction farther downstream. He didn't want the old man to see him too soon.

Hiding in the tall grass at the water's edge he yelled Johnny's name in the hope that the old man would hear him. He figured they were all three on the same side of the river but he peered upstream at the opposite bank for a few minutes before he yelled again. Something stung his neck; he slapped at it, brushed it off and crept down into the shallow water, dragging the vine. He wrapped it around his middle, wedged one end under itself and held the other out in his hand. It wasn't nearly as heavy as the snake but at a distance it might pass. He waded out into the water and stood on a rock. Looking up and down the river he didn't see anyone. He yelled Johnny's name again and waited, scanning the banks. He rubbed the welt on the back of his neck and shifted from foot to foot. Clouds were moving in, coming off the mountains.

49

A hundred yards upstream Johnny burst out of the bush and splashed into the river. Harlan called out and Johnny looked at him briefly as he crossed the water and ducked into the bush on the far side. The old man appeared on the bank, looking across the river at the place where Johnny had disappeared. Then he looked downstream and saw Harlan. There was a moment of recognition and Harlan paused—holding up the vine-head—before he slid into the water and continued across the river.

At the bank he looked back in anticipation. The old man was following from the other side. Harlan moved downstream, glancing across to check on the hunter's progress. The old man was steady but hampered by his dog, who couldn't keep up. Finally he carried the animal in his arms. And when Harlan decided he'd gone far enough he climbed a pile of rocks at the bank and waited in full view.

With the old man watching some thirty yards away Harlan carefully unwound the vine and lowered it down the side of the rocks. It floated away, unbending and straightening out on the surface. The old man left the dog and scurried ahead, wading out further into the water as Harlan went over the bank and into the bush. The old man stopped and studied the vine, drifting and turning with no movement of its own. He raised the gun—the vine caught on a protruding stick and bobbed inanimately—and then spun around, aiming into the bush where Harlan crouched, hidden, waiting for the ripping blast.

Clouds were darkening the sky as the old man lowered his gun and started walking back upstream. The river divided the men and the sound of it divided them moreover and the old hunter did not look across again as he passed.

The rain came. Far upstream the old man and the dog, again in his arms, blurred out of sight, obscured by a liquid, gray haze that linked the sky and the river. Harlan sat huddled under a tree, starting to relax a little, too wet already to be bothered by the weather. He shut his eyes and drifted off, half asleep in the roaring pour of leaf-slapping rain.

Then Johnny spoke. "You okay, mahn?"

He opened his eyes. "Yeah, fine. What about you?"

"Also."

Harlan wiped rain from his face. "What was that gunshot?"

"Dat crazy old mahn, he shoot at me."

"That's good," Harlan said, smiling.

"Good?" Johnny said, starting to laugh.

"That's right, man. Better you than a helpless Tet-Chien." They laughed together under the dripping trees.

"Where is your bag, mahn?"

"I guess I left it for the old man." He shook his head. "And now I'm hungry."

Johnny looked surprised. "You found no time to eat?"

"I was busy."

"You should have eaten dat snake."

"If I had it now I would." He nodded at Johnny's bag. "I'd even settle for a cup of tea."

"You lost de pot, mahn," Johnny said, laughing. "Too wet for fire anyway." He brought the rum out and handed it over. "Try dis. We can cook at home."

The rum permeated Harlan's tired body and seemed to warm every damp skin cell. They passed it back and forth quietly for a few minutes.

"Johnny?"

"What?"

"What did you yell to the old man when I first grabbed the snake?"

Johnny smiled, looking at the ground. "I tell him I am Tet-Chien, watchin him."

They found some guavas and ate them as they started home. The rain stopped and they maintained a good, steady pace and arrived at Johnny's house just prior to nightfall. He made tea first, then cooked rice and peas and added some canned fish they had left over. After dinner Harlan went home and slept. A deep, forest sleep where dreams came and went like shadows.

REMNANTS

Better if they had been born in the open pasture
and suckled by a wolf, that they might have seen
with clearer eyes what field they were called to labor in.
—Henry David Thoreau

Black frigatebirds swung down in gangly arcs, skimming the flat surface of the shallow water around the dock. A man wearing green shorts and a dingy white cap stood on the covered end of the dock rapidly scaling and gutting a pile of fish and flinging the bulbous strings of entrails into the water. Like prehistoric scavengers, the angular-winged birds turned and dove in continuous pendular motions plucking the fresh refuse from the surface before it could sink. Their raucous cries resounded off the flat water around the man. The water stretched out away from the dock for nearly a mile to an undulating strip of white froth where waves broke and foamed over the reef. This white surf line, constantly broken up and redrawn in fresh foam, ran the length of the horizon and revealed the long barrier reef that protected the cays—small offshore islands strung down the coast between the reef and the mainland. From the air they made a trail of green spots on the blue Caribbean Sea; at the water they were low humps of mangrove and palm.

From the dock the sound of crashing waves was faint but audible, like the sound in a large seashell held just away from the ear. Edging up between that muffled sound and the immediate shrieking of the birds came the distant high whine of a motorboat. The man glanced up, squinting over the shimmering blue surface. His sun-browned arms continued to move deftly, without much effort.

Nailed to the front of the dock was a sign that read: George's Reef Hotel. At the bottom of it, the words Dive Shop had been added in red letters and a red and white diver's flag had been painted on a dock post. Behind the dock, not twenty yards from shore, was one end of a two-story wing of rooms that adjoined the original wooden house at its other end. The entire building was painted yellow and along its length grew bushes of red and pink hibiscus. An aging rain tank, a huge brown barrel on stilts, leaned against the house. A row of tall coconut palms lined one edge of the property and their large brown nuts lay scattered in the sand like stones. A pile of stringy husks surrounded a waist-high beam of wood planted solidly in the ground; out of the end of the beam stuck a thick, metal spike. Close to the water's edge were several wide-slatted wooden armchairs, pale yellow and peeling.

As the boat approached the dock the man placed the last of the fish in a plastic bag and stepped out of the shade to catch a line thrown by the boy standing at the engine. There were four other people in the boat, two couples from Florida who'd been on the cay for nearly a week. They'd been diving every day and George's son, Manny, had taken them to a different spot each time. One of the divers, a tanned and wiry young man with sandy hair, sprang onto the dock with the bowline.

"How's it going, George?" he asked as he tied off the line. The boat gently bumped a smaller one in front of it.

"Okay, Ben," George said, pulling the boat up snug to the ladder. "Got a few jack today."

The other man, Bill, stood on the bow and hoisted a tank up to his shoulder. He was heavier than the others, large around the middle, with reddish hair and an excited red face. He banged the tank down on the dock and said loudly, "Your kid knows that reef like the back of his hand."

George smiled and said nothing as the three of them worked to get the heavy gear out of the boat. Bill grunted as he lifted another tank. Then he bellowed, "Yeah, he put us on a big funnel a ways south of here and we drifted around to a nice wall that must have dropped, what Ben, about sixty or seventy feet?"

The women, Pam and Nancy, collected all the shoes, stray articles of clothing, sunscreen bottles, trash and food remains, and climbed out of the boat. Manny brought over a two-wheeled cart from the end of the dock and helped his father arrange the tanks and weight belts for transport to the shop. After the vests and the mesh bags of regulators, masks, fins and snorkels were gathered, they all moved toward the hotel, where one back room held the diving equipment, a compressor and a tank bath.

Bill continued his story. "I came under a ledge, it was on that second dive, and came up face to face with a grouper— shit!—that must have been—" he pointed at George, then down at their feet, "—as long as this dock is wide." His wife snickered. Pam was a petite blond who laughed a lot, especially at Bill's descriptions. "I put on the brakes real quick," he said. "I mean, I sucked up some air in a hurry. But then I just eased back—" He dropped the gear and raised both hands to illustrate. "And sat there staring that big dude right in the eye."

At the edge of the dock Ben helped George lower the cart off the wood and into the sand. Bill stood with his arms raised as Manny passed him, looking up expectantly. Then he grabbed the boy's shoulder.

"If I'd had a spear gun—" He poked Manny in the stomach with his index finger. "Fffttt! We could've had this whole island over for dinner." The boy pulled away giggling.

Ben nodded to George and said, "Or Big Bill would still

be out there getting dragged along the bottom somewhere."

Bill stuck out a red arm. "Right between the eyes."

"An underwater towing service," Ben said, sending Pam into a fit of laughter.

The men helped unload the equipment and the women went up the back stairs to their rooms, which were above the dive shop and closest to the water. The toilets and showers were at the other end of the hallway. Outside her door Nancy said, "You're getting pretty dark."

Pam looked at her arm in the shade. "Yeah, my skin feels hot."

They heard Bill holler downstairs, "Damn if it isn't just about happy hour."

Nancy smiled and said, "He never tans, does he."

"Nope," Pam said. "Just stays red." Then she said, "See you in the shower," and winked at her friend.

After cool showers and aloe cream coatings the four of them sat in the wooden chairs facing the water and drank rum cocktails as the sun slowly sank behind them. Basking in the tranquil afternoon light they settled into a daily collective state of post-dive relaxation where the common ingredients were pleasantly tired muscles, the flush of warm skin, the smooth scent of coconut oil in the air, and the feel of a cold drink in the throat. Before them the water spread out soft and flat to the reef and their eyes were drawn there. A couple of boats were heading in. At first they didn't appear to be moving at all and their engine whines seemed far away. The foursome watched and listened as the noise gradually increased and the boats came at them, then veered away lazily to the north, to other docks, and stopped their engines—and the only sound left was the distant crashing of the reef waves.

Pam slapped her ankle. "Here come the no-see-ums."

Bill rubbed the back of his knee. "Damn these little assholes."

Nancy stood up. "I'll get the spray," she said, walking

toward the building.

Pam frowned. "Where's that lovely breeze this evening?"

"Don't forget," Ben said, "it's happy hour for the sand flies too." He wore long pants, shoes and socks and sat staring at the darkening water, stirring his drink with one finger. His eyes moved over the flecks of silvery waves, out to the ridges of luminescent froth glowing in the last light. Beyond that the horizon was beginning to dissolve. Nancy returned and sat down next to him.

"Here." She reached across and handed the can to Pam. "And I brought out some peanuts."

Bill leaned over and took the bag. "I'm starving," he said. "Nothing like a hard day diving to stimulate the old appetite." He slapped his leg. "Damn it."

"Yours doesn't need stimulating," Pam said, setting the can on the arm of his chair.

He took the can and sprayed his legs down to his wide red feet. "If the breeze goes, then so must we," he said solemnly, spraying his arms. "Or get eaten alive."

"If the breeze dies—" Ben muttered, glancing up at the still palm fronds. Nancy turned to look at him but he didn't finish. He slapped his forehead and gulped down the rest of his drink.

Twilight was upon them. Ice rattled in plastic cups and hands slapped at scalps and spots of assailable skin. The distant surf lost its glow but its sound seemed much clearer now, as if the boundary between the island and the sea had changed, come nearer for the night.

Bill lumbered out of his chair and over to the back porch table under the stairs where he refilled a plastic pitcher with the rum, mango and coconut milk concoction that had become his holiday trademark. "Drinks all round," he yelled, returning to the group. No one objected and he poured. "Yeah, it's been a great week." He slapped his neck, then picked up his own cup and topped it off. "Here's to it," he said, raising his cup.

"Good friends and good diving," Pam added, and they all drank. "Wow!" she said, gasping theatrically. "That's pretty strong, Bill."

"And good eatin and drinkin," Bill said loudly, walking around to face the chairs. He held the pitcher in one hand and his cup in the other and looked red even in the dim light cast from the porch. He suddenly shifted his weight, scratching one ankle with his other foot, and spilled some of his drink. He looked down at the dark spot in the sand. "And free drinks for the no-see-ums," he bellowed.

The two women started laughing, triggering an outbreak of hearty laughter from Bill, who then spilled more of his drink. This produced more laughs from the women and the chain reaction of hysteria continued until Bill handed the pitcher to Pam and sat down heavily. Struggling to catch his breath, he waved his hand to signal that he wasn't finished yet.

"Either—" He started laughing again, then sniffed and wiped his eyes. "Either they've gone somewhere else to drink, or—" He struggled to suppress his laughter but the women set him off again. "Or, or—" he squeaked.

"Sshhh," Pam said. "Or what?" She set the pitcher on the ground.

Bill gripped the chair arm and inhaled deeply. "Or we just can't feel 'em any more." The three of them laughed in unison and Bill fell back in his chair gasping. He finally looked up through wet eyes and noticed Ben staring at him. "The bugs, man, the bugs," he said.

"I'm laughing inside," Ben said.

Bill sat up. After a few seconds he looked over at his wife. "It's our last night," he said quietly.

Ben raised his cup. "To our last supper, then," he said and downed his drink. The other three stared at him and Nancy's face sank into a frown. He asked, "Could I have that pitcher please?" When no one moved, a look of mild surprise showed on his face. "Have you been seduced by tropical fruits?" he asked.

60

"Don't you smell that fish?" The sweet, delicate aroma drifted among them, floating on the warm night air and bringing to mind the dining room in the house where George's wife Amelda served fish or lobster or conch—whatever was freshest—nightly, to those who made reservations before noon. "That's right," Ben whispered, "Amelda's frying up those jacks."

Bill stood, his attention focused again. "She's a great cook," he said.

Turning her glare away from Ben, Nancy stood too and smiled at Bill. She touched his shoulder. "You really have to go tomorrow?"

Pam hopped up, knocking over a cup at her feet. As the three of them moved toward the building she spoke rapidly. "We thought we'd get the early boat into town and spend one more day over there, you know, shopping and stuff." They reached the stairs and started up. "Then we'll leave the next day." She groaned, adding the lament, "And then it's back to work bright and early Monday morning."

At the top of the stairs Nancy glanced down at Ben.

He sat watching them. As she turned away to open the door, he heard her say, "I suppose we'll stay a couple more days." Then heard Pam ask, "Where's Ben?" and Nancy answer, "He'll be along in a minute." Then the doors shut and there was only a murmur of voices.

He got up, poured the rest of the pitcher into his cup, and sat down again. He stared into the darkness and listened to the measured pounding of the surf. His breathing slowed to match the rhythm of the waves. The alcohol settled in his head as he settled in the chair, mesmerized by the offshore sounds. His eyes closed; in a hazy transition his mind slid down into an underwater world where he saw himself passing through huge schools of grunts and sergeant majors, where colorful parrotfish cut into his field of vision, watching him as they swam in silence. As he drifted in this quiet state of mind a soft sound intruded. It registered just loud enough to pull him out of the depths and back into the wooden chair so that the sound took shape and lodged itself in his memory. It was a squishy noise, something like the sound made by a shoe stepping in soft mud, and he opened his eyes not knowing what it was. Then he heard the crunch of shoes in sand and turned his head to look.

At the edge of the property a man emerged from the line of palms. Walking toward the water he stopped adjacent to the chairs and looked over at Ben, some twenty yards away. The man was tall and thin and dressed in dark clothes. He suddenly spoke in a deep, even voice.

"Do you have the time?"

At first Ben understood it to be an inquiry for help of some kind and he waited for an explanation while the man took him in. When he received none, he raised his watch and was about to answer when the man took off walking again, turned at the water's edge and moved away into the darkness. Ben was poised to announce the time but the man never looked back.

Nancy's voice startled him. "Who was that?" she asked from the upper landing.

He stood up and turned to face her. "I don't know. Some guy walking by."

She waited a moment, then said, "Dinner's ready," and walked into the hallway.

He collected the cups and the pitcher, put them on the back table, glanced out into the darkness beyond the palms once more and went inside.

The menu was fish, rice and beans, conch fritters and bread, served piping hot and island spicy in portions to match the ravenous appetites developed during the long, hot day. The divers' nightly feast was at hand and another couple, new to the island, joined them at the table. From the adjoining kitchen Amelda brought out the food on old china platters that didn't match. A lace tablecloth covered the large wooden table and a chipped crystal pitcher of ice water with droplets streaming down its sides sat in the middle. On a small table in one corner an oscillating fan rattled back and forth. Against the walls were a few other chairs and opposite the hallway door a large glass-fronted cupboard displayed its hodgepodge collection. On one side of it was an old photo of the house as it originally stood, without the added rooms, and on the other side was a standard representation of Christ gazing serenely over the room with one index finger delicately raised.

After a few simple queries from the new people Bill launched into his diving stories, and when the topic turned to the next day's dive he sadly disclosed his departure plans. He hated to leave, he told the new guy. "But," he said, "Ben and Nancy are sticking around for a couple days. Maybe you could go out with them."

Ben looked up from his plate at the new arrivals and stopped chewing; he took a sip of water and swallowed. "Actually," he said, "I think I'm about dived out."

Bill snorted loudly. "What the hell else is there to do here?"

Ben set his fork down and wiped his mouth. "Well," he said, gazing wistfully at the ceiling, "in the morning I might take a walk and maybe read awhile and then in the afternoon I thought I'd just lie in a hammock in the shade and watch lizards fuck."

There was a second of silence before Bill let out a guffaw. The new arrivals laughed politely and Pam smiled quizzically at Nancy, who looked from Ben to her plate. Bill pounded the table and chuckled; when Nancy looked at him he winked and said, "He might just get some ideas."

"That's right," said Ben. "In fact, lately I do feel the reptilian part of my brain could be taking over."

Nancy said, "That probably explains why you're acting so primitive."

Ben laughed and the new people laughed with him. "I do believe that life on a tropical island can change you," he said, looking seriously at the woman.

"I agree," she said, looking from Ben to the others

around the table. "Look what happened to Gauguin."

"I don't know," said her companion. "You could argue that he was already a savage inside."

Amelda brought out a coconut pie and put it on the table. When she'd returned to the kitchen Nancy said, "In any case, he died of syphilis."

"Brings out the best in some people," said Ben, as Amelda entered with a pot of coffee and a small, ceramic cream pitcher in the shape of a blowfish.

"The pie, you mean?" asked Bill. He pulled it toward him and grinned, raising his knife. "She'll probably bring one out for you people in a minute."

After dinner the six of them walked down the sandy, central road—a path really, since there were no cars on the small island—to a place called Elgin's Crab Hole that had a long bar, a scattering of wooden tables and chairs, a worn pool table with a surface like linoleum, and a good sound system that played a stream of year-old American pop songs. Local men, some Creole, some black, sat at the bar near the door. Several people were having late dinners and though the pool table went begging, there were two young girls dancing in the open space around it.

Bill selected a table in the center of the room. After they were seated a boy in jeans and a tee shirt came over and stood by the table. He took the drink order and walked away without a word. When the drinks came the three women were embroiled in a discussion of seafood recipes and Bill was presenting his views to the new man, in a voice loud enough to rival the music, on how the island might be improved. The time was ripe, he thought, for opening a larger hotel with greater amenities. Not luxury but very nice. A classy place that catered to divers and had a big, air-conditioned bar. Forget these crappy little flophouses and so-called drinking establishments.

Ben finished his beer in a few swallows and headed to the restroom. When he came out he went to the bar and ordered another beer. Through the open door he saw the moonglow on the sand and the dark water glimmering; farther out the reef spray flashed faintly. He downed the beer and decided to call it a night. He got the room key from Nancy, squeezed her shoulder and waved his goodnight to the others at the table, saying he was tired.

"Yeah, he's dived out alright," Bill said.

Ben went back along the water's edge; the moon was three quarters full and high enough to provide some illumination. He walked between a dock and a stack of lobster traps as high as his head. At the dock a fishing boat bumped against a post. Beyond the traps was a small wooden house raised on pilings several feet above the sand. The house was dark and quiet; as he looked over, a dog stepped out from under it into the moonlight. Ben kept walking and the dog stood watching him without moving farther or making a sound. Next door was another house, also dark, and another dock, this one warped and sagging on one side. Glancing back to check on the dog, Ben walked into a fishing net strung between two palms and jumped back, flinging up his arms. Realizing what it was, he brushed his hand down the coarse mesh, feeling the strands with his fingertips—and suddenly remembered an absurd scene from a Tarzan movie he'd seen as a child, where someone, probably Boy, was running through the jungle and got caught in a ridiculously large web; the screaming victim lay wrapped and writhing on the ground as a pack of menacing spiders inched closer. He smiled at the memory and crossed an empty lot, hearing his shoes on the sand, then passed the cemetery, its low, coral rock wall only thirty yards from the water's edge. Crosses and tilted grave markers shone feebly in the moonlight; between them weeds grew in wild tangles. Clouds covered the moon and he picked his way slowly through a dark acre of tall coconut palms, passing a house with a dim light burning inside. Out on the open sand the moon reappeared. He went around two boats beached beside a fisherman's shack. Up ahead he saw George's; the rear light was on, casting a pale pool of illumination nearly absorbed by moonlight. Ben walked up near the happy hour chairs. The house was quiet. He glanced over the yard, at coconuts on the ground, the pile of husks, the husking spike. He took a few more steps and stopped, looking at the spike; he saw something on the end of it. A piece of husk, he thought as he walked toward it. As he got closer he thought it looked like a fish. It was a fish. He stared at it: an angelfish. He bent closer. An angelfish impaled on the spike right through its side and drooping stiffly against the beam. He straightened up and looked around, down the row of trees, and saw no one. He bent forward again to examine the sight. The steel shaft was sequined with dozens of tiny scales that clung to it in clear streaks no longer viscous but dried shiny like household glue. The speared fish—the size of a dinner plate—was held horizontally, like a ticket on a lunch counter spike; at the puncture a pink, oozing fluid had sealed itself around the metal. Otherwise the fish was intact, its silvery gray side smooth as steel. The upward eye glinted, staring round at the moon overhead.

Ben turned away, thinking it was someone's idea of a joke. But no one local would waste this much food. He looked out at the water, hearing the surf, the relentless bashing at the reef. The familiar sound, over and over again. The waves, the waves, the waves, the fish. It flashed in his memory—the squish! The sound of the squish. He remembered himself in the chair. The man who had spoken and walked away. Looking down at the angelfish he tried to hear the sound again and tried to recall every detail—the sequence of events, how the man looked, the sound of his voice, if he had anything in his hands—but there wasn't much to recall. People ask for the time all the time. It was dark. Also, a doubt lingered in Ben's mind: if he was wrong about the sound, then the fish could have been there already, or been put there later, after he saw the man.

Ben went up the stairs and into his room, then went down the hallway to the bathroom. When he came back he turned off the light, undressed and lay on the bed with his eyes open. The fan hummed back and forth.

Later, as he was finally beginning to drift off, he heard Bill laugh across the hall. Then Nancy opened the door. Fumbling around for her toiletries, she asked, "You awake?"

"Yeah."

There was a pause, then she asked, "What's the matter?"

"What do you mean?"

"I mean why have you suddenly developed this monstrous rudeness?"

"I haven't developed anything. I've been having a great time, but now the trip is starting to seem a little one-dimensional."

"You mean the diving?"

"That, and the people."

"That's what we came for. And we came with friends."

"She's your friend, really. Bill and I got sort of thrown together."

"You've met him before."

"I know, but I didn't know him. As far as the diving went, he was fine."

"There's no need to be uncivil."

"I wouldn't call it uncivil. Maybe I've gotten a little impatient. I'd just like to see the pace change a bit."

She said, "We'll have the rest of the time to ourselves. But I wanted to go over with them in the morning. Do you want to go?"

"No."

"Alright. I'll just go then."

"Okay, but don't hang out by yourself over there."

"I won't. I'll be with them, we'll go to the market, and I'll take the afternoon boat back."

"Fine. I'll get up and see you off." He watched her move to the door. "And if you come to bed now, I'll see that you get off sooner."

"How generous," she said. "I'll be right back."

He waited on top of the sheets. She returned and stood in

front of the fan, undressing. Only the whiteness of her breasts and hips was visible and he got hard watching her put body lotion on. The smell of it filled the room as she stood over him rubbing herself with creamy hands, squeezing her nipples as he held himself ready. She climbed over him and slowly lowered herself; he slid into her and moved his hands to her slippery breasts. They rocked back and forth impatiently, neither wanting the other to last very long, and picked up speed, until the bed was banging at the wall. He thrust harder and she fell forward, pressing her face in the pillow as she came. Then he came too, holding the flesh of her butt tightly and breathing roughly in her hair. A couple of minutes later she raised her head, kissed him on the lips and rolled off him. They fell asleep almost immediately.

The next morning the two couples waited on the dock. It was Saturday, market day in town. The boat arrived already full but the sea was calm and the extra passengers and luggage were taken on. Bill had a hangover and was unnaturally quiet; Ben shook his hand, hugged Pam and kissed Nancy goodbye. He watched the boat round the southern end of the island. The sun was low and brilliant over the water. Going back to the room he noticed the angelfish was gone.

He felt like crawling back into bed but decided instead to start out on a walk around the perimeter of the cay before it got too hot. First he had coffee and toast alone in the dining room. Then he set off toward the southern end of the island, where after a few more stilt houses the land was undeveloped.

He followed a trail through the bush that came back to the water near the southern point. There, a thick mass of mangroves ended the trail; he waded into the shallow water, his shoes sucking out of the muck with each step. Under the mangroves small white crabs ducked into countless round holes which covered the bank like skin pores. Out on a sandbar a white heron stood poised for breakfast, still as a stick.

As he came around the thick clump of vegetation Ben caught sight of the next cay rising above the water a few miles away. After a few more steps the mangroves gave way to a clearing of long grasses and shrubs from which a dilapidated dock, full of gaps and broken boards, extended into the water. At its warped and rotten base a huge pile of white shells rose out of the sand—old, cracked conch shells heaped in a jagged, sun-bleached mound.

Across the clearing Ben noticed a thin plume of smoke rising above the shrubs. He advanced slowly, his wet shoes slurping. Peering around a bush he saw the back of a man squatting over the source of the smoke. The man's back muscles tensed and his head turned enough to look behind him. Ben stepped clear of the bush as the man stood and turned to face him. The man was tall and thin and had straight black hair, unevenly cut. His facial features were prominent—sharp cheekbones and chin, a long aquiline nose—and his eyes were darker than tar. His skin was uniformly browned; he was barefoot and wore only a pair of white shorts. Despite the brevity and the circumstances of their previous encounter, Ben recognized the man instantly.

On the ground behind the man a coconut husk smoked—a natural vessel for a small pile of smoldering embers—and a pungent odor marked the area. Looking up to meet the man's gaze Ben said, "I was just passing by."

The man was studying him closely. He turned and bent down, adding something to the fire, which had begun to die out. Ben started to leave.

"Where are you going?" the man asked without looking up.

Ben stopped. "I'm just walking around the island."

The man stood up. "Then you'll end up here again." A small green object on a leather cord hung around his neck.

Ben hesitated a few seconds, then moved closer and removed his sunglasses. The green object was a frog-shaped carving. "Is that jade?" he asked.

The man stared into Ben's eyes. "It's a little man in a frog suit."

Ben nodded, glancing down. Nearby was a patch of sand in which a circular arrangement of shells had been placed. Inside the circle was a pattern of black feathers and white bones, either those of a chicken or some smaller bird. Along the inner edge of the circle symbols were drawn in the sand. "What's that for?" he asked.

"The sun."

"Okay." Ben clasped his hands together. "A little sun worshiping, right?"

"Exactly."

"Most people lie on a beach."

"I'm not most people."

"That seems fairly evident."

The man squatted again to attend the small fire.

"What's cooking?" Ben asked.

"Copal." When Ben said nothing, the man added, "It comes from the resin of a tree in the jungle." He stood, watching Ben's face. "It's used as an incense by the Maya."

"Where'd you get it?"

"In the jungle."

"Are you a Maya?"

The man laughed. "They are a very short people."

Ben laughed too. "You could be an exception."

"I could very well be, but I'm not Maya."

Ben shrugged. "Why do you have it then?"

"I'm doing my doctoral thesis on the Maya." He paused. "And related subjects."

"Such as?"

"Such as whatever I can discover."

"What can you discover here?"

The man looked out at the water. After a few moments he returned his gaze to Ben. "I've been in the jungle for several weeks. Alone, for the most part, and deeply involved in my field work. I've visited known ruins and located unexcavated sites. It's been very productive so far but there is much more to do. I took a break and came here. As you said, a little sun-worshiping." He bent down and stoked the small fire.

"So you're going back?"

"Of course."

"When?"

"Tomorrow."

"Had enough relaxation, I guess."

The man straightened, stepped to a bush, reached under the lower branches and pulled out a nylon bag. He unzipped it and withdrew a bundle of cloth. Moving closer to Ben he carefully turned back the corners of the cloth to reveal a palm-sized object, a round piece of dark pottery with an open-mouthed, wide-eyed head sticking up from its center. Except for some scratches on the head and a few minor chips on the rim, the object was in good shape.

"I would say," Ben said, "it's the top of a dish of some sort."

"Precisely!" the man said, smiling. He picked it up by the head and showed the concave underside. "The lid of a bowl, probably a tripod bowl. And the handle—" He placed the lid back in his other hand, right-side up. "—is the head of a monkey."

Ben stared at the little face; it seemed to be startled, or howling.

The man seemed to read his thoughts. "Maybe a howler," he said, "but probably a spider monkey. The head is smoother. Less fur." He watched Ben examining the little head. "In any case, exquisitely preserved."

"How old is it?"

"About twelve hundred years."

"No kidding." He saw the piece in a new light. "Really amazing," he said, wanting to hold it as he watched the man rewrap it and place it carefully in the bag. "Do you have any other things like that?"

"Not with me," the man said. He glanced down at the trickle of smoke. "But I could show you something else later, if you're interested."

"I am," Ben said. He turned away for a few moments, cleaning his sunglasses, considering the offer, before looking back at the man. "Look, why don't you have dinner with us, me and my girlfriend, about seven."

"Where?"

"How about George's? The food's good there and it's homey. Sort of semiprivate."

The man lingered over the invitation, his sharp face turned on the other man as his dark eyes drew an appraisal. "Alright," he said.

"Good," Ben said, putting on his sunglasses. "See you there." He took a few steps and stopped, turning back to face the man. "I meant to ask you something." He looked out at the water and back again and cleared his throat; a few seconds dragged by. "What about the fish?" He saw in his mind the laden, misused husking spike and began to feel he had asked such a foolish question of a total stranger that an answer was undeserved. But he said anyway, "The angelfish."

"A simple offering," the man said.

"Kind of fast, wasn't it?"

"Not every offering takes a ceremony."

"Of course not."

A tiny trail of smoke rose from the coconut; the man knelt over it and blew gently. Ben continued along the shoreline, feeling the sun on his back. The day had gotten hot.

On the west side of the island he passed the icehouse and the generator shed and came to the fishing cooperative's building. He swam in the clear, deep water off the end of the pier there; beneath it several young boys played among the pilings. Afterward he stopped at Myrna's Kitchen for lobster salad, Creole bread and a beer. Walking again he retreated into the water at the edge of a bushy, unkempt yard after a brown dog ran out barking. From her house on stilts a woman watched him go by as she hung laundry on wires stretching away from the staircase to a pole in the yard; he heard the screen door slam behind her. In another yard an old man sat on a rusted kitchen chair in the shade of a tree, replacing the broken slats in a lobster trap. Hearing yelling voices, Ben walked down a dirt path to a soccer field and watched part of a game, leaning against the shaded wall of a store on which an advertisement for a rum distillery was printed in large letters that read: Drinking is Fun. When the shirtless team had made two goals in a row he left. He passed a school and a government office that were closed, and another store. On the north end of the cay a boy in a boat offered his services for a trip to the reef, and when Ben declined, the boy followed along puttering offshore, making periodic proposals: a fishing trip, a sightseeing tour, transportation to the next cay, or even passage to the mainland. Eventually he gave up, opening the throttle and peeling around the point out of sight, and Ben meandered along a path that took him between a row of houses and a sandy shallow-water beach. Then he passed Elgin's, where music blasted out into the still air, and a few minutes later he was home persuading Amelda to add one more evening plate. He got some ice water and a book, climbed into a shaded hammock near the water, and soon fell asleep.

The motorboat arriving at George's dock woke him. Nancy waved when she saw him, the boat took off with its noise and the area settled into quiet once more.

"Is this what you've been doing?" She bent over the hammock and kissed him, holding her straw hat in place with one hand. The brim bent against his head and her brown hair fell around his face.

"Nice hat," he said.

She kicked off her sandals and twirled in the sand. "Do you love it?" she asked, arching her back and hiking her white skirt up a few inches.

"I love it," he said, examining her tensed brown thighs.

"What's in the bag?"

"Fruit. I'm going to make a beautiful fruit salad."

"How was it over there?"

"Crazy after being here. The market was bustling." She laughed. "Bill haggled most of the morning over some little carvings. Then we had lunch upstairs on the terrace of an English pub sort of place, Sir Edmund's."

"No trouble?"

"No. They walked me to the boat. Pam told me they had a really great time." She smiled at him. "So what's on the agenda? Are you going to lie there all day?"

He clasped his hands behind his head and stretched his chest, took a deep breath and exhaled. "Why don't you put on your suit and let's take a swim."

"Okay." She picked up the bag. "I'll see if Amelda has room for some of this in the fridge."

She came back in fifteen minutes in her lavender bikini and the straw hat. "I'm ready."

He opened his eyes. "I met this guy today and invited him to have dinner with us."

"Oh yeah?" She put her lip out. "And I thought we were dining alone."

"Well, I know, but he's an interesting fellow and he's leaving tomorrow."

"A tourist?"

"Not really. He's down here doing research on the Maya culture."

"By himself?"

"Apparently."

"What's his name?"

"I just realized I forgot to ask."

"Oh well, a stranger comes to dinner."

"It should be educational. If he shows up."

"I can take anything for one night."

"I'm sure you can," he said, getting himself out of the

74

hammock. They walked up to the beach past Elgin's and frolicked in the shallow water for an hour or more, then came back and went upstairs to their room. The fan pulled a gentle breeze through the windows, fluttering the thin curtains, and the afternoon light bathed the room in a soft yellow glow as they made love. Afterward they fell asleep. They woke some time later glistening with sweat in a thick, dreamy atmosphere disturbed only by the strange, intermittent creaking of the fan.

As night approached the breeze became a cooling wind and the faraway roar of the surf was lost in the rush of air. Ben and Nancy waited outside by the chairs until seven-fifteen and when their guest hadn't arrived, went in to the dining room. Even though it was Saturday night the room was empty. At seven-thirty Amelda peeked in from the kitchen and Ben shrugged. "Anytime," he told her, and looked at Nancy. "We're dealing with a scientist."

The side door opened and the man came in; the night air ruffled the tablecloth and napkins. He shut the door and sat down opposite the others, smoothing his wind-blown hair as he looked at them across the table.

"Thought you weren't going to make it," Ben said, and when the man didn't answer, he added, "Somehow names didn't occur to me earlier today. This is Nancy Fleming and I'm Ben Cale."

"Kalal," the man said. "James Kalal."

"Nice to meet you," Nancy said.

"Like something to drink?" Ben asked.

"The water will be fine."

Ben ordered a beer and the meal began. The fish was baked grouper, served with rice and a spicy casserole made from pumpkin. Kalal took small portions—a spread of rice grains that could be covered with three fingers, a piece of fish the size of the toothpick box on the table, and a spot of casserole that wouldn't fill the salt shaker. He took small bites, eating quietly from the end of his fork and chewing very slowly.

"Ben tells me you're a student," Nancy said.

He looked at them for a moment as they watched him. "That doesn't describe my situation very accurately," he said, putting his fork down. "Are you familiar with the Maya?"

"A little," she said, feeling embarrassed. "There are some ruins in Mexico."

"Not only there." He placed his hands flat on the table and a few more seconds passed before he spoke again. "These Maya people settled in the jungles not far from here over two thousand years ago. They created an incredible civilization that grew out of what is now northern Guatemala and became the most widespread and advanced in Central America. Probably in the western hemisphere. They were astronomers and mathematicians who watched the movements of planets and built fantastic temples and highways in places that were practically inaccessible. And they did it without metal or wheels, using stone and wooden tools." He paused and the room was exceptionally quiet. "Then, a thousand years ago, the people vanished, the stone cities fell into disrepair and the places were reclaimed by the jungle. The civilization ended."

"But the Spanish—"

"It was over before they arrived," he said. "There were some Maya still around, as there are today, but they were not the same." He took a sip of water and they waited. "I have immersed myself in the study of this culture, using the relics and ideas that were left behind."

"And you'd like to know what happened?"

"Wouldn't you?"

"It was a long time ago. I'm more interested in what our civilization is doing."

His dark eyes studied her. "There might be connections you're not aware of."

Amelda came in with a pie. "Choclit-coconot," she said, putting it at the edge of the table. She looked at the food left uneaten, wrinkled her face and put her hands on her white-

76

aproned hips. "Food no good?"

"Delicious as always," Ben said. "We want to keep some for breakfast."

She wagged a finger at him and left the room; in a moment she returned with a coffee pot. "Too hot," she said, setting it down.

Ben and Nancy each had a big piece of pie with their coffee. Kalal had only black coffee. They heard Amelda cleaning up.

Kalal pulled a small cloth bag on a string from the front of his shirt and withdrew a pottery figurine about two inches tall. "This is not yet for public display," he said, handing it across the table. Ben took the piece in his palm, glancing at the kitchen doorway.

The little, gray piece was a standing figure, arms at its sides, wearing a headdress that swept back close to its head; the eyes and mouth were chips of inlaid shell. Ben offered it to Nancy but she only looked at it lying in his palm. He held it upright on the table next to his coffee cup and put his head down in front of it, lining up his eyes with the figure.

Nancy asked, "Is the local government aware of your research?"

"They are," Kalal told her, "but not every detail."

"It's beautiful," Ben said.

"A priest-ruler," said Kalal, plucking the figurine away from Ben and resting his own hand lightly over it as Amelda entered the room. She gathered some dishes and left as they sat in silence.

Ben spun the salt shaker slowly in one spot while he looked across the table at Kalal. "So where are you headed tomorrow?"

"A place near the Guatemalan border, a site with a spectacular pyramid. In fact, it's still the tallest building in the country."

"How long will it take you to get there?"

"I could be there tomorrow afternoon but I'll probably wait until the next morning to visit the ruins."

"Where will you stay?"

"On a farm a couple miles from the site."

"You mean anyone can stay there?"

"There are a few small cabins. Nothing fancy at all, but a river flows through the property. It's quite a beautiful setting." He slid the figurine into the bag and let it down inside his shirt.

Nancy's feet scraped the floorboards. "When do you think you'll finish this study?" she asked, leaning forward on her elbows.

His eyes darted to her for a second and returned to Ben. "A magnificent place, this site. And simple to get to."

"So we could make it there and back in two or three days," Ben said.

"That's correct. Of course, if you care to, you can come with me."

"We couldn't," Nancy said. "We wouldn't want to interfere with your work."

"Don't be silly," he said. "Once you get there you're on your own."

"Ben," she said, touching his arm, "I really don't think we have the time."

He faced her. "We have the time. We would just spend it somewhere else instead of here. I've seen this little island. I literally walked around it today."

"That sounds nice to me."

"This is a new opportunity that popped up."

"Lots of things pop up. You're not obligated—"

"Look!" He threw up his hands. "Let's not sit here arguing." He turned back to Kalal. "Thanks for the offer. If we decide to go we'll be on the dock out here, waiting for the seven A.M. boat." He saw Amelda in the doorway. "In fact," he said a little louder, "we'll settle our bill tonight, just in case we do want to leave early. That's simple enough."

Kalal stood up and took out his wallet.

"Wait a minute," Ben said. "I invited you for dinner."

The tall man placed a few dollars on the table, saying, "But it was my pleasure." He went to the door and opened it; the wind blew the money onto the floor. "See you in the morning," he said, shutting the door behind him.

Ben stood on the upstairs landing facing the sea, his hands on the wooden railing. Nancy was behind him, her arms folded and her hair blowing back as if it were being drawn into the hallway. A lightbulb threw their shadows down on the sand.

"It doesn't feel right," she said loudly into the wind.

He turned his head, allowing his voice to escape. "What does that mean?"

"The man's a little strange."

"He's dedicated to a project."

"He's weird."

"For Christ's sake, we don't need to get into a personality analysis. The man's an expert and we're close enough to see something worth seeing. Why don't you try a little flexibility once in a while?"

She moved up close behind him, put her hands on his shoulders and spoke softly in his ear. "I'm just telling you how I feel. And thinking about us being alone."

"I understand that." He pulled away a few feet to the head of the stairs. "But where's your sense of adventure? Don't you have any interest in any of this?"

"I'm interested in being with you."

"Then come with me."

She made a sour face. "I bought all that fruit for us."

He looked at her with an incredulous expression. "So we'll bring it with us."

"We have too much luggage."

"Then fuck the fruit," he said, and went past her into their room. He began to round up pieces of his clothing and fold them into a pile on the bed. When he was about finished she came in and stood holding the open door, watching. At the windows the wind whipped the curtains violently. She propped the door open with a shoe and bent down to look under the bed for its mate. She found the shoe and a pair of panties and noticed a spider moving along the baseboard. Ben had his back to her as she straightened up and threw the panties. They hit the side of his face; she laughed and reached for a pillow as he dumped his pile of clothes on her and jumped up on the bed. She swung the pillow at his stomach but he grabbed it and pulled her down. She wrapped her arms around his ankles; he fell on top of her and they wrestled into slow motion, finally switching off the lamp. The wind blew through the open room.

The morning was calm and the sea gentle as they left the cay and the reef behind, skirting Styrofoam lobster trap buoys and winding through a maze of mangrove clumps and skimming across open water to find the channel into the coast. As they entered the mouth of the river a few people moved around the quiet marketplace, sweeping out empty stalls; a man with a garden hose sprayed debris—fish scales, bits of fruit and shell, curls of straw—from the smooth stone tables and worn floor off the low wall into the dark, slow-moving river. They motored past single-masted fishing boats; wooden skiffs with Yamaha engines lined the wall in red and turquoise variations. The boat eased under the low bridge with its Sunday-morning pedestrians. A short distance upriver, boys jumped into the water off tires hanging from the seawall behind a gas station.

The boat was tied up against another one, which the passengers stepped across to reach the landing. With their bags, Ben and Nancy followed Kalal over a canal and down a narrow street between densely arranged, two-story wooden houses. People sat in the shade at street level and watched them pass. Cooking fires leaked smoke between the brown boards of kitchens and crowded the air with smells of fried seafood, curried meats and roasted chicken. They passed a little girl walking with a white basin full of tamales and boiled eggs. In the thin spaces between buildings they caught glimpses of women hanging laundry in backyards where palms and orange-flowered poincianas towered over red-rusted, corrugated roofs. Girls in green and pink and blue plastic curlers leaned out of upstairs windows. Snatches of reggae and calypso and American music drifted into the street where children and small, ordinary brown dogs moved at the same speed.

They passed stores with windows displaying records and radios, hardware and fabrics, and a Chinese restaurant—all closed—and came out into a wide street split down its middle by a canal of still, gray water in which scraps of food, plastic and paper floated in idle designs.

A jukebox played loudly from a bar with saloon-style doors. Inside, black youths brandished pool cues and drinks in semi-darkness to the din of music, voices and the sharp smack of billiard balls. Outside by the door a young man in a knit cap and mirrored sunglasses sat on a red barrel, leaning back against the wall with one knee up and one leg hanging down. He called out to the three travelers, then hopped down and sauntered over to them. He offered to show them whatever they were looking for but Kalal cut him short, pointing to the bus station two blocks away. The young man scowled and walked away muttering; he climbed back onto the barrel and watched them a moment, then called out, "Colonial cunts". A tall woman in a dark blue dress and hat walking by with two little girls in matching yellow dresses and white pocketbooks said something to the young man, who looked away and said nothing else.

A small crowd of people milled around the station where three well-used buses sat parked in a row. Inside, Kalal and Ben bought tickets and checked the bags; at an adjacent counter Nancy got coffee for herself and Ben. They went outside and stood at the edge of the canal. On the opposite side a large group of well-dressed people moved slowly down the road in a mass that stretched a block. Little girls in bright, frilly dresses and boys in sport coats paraded at the edges. A choir of women, some in white gloves and hats with lace, sang and clapped in unison. Behind them came a stiff procession of men in dark suits. In the midst of these men a shiny black coffin with gleaming silver handles rode high, rocking along above the heads as if it were floating on air. The pallbearers wore crisp black hats—trickles of sweat rolled down their solemn necks into white collars—but bore no expressions as they carried the box beside the fetid canal. Displaying a wider variety of dress and demeanor, a motley crowd of neighborhood people brought up the rear, and a lone drunk stumbled along singing a song no one else cared to sing.

Passengers boarded and sat; after a while the bus pulled away, lurching noisily through tight turns into narrow streets on its way out of town. When they'd gotten onto the western highway Nancy realized she'd forgotten her new straw hat in the restroom at the station. As they passed the sign to the airport her initial sadness changed to distress and she settled into a gloomy silence. They were leaving the coast. She stared out the window as the landscape turned from marsh to grassland to oak and pine; ahead of them the country undulated in distant ridges and green hills. The sea was gone.

The bus stopped to take on and let off passengers. People got out to walk around or buy refreshments. Through her window Nancy watched Ben and Kalal talking outside. She stayed in her seat. The bus plunged on into the highway's dusty heat. Mountains rose in the south; forests grew across the horizon. The farther they went, the less safe she felt. She looked around the bus and felt a strange isolation, as if she were becoming mute. The passengers had changed. There were no more islanders; the people were Latin or Indian. And the bus moved on, rolling into Central America with the jungle closing behind it. She had a sensation of being cut off, of flowing with an unseen current; the Caribbean was already a distant memory and she was adrift on land.

The bus slowed through a small town and lumbered over a suspension bridge high above a wide, smooth river. Below, a dozen people stood in the shallows bathing and watching the bus. Horses stood in the shade of tall trees near the water. A few hundred yards upstream the bending river was met by the slopes of rolling meadows; downstream the banks were lost in the thick choke of crowding trees. On the other side of the bridge the bus circled a plaza and stopped; the center of the plaza contained a circle of trees and stone benches. Across the street a long stucco building with a clock tower and a flag housed the government's district office and the police station. One man in uniform sat on the steps watching as everyone got off the bus.

"End of the line," Kalal said. They stood in the plaza looking at the town. "The farm is a few miles farther. I suggest we wait out the heat here and then either get a ride or walk the rest of the way."

They left their bags in the police station and walked up the main street. It had the look of the Old West—shops with swinging double doors and wooden-railed balconies that overlooked the street and shaded the worn, dusty planks of front stoops where men in farm hats leaned against walls. In the street a horse was hitched to a wagon and tied to a post. Above it they saw tables with beer bottles and people taking their midday meal.

At the top of the stairs the newcomers were met by an olive-skinned old man in a long-sleeved, floor-length brown robe. He had a great beak of a nose and close-cut gray hair that showed beneath a floppy cloth cap. Along the wall were pictures—a mosque, a city of gleaming spires by the sea, camels beside date palms in the desert—with Arabic inscriptions on them. Scuffing softly in old slippers, he took them to a balcony table.

"You would like tea?" he asked, smiling with stained teeth. A local Indian boy in a white jacket entered the room holding a woven tray. The old man took cups from the tray, placed them on the table and poured the hot tea from a ceramic pot; his long hands, yellowed at the fingertips, hovered briefly over each cup. "I am serving today roasted chicken with beans and rice. You would like three?"

"Only tea for me," said Kalal.

Ben looked at Nancy and she nodded. "We'll have two," he said. The old man put the teapot down and left.

The two men drinking beer at the next table wore straw hats folded up on both sides. A large family occupied a table along the railing. Against the wall at the other end of the open room a stout Indian woman held a baby who began to cry.

"You're not hungry?" Ben asked.

Kalal regarded him passively for several moments. "I'm fasting," he said, "in preparation for our visit to the temple tomorrow." He sipped the tea. "You might consider the same."

"What difference does it make?" Nancy asked.

His face was smooth as he examined her. "That is what was done." He paused and smiled at her. "We'll visit a ceremonial site, a religious center. To understand what went on there, you must know how it was done. And you must make the journey yourself."

"Where?"

"Inside."

"What? A dead culture?"

He refilled his cup; the stream of tea wavered slightly. "If you allow yourself to sink into it far enough, you can experience a—" He paused to think. "—a transference that is quite alive." He looked across the room at the woman and the baby.

Nancy smirked at Ben. The food came but Ben kept his hand on the warm teacup. Nancy began to eat; the tender chicken fell from the bones.

"Look at that woman with the baby," said Kalal, resting one hand over the other on the table. "She's Maya. Notice how round the baby's head is. When their culture dominated this area the ruling families had high, sloping foreheads. They gave themselves longer heads." He pressed one palm against his own forehead. "They would flatten the skulls of their newborn by keeping a board tied against the soft, young head."

Nancy put her fork down, making a face. "That's

84

disgusting."

He put his hand back on his other one. "In this way they distinguished themselves from the ordinary people."

"After a couple generations they must have had some brain-damaged leaders," Nancy said, looking at Ben.

"Like today, you mean," Ben said.

"That's not what I meant."

The horse snorted loudly below them. Ben looked over the railing and saw a man placing a box in the wagon; he untied the tether and climbed up on the seat as Nancy leaned over to see. They looked down on a wide-brimmed round hat and a solid figure in plain black pants and a long-sleeved white shirt. His brown beard hung halfway down the front of his shirt.

"Looks like a farmer from the last century," Ben said.

Kalal peered over the railing. "He is a farmer. A Mennonite."

With the horse clopping over the hard dirt the wagon moved down the street, throwing up a little dust behind the wheels. The back of the man with the reins was as straight as a corner post.

Ben had only picked at his plate. He paid the bill and they walked back toward the plaza. Across from it they passed a man opening his shop; it contained a single, tarnished barber's chair, shelves of cans and jars, a fan, and two wooden chairs against a wall. The middle-aged barber, sporting a crisp Panama hat and a neatly trimmed mustache, flung open a window that faced the river. He began to sharpen a silver straight razor against an old leather strap hanging from the chair. The sound of the short, sharp scrapes seemed to summon two elderly men sitting in the plaza; they walked over and stood in the doorway.

Kalal put a hand to his black-stubbled face and neck, and said, "I think it's time for a close shave."

"Suit yourself," Ben said. "We're going down to the river. We'll meet you here at the plaza in an hour or so."

As they started away Nancy looked back and said, "Don't

85

make any sudden moves."

At the base of the bridge they could see a trail on the opposite side that led down the grassy bank to a wide, rocky shore where some children were splashing about. They crossed the bridge on the planks of a raised walkway along the girders at the side. A car rattled past and the boards vibrated under their feet. They stepped off and went down the trail.

The children stopped playing to stare at the two strangers. Up on the bridge the bus from the coast clattered by, beginning its return trip.

"There it goes," Nancy said.

"And it'll be back," Ben said, removing his shoes.

"You're not going in!" Her voice surrendered some of the apprehension she was holding inside.

"You couldn't keep me out," he said, pulling his shirt off. He bent down and put the contents of his pockets into a shoe.

"You don't know what's in that water."

He walked gingerly on the round rocks, arms outstretched for balance. "I see all these people in it."

She folded her arms. "It looks too brown."

"That's the bottom." He cupped some water in his hands and extended it toward her. "You've never even seen water this clean." He waded out waist-deep. "Ahhh, yes." Looking back at her, he said, "Nice and cool."

He plunged in and swam, his bright, chopping wake smoothly erased by the slow-flowing river. Nancy waded in up to her knees and watched him crossing the current. A short distance downstream a group of women stood neck-deep, talking. Their round heads—with hair pulled back in buns or wound up tightly in colored curlers—were like animated floats turning and bobbing on the water.

At the other side, where the bank dropped into deeper water, Ben swam along the bottom, pulling himself over slimy branches and rocks in the murky coolness. Gliding upward into streaks of sunlight filtered through eddies of sediment, he broke the surface. A narrow dugout canoe, long and rough-hewn, slid over the water along the deep bank, barely slicing the surface. At the rear an old, brown-skinned man cut the water with a dark, wooden paddle; his wiry arms, tough and dark as the worn wood of the vessel, brushed at the water in a rhythm of quiet strokes. A straw hat shaded his face. In seconds he was under the bridge and moving through scattered light, blending into the dark shadows of the riverbank jungle.

At the plaza Ben and Nancy saw no sign of Kalal. They bought sodas and waited in the shade among the townspeople. Children ran and screamed in an adjacent park and Ben grew drowsy watching them. The shadow of a church steeple crept toward the center of the plaza while Nancy slowly tore her drinking straw into pieces.

Appearing out of the people of the plaza, Kalal towered over everyone as he walked up to the low wall where his companions sat. He was very clean-shaven with several red nicks at the base of his neck.

Nancy said, "We thought you got lost."

He looked down at her briefly. "I'm not the one who is lost," he said, and they followed him across the street.

They retrieved their luggage and took the road out of town that the bus would have taken had it continued onward instead of turning back. In the afternoon heat they walked slowly. Two cars passed without stopping. After half an hour Nancy dropped her bag. The men kept walking.

"We should've taken a taxi," she said, and looked back the way they'd come. She saw something on the road moving slowly toward them. In a minute she realized it was a horse and wagon, and soon after, she recognized the driver's hat and beard. "Hey!" she yelled at the men, "it's that farmer."

She waited until he came up beside her and stopped the horse. "Hi," she said cheerily, looking up at the pale blue eyes under the brim of the hat.

"Hullo," he said.

"Can we get a lift?"

He looked up the road at the two men looking back at them. "Where are you going?"

"A farm up the road, on a river."

He held the reins loosely in big, calloused hands as he watched her. "The Pazos farm?"

"I don't know the name."

He looked at the men, and then at her again. "Get on," he said.

She put her bag in the wagon and climbed up on the seat beside him. "Thanks," she said.

He made a clucking sound as he rippled the reins and the horse started walking. He stopped the wagon once more to allow Ben and Kalal to get in the back and started again at the same leisurely pace, the horse breathing a little harder now.

They plodded along the rocky, rutted road; rolling tree-studded pastureland sloped down on one side and wooden fence posts began to parallel the road. Rough outcrops of rock dotted green meadows; cattle grazed in the open or stood bunched together in the shade of great, spreading trees. Beyond the farmland dark green hills rose in a thick mass and heavy white clouds trailed over them.

Nancy turned to the farmer. "What kinds of things do you grow out here?"

He looked at her. "Vegetables," he said, "tomatoes we grow." He pointed to the pasture. "We have animals too. Cows, sheep, chickens. So we have eggs and milk. We make cheese." He smiled at her. "We make a lot of cheese." He reached down into a bag at his feet and handed her a bundle of wax paper. "Take it," he said.

She unwrapped the paper, broke a piece off the chunk of hard white cheese and nibbled at it. "It's good," she said, wrapping it back up. "Thank you."

He stopped the wagon next to a log gate in front of a long, rocky track. Wire fencing ran along the road in both directions. The farmer pointed. "Two kilometers to the river and the farm of Pazos." There were no houses in sight. Kalal and Ben hopped out and grabbed their bags.

"Thanks," Ben said.

Nancy sat staring at the open land. A small bird chirped at them from a fence post. White thistles grew along the road. "Where are you going?" she asked the man.

He pointed up the road. "The next farm is mine."

She stepped down. "We appreciate the ride."

He nodded and shook the reins; the wagon wheels turned.

"Hey!" she called, and the wagon stopped. "What's your name?"

"Ezekiel."

She held up the wax paper package. "Well, thanks for the cheese, Ezekiel."

She watched the wagon slowly climb a rise and descend the other side until finally the man's hat dropped out of sight. Then she picked up her bag and trudged down the track, way behind the two men.

The track rose and fell gently over the land and made a long curve that corresponded to one in the river. Thick vegetation lined both banks and indicated the river's twisting course over a vast section of the countryside. At its end the track cut back sharply to intersect the water and at that point a farmhouse was visible across the river. Downstream the river curved back toward the house. It was apparent that the house stood inside a loop in the river and was, in effect, surrounded by moving water on three sides.

Kalal stood on the bank and yelled across the river. Two black dogs ran out of the trees barking; they paced back and forth at the bank, watching the intruders across the water and sniffing the air.

A few minutes later a boy came from the house and approached the bank. Kalal raised his hand, calling out, "Pablo!"

and the boy descended the bank to a flat wooden boat. A line to the boat hung down from a ring around a taut cable suspended over the river and anchored to trees on both sides. A rope below the cable was attached to stakes imbedded in each bank; pulling hand over hand on the rope, the boy transported the boat across the river in a straight line.

Holding the rope firmly, he kept the boat against the bank while the passengers got in. Then he pushed off and began to pull in the other direction. He was only about ten years old, dressed in leather sandals and cut-off jeans, but his back muscles stood out like a man's as he pulled the heavy boat across the wide current. His soft brown eyes were the color of the riverbank mud.

"Where's your father?" Kalal asked.

"In the field."

"But it's Sunday," Nancy said, smiling at him.

The boy didn't answer, though he looked at her face as he pulled on the rope.

Kalal asked, "Are there other people staying here now?"

"No one," the boy said.

They reached the bank and Pablo tied the boat to a small dock made from split logs. They followed him up steps cut into the steep bank, and flanked by the pair of dogs, walked along a trail through short brown grass to the house.

The house was a simple, solid-looking structure—a cement block foundation with heavy beams and wooden walls supported a corrugated, galvanized iron roof that sloped down two sides from a middle peak. The kitchen, adjoining the house like a screened porch, protruded off one side of the living area, which was furnished with several sturdy chairs and tables and a few throw rugs. A wall divided the main room from the two bedrooms and the loft area above them. A variety of kerosene lamps were scattered around and abundant windows, shuttered and screened, without glass, allowed ample light and air to fill the small house.

Outside at the back corner behind the kitchen, a huge water barrel, fed by rain gutters along the edges of the roof, sat on an elevated platform above a shower room. A pipe ran from the barrel to the kitchen. Some distance away an outhouse stood alone. Beyond that, some horses and cattle roamed a fenced pasture. In a corner of the pasture opposite the house a separate pen with a low, slanted shelter held several goats.

Downstream from the house, four small, thatched-roofed cottages were arranged in a stand of trees that largely shielded them from view. Nearby but apart from the cottages another outhouse stood.

In the kitchen Pablo offered the guests water and then showed them their cottage rooms, throwing open the windows to let sunlight in. Each room had two single beds, a chair, some shelves and a bedside table with a lamp, a box of matches, a bottle of water and a basin. Nancy wrinkled her nose at the musty smell and stepped outside with the others. She tapped the boy's shoulder.

"Where's the bathroom?"

He pointed to the outhouse.

"I mean for bathing."

"The river is there," he said.

"That's fine," Ben said.

The boy left. Kalal went into his room and closed the door. Inside their room Nancy sat on a bed with her hands in her lap while Ben unzipped his bag and took out a few things. The late afternoon light made a yellow patch on the wall and lit strands of web in the corner of the window screen. One of the black dogs trotted by the open door. Nancy lay back on the bed and closed her eyes. She heard the goats bleating loudly, as if they were right under the window behind her head.

Leaving Nancy asleep in the room, Ben followed a narrow path through the trees to the river. Carrying his bag of toiletries he went down the bank to the shallower inner curve of the bend. A long, smooth log lay dry at the water's edge; he sat down to remove his shoes. The sun slanting through the trees cast broad stripes over the water and up the opposite bank. He draped his clothes over the log and stepped into the cool, flowing water, sliding forward as he found its depth. He swam through the current to the other side; coming back he relaxed in the middle and drifted at the surface like a stick, letting the river take him with it and seeing how fast it would. Then he fought against it, returning to the log, and sat down panting. He lathered his hair and his body, whistling in imitation of a bird he heard but didn't see. The current rinsed him and he sat dripping as he brushed his teeth. Combing his hair back, he felt water droplets trailing down his shoulders and along his spine; his skin tingled. When he stood his head felt light and clear, and sudden waves of hunger coursed through his middle. Walking back to the cottage, he pictured them as the harmless ripples a leaf makes falling on a pond. At that moment he decided to stop eating for a short time, not to seek sustenance elsewhere, but simply to empty himself.

He found the room empty, the light fading inside. He put on long pants and a shirt and walked to the house. The sun had dropped below the hills. Nancy was alone at the kitchen table reading a magazine between a water bottle and a basket of bananas. Ben went past her to the rear door and looked out at the land beyond the fence. He saw a figure—Pablo, he thought—heading across the field toward the house.

A short, swarthy man walked into the kitchen from the house. He wore sandals, khaki pants and a white shirt with rolled-up sleeves. His face was deeply lined, his eyes dark slits, his black hair dripping wet. A heavy black mustache hid his mouth; it seemed to rest on his face like a charred stick. To Nancy he resembled a Western movie version of a Mexican bandito without his sombrero. He glanced over the long wooden table at Ben and nodded.

"Hello," Ben said.

"Bienvenidos," the man said. He moved to a cutting table next to an old black stove. A gas canister sat on the floor beside

92

it, and a covered pot gurgled over a flame on the stove, the lid rattling, metal on metal. The man squinted at Ben, who stood with his hands in his pockets, watching. "Everything okay?" the man asked.

"I think so," Ben said, leaning forward with his knuckles on the table. He felt a little weak, smelling the food he would deny himself.

Nancy put down the magazine and pushed it away. "Beautiful place you have, Mr. Pazos."

He pulled a block of hard cheese from its wax paper and cut into it, holding a kitchen knife and pushing the blade down with the palm of his other hand. "You sign the book, on the table—" He nodded toward the living room. "—and put the money in the box." He looked at them both. "Each night you pay ten dollars, each person." He cut another piece. "Para comida— to eat here at night—" He pointed at the table with his knife. "—you must put four dollars more." Then he smiled at them briefly and returned to his task. From the wall of shelves in front of him, he brought down a basket of onions, picked out a couple, quickly sliced them to bits, and knocked the skins into a can at his feet.

Pablo came across the yard carrying a gray-green iguana by the base of its tail. The dead lizard was three feet long; its head swung back and forth just off the ground and its legs flopped out to the sides, the long, jointed toes limply scratching the air. The boy entered the kitchen—Nancy sat up stiffly at the sight of the lizard—and tossed the animal into a tin basin below the water pipe. The body banged against the metal and slid down, the back spines bending as they scraped the side. The long tail hung out over the rim. Outside, a pale red stained the western sky and the goats began bleating for their supper.

Pablo lit two lamps, brought one to the kitchen table and left the room with the other. The smell of kerosene invaded the kitchen and the flickering light bounced off the ridges of the corrugated roof. Moths fluttered into the screens as darkness slowly closed around the house.

93

Ben held the lamp over the lizard. He didn't see any marks. "How'd he get it?" he asked.

Pazos bent into the light and ran some water in the basin. "A stone on the head."

"He threw it?"

"Slingshot."

Nancy stood behind them, peering over their shoulders. "What are you going to do with it?"

Pazos laughed, turning the lizard over in the water. "That's bamboo chicken," he said. "Good food."

"Oh," she said, and went to the other side of the table and sat down.

Pazos pulled a bag out of a cupboard below the shelves and put several handfuls of rice into the pot on the stove. He took the iguana out of the water, shook it, cut off the blunt head and the extremities and slit the tough skin along the ridge of the back. He cut down to the belly and removed the organs; at the door he tossed them to the black dogs, hovering like shadows at the edge of the kitchen. The entrails were snapped out of the air; some low growling ensued over the division, before the end of the tail and the feet were thrown out and a few quick crunches finished the discussion. Slicing and pulling, Pazos carefully separated the meat from the skin, which he removed in one piece and put in the basin of water. Cutting the white meat into chunks he cooked them in a skillet with oil and onions, adding spices from the shelf over the stove. He stirred the sizzling meat with a wooden spoon and shook in spurts of pepper sauce. Setting the skillet aside, he stirred the pot of rice and beans, then took the lizard's head from the cutting table to the outside of the kitchen and stuck it on a nail high above the ground. As he walked by the table, Nancy stared at him and wrinkled her brow.

"For the ants," he said. "They do not sleep." The dogs sat back on their haunches, looking up at the stark, bony head of the iguana.

Pazos heaped rice and beans into the skillet and stirred it

together with the meat. Ben paced at the far end of the table, water springing up in his mouth like dew on morning grass; his nostrils consumed the odors from the stove while the thought of purposeful hunger kept him silent. Pazos took a loaf of bread from a dented tin, brushed off some small black ants, and put it on the table with the cheese.

Nancy said, "Pablo is a quiet boy."

Pazos looked at her thoughtfully before he spoke. "His mother died two years ago."

"Oh—" She touched her bottom lip. "I'm sorry."

He stared into the lamp between them. "She was a beautiful Mestiza woman. She came with me here and we made this house." His eyes smiled briefly in the flame. "One day we are together and the next day she is dead." The smile vanished; he turned away and got plates from a shelf.

Nancy asked, "What happened?"

He put the plates down on the table. "She was bitten by a snake. The barba amarilla. You know it?" She said nothing, watching his eyes for sadness. "No? Maybe you know the other name. Fer-de-lance." She shook her head. He looked down the room at Ben, who stood motionless by the door. Pazos nodded. "You should be careful." He smiled at both of them. "He has a yellow mouth here," he said, patting his chin.

Ben walked out into the yard behind the house, away from the glow of the kitchen. The oily-sweet aroma of the hot food followed him on currents of night air and clung to his clothes. He gripped his stomach and walked farther in the dark, holding his breath. Oblivious to the ground, he looked up at the sky, his pants brushing through the grass. When he felt his lungs would burst, he exhaled and stopped, dragging air in deeply through his nose. An acrid smell cut into his nasal passages and he glanced around, fearing an animal presence. The outhouse loomed beside him; its fumes filled his lungs and choked him. He gagged and covered his mouth. Running to the fence, he grabbed a strand of wire with both hands and leaned forward coughing.

He hung his head, feeling a tightness in his stomach, and stared at the grass, taking deep, deliberate breaths.

In a few minutes he felt better and straightened up. An oval white moon was creeping over a hill, lighting the puffs of clouds above the field and spreading a soft glow across the grasses. A few yards away, under a tree by the fence, a dozen cows sat on the ground watching him in silence, their round eyes wide in the moonlight. He let go of the fence, smelling the cows for the first time, and raised his arms over his head, exhaling completely. The moon moved behind a cloud and he walked back to the kitchen feeling calm but weak.

Pablo sat next to his father, across from Nancy. His plate was scraped clean; he rested his chin in one hand, elbow on the table, and watched Nancy eat. She looked up as Ben came in. "If you're going to go walking," she said, "take a flashlight."

He took the water bottle and a glass and sat down at the end of the table.

Pazos gestured with his fork toward the stove. "There is enough food."

"I'll pass, thanks," he said, and drank some water.

Nancy held up her fork with a tiny piece of white meat on it. "It smelled so good I tasted it," she said. A brown beetle hit the lamp's glass chimney with a tink and fell onto her plate. She flicked it off with a finger and it spun to a stop at the edge of Pablo's plate. He flicked it back and it bounced off her shirt to the floor. "It's not bad for a lizard," she said. "You just can't think about it."

Pazos wiped his mustache. "If you don't like the meat, there is bread and goat cheese." He pushed the loaf a little way down the table.

"I could probably eat goat horns," Ben said, "but I'm just going to pass on the food right now. Okay?"

One of the dogs growled just loud enough to be heard at the table. A flashlight beam zigzagged over the ground, moving toward the kitchen. "The Maya man comes," said Pazos, cleaning his plate with a piece of bread.

Kalal stood in the front doorway by the stove and met the stares of the others one at a time. "Hola, Pazos," he said, looking pale in the lantern light.

"Señor Kalal," said Pazos. "Como van las cosas?"

Kalal stepped forward and Nancy noticed a line of sweat on his upper lip, and then more on his forehead. "No malo, amigo. I am drawn here again," he said, staring into the lantern, "like an insect to the flame." His eyes lifted and focused on Ben's. "You want some tea? Pazos keeps a good blend on hand."

Pablo filled two bowls from the stove and fed the dogs. For several seconds the moon bathed the yard and the standing dogs in bright light before the gap in the clouds closed again. Pazos rinsed the iguana skin and trimmed away the ridge of spines; he stretched the skin on a board, inside up, pulling and pinning its edges, then shook a handful of salt from a box and covered the raw shape, patting the crystals into a smooth layer.

Kalal poured boiling water and floating herbs through a cloth sack into cups he brought steaming to the table. Ben sat hunched over his cup, holding it loosely as the soothing heat rose to his face. After a few sips he felt less hungry.

Pazos lit a cigarette and blew smoke over the lantern; the smoke was pushed upward, caught in the column of heat rising out of the chimney. He watched a spot on the ceiling. Behind him Pablo washed dishes in the basin. Drawing tenderly on his cigarette—thin fingers of smoke curled up over his mustache—Pazos exhaled into the light and broke the silence hanging like a vapor in the dim kitchen.

"At times—" He cleared his throat softly. "—the moon is very strong here." He squinted through the smoke, not looking at any of them. "The light can crack mahogany trees." He drew on his cigarette again, watching the ceiling. "Frogs are touched by the light and they don't move. The next day they are swollen by the sun." He puffed out his cheeks as his eyes moved down to meet Nancy's. She had begun to like him, though with the cigarette he looked more like a bandito than ever, and she thought now he was trying to scare her for no good reason. He turned his head to look at Ben. "Tomorrow is your first trip to the ruins?"

"That's right."

Still squinting, Pazos smiled without opening his mouth, so that his mustache seemed even longer. He puffed on the cigarette once more and stubbed it out. "And you arrive with a strong moon."

"I get lucky once in a while."

"He wants to have a Mayan experience," Nancy said, "so he's playing follow the leader."

In the short silence that followed, Ben cocked his head slightly and watched her as if she were a figure on the horizon.

"And that's the perfect attitude for approaching the Maya," Kalal's deep voice informed them. "Isn't that why we're here?" The question got their attention; the voice demanded it, and his sharp, glistening face assumed a rhetorical intensity to match, barring interruption. "To understand something of their mystery? To walk in their place?" He stood and backed away from the table, bending toward his companions as they were drawn forward to meet his enunciated whisper. "Even, for one bright moment, to be them?"

Having taken the stage, he paused, savoring the moment, extending his arms to hold them. "Imagine you're one of thousands of people gathered in the great plaza—only two miles from here, incidentally, and there was certainly a farm, people living right where you now sit—and like everyone you are looking up at a temple on the top of a giant pyramid. High above you, higher even than the roof of the jungle, stands a man. He is adorned with long, beautiful feathers and heavy jade ornaments and he is one of your leaders, a priest who is about to tell you what is in store for you."

Kalal held them without mercy, a stern minister of truth dragging the captured back into history. He clapped his hands sharply and began to move slowly around the table, towering over the seated listeners. "You are part of a great society—of astronomers, artists, builders—but you're just a regular guy, someone who grows corn or cuts limestone block. Still, you've answered the call to worship and gathered with the rest for an important occasion. You've come for the latest news and the chances are good that it won't be great." As he walked, looking at the floor, sweat dripped off his face. Pablo stood very still at the basin, peering over his shoulder at the storyteller. "Because it's not easy to keep the gods on your side. There are always problems. The corn crop, your mainstay, depends on rain that's too unpredictable, and a crop failure could mean disaster. Disease and sickness could invade your community at any time. Or people from outside your region could attack, steal your food and wreak havoc on your city, where life is so delicately and beautifully balanced between harmony and danger." The low voice grew quieter, projecting sympathy. "Because death lurks everywhere, not only on the earth, but in the sky as well. Just look at the storms and the lightning if you need to be reminded. There is no escape from such primal and malevolent forces." He stopped and raised his hands overhead, palms upward. His hair, stuck to his forehead and the sides of his face, created a dark cowl around his eyes.

"Your priests are astronomers who watch the heavens intensely. Buildings are constructed in relation to the sun's movement. These men track each day and name it. They give it a number. Days, events, and prophesies are recorded in folding books of bark paper using a complex, hieroglyphic language. Numbers are very important in the recorded history of Maya time, so the priests check their figures often with the beads and shells of counting boxes. They know the earth travels around the sun every year, sustained by the relationship. They know the path of the moon and believe in its effect on the earth. They understand the magnitude of these celestial events and are deeply concerned with their own place in the overwhelming scheme of cosmic interactions."

He began to walk again, his voice deep and resonant. "They expect change and calamity. Potential disaster looms large in their observations. They worry over every solstice and every dark and dreaded eclipse. Meteor showers produce hysteria. There is nowhere to hide from such power." He paused to catch his breath, moving back and forth at the end of the room. "The only hope, the only way to keep luck on their side, is to appease these forces—these gods—with a constant barrage of prayers, rituals and offerings."

Kalal turned his back to the table and stood at the doorway trembling, taking in the night air. Across the yard crickets in the trees produced a loud, steady whirring. The dogs lay at the outskirts of the lamplight, their heads resting on the ground. Through the outer darkness moonlight splashed onto the yard, stopping the crickets momentarily as it spread out and washed over the house. On the outside of the kitchen black ants worked on the iguana's head, attacking the open neck and the eyes.

Kalal came back to the table, speaking with fresh passion. "So you've come to see your priest—" He put a hand on Ben's shoulder. "—and you've brought an offering, though you, like many others here, have not eaten for a third day now. You honor this priest, this ruler, this astronomer, because he honors the gods for you. Even now, way up there, he is closer to them, almost in the clouds, and he is dressed like a god himself. You are not surprised by what he says or does. It isn't easy to deal directly with these fickle gods who smile while they're angry." He walked to the other end of the table, pushing his wet hair away from his face. "But the ceremony you are about to witness will help keep things running smoothly."

Pazos caught the attention of his son. "You finish there?" he asked, extending a hand. "Time for bed now."

The boy stood still a moment, looking at the basin, then went to his father and hugged him. He went around the table past

Ben and as he came near Nancy she held out her hand; he touched it and then hugged her too. She held him, kissed his cheek and whispered in his ear, "Sweet dreams," and he went quietly into the house.

Kalal leaned on the table staring at Nancy. "Submission to these gods doesn't come automatically, just because they control your life." He laughed, hanging his head, and then abruptly slapped the table. "You must earn submission, and the priest up there—" He pointed at the ceiling behind him. "—demands your payment." He straightened up, rubbing a hand down his face, and stared at his wet palm. "You see, it's his place, as your link to salvation, to exact the toll." He glared at the three of them in turn. "And that takes some blood."

He picked up a glass and sipped water, grimacing as he swallowed. He set it down with a knock on the wood and pointed at Ben. "As you stand waiting for the ceremony you endure the pain lingering from an early morning visit to the palace. You were taken into the candlelit recesses of inner chambers where religious leaders prepared for the day's affairs. Strong tobacco smoke hung in the dark hallways; you heard unusual cries and moans from unseen rooms. Your priest had already entered a state of hallucinogenic detachment and you were frightened in his presence. Someone in the room handed you a bowl of corn liquor which you were only too happy to drink. This before you underwent a purification—of course you had already volunteered—during which you stuck the sharp tail spine of a stingray through your lips and watched the blood drip into a wooden bowl." Kalal cupped his hands. "As an ordinary citizen you were honored. Lucky to have the chance. A distant cousin of yours, one of the god impersonators who wears a paper mache jaguar mask in today's ceremony, had the privilege of pulling a barbed cord through his tongue." Nancy groaned, turning her head toward Ben, whose eyes stayed on the speaker. "But in his role today he will not need to speak." Kalal smiled slightly, his eyes directed at the base of the lantern. "Others have pierced

101

their penises with stingray spines but they will not need these right away either—there are more important things on the agenda."

He cleared his throat and drank again, then stepped back and faced the length of the table. "And now the ceremony begins," he said, his eyes fastened on the lamp at the center.

"Along the base of the main pyramid musicians are shaking turtle-shell rattles and pounding drum skins with bones and antlers. The high, chaotic notes of ceramic flutes are laced between the deep blasts of conch shell trumpets resounding off the stone walls of the massive structures around the great plaza. It is very hot under the tropical sun and on the lower steps of the temple the god impersonators sweat beneath their masks, and in the crowd of spectators people stir around you and shift their restless feet. Finally a procession begins to enter the plaza. Bearing elaborately crafted gifts and splendid offerings of food, figures dressed as forest animals parade through the open lane in the midst of the throng. Columns of painted warriors file into the plaza to flank the path to the Temple of the Jaguar God. Dignitaries and noblemen follow in jaguar pelts, shielded from the sun by consorts holding basketry parasols. The great ruler rides under the thatched canopy of a chair on bamboo poles carried by the warrior elite and he wears a spectacular headdress made of red macaw feathers and the brilliant, iridescent green tail feathers of the sacred quetzal bird. A huge jade necklace covers his chest and he wears wide jade circlets on his forearms and ankles. As he is taken to the base of an adjacent temple he passes his stela—a carved, stone slab standing upright and weighing several tons—proclaiming him in image and language the rightful ruler, predestined for his place in the lineage of great Maya rulers.

"The chair is lowered. He climbs out and slowly mounts a few steps to a throne covered with jaguar skins. His entourage takes its place around him and, from a dark doorway, women come forth in attendance. When he is ready he lifts his hand and the music stops. He stands and speaks to the waiting multitude.

He reads from a book concerning the significance of today's date. He talks about the many days without rain and the danger to the cornfields and the people. At last he says a prayer to the Maize God and returns to his throne, signaling the high priest at the summit of the great pyramid, far above them all, where the crowd now shifts its attention.

"The priest steps to the edge of the temple platform holding a large carving of the fierce-faced Rain God. In a booming voice he speaks of the drought and then prays to the Rain God. A torch is brought to him and he turns to light an incense burner, a statue of the same god. Smoke drifts into the clear sky and drums sound again as a dozen captives taken in the last raid are brought out by the temple guards. They are bound hand and foot and wear only white loincloths. The long black hair of each has been tied back and their faces are like fright masks, hardly visible to those of you pressed together down in the plaza. But you know the routine and the next part of the ceremony—the humbling of the captives. The hands of the first one are freed and he is encouraged to crawl to the edge of the long flight of stairs and kneel before the crowd. The drums become a chant. The priest presents the sharpened edge of a turtle shell to the prisoner, who is allowed to cut himself—his arms, his chest, his stomach—and bleed for the Rain God."

"My God!" Nancy said. "This is sickening." She looked around the table for support and found none. Across from her Pazos put a finger to his lips and Kalal continued as if he had heard nothing.

"On this day, four of the captives choose to comply with the expectations of their captors and are then retied and taken out of sight. Another, when his bonds are released, grovels and clutches at the ankles of the high priest. He is quickly pulled away and held by the guards. The priest says more prayers, this time to the Lords of the Underworld, the Death Gods. He mentions the Jaguar God; the crowd grows very quiet. Beside the priest a heavy, round stone sits on a short pedestal. In the middle of the stone the sun is carved, its rays and border of clouds forming a pattern of concentric circles on the surface of the altar. The captive is placed on the stone, face toward the sky, and his hands and feet are tied underneath so that the ropes cross between the legs of the pedestal. Meanwhile the drums are beating a slow, steady rhythm of appreciation."

Kalal approached the table and closed his eyes; his voice was nearly a whisper, as if he spoke in confidence. "A box is brought to the priest. He takes out a knife, the handle a polished hardwood, the long obsidian blade sparkling in the sun. The drums quicken and grow louder as the priest steps to the altar and the wailing of the victim is almost drowned out. Holding it above his head with both hands the priest plunges the knife into the chest of the man—the drums stop at once—and the screams fade away in echoes beyond the plaza. Monkeys cry out in answer and birds screech as the priest labors to cut out the heart."

"Oh my God," Nancy cried, covering her face.

Eyes still closed, Kalal raised a fist over his head. "He holds the beating heart over his head to the sky and the blood runs down his arm as the crowd cries out its praises for the Gods of the Underworld. The body is taken off the altar by several subpriests and heaved out over the stairs. It tumbles in a flailing heap and finally comes to rest near the bottom. People can see the body—a contorted mess—more clearly now. At the top the priest places the warm heart in a sacred bowl. A subpriest washes the knife and another washes the hands and arms of the high priest as the next victim is placed on the altar. The drums build to another crescendo and the ritual is repeated. And then again and again, the blood and the expected screams of the victims, the hearts collected, the crowd's roaring approval, the bodies tumbled down, the priest perfect in his execution, the grateful populace numbed and pacified with spectacle.

"Across the pyramid's corner, almost level with the dead men, the great ruler stands and motions to another priest at the base of the stairs. This priest stands on a platform surrounded by his assistants; they wear thick jade earplugs and their teeth are filed to fearsome points and inlaid with bits of jade. At his word they move up the stairs and drag the bodies down to the platform. The crowd presses in as close as possible but the area is cordoned off by guards armed with spears. Some of the people move up the steps of other buildings for a better view as the first body is positioned on a stone table so that the head hangs off the end. Another priest appears; he wears a spotted mask of ocelot fur and wields a special wooden axe with sharp-edged obsidian blades. As people yell and drums are beaten he swings the axe and chops at the neck until the head falls into an urn below the table. And thus begins the dance of flames." With his hands spread Kalal directed their attention to the lamp while he moistened his lips. His eyes remained closed as he took breaths through his dry mouth, making little sounds like hollow beetles blown along a window sill.

"In the center of the plaza a bonfire is lit. As the flames rise and the fire crackles the decapitations continue. Costumed dancers move around the blaze blowing shrill pottery whistles. All around the great plaza people begin to move, singing and dancing with relief as the sun beats down and the fire roars. In their long black hair and white loincloths they resemble the victims and they shake and sweat, happy to live. Animal figures and crazed, drunken god-men drive the crowd to bedlam. The noise is deafening: drums and whistles and screams of optimism. In the afternoon heat the dance of flames becomes a frenzy of elation, the people feeling closer to the gods and the blessings of good fortune, farther from hardship and uncertainty.

"As the sun drops behind the forest trees and the emotions of the day gradually subside, the great ruler disappears into a room behind the throne and the people begin to drift away from the plaza. A series of deep drum rolls sounds something like distant thunder, the rumble of hope. Off to the side priests prepare to burn the sacrificial heads, breaking off the bottom jaws to finish the ritual. A perverse happiness lingers in the plaza, drifting with the smoke and the smell of blood."

Kalal's eyes opened but remained in a fixed position, as if he did not yet see what was in front of him; he took a long, deep breath and concluded. "Out in the settlement women are cooking tortillas, squash and beans in the shade. Deer and forest pig are roasting over fires. People murmur about the steep price of rain as they pass through the last smoky rays of daylight."

He stood looking at the floor and no one said anything. When he sat down Pazos passed him a water bottle. He drank a mouthful, set the bottle on the table and looked around at each of them. In the flickering lamplight his dark eyes were like shiny chips of obsidian.

Ben shook his head. "I feel like I've been there."

"Perhaps you have," Pazos said, standing. He stepped over the bench; outside, one of the dogs raised its head. "I rise before Lord Sun returns from the underworld," he said, smiling at the table, "so I will say goodnight. Sleep well. Buenas noches." He went inside and lit a lantern; its glow receded to the back of the house.

The other three sat quietly around their lantern as more insects found their way into the kitchen. Ben stared at a mango on the shelf above the stove; he could smell the ripe bananas on the table.

Nancy sighed. "It's no wonder those people vanished," she said, brushing at her sleeve, "with all their horrible practices."

Kalal had been looking out the door and now he turned to see her. "What do you mean?" His voice sounded a little hoarse. "They didn't propitiate the gods correctly?"

"I mean they were punished by God."

"Which god?"

"The only God."

"And which god is that?"

"The God in heaven."

"You mean the god of mercy."

"Yes, I do."

"So what do you suppose he did with them?"

She shrugged. "Probably made them all bleed to death. Like maybe sent a plague through and wiped them out."

He nodded, stern-faced. "Yes, well, that certainly would have been merciful."

"People bring things on themselves."

"If only they had known about this one god," he said.

"They were heathens."

He nearly laughed. "Religion was the core of their existence." A look of bewilderment settled on his face. "Don't you see that? They were phenomenal. They had it all figured out. They watched the planets and the sun and saw that they came around at prescribed times. They knew they themselves were in orbit and could predict their relationship to other heavenly bodies. The repetition meant predestination to them. Beginning and end. They equated the cycles of life—day and night, birth and death—not just to themselves, but to other planets as well. Their astronomers saw the big picture and felt helpless. Anxiety got the better of them and they passed it along to the people, convinced them it was real. They taught their people to be afraid, to fear the gods, to fear the sun and the moon, to fear the Earth itself. To fear nature. What they knew, and of course what they didn't know, scared them. This fear propelled their religion which in turn fed the culture. But regardless of the reasons, what they produced was absolutely extraordinary for the time and place in which it occurred." He glanced at Ben and then brought his eyes back to Nancy. "It was civilization."

She looked over at Ben, who was tapping his fingers on the table. "You've got some strange ideas," she said, drawing herself back to Kalal's dark stare.

"Tomorrow you can take a look for yourself," he said.

"I expect to see a pile of rocks. Maybe an old building."

It was quiet for ten seconds, before Kalal said, "I expect you won't see anything at all."

She opened her mouth to say something as a beetle, flying

erratically toward the light, grazed her lip. She jerked her head sharply, catching the insect in her hair, and frantically slapped at it, turning the back of her head so Ben could see. "Is it out?" she asked, flipping up the underside of her hair.

"I don't see it."

"It almost went in my mouth."

He laughed softly. "Please don't mention any food."

Her face hardened. "Why don't you just eat something, for Christ's sake?"

"Take it easy," he said. "I'll eat tomorrow night."

She looked back and forth between him and Kalal. Abruptly she stood up. "Are you ready for bed yet?"

Ben pushed a hand through his hair, feeling the shape of his head. "I think I'll stay up awhile."

She blinked at him. "You want me to go over there alone?"

He dug into his pants pocket and pulled out a small flashlight. "Here," he said, holding it out.

She didn't move. He set it on the table.

She snatched the flashlight as she left. Passing through the doorway she said, "See you at breakfast," and clicked on the light. A few steps outside the kitchen she said, "We're having western omelettes with potatoes and bacon. And fresh orange juice." The light beam followed the trail. "Blueberry pancakes with butter and syrup." Ben laughed. A few seconds later her voice reached them again, fainter now. "Filet mignon, asparagus tips, French fries, barbecued chicken, corn on the cob." Then she yelled out, "With butter and salt." The light was no longer visible to them, but the words were still clear. "Peach melba, chocolate ice cream, strawberry shortcake." The taunts trailed off but Ben was sure he heard "Fettuccini Alfredo," a favorite of his, just before the sounds of night settled in around them again.

"She's funny," he said.

Kalal nodded. "She's frightened."

"Yeah, that too."

"And you?"

"Not me."

Kalal smiled, getting up. He went to the stove with a bottle and poured some water into a pot. He turned on the gas, struck a match and the burner flared to life. Ben watched from his seat, aware that he hadn't moved in a long time. The flame hissed as they waited. One of the dogs exhaled loudly.

Kalal pulled out the cloth bag hanging around his neck, withdrew an object and placed it on the table. Ben picked it up and turned it over in his hands. It was a piece of hard, smooth, yellowed material, four inches long and an inch wide, with a scene etched into its rounded surface.

"This is bone," Ben said, "and these—" He peered closely at it. "—are animals in a canoe. Except this one guy."

"And what's different about him?"

"Well—" He set the piece down, closer to the light "—his arms are up. Ahh! His hands are tied. He's a captive of these masked fellows and they're taking him by river back to their city." He touched the bone lightly with a finger. "This one is, what, a deer maybe?"

"Yes."

"And a pig?"

"A peccary."

"A peccary then. I don't know about this one."

"An armadillo."

"So this man is up the creek without a paddle, in the company of animal-men on their way to the altar. This is truly bad luck."

"His time is running out," Kalal said. "That's all."

"You don't believe in fate."

"Time is the only fate. The only limitation." The water was boiling; he poured it, brought the cups to the table and sat down. "The Maya measured time. All civilizations measure time. But at particular periods, it moves ahead too rapidly, out of control, like a river going over the falls. It plummets into the future. Into uncertainty."

"So the rituals were an attempt to conquer this uncertainty."

"To put it off, even as they realized it was impossible. Beyond their scope." He blew the steam away from his cup. "So they ended up constantly fulfilling their own prophesy of human inferiority in the face of time."

Moonlight fell again over the house. The black dogs lay asleep in the dirt. Outside the kitchen screen, bats picked winged insects out of the silky air, and on the post, the ants worked in a furious silence, stripping the iguana's head. A night wind blew down from the hills, cooling the river and rustling the trees around the house. Ben shivered a little and sipped the tea, savoring its bland warmth while the act of swallowing reminded him of the hunger gnawing at his stomach. He invented images of food without wanting to, then dwelled on them before he could push them away. The tea became the rich broth of a soup. When an insect fell into the lantern and sizzled beside the flame, he smelled meat cooking on a grill. Hit by a wave of fatigue, he suddenly welcomed the thought of sleep but felt so weak that he momentarily doubted he could stand. His eyes closed; he imagined himself on a crowded bus. The bus stopped and everyone rushed out to form a line. He saw a table with bowls of grapes and apples, platters of whole baked fish and loaves of bread. When he got to the table there was only one fish head left. He put the piece to his mouth. With a jerk he opened his eyes and saw Kalal across the table with his head bent down, holding the ancient bone sliver in both hands. Ben stood up and stumbled away from the table. As he came outside both dogs stood up; he stopped a moment, swaying as he looked at the sky, waiting for his sense of balance to return. The moon was almost round, a stark disk overhead, and bright clouds passed near it, swiftly drawn and pulled with the wind.

He looked at the kitchen—Kalal hadn't moved at all—and staggered down the path to the bungalows. The dogs watched him go and returned to their prone positions on the ground.

Around the bungalows crickets were close and loud and the trees cast dark, irregular shadows that moved unexpectedly over the ground. At his room pale light shone from the windows and at the edges of the door. He clicked the latch up and pulled the door open. Nancy, lying on the bed, jumped and caught her breath.

"You could've knocked," she said.

"And that wouldn't have scared you?" He crossed to where she lay by the lamp, still fully clothed. "I thought you'd be asleep by now."

"The bugs are too noisy."

"That's music to sleep by." He drank from the water bottle beside the bed. "I don't think I'll have any trouble." He squeezed toothpaste onto his brush, grabbed the water bottle and stepped outside. He brushed a long time, enjoying the mint taste immensely. He set the bottle down and urinated in the moonlight. The crickets were deafening. He went back in and closed the door. "We have to get up early," he said, "so let's turn off the light and get some sleep." He bent down and kissed her, then sat on her bed to remove his shoes.

"He's losing it," she said.

"Who?"

"Who do you think?"

"Pablo?"

"Very funny."

He stood up and undressed. "The flashlight's right here. And so are the matches." He turned the lamp's flame down until it went out. "It's a beautiful night. The moon's watching over us." His bed creaked as he sat down. "The bed feels good." He stretched out and groaned. "Just relax and welcome the sleep of the dead."

"Thanks. That's a big help."

"Go to sleep." He was already slipping away.

"Goodnight."

"Goodnight, Nancy." A few minutes later he was gone.

Two hours passed, during which Ben slept deeply, hardly moving. Moonlight crept in through a window. Nancy woke from a light sleep and lay still, listening. The room was brighter. The crickets were quieter. Somewhere near the river a frog croaked and another answered. She became aware of the pressure on her bladder and got out of bed to relieve it. More frogs joined the calling. She bent down and found a tennis shoe. Something stung her hand—she screamed, dropping the shoe, and fell back against the wall, shaking the entire room.

The scream shattered Ben's deep sleep. He sat upright and had no idea where he was. He heard his name yelled and scrambled to his feet, his eyes adjusting to the moonlit room. Nancy was leaning against the wall gasping.

"What is it?" he asked hoarsely, hunched forward, eyes darting over the room from windows to door to Nancy on the other side of the beds.

She was holding her hand, bent over. "Something bit me," she said.

"Don't move," he said, scrutinizing the floor. "Where is it?"

"I don't know," she said. "On the floor somewhere."

He climbed back on his bed and leaned over to find the flashlight on the table. He directed the thin beam across her bed as he stood and leapt over to it, then found her feet with the light and passed over her shoe and stopped on a black scorpion five inches long.

"Oh, God!" Nancy cried. With its pincers raised in defense, the scorpion was motionless, the menacing tail arched over its back.

Ben examined the floor around and under the beds, then struck a match and lit the lantern. "Let me see your hand," he said.

Turning toward the light she extended her arm and let it rest in his hands. The small wound was on the soft inside flesh of her right thumb. Her entire hand was red and beginning to swell, fingers thickening. "It hurts, Ben." Her face was pinched; tears ran down her cheeks. "It really hurts." Her breath was coming in short, sharp gasps. "I don't feel good," she said, closing her eyes.

"I want you to sit down on the bed." He put an arm around her shoulders. "And breathe deeply and slowly."

She took a step. "Aren't you going to kill it?"

"Yes." He touched her face as she sat. "And then I'm going to get Pazos. Okay? Just take it easy. I'll be right back." He brushed her forehead. "You're going to be fine." She held the hand lightly—looking at it like it was something fragile she'd found—as the swelling moved up the wrist.

With the flashlight in one hand, Ben picked up her shoe and knocked the scorpion toward the door. It spun and skidded to a stop. He hit it again; it banged into the bottom of the door. He opened it, flipped the scorpion outside, and shone the light around the ground before he stepped out. In the dirt the scorpion struggled to orient itself, moving its legs and curling its tail for battle. Ben knelt and nudged it onto a rock. Nancy staggered to the doorway as he brought the shoe down flat, smashing the hard exoskeleton, spilling the body fluids, delivering the death blow in a crunch that sounded like a bite into a crisp apple.

Nancy lurched forward and vomited on the grass, sinking to her knees and uninjured hand. Ben dropped the light and the shoe, turning to catch her shoulders as she listed to the weak side. He stood and straddled her waist, keeping her up while she heaved and gagged, her swollen hand hanging limply in the grass. Around them the air was still and cool and in the moonlight the ground looked soft as down.

He helped her up and back to the bed, where he wiped her face, gave her a sip of water, and got her stretched out with the sore arm resting on a pillow. She was pale.

"I feel sick," she said.

He pulled the sheet up to her neck. "Just be still," he said.

"I'm going to get Pazos now." He put on pants and shoes, got the flashlight as he left, and kept the light on the path even though it was bright enough to see without it. He saw a light in the house and the dogs standing at the head of the path. He went through the kitchen and into the living room. Pazos stood at a front window.

"What's the problem?" he asked.

"Nancy got stung by a scorpion."

"You see it?"

"Yeah, I killed it."

"She is okay?"

"She looks pretty sick."

Pazos frowned. "Most people are not bothered much."

"Why don't you come tell her that."

The dogs followed them to the bungalows. Ben put the light on the scorpion. "There it is," he said. Pazos nodded and they went inside. The dogs found the spread of vomit and licked at it, picking out bits of iguana meat.

Nancy opened her eyes. Ben put his palm on her forehead. "How you doing?" he asked. Her eyes were scared. "Show Pazos your hand." She stared at Pazos and lifted her arm; the hand was a red lump, the arm puffed out to the elbow, wobbling as she held it up. She let it down, moaning as it sank into the pillow.

"I have been stung by this thing many times," Pazos said. "It is nothing to worry about."

Her voice was hushed. "I'm allergic to stings."

Pazos put his hand on her shoulder. "It's okay. I will make you a drink and you will feel better." He looked at Ben and nodded. "This will pass." At the door he said, "Give her water."

She took a few sips from Ben's hand and fell back, water rolling down her neck. "I need Benadryl," she said.

"If you didn't bring it, we don't have it."

"I need Benadryl." She was gazing at the ceiling.

"Alright, Nancy. I'll hop in the car and drive over to the

all-night drugstore. Shouldn't be gone more than ten minutes." Her sad red eyes turned on him and he looked away for a moment. "I'm sorry." He felt her forehead again. "You heard what he said. You'll be fine." Her eyes closed and he said, "You'll be fine."

He sat down heavily on his bed, laid his arms across his knees and put his head down. He felt a touch of anger at her carelessness but told himself it was an accident. She'll be fine. She might miss the ruins but she'll be fine. He felt a dull ache in the front of his head. In sleep there had been no hunger; now his stomach rumbled for attention. I don't need food yet, he told himself, just sleep. She'll be fine after a good night's sleep. He pictured a can of peas he'd seen in the kitchen, and the mango. Now there's a feast, he thought. Tomorrow, after I get back. No, not tomorrow, today. Today we go to the ruins. After we get some sleep. She'll be fine.

He jerked his head up when Pazos came in, and for a second he thought it was morning. He looked at his watch. Five past three. He got up and went to the other bed. Pazos carried two cups—one steaming, one empty—and a bottle of lotion. "Something for the skin," he said, setting the bottle on the table. He handed Ben the hot cup. "This will help the pain and make her sleep."

"Thanks."

Nancy's eyes were directed straight above. Her front teeth were pressed into her bottom lip. Pazos took a long look at her and left, shutting the door behind him.

"Drink this," Ben said, bracing her neck and tipping the cup to her mouth. He smelled mint; bits of leaves and brown particles floated in the thin, amber-colored liquid.

She sputtered. "Ehh. What is that?"

"Tea."

"It's not tea."

"It's bark tea. It's natural medicine. Drink it."

She took a mouthful, swallowed and coughed once. "That

sucks. My arm hurts."

"This will help."

She took another swallow and shook her head, making a disgusted face. "I could throw up."

He rummaged through his shaving kit and found the aspirin. "Take these," he said, putting three in her mouth. He poured water in the empty cup and she sipped a little. Then he took three himself. He poured some lotion in his hand—it smelled like calamine—and gently spread it over her fat hand, up the stretched skin of her arm to her shoulder. The misshapen extremity didn't seem to belong to her; it was more like some reddish object, hot to the touch, that lay beside her on the bed. He wiped his hands on the sheet. "Now sleep," he said. He bent over and kissed her forehead. "This is no big deal." He turned the lantern down low; there was no moonlight now. Her voice came to him weakly.

"Ben?"

"What?"

"Don't leave me here."

"Don't worry," he said.

He sat on his bed and tasted the amber drink; it was warm and bitter and earthy as rotting bark, the trace of mint doing little to flavor it. He drank the rest of the cup holding his breath, swallowing hard as he finished. He wiped the solid particles from his mouth, spit out some, and set the cup on the floor. Stretching out on top of the sheet, he closed his eyes and lay still with his hands by his sides. He felt relaxed and drowsy listening to the night sounds, the croaks and whistles, the whirring of peace and quiet. A long time seemed to pass; he wasn't sure if he'd slept any but he didn't feel worried. After a while, he thought he might be sleeping. He might be dreaming of lying in bed listening. He felt fine, he realized. He had no headache. Nor was he hungry any more. He was light, not in need of anything. He was very light, pleasantly sleeping in mind of himself. He heard a voice but saw no one in his sleep.

Someone was speaking. The words formed in his mind—he wants to kill you—but made no sense.

"What?" He heard himself speak.

"He wants to kill you."

It was Nancy's voice. He sat up and looked over at her bed, where she lay as before in faint lamplight. "Nancy!"

"He'll kill you."

He got up and went to her bedside. Sweat covered her pale face; her breath was jerky, her eyes closed.

"Who?" he asked.

"You."

"Who will?"

Her voice rose, raspy and strident. "He'll kill you."

"Who will?"

"Him."

Ben swung around involuntarily. The door was closed; they were alone.

Her mouth opened and closed. She began to shudder; sweat fell on the pillow. Ben clamped his hand on her hot forehead and pushed her hair back. Her eyes popped open and her shoulders drew up tightly beside her neck. Her eyes shifted to Ben but they were wide and shocked.

He removed his hand. "Nancy. You're awake."

The large pupils remained fixed on him, not showing recognition.

"Nancy!"

Her words were barely audible. "She's dying."

He grabbed her shoulders and shook her. "Knock off the bullshit!" he said. She turned her head away; strands of wet hair clung to her cheek and her chin rested on the shoulder of the disfigured arm. He stood looking down at her and felt heat rising into his head. "Is that what you want?" he asked. "To be a fucking martyr." He walked to the door and back to the bed. The room felt hot. He went back to the door, threw it open and turned around. He came back to the bed, bent close to her ear

117

and whispered, "Think about it." The lantern flickered, making his shadow jump up and down the wall. "The lamp's going out." He turned her face toward him. "You have a fever," he said. "You're not dying."

He shook three more aspirin out of the bottle and pushed them into her mouth; he slid a hand to the back of her neck and pulled her forward as he raised the cup. She took the pills without looking at him. As he stood watching her, the light fluttered and went out. He closed the door, went to his bed, lay down in the dark and shut his eyes. For a while he remained perched at the edge of nervous exhaustion before plummeting into a few hours of fitful sleep.

Far away he heard bleating; gradually the sound came closer and he woke. Light seeped in through the windows. He heard a light knock. He swung his legs over the side of the bed and sat staring at the floor for a few minutes before he stood. Nancy was still, her eyes closed; he bent close enough to see the pulse in her neck. He drained the water bottle, walked unsteadily across the room, and opened the door. Pablo stood waiting. Ben handed the water bottle to the boy, who ran toward the house with it.

Ben turned his shoes upside down and tapped them on the floor, knocking out some sand and bits of dried grass. He put them on and followed the path to the river. The sky was overcast, the grass wet against his legs. Going down the bank, he shivered. He didn't feel well this morning. He found his muscles tired, his concentration weak, his plans vague. In an effort to clarify the situation, he lined up three simple thoughts: I'll visit the ruins; she'll recover; we'll leave. This was the framework of his future; he saw no details.

The water was cold and wisps of mist floated above the running surface. Kneeling in rocky sand, Ben brought handfuls of the clear water to his face and head; he rubbed his neck and shoulders and kneaded his scalp vigorously. When he stood up a dragonfly cut through his field of view and his eyes locked on something in the grass along the river. Climbing the bank he could see what it was—a dead frog—and stopped to look closer; it was a distended gray frog, puffed up so tightly its bubbly skin was almost smooth. Parting the grass with his foot, he saw another one. They were inanimate objects with legs sticking straight out and eyes wide open, without visible damage or unpleasant odors—like lightweight, round replicas, tilted at odd angles. Toys with too much air.

When he got to the bungalow the door was open and he saw the water bottle inside on the floor. Pablo stood against the far wall watching Nancy. Squatting outside the door Ben motioned to the boy, who came over to look where he was pointing. The scorpion, tail unfurled in the dirt, was covered with ants working to dismantle the hard, jointed carcass. The boy gave Ben a long look and went back inside to the sleeping woman.

Ben sat on his bed and wiped his face with a shirt. The air was already warming. A fly flew in the open door, circled the room and landed on a window screen. Nancy moaned and the boy leaned forward.

"Pablo?" she said, sounding surprised.

He moved to the side of the bed.

"Pablo," she said.

He looked at her with sad eyes but didn't speak.

Her left hand came out from under the sheet. He hesitated at first and then slowly lifted his arm and placed his small hand in hers; his eyes grew wider as her fingers closed on his and he felt the heat of her flushed skin.

"No one is helping me," she told him. Tears welled in her eyes and she swallowed hard. She took several breaths through her mouth; her bottom lip quivered. "Will you help me, Pablo?"

He had not yet looked away from her pained expression but his brow knitted as her tears rolled onto the pillow and he stole a quick glance at Ben, who was sitting with his chin in his hands, watching him. Nancy blinked a few more tears out of her eyes as she pulled Pablo closer, gripped his hand tightly and whispered, "Please get help."

When she released his hand he stayed there with her. He looked at Ben and then her again, back and forth between them several times. She closed her eyes and he backed up a couple of steps. Finally he turned and walked to the door very slowly, as if the floor were too thin to support his weight. Holding his bottom lip with two fingers he looked back at them once more and left.

"Ben," she called.

"Good morning."

"I have to pee."

He got up, shut the door and went to her. "How are you feeling?"

"Terrible."

He leaned over and turned the sheet back. The arm looked worse in daylight. She lifted her hips and he pulled her shorts and panties off. They got her legs over the edge of the low bed, dragging the injured arm off its pillow; she held it against her side and groaned as he helped her into a sitting position. He put the basin on the floor between her feet and supported her weight from one side as she moved forward to straddle it. She scooted off the bed and he braced himself against it, holding her under one shoulder and around her waist as she squatted awkwardly over the target. They waited there a minute and a few drops fell; the trickle became a stream that spattered their feet and drummed a ringing off the sides of the metal basin.

When she was settled back in bed he administered aspirin and lotion and gave her more water. He took the basin outside and dumped it near the outhouse. The sun had burned away the mist and was slanting through the trees. He returned to the room in a warm daze.

"You probably frightened the boy," he said.

Nancy stared at the ceiling.

Sitting on his bed Ben was thinking about having some tea. He heard several flies buzzing now. He'd seen the room getting brighter for a while but he'd taken off his watch and put it in his pocket so he couldn't see it. He felt tired but not sleepy, though he had no trouble picturing himself sleeping. He pictured other images too, cropping up over and over again in his idling mind: swollen frogs, a bonfire with great clouds of smoke, round heads floating on a river.

There was a knock at the door.

"What?" Ben asked.

The door opened and Kalal stood in a rectangle of sunlight.

Nancy stiffened under the sheet.

He took a couple of steps inside, appearing taller than usual in the small room; his features were gaunt, his eyes glowering. He said, "I heard about—"

"Please leave." Nancy gripped the sheet at her chin.

He watched her anxious face a few seconds. "I thought there might be something—"

"I don't want your help. If it wasn't for you I wouldn't even be here."

"I believe you had a choice."

"Please get out."

He looked at Ben and said, "The poison seems to be spreading," then turned and left, closing the door behind him.

Ben got up and walked outside. Kalal stopped and they stood in the sun among the bungalows. "I still want to go," Ben said. "I just want to make sure she's okay first."

"You might have a long wait."

"I think by this afternoon—"

"It's a long walk." Kalal craned his head around looking at the sky, the clouds. "We'll probably get some rain." His eyes lowered to Ben's haggard face. "Alright. Look for me about two or three and we'll go then, as long as you don't mind returning after dark."

"I don't."

They walked along the path to the house. One of the black dogs trotted over from the fence behind the house and sat on its haunches under a banana tree. The house was empty. In the kitchen they sipped tea with honey.

"How are you feeling?" Kalal asked.

"I've been better."

Kalal studied him a moment. "By this evening you'll transcend it."

"Then I'm sure I'll be a happy man."

"A man who doesn't think?"

"A man who feels at home," Ben said.

"A man at peace?"

"A man who remains hungry."

Kalal smiled. Ben finished the tea and wiped his finger around the inside of the cup to get the last traces of honey. Then he washed their cups and set them on the draining board. "See you later, I guess," Ben said.

"Conserve your strength," Kalal said.

Inside the bungalow Ben examined Nancy as she slept. The swelling and redness in her right arm had moved up the side of her neck where a pink stripe disappeared under her hair. In a disturbed sleep her breath was noisy and irregular; once in a while her head twitched or her left arm jerked under the sheet. Ben lay down on his own bed and felt the closeness of sleep. In a state of unaccustomed hunger there seemed nothing better to feel. A slight breeze came through the windows and except for the wind in the treetops the day was quiet. Great shadows of fast-moving clouds rolled over the bungalows as the sun ascended the sky over the farm and the river.

Drifting in and out of a light sleep Ben heard someone humming. A lilting tune came in the window. A woman's humming. He sat up; his throat was dry as dust. The gentle song neared and the woman passed the window; down at the sill, Ben saw Pablo's head pass behind her. They stopped outside the door.

"Hello," the woman's voice called out.

Ben got up—he saw that Nancy was awake—and opened

the door. The woman with Pablo was holding a package and a book and her fleshy white face was fixed in a tight smile. Behind wire-rimmed glasses, her crinkled little eyes jumped from Ben's near-naked body, away from his tired, unshaven face, and lit on the form of the sick girl in the bed behind him. In her bulky gray dress, long-sleeved and buttoned to the neck, the woman seemed shapeless; below the long hem, her thick ankles were covered by black stockings, her feet encased in blunt black shoes. To Ben she appeared to be an old woman but he could tell by her hands that she wasn't. Her hair was gray-brown, pulled back in a smooth, seamless bun and sitting up on the back of her head was a white, mesh bonnet, the strings of which hung loosely down her neck.

"I'm coming from the next farm," she said. "Pablo has told me the girl is ill."

Ben looked down at the boy and stepped away from the door. "Come in," he said.

She brushed past him, followed by Pablo, and stood beside the bed. Her expression was grave. "How are you, child?" she asked.

Nancy pulled back the sheet and displayed the arm. The older woman nodded solemnly and placed a hand on Nancy's forehead. "I brought you something to eat," she said. She stroked Nancy's hair gently. "And I have prayed for you."

Ben stood out of the way, behind the woman. He picked up the water bottle and drank, gulping mouthfuls and letting the water run out the corners of his mouth and down his neck and chest.

"Thank you," Nancy said.

"Are you a Christian?"

"Yes, yes I am."

The woman smiled, holding up the book in her other hand. "Then we will pray together. The Lord will make you well."

Nancy's eyes filled with water—the woman's face became blurry—and she felt a tiny spring of joy bubble in her chest and rise into her throat. When she tried to speak, a little squeak of air came first. She swallowed. "Do you know Ezekiel?"

"He is my husband."

"Oh!" Nancy smiled. "He's a kind man." The woman's face loomed like a cloud over her.

"He is a man of God," the woman said, and held Nancy's hand. "He is coming soon to see you."

Tears began to roll down Nancy's face and then poured unrestrained from the wellspring she let open. She sobbed into a blind fog that seemed to fill the room until she was aware only of the tight grip on her left hand and the throbbing in her right arm.

The woman dragged the bungalow's chair next to the bed and settled herself with the package and the Bible on her lap. Pablo stood behind her against the wall and Ben sat on his bed.

The woman closed her eyes. "'Our Father which art in heaven, Hallowed be thy name. Thy kingdom come, Thy will be done in earth, as it is heaven. Give us this day our daily bread. And forgive us our debts, as we forgive our debtors. And lead us not into temptation, but deliver us from evil: For thine is the kingdom, and the power, and the glory, for ever. Amen.'" She opened her eyes and then the package. "I have banana bread and cheese strudel."

"I don't—" Nancy hated to be impolite "—I don't think I can eat right now."

"You must try, child." She leaned forward with a piece of bread. "We must nourish the body and the soul."

Nancy struggled to sit up straighter. Taking the bread, she nibbled half-heartedly; some crumbs fell down the neck of her shirt. The woman set the package on the edge of the bed and opened the Bible. Nancy coughed lightly and cleared her throat. "Water, please," she said. The woman handed her a cup and watched her drink it. Holding out the empty cup, Nancy said, "Thank you. I don't even know your name."

"Martha."

"Thank you, Martha, for your kindness."

The woman looked at her lap. "I am only a servant of the

Lord." She flipped a few pages and quietly read, "'But they that wait upon the Lord shall renew their strength; they shall mount up with wings as eagles; they shall run, and not be weary; and they shall walk, and not faint.'"

Nancy lay back on the pillow and closed her eyes. The room was hot now. Pablo moved to the foot of her bed. Ben had been staring out the window, his mind wandering over the land. He stretched out now, languid in the heat, as his imagination drifted into a part of the river he had not seen. He heard the squawks of parrots overhead; monkeys peered out from branches above the banks he passed silently, sleeping in the bottom of a long canoe. Yellow fruit dropped into the water but the splashes did not wake him.

Nancy's voice was soft. "I still remember the psalm, the twenty-third psalm, that I prayed when I was a little girl." She licked her lips. Pablo's hands rested on the foot of the bed and he watched her closed eyes and her mouth as she recited, "'The Lord is my shepherd; I shall not want. He maketh me to lie down in green pastures: he leadeth me beside the still waters. He restoreth my soul: he leadeth me in the paths of righteousness for his name's sake. Yea, though I walk through the valley of the shadow of death, I will fear no evil: for thou art with me; thy rod and thy staff they comfort me. Thou preparest a table before me—'"

"'In the presence of mine enemies,'" Martha said.

"'In the presence of mine enemies: thou anointest my head with oil; my cup runneth over. Surely goodness and mercy shall follow me all the days of my life: and I will dwell in the house of the Lord for ever.'" She opened her eyes and saw Pablo's round face. Behind him stood Ezekiel, framed in the doorway, much larger than he had seemed sitting in the wagon, but dressed as he had been then. She smiled at him and he removed his straw hat and came into the room, bringing the smell of horses and fields with him. As he clumped across the floor he glanced down and nodded at Ben, who regarded him

125

from his prone position on the bed.

Ezekiel stood beside his wife, set his hat on the bed and squeezed the hand Nancy extended, covering it with his thick fingers. He leaned over and placed his other rough hand on her forehead; it was too warm and her cheeks were flushed.

"It's good to see you again," she said.

Martha recited, "'And he touched her hand and the fever left her; and she arose, and ministered unto them.'"

Ezekiel took a handkerchief from his back pocket, poured water over it and wrung the excess into the basin, then carefully folded it and placed it across Nancy's forehead. She shivered a little and her faint smile became a grimace. "I'm afraid," she whispered, "that God won't hear me."

He wiped his hands on his pants to dry them. "Take comfort," he said, reaching down and raising the Bible from his wife's hands. He turned the pages and stopped to see Nancy's eyes before he read. "'And when he putteth forth his own sheep, he goeth before them, and the sheep follow him: for they know his voice. And a stranger will they not follow, but will flee from him; for they know not the voice of strangers. Then said Jesus unto them again, Verily verily I say unto you I am the door of the sheep.'" He stopped to look at her again, then his eyes returned to the page, moving over the familiar words as a man walks the path to his garden gate. "'My sheep hear my voice, and I know them and they follow me: And I give unto them eternal life; and they shall never perish, neither shall any man pluck them out of my hand. My Father, which gave them me, is greater than all; and no man is able to pluck them out of my Father's hand. I and my Father are one.'"

Ben lay with his hands behind his head staring up at the thatchwork of the ceiling. "You want to be a sheep, Pablo?"

The boy spun around, eyes round as marbles. Martha looked over at Ben too but his gaze didn't change.

Ezekiel cleared his throat, finding another passage. "'And Jesus said unto them I am the bread of life: he that cometh to me shall never hunger; and he that believeth on me shall never thirst.'"

Ben groaned and turned away from them holding his stomach.

Ezekiel continued, his deep voice reverberating in the wooden room. "'I am the living bread which came down from heaven: if any man eat of this bread, he shall live for ever: and the bread that I will give is my flesh, which I will give for the life of the world.'"

"Pablo, did you ever see a sandwich fall from the sky?" Ben asked.

The boy looked up at the face of the big, bearded man with the book and saw the face form a scowl.

"You hear the Word of God," Ezekiel proclaimed.

Ben rolled over onto his back again. "I hear the words of men."

Ezekiel's face straightened. "You can mock God's Word?"

"I can mock a best seller."

"Ben! Please!" Nancy cried.

"You would blaspheme even as your woman is held in the embrace of the Savior?"

"She's the one who asked for help. I ask for nothing."

"Oh, Jesus!" Nancy turned her face to the pillow.

Martha jumped up, laying one hand on Nancy's shoulder and the other on the side of her face. Pablo backed away from the bed and stood by the wall.

For a moment Ezekiel was taken aback. Pulling at his long beard he shut the book with his other hand. Staring across at Ben his eyes slowly moved to the foot of Nancy's bed and over her covered body to her tearful face, and she turned her head to see him. When he spoke again his voice was calm and reassuring. "'Then shall two be in the field; the one shall be taken, and the other left. Watch therefore; for ye know not what hour your Lord doth come.'"

127

Ben got up, took his shirt and sunglasses off the bed, pushed his feet into his tennis shoes, and walked out. He shut the door, went across the clearing to Kalal's room and knocked. There was no answer. He tried the latch and pulled the door open. Kalal wasn't there. Ben held the door, staring into the neat little room. With a shock he realized the man's belongings were also gone. He went inside and looked under the beds. Nothing. The water bottle was empty; the table held only what came with the room. He sat on a bed, elbows on his knees, and stared at the floor. He exhaled a long sigh of disappointment and for a few moments his mind went blank.

It was hot in the room; his body was covered in a layer of sweat. He felt a little feverish himself. He wouldn't mind some aspirin but they were in the other room and he wasn't inclined to return there now. He sat grasping at thoughts. There was nothing to be done. What about the ruins? Maybe he could find them alone. Not today. With an early start tomorrow he might, though. Sure. Why not? There was nothing else to be done. He felt a little too warm. But there was the river. He stood up. There was always the river.

The air was humid; a layer of clouds distorted the sunlight, making it harsh to the eyes. He put on his sunglasses and walked away from the bungalows to the main path between the river and the house.

Above the dock where the boat was tied, he stood on the bank looking back at the farm. The place seemed deserted. He went down the steps, removed his shoes and waded into the water holding his shirt and shoes over his head. The river was delightfully cool and soothing; he was soon treading water and drifting with the current. A short way downstream a tree grew diagonally out of the far bank; its branches hung over a sandy spot and brushed the surface of the water. As he approached the tree he maneuvered himself toward the side and stepped up into shallow water, then tossed his things onto the sand and plunged back into the deeper water, sinking to the cool bottom softness, where in the murky flow fever and fatigue were washed away and he felt the smooth regeneration of his sagging spirit. As if he could absorb the course and current of the river's life and benefit from its steady journey through his soul.

He swam to shore, crawled onto the sand and stretched out in the shade of the low-hanging limbs. He rested there, examining the branches above him for hidden creatures.

After a while he heard the sound of talking, and getting up on one elbow he peered through the leaves. He saw Martha approaching the bank above the dock and behind her a few steps came Ezekiel, cradling Nancy in his arms. A shock of horrible disbelief shot through Ben—she couldn't die that easily—and sat him up with a jolt before he saw her head move.

They made their way carefully down to the water's edge, Martha first, carrying the Bible. Ezekiel was barefoot; Nancy wore her white cotton dress and was also shoeless. Her right arm rested on her stomach and the left one was hooked around Ezekiel's neck. In his hat and clothes he waded into the river to his waist and, facing upstream, bent forward and eased Nancy into the water. Martha read from the book; she couldn't see Ben and he couldn't hear what she was saying.

He crawled into the water on the other side of the tree and submerged. He swam across and came up quietly beside the roots and grasses at the other bank. A pair of damselflies darted away. Nancy had gotten her footing; Ezekiel held her left hand and steadied her with his other hand against her back. Her swollen right arm hung away from her in the water and the white dress floated out on the surface behind her.

Ben went under again and swam into the current, feeling his way around sticks and roots, and came up close enough to hear their words. This time he saw Pablo, still as a post up on the bank, and the boy saw him. Martha held the open book and adjusted her glasses; the sun glinted off the lenses. A wasp flew over the water between her and Ben. Somewhere downstream a bird whistled like a tolling bell.

"'Jesus saith unto him, I am the way, the truth, and the life: no man cometh unto the Father, but by me,'" she read. "'I will not leave you comfortless: I will come to you. Yet a little while, and the world seeth me no more; but ye see me: because I live, ye shall live also.'"

With water droplets running down his face Ben watched Nancy's back; the white of her dress was bright in the hazy sunlight but she trembled in the cool water. Ezekiel moved his hand up behind her neck and his voice rang out over the river as if to a congregation of weeds and water bugs lining the shores. "'For God so loved the world, that he gave his only begotten Son, that whosoever believeth in him should not perish, but have everlasting life.'" He paused, shifting his weight slightly. "Almighty God, we are gathered here to witness this woman, Nancy, who has taken Jesus Christ as her Lord and Savior." She tilted her head back; her brown hair hung down toward the water and her face was lifted to the sky. Ezekiel braced himself and spoke with authority. "I baptize you in the name of the Father, the Son and the Holy Spirit." He supported her neck and bent her backward into the water until her head was fully immersed. He pulled her up, streaming hair and water, and held her upright—sputtering and quaking and then coughing—as sparkling droplets shook loose and showered back into the river.

Ben stood up; he saw one of the black dogs with Pablo. And then he was able to see Kalal standing back a few feet from the bank above Martha. Kalal saw him at the same time and Martha did also, jerking her shoulders in surprise.

Supported around the waist, Nancy took a short step toward the shore. Looking up at Martha, she noticed Kalal and faltered, losing her balance on a stone. Ezekiel caught her with the arm against her back as he reached down under the water behind her legs and pulled her up out of the river; cradling her like an armload of wood, he splashed to shore with her head lolling against his chest.

Standing in the soft, sandy mud, Martha motioned to her

husband and he turned to see Ben in the water. Ben hadn't moved at all; his arms hung at his sides as he watched them, not knowing what to say. Nancy lifted her head and saw him. She didn't recognize the look on his face but her viewpoint was not quite horizontal. She stared at him but he seemed like a stranger; she felt a cold fear in her heart and started shivering as she tried to sit up straighter.

Ezekiel took a step and she cried, "Wait!" He stopped and turned so she could see Ben more easily. She opened her mouth and nothing came out; the sound of moving water filled the space between them and would not stop. "I wanted to do this," she managed to say. For a few seconds their eyes stayed on each other, then he looked away, up above her.

Kalal came forward to the edge of the bank. "Are you ready to go?"

"I am," Ben said.

Nancy looked up at Kalal and found his eyes on hers. His face was impassive, like a hawk's; she expected to see pity, but did not. For a moment she felt a sense of tremendous loss, a loss of human contact, and her own quickening heartbeat scared her. She had always expected the comfort of strangers but now she saw herself smaller than a child and helpless in the arms of the Savior. She suddenly felt an intense loneliness pulsing in her chest and looked away in tears to see her arm hanging down—an ugly red stranger—and felt each throbbing ache her own blood delivered to it. Her blurry eyes blinked at Ben as she asked, "Where are you going?"

"The ruins," he said.

She looked at Martha's little eyes behind the glasses, the mouth pinched shut. Then she craned her neck up to see over the long brown beard and into the watery blue eyes of Ezekiel. "The Maya," she said.

He regarded her for a moment and then said harshly, loud enough for all of them to hear, "Pagans!"

"Pagans?" The word echoed off the opposite bank as

Kalal shouted down to the river. "We're all seekers here."

Nancy heard Ezekiel's breath rushing from his nostrils and felt his chest pushing against her face as he declared, "'I will love thee O Lord my strength.'" His beard jumped back and forth over her. "'The Lord is my rock, and my fortress and my deliverer; my God, my strength, in whom I will trust; my buckler, and the horn of my salvation, and my high tower.'"

Martha started up the bank; she did not care for public conflict and wished to return home. With the girl, if need be.

Kalal said, "'The Lord taketh pleasure in them that fear him, in those that hope in his mercy.'"

Martha stopped halfway up, clutching the Bible tightly, and looked back at her husband. His cheeks were red; he quivered with anger and looked at his wife as he spoke. "'Praise ye the Lord. Praise ye the Lord from the heavens: praise him in the heights. Praise ye him, all his angels: praise ye him, all his hosts.'" He looked up at Kalal, then over at Ben, motionless in the water. "'Praise ye him, sun and moon: praise him, all ye stars of light.'" Nancy pulled herself closer to him, clutching at his neck.

Kalal surveyed his audience. The boy stood off to his side, absorbed and a little frightened—this was the way people died. His dog sat beside him, watching a yellow butterfly zigzag over the river. Kalal raised his hands. "'Let the saints be joyful in glory: let them sing aloud upon their beds. Let the high praises of God be in their mouth and a two-edged sword in their hand; To execute vengeance upon the heathen and punishments upon the people; To bind their kings with chains and their nobles with fetters of iron.'" He clapped his hands loudly and the dog watched him also. "'To execute upon them the judgment written: this honor have all his saints. Praise ye the Lord.'"

They were all silent then. Nancy felt herself slip down a fraction. She looked up at Ezekiel's face but he wasn't looking at her. She squirmed a little; he brought a knee up and repositioned her weight, jostling her bad arm. Pain shot through it like electrical current and found its way out of her mouth in one sharp cry—and then she was quiet.

Martha went up the bank and waited; Ezekiel followed carefully with his quiet burden and stopped a few feet from Kalal. They watched each other for several moments and then Ezekiel moved closer, so that Nancy—curled up and withdrawn around her afflicted arm—was almost touching the other man. To Ben it looked as though she were being given away.

Ezekiel said, "'I am the vine, ye are the branches. He that abideth in me, and I in him, the same bringeth forth much fruit; for without me ye can do nothing.'" He glanced down at Ben, then turned and began to walk away.

Kalal said, "'And my name is dreadful among the heathen.'"

With his wife beside him Ezekiel kept walking, feeling the slack weight of the carried woman in every step. The boy watched them go.

"Pablo," Ben called, "I'd appreciate it if you'd get my bag and put it in his room." He pointed at Kalal. The boy looked at them both, then bent down to pet his black dog; after a moment he stood and trotted after the others, the dog following. Ben dove into the water and swam to get his shoes and shirt.

They followed the general upstream direction of the river, and though its actual course would have taken them very near the ruins, they cut away and traveled in a straighter line across fields and farmland toward the treeline and the hills.

The afternoon brought heavier clouds and the wind bent the long grasses of the pasture through which the two men moved. In another section of the fenced land, horses grazed in a group; far beyond them were some white buildings—a house, a barn, a shed or two.

They proceeded steadily, not lingering anywhere, and carried very little aside from water. They talked hardly at all, putting distance behind them silently; the physical exertion across uneven terrain demanded their attention and took their energy. Walking empty, they traveled without the burden of food or the mention of it.

Ben trudged along, barely noticing the sky, the distant hills, the fields, the wind, or the occasional appearance of sunlight on the grass. The fever of the quest forestalled any discomfort; emotional grapplings were abandoned in the pursuit. Without understanding why, he felt drawn toward a mystery. In this manner he moved ahead, his mind wandering, sometimes imagining the place they sought.

They walked along rows of beans and squash and came to a cornfield at the edge of the jungle. They moved between the tall plants, an orderly forest of stalks and long green leaves that waved over their heads. Kalal broke off an ear of corn and put it in his pocket. Then they left the field, parting the strands of a fence and going through into the trees, leaving the wind and the sky behind.

Treading on a moist mat of soft leaves and sticks, they pushed through the fronds and shrubs of the understory and penetrated the deep tree-world. Moving under the high green canopy they seemed reduced now, cautiously sheltered like any small animal crawling through the towering gloom at the forest floor. They stopped at the huge, buttressed base of a ceiba tree whose trunk rose straight up over a hundred feet before its branches flared out in a dense crown. "Sacred to the Maya," Kalal said, laying a hand on the tree. There was a raucous screeching overhead—a pair of black toucans leaving the tree, sloping downward through space, their long yellow bills nose-diving them to a lower tree, where they disappeared from view but continued to squawk.

All directions were the same, a maze of thin, light-seeking trees, palms, fallen limbs, wide, moss-covered trunks, vines, leaves, peeling bark, logs and rotting stumps. Ben followed Kalal deeper into the tall trees, into mahogany, cedar, sapodilla, wild fig. Pink and scarlet bromeliads blossomed from tree forks;

purple and white orchids drooped from branches. Clusters of ferns grew up the sides of trunks and out over thick limbs. Brittle wood snapped under Ben's feet; his pants snagged and pulled thin, thorny vines, ripping them through crisp leaves. Brown fronds crashed together to drown out all but the sound of his own movement. He stopped to listen and heard Kalal up ahead. Here and there squeaks and whistles sounded in the underbrush. Partridges scurried over leaves on the ground. Wood wrens flitted around, chirping close at hand. He took one precious swallow of his water and closed the bottle tightly.

He came to a clearing below a hole in the canopy. The sky was the color of slate; clouds blew across the opening. Grass grew in the clearing and several trees on one side showed the remains of fire damage. One huge tree was dead, its limbs gray and spindly, some of its bark still charred. A piece from the top of the tree lay on the ground and Ben understood that lightning had struck there, that he'd seen no sign of man since he'd entered the forest.

Out of the corner of his eye he caught a movement just outside the clearing. He tensed involuntarily and leaned forward, peering around the tree nearest him. He saw a young goat—a brown and white kid—standing timidly and watching him. He moved closer; the kid made a little bleating cry, like a baby, and pulled against a tether tied to a tree at the edge of the clearing. Surprised, Ben looked around for the owner; he heard a low whistle and snapped his head toward the sound. He saw Kalal not far away, waving his arm.

As he approached the place where Kalal waited Ben saw a lean-to shelter about four feet high, a slanted, branch-framed roof of palm fronds lashed between two trees. The open side faced a circle of burnt stones that surrounded a bed of ashes. A small pile of firewood and a log with a flat spot cut into one end lay beside the fireplace. Kalal sat on the log.

"Where are we?" Ben asked.

"Close." Kalal pointed into the trees. "Just over there."

135

Then he gestured in the other direction, toward the clearing. "We're lucky the goat's still here."

Ben looked back the way they'd come. The light was slipping away. "What do you mean?"

Kalal rubbed his hand over the smooth surface of the log. "I mean we're in the land of the jaguar."

Ben stared blankly at Kalal for a few seconds, then looked toward the clearing. "You knew it was here?"

"I brought it here. This morning."

In the following silence the noise of insects became apparent. "You mean the goat belongs to Pazos?" A mosquito hummed in Ben's ear and he brushed it away.

"It did, yes." Kalal stood up and walked a few yards from the campsite to the base of a tree; he bent down, scooped away some leaves, and took hold of a taut length of twine running up the trunk. Yanking down on it he dislodged the twine at the roots and with both hands lowered his backpack to the ground. He pulled the twine down from the branch it hung over, brought the pack to the campsite and leaned it against the log.

"Why do you want the goat?" Ben asked.

Kalal stuffed the twine into the pack and removed a flashlight. "To summon the jaguar." Bent over the pack he laughed. "Actually, I thought we could use it to break the fast." He looked up at Ben. "How does that sound? Fresh roasted kid." He flicked on the flashlight and set it on the flat of the log with the beam directed over the fireplace. Reaching inside the lean-to he withdrew a calabash gourd bowl and set it on the log. From his pocket he took the ear of corn and a knife; he shucked the corn and cut the kernels into the bowl, then poured in a little water and stirred it with the blade of the knife. Ben squatted beside the ring of stones to watch. From a side pocket of his pack Kalal took out a small jar, a box of matches and a scrap of paper. In the light he tapped a couple of tiny lumps from the jar onto the paper, carefully wrapped it around its contents and twisted the ends closed like a piece of candy. He put it in the ashes, struck a match and lit the paper.

"For the God of Rain," he said, and blew out the match. A tiny trail of smoke rose through the beam of light, followed by the piney smell of copal. Kneeling by the stones, Kalal began to mumble. It was nothing intelligible to Ben. He felt a tickle on his forearm and held it into the light beam; a tick wiggled among the hairs. He pinched it off and crushed it between his thumbnail and a rock.

Two little spots glowed red in the ashes; the smoke was gone. Kalal dipped his hand in the bowl and touched his lips. Ben stood, drank from his bottle and hung it back on his belt. "It's getting dark," he said.

Kalal stood beside him. "It's still light on the outside," he said. He put on his pack, picked up the flashlight and walked back toward the clearing. Ben took out his own flashlight and clicked it on. In a moment Kalal came back holding the tether and led the kid past the campsite. Ben followed the little animal through the darkening forest. For a time he heard the short staccato bleats every few seconds—like a sentence started over and over but never finished—until they were finally drowned out by the rising cacophony of insects.

They came to the river and followed it a short distance to a shallow area where their lights shone on the sandy bottom, and Kalal pointed out a series of broad stones. Amid the screams of tree frogs they crossed—the kid splashing uncertainly through the stream—and scrambled up the steep bank with wet feet and muddy hands. The ground continued upward on a slope; as they climbed the hillside the forest thinned out and the lightness of the sky began to seep through. Ahead of them the air glowed between the trees, and they stepped out into the remaining daylight on the open summit of a hill.

In front of them, a squat, rectangular structure on a grassy mound blocked the view ahead. Ben stood catching his breath before the thick limestone and worn mortar of the building; his eyes, moving over the rough surface, could almost feel the texture of the walls. He wanted to feel it with his hands, touch the historic stonework with his own fingertips. Now he could enter this solid place, so intact and so silent, enduring the slow crumble of centuries. The building waited for him, its dark, open doorways like narrow black slots into the past.

He headed across the grass, the whine of mosquitoes around his face.

"Listen!" Kalal said. "It's late and probably no one else is here but before you go into the open make sure there are no caretakers or tourists still around. We want the place to ourselves."

Ben nodded and scampered up the incline to the building; he moved along the rear wall to a dark entrance. In the doorway he smelled the dank air and stepped inside, feeling the tight confines of the space before his eyes could see into its empty corners. Breathing the hollow smell of long-forgotten lives. Hearing in the sudden solitude the distant sighs of ancient times; and still the insects outside, the unchanging buzz and hum of a million generations since. Then he was leaving—anxious for more before this day of discovery was gone forever—and moving again along the base of the back wall. With his hands in the crevices his blind fingers found, he peered around the edge of a cornerstone and felt his heart pounding.

The clearing was immense. He crept forward, hugging the wall. The mound he was on fell away to level ground; stone steps led down to smaller buildings, one a mere foundation, that remained at the base of the rise. From there an open field—a plateau dotted with a few bushes and broken stones—stretched away over the top of the hill. All this he saw instantly, then his eyes stopped at the other end of the field. Rising higher than the surrounding trees was a rough pyramid—a hill itself, not wholly excavated, whose broad base was covered in grass, as yet unstripped of the soil of centuries. On land long ago reclaimed by the jungle the building stood apart once again, a man-made mountain cut free by men. The doorways of its crowning temple stared out over the ever-encroaching vegetation—eye sockets into chambers of secrecy where jade-laden men orchestrated the life of a civilization a thousand years earlier.

For a few minutes the improbability, the puzzlement of the place was so overwhelming that Ben noticed nothing else, neither the noise of the katydids nor the waning light. The wind blew cool over the treetops and across the field into his face. But he felt only the presence of the past, saw only this ancient monument, this standing testament to questions asked and feats performed—a strange reminder of human power and frailty and mystery. A remnant of history's weight.

He walked down the steps into the field; going through the grass he tripped over a rooting armadillo. The startled animal jumped straight up off the ground and bolted for the trees as Ben stumbled forward, catching his balance. He looked around wildly, suddenly feeling conspicuous in the open field, and followed the armadillo toward the trees. Walking along the edge of the clearing he passed an open thatched-roof shelter; under it, a few stone blocks lay scattered, white shapes at dusk.

Above him the temple loomed against the sky. The pale stripe of a path cut across the grassy slopes at the bottom of the hillock and wound around the other side. He peered up at the black doorways at the top; the place certainly seemed deserted. There was a rustling behind him and he turned quickly to see the dark, huddling shapes of wild turkeys moving in a row up the slant of a fallen tree.

Climbing the rocky path he cleared the thickening gloom of the field, ascending in a wide spiral around the hill of stones. On the east side the dusky plateau spread out below him; on the other side streaks of light traversed the low clouds of the western sky and illuminated the tops of trees. The path ended below the temple; he climbed the cracked, uneven steps and stood on the ledge outside the rooms at the summit.

He saw an endless green expanse; the place where he stood was a lone and resolute island in a sea of lowland jungle. A hill growing out of a hill where stones rose into the air and connected the earth to the space above it. He reached up to touch the infinite sky; it was the color of berry stains on the inside of a tin bucket.

From the east the edge of darkness approached; there was a dampness in the air. Birds went winging over the clearing; in the trees their twitterings, whistlings and squawks joined the screeching of countless insects. Standing alone above the jungle, between day and night, Ben felt a quiescent solitude, a profound awe that grew to filter the orchestra of natural sounds, transforming the noise into faint background music, and continued to expand until all vestiges of sound were absorbed and he was left with the impression that time itself might have gone on without him.

The sound of feet scraping on the path below broke the silence. He looked down over the ledge and saw Kalal coming up, leading the goat by its rope; the kid trailed reluctantly, pulling to the side and slipping on loose rocks.

Ben stepped into the high doorway of the closest of the two western rooms. In peculiar flight swallows swooped and curved over his head, entering the chamber only to loop and dive out into space without pause, returning in seconds, their small, humming wings blurring through the narrow doorway with the edgy speed of aerial maneuvers and a frenetic sound of near-collision. Inside there were no windows, no other exits, no passageways to any of the other three rooms; there was the smell of urine. He flipped his flashlight on; the beam climbed the rocks, jabbing into corner recesses. High up, straw spilled from crevices, revealing the nests of the birds. On the ceiling were adjoining rows of clay cylinders, the tubular nests of mud daubers. Down the wall the smooth work of the builders was evident in the great, fitted blocks, the lower ones full of the scratched-in names and dates left by more recent visitors. On the floor: a layer of dusty dirt, a gum wrapper, a crushed film box, bits of rock, a small lizard ducking into the wall as the light passed over it.

Outside, pale light still washed the western face of the temple. Kalal passed the bottom of the steps and went around to the southern side where the hill flattened below the temple into a small, grassy terrace—the only level area on the pyramid's broad slopes. Ben stood at the lip of the temple's southern ledge, twenty feet above Kalal, and watched him tie the kid to a rock, remove his pack and face the wall with raised arms. Ben leaned out to look down the surface; the wall was a carving in deep relief that covered the side of the building. As he stared down at the carving and the man before it, something else caught his eye—just off the wall a distortion formed, a mass of vibrating particles—and he tried to focus on it. A wavering cloud materialized in the air; then he heard the droning. A living cloud, he realized, hornets coming and going from a fissure in the wall. A swarm at dusk, the droning became a furious buzz, like tension in the air.

"The heartland," Kalal said through the buzzing. He waved his arm toward the west, talking to himself it appeared to Ben.

The droning grew louder. Ben stepped back from the ledge, covering his ears, and the sound diminished. Walking down the steps he dropped his hands and the droning intensified. He shook his head, trying to ignore it, but it was like someone was humming a tuneless song in his ear. As he walked onto the grassy terrace the kid moved out of his way. He joined Kalal at the wall, and looking up thought he heard the man humming.

The wall was a massive sculpture of pictographs, images boxed and bordered by the decorative patterns of simple motifs—dots, slashes, swirls and rounded glyphs—that stretched horizontally the width of the building and extended halfway down to the terrace from the temple ledge. The framed images—monkey, serpent, bat and bird deities, human-like animal figures—and the surrounding strips of hieroglyphics fit together in an orderly arrangement, a pictorial design of beauty and balance, like a stone tapestry. It was a grand statement, a work of art, an astronomical frieze, a chipped and cracked puzzle of pieces, interlocking and incomprehensible.

Ten feet up the hornets hung like a dark gas, undulating in the air in front of the wall. The vibrating sound seemed to come from an individual source; it formed swirling patterns in Ben's mind. As he listened it became a voice, unintelligible words escaping from a crack in the wall. He shook his head violently. Next to him Kalal was speaking. "—and aligned with the summer sun," he said, looking over at Ben.

Ben looked toward the sunset; he saw faint streaks in the sky and clouds moving on the horizon. In confusion he looked back at the wall, groping for a train of thought. "It was peaceful," he said, "so peaceful up here."

Kalal made a sound, a laugh in one note. "Not here," he said. "The people lived out there." His arm swept at the treetops. "Daily life happened out there." He leaned forward, placing his hands on the wall. "They came here for ceremonies, to overcome the anxiety of living. Because they believed time was not on their side."

He backed away and looked up at the carving. "Despite their knowledge, their accomplishments, their language and art, the civilization ended." He looked sideways at Ben. "Civilization ends." He looked down and nudged a rock with his foot. "You start with nothing and you end up with nothing. Except these." He stamped his foot. "Overgrown remnants." He moved to the edge and looked over at the dark ground below. "They came here for the ritual. To get the gods off their backs." Turning back he asked, "Who can accept the end?" and began to walk in a circle around the terrace, keeping one hand by his side and the other on the back of his neck, directing his head toward the ground.

"What could they do? Kill the priests and run off into the jungle? What for? The end was always near. So they let the priests control them, let them create a terrible anxiety. The priests told them they were powerless. The gods could turn on them anytime. Smash the planet. Extinguish the sun. Or better yet, kill them in small doses." His hand was pressed against his hip; he seemed to be limping. "Stop the rain. Starve them with drought. Strangle their jungle world." He raised his head and laughed. "Look out there."

Ben looked. Darkness had crept up from the ground, taken the trees and made them all one; it had closed in on the ruins and spread out everywhere, meeting the deepening sky at the horizon. He heard the hornets but could no longer see them. Shouldn't they be inside now? he wondered.

Kalal's voice took over again. "They became overpopulated. Can you believe it? With all this land? Their city-states grew and they couldn't grow enough corn. The crops weren't always good; the land wasn't suitable for great farming. New fields were always needed. They struggled under their own weight."

At his feet Ben heard the kid eating, ripping out clumps of grass—a sound like cloth being torn—and chewing noisily in the dark.

"A mysterious problem?" Kalal asked. "Cultural exhaustion perhaps? Or a civilization growing into its future, where the end is certain. There was no doubt about it. The only question was when. And finally the priests told them. After keeping themselves on the edge of uncertainty for centuries they finally answered the big question: when is it over? Tell us, the people cried."

Kalal cupped his hands around his mouth and yelled out to the dark plaza, "Tell us!" The echo came back—"tell us"—and rebounded off the stone, scattering into the softer places between trees, absorbed by the moist air. The nearest insects shut down for a moment and then revived at once, louder and more insistent. Kalal continued. "We're dying to know." He laughed at the ground, a short laugh like a cough. "And the answer is simple. It's over now." He walked up to Ben and bent down so their faces were close; his jaws were clenched, the skin between his eyebrows bunched into grooves. "Imagine the relief," he said.

Ben stepped aside; he smelled the rank sweat of fasting

from the other man. In the east he saw the beginning of a glow creeping over the treeline. He touched his water bottle, light against his hip, and considered taking a sip. A breeze came steadily at his back but he smelled his own rank sweat too.

"The uncertainty is over," Kalal said. "Civilization has served its purpose. But what is it? What's the point of doomsday?"

No point, Ben thought.

"Just a span of life," Kalal said. "Time runs out."

And Ben thought, nobody stays on top forever.

"But even if it's the will of the gods," Kalal said, throwing out his arms, "who can accept the end of time?" He held his forehead with both hands and moved around the grassy area. "The relief of knowing doesn't last. It doesn't stick. The idea of fate becomes repulsive. It creates a conflict in the heart." He wrapped his arms across his chest and moved in a circle around Ben and the kid, bobbing forward slightly as he walked.

At last a sliver of moon lifted over the treeline; it grew large in seconds, splashing silver over the trees and the stone of the temple. Kalal stopped walking; he faced the east as the moon cleared the trees and its radiance rolled down the pyramid and over the field. The two men stood still in the gauzy light as the enormous round bulk of the moon rose like a great, luminous jellyfish floating up through warm, night water. In the jungle all around the plaza the nocturnal creatures voiced their approval.

Kalal was moving again, holding his throat and pressing his thigh, limping slightly. "What happens when your world no longer contains you?" He stopped to stare again at the moon over the plaza. "You get chaos. You get madness. You get death." He spun around, clenching his fist at Ben. "More and more hearts offered to stop the madness. But where is it coming from? The gods? Is it in us, Ben? A part of us?" Tears rolled out of his bloodshot eyes.

"Listen!" Ben said. He felt the humming in his stomach now. "Listen!" He held out his hands, patting the air.

The rumble was low, barely audible over the jungle noise. Seconds later another wave rolled out of the west, a little louder. Ben sniffed the breeze as he turned into it and smelled the rain. He could see the dark outlines of clouds moving closer.

Kalal stared into the distance, his face drawn in the moonlight. "The Rain God comes," he said.

The breeze was cooler; Ben swayed, holding his arms tight across his chest, watching the other man.

"He comes from the west," Kalal said, not looking at Ben. "The direction of death." His eyes darted around the western sky and he appeared to be listening. His mouth opened slowly as his head turned toward the wall; the moon shone behind him, highlighting in profile his alarmed expression.

Distant thunder rippled the air. Ben shifted his feet. He felt the sound in the blocks of the pyramid. The stones hummed under his feet; the building seemed unstable. Abruptly he felt off balance, as though he might fall, and slowly sank to his knees and spread his hands on the grass. The wall was blurry in his eyes.

Kalal brushed past him and picked up his pack.

"What does it mean?" Ben yelled.

Kalal stepped onto the path, moving away.

"Kalal!"

He stopped and looked back at Ben as if he'd just remembered something.

Ben pointed at the wall. "Can you read it?" His finger stabbed at the air.

"It's a blueprint."

"A blueprint? For what?" But the man had disappeared around the corner. "For what?" Ben shouted after him, and waited, hearing for a few seconds the scraping of Kalal's feet on the path. He noticed the kid straining toward him, pulling on the rope, its head touching the ground near his foot. Overhead the dark clouds advanced toward the moon. The humming grew more intense, blending into the shrill sound of screaming insects. He wondered if the noise actually stopped or if there were times when he didn't hear it. He shuddered, feeling faint, and rolled over onto his back, thinking the humming in his stomach was hunger; it moved to his head and became pain, then sprang to full force and hit him like a breaking wave. He thought of water and fumbled for the bottle at his side, then sat up to a wrenching headache and drank the few swallows remaining. He dropped the bottle and lay back in the grass again, shutting his eyes, thinking of resting through the headache. Then starting back to the farm. Going to the river. He shut his eyes, put his fingers to his temples and pressed.

Thunder rumbled over the hills—a ball on a wooden floor. Raindrops hit his face; a slow pelting began. I can't move, he thought. I'm too near the edge. He opened his eyes and saw the dark sky; out of its void fell single, stinging drops, rushing to earth, beating his body, the grass and the stones. A heavy drop hit his open eye; pain bolted into his head. Lightning could strike me through the heart, he thought. He shut his eyes and let raindrops fall into his mouth. Sweet sky water. Tap tap tap, bursting on eyelids and teeth. Tap tap, drops on the forehead. More and more. Let it come, he thought, as a pounding torrent drenched the hill. Water slid down the walls and covered the terrace, threatening to wash him away. Tread water, he thought, swim to the side.

The flash of light burned his eyelids red—he rolled over—and the explosion came like the crack of a colossal bat above the building, ripping the air with deafening tremors. He jumped, lifted by fear, and staggered to his feet. Rain slashed his back. Impenetrable blackness was everywhere; he stumbled to the wall and held it to stand. His light flicked on, jerking over the ground, and found the kid huddled in a soft, wet bundle against the wall. The light raked across the wall of symbols and returned to the ground; he followed the erratic beam to the path. Lightning erupted in a brilliant, jagged blaze, striking the roof of the temple, vanishing in grounded stone as the clap of shockwaves threw him down, the outlines of trees burned into his retinas and reverberations rocking his eardrums. He uncovered his head, saw the beam shining at him from the base of the steps, scooped it up and ran bent over up the slick steps, one hand grabbing at the stone in front of him. Sheets of water slid off the roof, slapping the surfaces below. He dove into the moist dirt of the first doorway—a flicker of light danced on the wall there—as rain lashed at the trees behind him.

He stood up dripping, shivering with fear and cold, and pushed the water off his face. His light cut through a haze that clung to his skin and entered his lungs. Thick smoke filled the upper portion of the room, tumbled down the walls and curled under the top of the doorway. Incense choked him and he coughed, peering into the room, wanting the fire. Kalal's pack leaned against the wall, his shirt draped over it. Ben turned off his light, stuffed it in his pocket and bent down under the smoke, pulling the bottom of his wet shirt up over his mouth and nose. On his knees and one hand, he crawled to the end wall where Kalal sat cross-legged before a small fire of paper scraps, sticks and cloth. Ben pulled himself close to the heat and put his shaking hands out; with his eyes stoking the dying fire, he hardly realized Kalal was mumbling and when he looked up, seeing the man in the smoky half-light of the tiny flame, he jerked spasmodically and pushed himself back against the opposite wall.

Kalal sat murmuring steadily with his eyes closed, his face serene and spotted with black smudges; two lines ran down his neck from a metal spike there. Ben leaned forward to see it: a thin tent stake pushed through a pinch of skin taken at the throat; from the punctures, twin red lines ran down an inch apart over his bare chest to his stomach. The man was so still—his skin powder-gray and charcoal-spotted, his congealed blood like painted stripes—that he seemed a wax figure decorated for the occasion.

Ben sat back against the wall, chilled and shaking, his teeth chattering violently. The fire dwindled to specks of red nothing; smoke hung in the darkness. He coughed raggedly, each raw exhalation of forced air a wretched renewal of the pain in his head.

The rumbling gathered again, crashed not so close, and the brief flash left darker darkness inside. Ben put his beam on the wall beside Kalal; the backwash of light sifted through the slow-turning swirls of smoke. Kalal's eyes were open. Ben clenched his jaws against the chattering as Kalal watched him, spotted face immobile, his eyes two more black spots. Rain spattered loudly at the doorway.

Ben lay on his side with chills and a hot face. His eyes watered, smoke-stung, and warm tears ran from them; he shut his eyes on the warmth and imagined a crackling blaze, himself on a mat before it. He saw the temple room furnished with chair, table, pictures on the wall, torches. Sleepily he wondered how long he'd been there. A long time? Some time? And he thought, what time is it? Is it time yet? Time for what? Like someone hopping across river stones to stay dry, he moved from phrase to phrase to stay awake: Time to go. Time's up. No time like the present. Time waits for no man. The wrong place at the wrong time. Time heals all wounds. Time flies. Killing time. Father Time.

"Water," he said, opening his eyes. Kalal was quite still, watching the doorway. Ben saw a white candle burning beside the dead fire and sat up. His flashlight lay shining across the floor. He touched his lips, not knowing if he had spoken aloud or in his mind. "Water," he said, feeling the breath on his fingers.

Kalal's voice was raspy. "Not the Rain God."

"It's no one," Ben said.

Kalal looked at him. "A Death God in disguise."

"There's no one here but us."

"The Jaguar God of the Underworld. He's a slippery one." Kalal's voice was low and stern, a hoarse whisper. "You can't turn your back." He stood up slowly into the hovering smoke. "He's not one you can ignore." He moved toward the door and bent over his pack in the faltering light. The rain appeared to have stopped and in the hazy quiet of the room his words drifted along the walls like cool, moist air. "One must prepare for the afterlife."

Ben held his hands over the candle flame and rubbed them together. "The Sun God went to bed," he said, "but he woke up the Moon God and sent the Rain God too. They were joined by the God of Storms, the God of Lightning, the God of Thunder—that's Thor's twin, right?—the God of Wind and the God of Bending Trees." He paused for a coughing fit and then rubbed his hands faster. "And let's not forget the God of Assholes." He looked up to see Kalal facing him, holding something in his hand. Ben picked up the dimming light and shone it on the man, on the object glinting in his hand. "What's that?"

"Obsidian."

"Obsidian what?"

"Obsidian blade, bone handle."

"A knife," Ben said.

"Sacrificial knife, very old."

"You think it'll still cut?"

"I sharpened it."

In the circle of light Kalal stood like an exhibit in a room between times—a tall figure in boots and jeans; long bare chest with two dark lines down the middle; sinewy neck holding a thin, metal spike; angular, brooding face marked with spots and plastered with coarse black hair; long, bony arm ending in a museum knife—and Ben laughed loudly in the stone room, lapsing into another coughing spell. He pushed himself up, straightening his stiff legs, keeping the light on Kalal, and fell against the wall; he stayed there, coughing softly until he caught his breath.

"Are you planning a sacrifice?" Ben asked. He heard water dripping at the door; in his hand the light fluttered as he felt the cold return. He pushed away from the wall and stood upright.

"I'm going to sacrifice the kid."

"The little man in the goat suit?"

"He's the one."

The room became sharp in the bad light, its details crystal clear; each block, every crack and line was visible. The smoke had dissipated, drawn out the door or sucked into the walls.

"Why not a real human?" The room smelled of old, smoked stone and the acrid sweat of fasting bodies. "That's what you really want, isn't it?"

"Are you a volunteer?"

"No, I'm an unbound captive."

"Of who?"

"Of myself. The god of nothing else."

Kalal looked at the doorway, then cocked his head, staring into the corners of the ceiling. After a few moments, his eyes came down and he peered closely at Ben. "You're a free man," he said, "free to go."

"And what are you, a student or a priest?"

Kalal stared at him a little longer and turned toward the door. "We've always been able to destroy each other," he said, and stepped out of the circle of light.

Ben's voice rose. "You can stop this game anytime."

"How do you stop the end?" Kalal said, scraping the wall with the knife as he went out.

The rain had quit completely. Ben stood in the doorway and took off his wet shirt. Aside from the tap tapping of falling drops he heard nothing. The sky was dark, the wind gone and the trees still. The air was thick and heavy, a blanket of moisture that smothered sound. The jungle waited, its silence conspicuous, like a missing pallbearer. Ben forgot the gooseflesh on his chest and arms and gazed out over the solid expanse of trees melding with the sky. There was no light; he saw nothing distinctly, yet his eyes were clear. And for a few fleeting moments in the surreal dead of night he came under the illusion that an unyielding jungle went on and on, retaking the land, covering empty cities, highways, airports and cemeteries. He forgot his trembling and hunger and saw the shape of the silent earth. And the jungle that followed the curve over the edge.

Far away the darkness lightened; he watched the lightness move toward him and soon he saw the trees clearly, the leaves, and then the dirt at his feet grew bright. He extended his arm and a shadow appeared beneath it. Backing inside he took Kalal's shirt off the pack; it stank, but was only damp. He put it on, wrung out his own and spread it over the pack. Out in the cool, bright moonlight a few chirps greeted him. Within seconds the isolated calls became a contest of thousands.

Kalal came up the steps carrying the goat. At the southern end of the ledge he put it down and wedged its knotted tether between two cornerstones. The animal pulled away until the rope was taut and stood looking over the ledge. Kalal went past Ben into the chamber and removed the twine from his pack. Returning to the kid he knelt beside it, wrapped the twine around its belly and tied it snugly. Then he unwound the twine along the ledge, backing up as he measured out a length, until he was squatting at Ben's feet. He pulled the obsidian knife from his waist, cut the twine and stood up. At his neck the two wounds had merged into one dark stain; the metal spike pointed at Ben's head. As Kalal turned toward him Ben sensed the knife below and in his mind he saw it. Black glass, like the black eyes shining back at him. But he was not tense. He felt as though he were watching from deep inside himself, looking out through the holes of his own eyes, while all around the night screaming escalated and the moon poured down, filling the air.

Kalal opened his mouth wide, without a sound, and the veins in his neck stood out. He twisted around, looking at the top of the temple, as he shoved the knife under his belt. He tied the twine around his left wrist, pulling the knot tight with his teeth and right hand. Then he yanked the goat's tether out of the rocks and dropped it, stepping up onto a cornerstone and pulling himself up with long arms as his other leg swung out and found a foothold. Reaching high into cracks and grabbing the edges of stone, he climbed the southern face of the temple like a spider.

The kid stood biting at the twine around its middle. Kalal reached the top and stood up; he peered over the edge at Ben and the kid, wrapped the excess twine around his hands, braced himself and pulled. The kid staggered sideways around the corner, bumping along the wall. The taut length of cord cut into the roof, broke free and caught again, knocking bits of dirt and rock down on Ben as the weight came to bear. Crying loudly the kid struggled to keep its feet as they lifted off the ledge and it swung free, kicking at the wall and then banging into it. Kalal leaned out over the edge of the roof grimacing, his thin limbs straining as he pulled hand over hand, raising the goat in jerky increments up the stone wall.

Ben stepped forward as the animal rose past him. He smelled the foul odor of wet, dirty fur, saw the round eyes and open mouth, and touched the soft flanks moving up through his hands. Dangling hooves brushed his fingertips. Coils of twine were buried in the moist skin of its belly. And all the while its high-pitched, plaintive cries filled his ears and flowed into the night, weaving into the tropical uproar that surrounded the clearing like the clamor at an arena.

Ben followed the example and climbed the corner slowly, his face close to the cool stone. He kept his mind on what he was doing and also thought: a fall from here would only be as far as the grassy plateau. He looked along the surface of the wall and remembered the hornets; they were below him at the other end of the pictograph but with the memory came the sound and as he rose the decibel level seemed to climb with him. By the time he pulled himself over the edge and lay spread-eagle on the top, his ears were ringing.

A ridge of additional stonework ran in a north-south line across the roof, like a wall with gaps in it. Each of the five sections was several feet thick and roughly eight feet high; they were evenly spaced, the gaps between them about the width of a man. Together they formed a crude, serrated crest—a crowning comb displayed to the sky—that divided the roof down its center and added height and purpose to the pyramid temple.

He crawled into the space of the nearest gap and heard Kalal's voice somewhere ahead. "We do what we can." There was a pause. Then he heard, "Nothing," and then, "Time is upon us." He squatted at the edge of the gap, hearing spoken words despite the ringing he couldn't shake. "I know that," Kalal said. And a few seconds later, louder, "It can't wait!" followed by a shout: "Annihilation then!" Ben stood up and stepped out of the space; he was ten feet from the eastern edge of the roof and the whole moon-drenched plaza seemed to open in front of him.

Kalal was squatting against the middle section of the crest with his head tilted to the sky; he held the knife with the flat of the blade against his neck and from his other hand the twine stretched away into the last break in the crest. "I know the time—" he said, and began to pull in the twine as he stood, the goat offering timid, questioning bleats as its hooves tapped across the stones. "—when the gods are ready."

"Kalal, c'mon!" Ben said.

Then the goat was beside him, smelling his leg.

"This won't do any good," Ben cried.

"When the world begins to die," Kalal said.

"Goddamn it, man!" Ben yelled. "There's nothing you can do."

Kalal grasped the twine wound around the kid's back and hoisted the animal with both hands and held it out in front of him.

"Wait a minute!" Ben shouted.

Kalal raised the animal over his head like a trophy as he moved across the roof. Under the twine his fingers dug into the animal's back. Its strident cries triggered the maddening shrieks of mammals and with the hum and drone of insects and the croaks of contesting amphibians a frenzied dissonance rained down on the ruins like an alarm.

153

To Ben it was a sonic assault—the sound of panic and pain racked his head; the noise fit him like leather bindings. He moved toward Kalal, waving his hands in the air. "Go ahead, preacher," he shouted at the man's back. "Kill the fucking goat!"

Kalal turned halfway around. The shadow of the lifted animal fell across him. One black eye gleamed and his torso shone with running sweat. "History stops!" he cried above the din.

Swift clouds covered the moon and erased its light. Ben stumbled backward for safety. His back hit stone and his hands gripped the wall. In stillness he remained fixed to the spot, enveloped by darkness.

In the sky a wavy, luminous line appeared, the trailing edge of the cloud mass moving across the moon. The line brightened and vanished and the moon washed over the clearing.

Kalal was waiting for the light, bent over, holding the squirming animal down by its neck with the knife poised above it. Ben lurched forward. The air crackled and buzzed, vibrating against his inner ear; his equilibrium left him, rolling away like droplets down a windowpane, and he fell. Lying on his side, watching the man and the goat, feeling the vibrations in his head and in the cool stones under him, he felt caught in a vortex of sound.

Kalal had frozen; he glanced at Ben, then turned his head to look into the light above. The kid slipped from his hand and ran. The twine snaking away tangled around his boot and he lifted his foot to loosen it; the twine sprang taut—the kid jerked to a halt and fell—and the man yanked it back too hard. He brought his foot down wide, hitting the edge of the roof; a stone broke loose, he dropped the knife, clutching at the twine as he pitched backward off the edge.

Attached to him, the kid—thin neck stretched, ears flat, teeth bared—slid away too. Kalal hit the ledge below, the kid landed over him at the top of the slope and they tumbled down the steep bank together—like two rag dolls on a string—until they hit the upper path and the kid bounced out, snapping the twine. They rolled down separately to the lower slope of the hill, where the kid came to a stop in the thick clumps of grass. Kalal continued down the bottom tier, limbs flailing loosely, and lay sprawled at the base of the pyramid.

On his stomach Ben looked down over the edge; he raised up on his hands and knees and yelled, "Hey!" His head throbbed like it had been cracked open. He crawled back from the edge and stood up. He peered over again, rubbed his face hard and shouted, "Kalal!"

He went back to the southern face and descended very carefully, his head pounding, his hands trembling in dark cracks, his feet nudging into places he didn't trust.

Walking downhill on the path he picked up speed until he was running, circling the pyramid, scrambling down the last section, sliding hand and foot over grass and rock to the place where the body lay. Kalal was face-up, chest and arms badly scraped, one leg bent under him. His neck was twisted unnaturally. Blood oozed from a gash on the side of his head and from a split cheek. His eyes were open—black and empty.

Ben took a few steps, holding his head, glancing at the body and looking away. He paced back and forth, leaned over the dead man, removed the metal stake still stuck in his neck, and flung it toward the trees.

The kid cried out. Thirty feet up the slope it lay on its side trying to lift its head. Ben trudged up the hill and stood over the young goat. Unable to stand, the animal began to cry repeatedly, bobbing its head with each plea, watching Ben, its eyes rolled back. He turned away, searching the ground, and picked up a rock that wasn't large enough; he threw it aside and wandered down the slope. The animal continued to cry, each feeble bleat sickening Ben. He kicked at a large chunk of stone sticking out of the hill but couldn't dislodge it; at the bottom he settled on a brick-sized piece and went back up. He knelt beside the kid, watching its face while he held the stone, feeling its weight. The animal rested its head on the grass, one round eye fixed on Ben. It let out a little bleat as he raised the stone above his head.

"Jesus fucking Christ!" he yelled, throwing the stone down the side of the hill. He stood up and walked away, slipping on the incline. He locked his fingers behind his neck and stared at the ground. He suddenly spun around and went back to the goat. He took out his pocketknife, opened it and felt the blade with his thumb. Dropping to his knees he closed his left hand around the kid's face, covering the eye, holding its mouth shut, and lifted its head off the ground. He slit its throat and looked away into the trees until it quit twitching. He wiped the blade on its fur and dragged the dead animal down the hill by the twine tied around its middle.

He stood at the edge of the clearing, looking back at the bodies, waiting for the nausea to pass. He pictured his head as a split coconut and thought: I've nothing to vomit. He stayed there awhile, doing nothing, watching the moonlight on the grass. The jungle noise didn't seem particularly loud. Mosquitoes bit his neck and arms. He looked at his watch: ten to one.

He cut the twine off the goat, tied Kalal's ankles together, and using the piece trailing from the man's wrist, tied his hands too. In Kalal's pockets he found a wallet, a pocketknife, a broken compass and the jade frog. He left the compass and put the rest in his own pockets, then dragged the body up the slope by the wrists until it lay fully stretched out. He turned on his flashlight and looped its lanyard around his wrist. Standing sideways on the slope, holding the arms out by the twine, he took a deep breath, pulled the body forward and crouched as it fell on him. He caught it over his shoulders, threw his left arm around the legs and shifted his feet, struggling to balance the weight across his upper back. He remained in a squat, catching his breath; the long legs and arms draped to the ground on either side. Finally he counted to five and stood all at once, feeling a pain in his back. Groaning loudly, he staggered back and forth to the bottom of the hill, nearly buckling under the weight, and started walking toward the trees.

Getting the flashlight into his hand he followed the beam into the jungle, weaving between trees and watching the ground with each stiff step for the course of least resistance. The stumbling effort took all of his concentration. Vines caught on the body; he swung it around, shuffling through leaves and sticks. Thorns dragged across his pants, holding him back. Seeking the light, winged insects flew into his face. Over his own rasping breath, he heard little else except the high-pitched whine of mosquitoes at his ears; they bit his head and face and pierced the shirt on his back. He felt like screaming but instead made strange guttural sounds, drawing deep breaths of seething tropical air and pushing them out as growls. He stepped in a leaf-filled hole and fell sideways, dumping the body over his head and pushing his own face into the damp ground. He jumped up, grabbing the dangling light, and shone the beam in every direction. Brushing off his face, he looked back, trying to estimate how far he'd come. Twenty, maybe thirty yards; not far enough. He pushed his wet hair back and wiped his hands on his pants, then picked up the feet by the twine around the ankles and began to drag the body inch by inch over the jungle floor. Exhausted after five more yards, he quit; his head, neck, shoulders and back ached. Feeling dizzy, he stood resting a minute. In the branches above him there was a movement; he brought the light up and spotted two shining, round eyes. A kinkajou, still as a stuffed animal, stared down into the light, blinking curiously.

Using a heavy stick to scoop out leaves and topsoil, he dug a shallow trench and rolled the body into it. He covered it thoroughly, raking dirt and leaves and sticks, exposing ants and spiders in the process, until there was nothing to see but a mound of jungle matter. Overhead, the fuzzy brown mammal watched, a quiet witness nibbling a piece of fruit, its long tail wrapped around the branch behind it.

Outside the trees, the clearing and the buildings were flooded in brilliant moonlight. Ben carried the dead goat to the backside of the pyramid where the forest grew close; a little way into the trees he dropped the carcass, thinking: it'll be gone by morning, maybe they both will. He went up the hill to the path and trudged to the top, moving like a man in a trance. He was filthy and feverish, his shirt blood-stained, his face and neck puffy with bites, his head throbbing. A light breeze blew and he shivered, feeling cold and warm at once.

Inside the chamber he leaned on the wall over Kalal's pack; he dragged it farther into the room and unzipped it. From a side pocket he withdrew matches and candles, set one on the floor and lit it. He found the canteen, a quarter full, and drained it. He went through clothes, camping gear, the nylon bag of artifacts, a plastic bag of toiletries, a small pouch of tools, a notebook, a passport and traveler's checks. He put on a dry tee shirt and a lightweight jacket, spread a ground sheet out on the floor and sat down on the edge of it. He emptied Kalal's wallet, transferred the cash to his pocket, and started a fire with the checks; he burned the contents of the wallet—an Illinois driver's license, a library card from Chicago, some scribbled addresses, a bus schedule—and then burned the passport. When there was nothing left, he scattered the ashes over the floor and lay down on the ground sheet in front of the flickering candle. Overcome with fatigue, he fell into a febrile sleep long before the small flame burned out.

In the dream he is standing on the roof with Kalal and the kid. The edge of the roof crumbles and they all fall together. On impact he hears an awful crack and winces as they tumble downhill in slow motion. He feels nothing and wonders if he's paralyzed; he is not concerned, just curious. He comes to a stop and gets up, mildly surprised to see that he is not hurt at all. Kalal lies beside him, alive but unable to move; he stares up at Ben and hisses through broken, bloody teeth, "Show me." Ben looks over at the kid and sees that it's already dead. He looks down at Kalal, who repeats, "Show me." Ben decides to get help and takes a step away. In a louder, insistent voice, Kalal says again, "Show me!"

Ben shakes his head but then sees that he is already holding a knife. He bends down and casually brings the blade across Kalal's throat. The action is nonchalant but the knife slices easily, like a spoon through pudding, and a gaping wound springs open. Blood flows freely and Kalal begins to yell. The yelling comes in short grunts and then becomes a deep, sustained howl.

He opened his eyes and lay still in the dark. He felt the hard floor under him and touched the plastic ground sheet with his hand as the yelling came again, a series of raucous bellows that stretched into one long howl. He sat up, alarmed at Kalal's screaming, and felt around for the knife as his memory searched for facts. He went to the doorway and listened. The air was cool and gray; mist hovered over the treetops. The tremendous yells came again—howler monkeys announcing the coming dawn.

The sky began to lighten. Ben stood on the ledge and yawned, stretching his arms overhead; his back and shoulders were stiff but his head no longer ached. He felt light, hollow as a gourd, and extremely thirsty.

He folded up the ground sheet, put everything back into the pack and zipped it up. He put his flashlight in his back pocket, carried the pack outside, leaned it against the wall and went around the ledge to the eastern side. Above the mist-filled clearing he waited for the sun. Roseate streaks crept into the pale blue as swallows darted out of doorways. Saffron rays flashed over the treeline as the rim of the sun came into view. The warmth struck his face and he smiled, relief surging through him like a current; he began to giggle joyously and soon he was laughing so hard that tears streamed down his face. He was light-headed, holding his sides, leaning back against the wall, hearing the laughter of birds. As the full dazzling disk of the sun lifted free, he took the jade frog from his pocket and hung it around his neck.

The pack felt light on his back. Near the bottom of the hill he left the path and moved down the southwestern corner. The grass was heavy with moisture. At the edge of the trees he looked up once more at the wall of inscriptions on the southern face. He stared blankly at the symbols for a few minutes. His mind formed a jumpy rhyme:

House of the sun. House of the bees. The temple brings you to your knees. Easy come, easy go, born so fast and die so slow. Carry the flesh and leave the bone, all together and all alone. First you're here, then you're gone. This you know all along.

He turned around and walked into the jungle.

The light trickled in without touching the brown forest floor. Overhead, gray turned to green, brightened here and there by flowers, crimson and white. The talkative chatter of chirping birds drifted through the damp air. He set the pack down and removed the bag of artifacts, the ground sheet, the notebook and his dirty shirt. He took off the jacket and tee shirt he was wearing, stuffed them inside the pack, covered it with branches and leaves, and put on his own clammy shirt. He stopped abruptly, remembering the obsidian knife. Okay, it's gone, he thought. It's history. He brushed off his hands, picked up the things he'd kept and started to the east on a course that would intersect the river.

The ground sloped downward to the south. He moved lightly through the trees, hopping over logs, side-stepping vines, his eyes noticing where his feet touched. He felt weightless, made of air, as if he were floating. He had no hunger, only thirst; he was aware of it without concern. Suddenly he was at the edge of a dirt road; he stopped in the trees and cautiously peered out. The road was a narrow track—deeply rutted along the sides—that ran up the slope toward the ruins. A short distance downhill a small deer stood poised at the side of the road. As he watched, its head turned sharply and in the next instant it leapt into cover and was gone from sight. A few seconds later he heard an engine; he backed up and crouched low in the undergrowth. A Land Rover came bumping up the hill, grinding in low gear, banging over ruts. He saw a woman with long blond hair in the passenger seat and she looked out the window in his direction as they passed. There were other people in the back; he heard them talking as the vehicle went around a bend. The engine noise diminished and then he no longer heard it.

He stayed where he was, hiding in the underbrush for several minutes. He imagined the woman taking pictures of her friends on the pyramid, finding the obsidian knife and traces of blood. He stood up and walked across the road into the trees, moving with great deliberation toward the river.

The river flowed peacefully through the jungle, its shallow passage lapping and gurgling over sand and stones, beckoning Ben down its tangled bank. On his knees he drank from a rock-funneled current, gulping handfuls of the cool, clear water. He submerged his head, slung his hair back and rubbed the water into his face and neck, cleansing himself of dirt and sweat.

He sloshed downriver in the stream bed, reveling in patches of sunlight. Turtles on logs crashed into the water at his approach. Tiny fish scattered over the bottom. He came to a place where the river split around an island of boulders and bamboo and he climbed out of the water opposite. At the base of a ceiba tree he took out his knife, dug a hole in the soft earth and buried the bag of artifacts wrapped tightly in the plastic ground sheet. He brought a large stone from the river and put it on the spot, then brought two more and placed them so that the three formed a triangle. He folded the notebook, stuck it in his pocket and went back down to the water; a kingfisher eyed him from a high, leafless branch. As he stood knee-deep in the stream the bird dove like a shot, pierced the water and resurfaced, climbing back to the same branch with a flashing fish in its beak. In amazement, Ben thought: I can eat anytime I want.

Soon the river came out of the jungle. Ben stood on the bank under a frangipani tree; sweet white blossoms fell on the water and twirled away in the current. The stream meandered through soft, rolling fields in the distance, shining in the morning sun like a ribbon of glass cut into the land. A cluster of papaya trees grew at the edge of the jungle; the ground underneath was littered with pieces of fruit, bitten and pecked to yellow bits.

Insects buzzed and crawled over the area. At the tops of the tall stalks, large yellow and green fruit hung under the leaves. He pulled on a smaller tree, bending it down enough to grasp one ripe fruit and twist it off. He sat down by the river and cut it open, exposing the deep-yellow flesh and the round black seeds, marveling at it a minute and smelling its tangy ripeness before slicing a thin piece. The meat dissolved in his mouth; he laughed. Sitting in the grass, watching the river and the sky, he ate slowly, the sticky juice running down his fingers and chin. A hawk circled high over the fields.

He continued along the bank. His shoes and pants were wet and heavy, mud-streaked and covered with clinging weeds. His arms and neck were scratched and itchy with welts; his back was stiff and a blister had formed on the ball of his right foot. He stayed out of the water, drying as he walked, and sang nonsensical songs. The sun grew hotter; he took off his shirt, dipped it in the river and draped it over his head and shoulders. Tired one minute, jubilant the next, he plodded along, watching the ground, singing, rubbing his inflamed skin, limping and daydreaming.

He came to a fence; on the other side a number of cows watched him from the field. Up ahead he saw a house and the lavender petals of a huge jacaranda tree and then realized where he was. He walked on, cutting under the fence and away from the river, and heard barking; as he headed for the house, one of the black dogs ran toward him across the land. Growling and barking intermittently, the dog approached and then circled behind him, coming closer as he spoke to it. He climbed over the next fence and crossed the yard between the banana trees with the dog walking quietly beside him. He saw Nancy standing at the kitchen doorway. She came out, looking well, smiling and clean in a white tee shirt and shorts, her right arm slightly puffy. She threw her left arm around his neck and he hugged her.

"I dreamed you were dead," she said.

"Not quite," he said. "How are you feeling?"

"Better. I'm recuperating." She pulled away from him.

"You smell bad."

"Really?"

"God, you look awful too."

"You don't have to call me God."

She pulled the shirt off his head, staring at his face, the bloodshot eyes and blank smile. "I don't find that particularly amusing."

"What do you find particularly amusing these days?"

She examined him, her eyes moving over the dirt, the abrasions, the jade frog hanging at his chest. "I find it strange, funny in an odd way I guess, that any of this happened. At first I did, I mean." She was looking into his tired eyes. "But now I think it's God's will."

"I think it's utter fucking madness," he said, "but maybe we're talking about the same thing."

"Are you angry?"

"No."

"Are you sorry?" she asked.

"About what?"

"About us."

"I don't regret anything, Nancy. We follow our paths and sometimes they run parallel, sometimes they separate."

She searched his eyes and looked away, down at the dog. "So where's Kalal?"

"He's gone."

"Where?"

"Guatemala."

She nodded at the frog. "He gave you that?"

"Yeah—a parting gift."

"I see." She shrugged. "And how was the trip?"

"Fine."

"You don't sound very enthusiastic."

"It was a subtle experience."

She hung the stinking shirt over his shoulder. "Well, I'm glad you're alright."

"I'm glad you are too."

In the bungalow he found his things as he'd left them. The water bottle was full and he drank from it. He put Kalal's notebook in his bag, stripped and threw his clothes in a corner. Wearing a towel he took his shaving kit down to the river, shampooed and bathed meticulously, then stood dripping, naked in the sun, brushing his teeth for a long time. He shaved using a hand mirror and cut himself several times; in the little, square mirror he watched curiously as thin, watery lines of blood ran down his neck. He rinsed his face and dried off, went back to the room, shut the door and stretched out on the bed; sleep was instantaneous and bare.

He woke in the yellow light of afternoon and lay still, staring at the ceiling. The room was warm; his hair was damp at the roots. He sat up and drank more water, feeling ill at ease, as if he'd forgotten something. He put on shorts, gathered his dirty clothes into a bundle, took his bar of soap and went back to the river. Sitting on the log he washed and wrung each item, tossing it up on the grass as he finished and taking care, if not delight, in the task. He strung a line in the breeze and hung the clothes over it.

The kitchen was empty; a pot of beans cooked on the stove, flavoring the air. Ben made tea and sat on the end of the table, watching twilight come to the fields. He heard the shower spattering and stopping and a few minutes later Pazos came out with wet hair.

"Buenas," he said, going to the stove.

"Evening, Pazos. How's everything?"

"It goes," he said, looking over his shoulder. "You had a good walk."

"We did. An interesting time."

Pazos nodded, stirring the beans. "Where's the Maya man?"

Ben waved his hand toward the fields. "He kept going."

Pazos put on a pot of water for the rice. "I lost one

164

animal," he said, watching the other man.

Ben sipped the tea. "I know that," he said, meeting the stare. "He took it. I guess maybe for food." He paused, believing his own sincerity. "He asked me to pay you for it." The dogs trotted up out of the dusk and sat down outside the door. Pablo came in carrying a bag, glancing and grinning at Ben.

"There he is," Ben said. "How are you, little man?"

The boy set the bag on the table. "Good," he said, and took out eggs, bread, tomatoes and a block of cheese.

"And how are the neighbors?"

"Good." He put the eggs in a basket and handed it to his father.

Pazos poured rice into the pot on the stove and put a lid on it. "You hungry?" he asked, cracking an egg into a bowl.

"I could eat something," Ben said.

Pablo was washing his hands at the basin as Nancy walked in, waving a flashlight around. "You people going to eat in the dark?" she asked. She set the light on the table and lit the lantern; a cocoon of light enveloped the kitchen. She smiled at Ben. "Good evening," she said, standing demurely in her clean white dress. She looked soft in the lamplight and her hair was silky, pulled back and tied with a white ribbon.

"You look nice," he said.

"Thank you." She put the flashlight in her shoulder bag and took out a small Bible.

Pablo set plates and forks on the table, put the bread on a plate and brought a water pitcher and glasses. He sat down across from Nancy. Pazos dished out rice and beans and eggs with cheese, tomatoes and onions, then put a bottle of hot pepper sauce on the table and sat down. Nancy said a blessing over the steaming food; as she spoke, Pablo looked up at Ben, who winked at him. The boy smiled and dropped his head.

Outside the door the dogs watched expectantly, occasionally snapping at flying insects. Ben finished half his food and took his plate out to the dogs. Pazos lit a cigarette and smoked, leaning forward with his elbows on the table. Nancy pushed her empty plate aside and opened the Bible.

"This is from the Book of Psalms," she said to Pablo. "'Blessed is the man that walketh not in the counsel of the ungodly; nor standeth in the way of sinners, nor sitteth in the seat of the scornful.'" She cleared her throat and took a sip of water. "'But his delight is in the law of the Lord; and in his law doth he meditate day and night.'" She held the book up and tapped it with her finger. "'And he shall be like a tree planted by the rivers of water, that bringeth forth his fruit in his season; his leaf also shall not whither; and whatsoever he doeth shall prosper.'"

Outside, Ben knelt between the dogs; he scratched their heads and rubbed their bellies and they rolled in the dirt.

Nancy continued at the table. "'The ungodly are not so: but are like the chaff which the wind driveth away. Therefore the ungodly shall not stand in the judgment, nor sinners in the congregation of the righteous.'" She licked her lips; her face glistened in the lamp glow. Pablo watched her, his chin resting in his hands, one foot swinging lightly over the floor. "'For the Lord knoweth the way of the righteous: but the way of the ungodly shall perish.'" She looked up, took a cloth from her bag and dabbed her cheeks and upper lip.

Ben came in and set his plate in the basin. "I hope that's not the only book around here."

"He likes to be read to," she said. "Alright?"

Pazos smiled as he stood up. "He can listen while he cleans." He went into the living room and lit another lamp as Pablo began to gather the dishes from the table.

Nancy read: "'I will not be afraid of ten thousands of people, that have set themselves against me round about. Arise, O Lord; save me, O my God: for thou hast smitten all mine enemies upon the cheek bone; thou hast broken the teeth of the ungodly.'"

"He'll like that part," Ben said.

"Do you mind?" she said.

She read to Pablo as he worked at the basin; from time to time he looked over his shoulder to watch her face as she spoke.

Inside, Ben and Pazos reached a quick financial agreement; afterward Pazos smoked, talking about some of the guests he'd had at the farm and the countries they came from. They could hear the drone of the reading in the kitchen.

When he went back out Ben roughed up the boy's hair. "Goodnight, Pablo. Sleep tight."

"Buenas noches," the boy said.

The moon was up. Around the bungalows crickets played their songs. In his room Ben sat on the edge of the bed near the lamp. With a knife point he drained the blister on his foot and covered it with a bandage. He put on a sock and walked around the room to test the feeling. There was a light tap at the door and an accompanying voice, "Ben?"

"Yes?"

Nancy opened the door. "I wanted to talk to you."

"I don't want to hear any scriptures."

"No, I know. I didn't come to read." She came in and shut the door. Ben sat down on the bed; she came a little closer and stood looking at him. "I'm just trying to understand—" she said, folding her hands. She paused and started again. "It's been a strange vacation."

"It's not the vacation," he said. "It's life."

She hesitated. "I feel like God saved mine."

"Don't be ridiculous. You weren't going to die."

"In a manner of speaking my life was saved."

"So now in return I suppose you'll waste it."

"You're so cynical!"

He looked at her for a few moments, then down at the floor. "I'm sorry," he said. "I don't really even know what it means to waste a life. I imagine that by the time you find out, it's over."

"But if you've done God's will, you go on."

"To that magical place where everything's cool? Where

there's no frustration, uncertainty or anxiety?"

"You can reject it or have everlasting life, Ben."

"I know the routine—the instillation of fear, followed by repentance, then salvation—the die now, live later plan. It doesn't work for me, Nancy."

"It's comforting."

"It's crap! I can't go around believing crap just to be comfortable. I can't pretend."

She didn't say anything for a minute. She frowned, looking at her hands, and unclasped them. "What's the plan?"

"I'm leaving tomorrow." He tried to smile. "What about you?"

She stood there nodding to herself, fighting the implication of his question even though she had expected it and wasn't afraid. "I told Martha—she stayed with me last night—that I would visit them before I left." She smoothed the front of her dress. "I have a low-grade fever. I should probably stay another day anyway, before I travel." She lifted her injured arm a little, to illustrate. "Would you mind waiting?"

"I should get going," he said, squeezing the back of his neck. "I'll just see you back at home."

They were silent for a time. She went to the table and picked up the water bottle. He asked, "Do you need anything? Money or anything?" She raised the bottle and drank. With the lamp behind her, he saw the outline of her body through the white dress.

She set the bottle down. "No," she said. She stepped closer and stood looking down at him. "Isn't there anything left?" she asked.

He stared at her parted lips and his eyes moved down over the front of her dress. "I don't know," he said, placing his hands lightly on her hips. After a few moments his fingers inched over her stomach and gathered the dress in handfuls; he tugged downward, pulling the light material tight over her chest, making the curves of her breasts press out against the cloth. As he watched, her breaths came quicker. "Maybe there's a little something left," he said, pulling her closer and leaning forward. He put his mouth on the dress, on the roundness under it, and sucked her through the thin cotton, pulling her nipple up hard against his tongue. She pulled back and turned, offering her other side; he drew her in with his teeth, moving his hands to her back, pressing her toward him as he pulled with his mouth. Squirming against him, she groaned in pain; he released her and she stood with her head back, chest heaving, her dark nipples pushing out against the wet cloth clinging to them. He put his hand under the dress, between her legs, and held it there as she squeezed her thighs together over and over, clamping and releasing his hand. He pulled her panties away and slipped his fingers inside, feeling the wet swelling, stroking her as she leaned on him. He stripped the panties down to her feet and stood up, pulling the dress over her head. She lay down on the bed; he got his shorts off and knelt between her legs, kissing and licking her while she touched his hair lightly.

He kissed her stomach; her eyes were shut. "I guess the only proper thing," he whispered, "would be the missionary position."

Her eyes opened. "This isn't a good time to make fun of me," she said, taking a look at him as he eased down on her.

He reached over and turned the lamp out. "I never fucked a fanatic before," he said.

"And you're about to let the chance slip away."

"Open up before I say anything else."

She widened her legs, spread herself open, sighed as he slid inside. "Be nice," she whispered.

"Doesn't this make you a hypocrite?"

"What?"

"Fornicating with the ungodly." He pressed his mouth on hers, muffling her protest as she bucked up against him. He pushed deeper into her and she hit him on the back with one arm; he fucked her harder, rocking her hips until she wrapped her

169

arm around his neck, hanging on to him as she arched her back in carnal pleasure and their violent rhythm accelerated. In their hybrid passion they withheld judgment, forgot the fatigue of travel and fate, the strain of separation and danger, and gave up the power of possible belief for temporal satisfaction. With a low, sinking moan she felt herself unleashing around him; and he, still pounding roughly in the smooth fitting, cried out with his sharp release. Energy faded like steam on a mirror and they oozed through a hazy relief into the gray doorway of sleep.

In the stone-colored light of pre-dawn he eased quietly out of bed and got his flashlight. He trotted down to the misty river and washed himself rapidly in the brisk water, awakening his brain and quickening his heart. With his skin tingling he grabbed his damp clothes, took down the line and slipped back into the room. He dressed and packed by flashlight; Nancy lay on her side breathing deeply, her hair splayed over the pillow.

In the kitchen Pazos stirred sugar into a dented pot and Ben waited quietly, smelling the sweet steam. A minute later they stood at the stove sipping strong, hot coffee from small glasses. Pazos lit a cigarette and blew a cloud of smoke into the cool air.

Ben finished his coffee and said, "I have to go."

Pazos called into the house, "Pablo!"

The boy came out rubbing his eyes. Ben picked up his bag and Pazos asked, "You leaving the woman?"

"We're not going the same direction," Ben said, glancing at the dogs outside. "It's better this way."

"She staying here?"

"Make her an offer."

"Can she cook?"

"She can, pretty well, actually."

Pazos smiled and they shook hands. Ben went through the door and Pazos said, "Buen viaje."

"Adiós, amigo," Ben said, and started down the path with Pablo and the dogs. They went down the bank to the steely river and got in the boat. Pablo pulled them into the current and the dogs stood in the bow, looking down into the rushing water. In the east the sky was blue-gray, like metal.

"Take care of your father," Ben said.

The boy nodded.

"And your animals."

The boy stared at him.

"Will you do that?"

"Yes."

The boat approached the other bank. "And take care of yourself. Okay?"

"Okay," the boy said.

They shook hands and Ben climbed out. He went up the bank and stood looking at the river and the farm. When the boat was halfway across he waved and the boy waved back, then he turned and left, heading up the rocky track. He walked in a daze; morning arrived and birds took wing across the rugged pastures. By the time he reached the road his foot was hurting and he sat by the gate for a few minutes, looking up and down the empty road. It looked the same both ways. He stood up and threw his bag over one shoulder, looking back to where he'd come from, toward the town and the bus to the coast, and began to walk in the other direction.

After a while he passed another gate, the next farm. He kept walking. A car passed, going the other direction. The vegetation grew thicker on both sides of the road. Ahead, to the north above the trees, he saw the flat black shapes of slow-spiraling vultures. Soon he came to a rutted side road and stopped. A small wooden sign stood in the weeds; its faded letters read: Archaeologic Zone. He moved on, feeling the heat. A car came his way and he motioned for a ride but it passed without slowing.

He came to a small village. Several men mingled outside a green café with bright blue saloon doors. A huge black and white hog nosed in the dirt at the corner of the building. From where he stood on the road Ben could see a sign farther ahead and he walked close enough to read it—Guatemala frontier: 2 kilometers. He went back to the café to get some breakfast. At the door the men moved aside to let him enter.

MOHO BIGHT

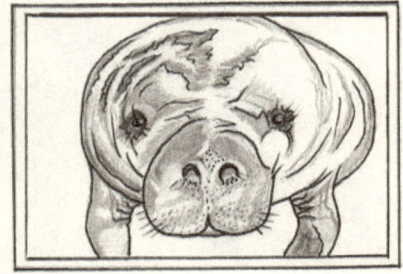

The gods first lived in superhuman power and beauty on the top of snow-clad mountains or in the darkness of caves, woods and seas. Later on they drew together into one god, and then that god became man.
—Carl Jung

Through the winding channel they tear, the captain out for adrenalin and terror and the sheer exuberance of speed on the water, a joyride for the visitor. In the staggering late-morning heat the sun shines across the hot green land and strikes the surface in shifting planes of flat, blinding light, the boat seeming to glide through the channel's curves between brilliant parabolas of rolling mercury. The Boston Whaler roars and banks along its serpentine path, the wind blows the heat past the men behind the console, and the engine's vibrations course through their limbs. When the visitor leans out the wind ripples the skin of his face and forces water from his eyes, forces his tight smile, threatens to rip the hat and sunglasses from his head. At the wheel the captain is grinning at all he surveys.

Herons lift silently like avian spirits, their squawks of disturbance drowned out by the engine's forceful cry. The watery land stretches away in all directions but after several days the visitor knows some channel patterns, senses as they turn east and then north again that the vast lagoon lies just beyond the mangrove ridge to their right, remembers the main creek ahead and the final turn that will take them back into Laguna Vaca and home.

Directly in their path a rounded shape breaks the surface, an island in the narrow channel. The visitor points, expecting the captain to throttle down, shouts "Slow down!" His words are lost as the boat remains on target, the throttle pushed forward, the visitor gripping the console rail with both hands as the impact lifts the boat and throws its hull starboard, the engine's brief, airborne whine obliterating his shouts, the captain pulling back as the boat regains the water, struggling to correct the trajectory and make the turn as they enter the creek.

The visitor steps wide for balance—one hand on the rail, his arm stretched as the aft end slides around—glimpses another vessel, a flash of white passing with two other men, faces frozen in shock before the cracking collision, then his head slams, impact and momentum, a sliding sensation, loss of cognition, the tropical water pulling him into its solemn and turbid embrace—these last fragments of time lost to him forever.

ONE

Turtles in a row.

He lies on his back too, not sleeping, not dreaming, but seeing these dozen or more dead on their rounded backs, two hundred pounds each, he'd guess, the series of flat shell-bellies like a line of plated tables under a long table of watered concrete, all turned the same direction, their yellowish heads one after another, side by side and identical in a repetition of images that seem cast by opposing mirrors and make these few appear many in this picture in his mind. Turtles in a row. Water drips to the floor beside the nearest and he, the observer, bends closer to the inverted head, the configuration of scales around the thick-lidded eye as clear as the cracks in the intricate ceiling above his bed. Down the line of heads, movement travels trance-like, all the left eyes slow-blinking, all the white throats rising in feeble breaths, each alive in its own hard coffin, each pair of tough fore-flippers pierced and drawn together, strung and bound in blue monofilament.

When he coughs his lungs cave in and push out, expectorating the buried memory of a mud-water filling, this action like a grater taken to his tender, worn throat while the incident itself is not seen, only tasted. His head aches constantly and he has all but given up trying to remember. It's been nearly a week, the nurse tells him, most of it slept, which is fine for a head injury. Though the pervasive smell of the sea is rank, so something is not right. The doctor will see him again tomorrow, he's told, but she with her silver cart, clean white dress and shiny black face is all he knows here; he watches her precise bedside motions and listens and takes his medication. She smiles and tells him how lucky he is and he does not need to answer. The swelling is down, just you rest. She has no name tag but he knows her by sight. Meanwhile the man in the next bed has bandaged eyes and someone down the room emits low moans with every breath.

A woman comes through the ward and finds him in his corner bed sitting up and watching the window, and through it the sea and sky, with half-closed eyes. She stands in his view at the foot of the bed; her tee shirt has a drawing of a parrotfish and a slogan that reads: No Teef De Reef. Above it are long curls of blond hair and a genuine smile that he is both glad and surprised to see. "California dreamin," he says in a raspy, unfamiliar whisper. "Have a seat."

"Hello, Reese," she says, sitting on the edge of the bed. "How are you?" And when he nods, she does too. "Yeah, the nurse tells me you're nearly ready to walk out."

He watches her a few moments, enjoying her sunny demeanor and feminine presence, then points at the water pitcher next to the bed. She pours him a cup; he sips, gently clears his throat, coughs lightly. "I'm surprised to see you, Heather."

"Well, I came another time and you were sleeping. I was going to bring your stuff up—Dale still has it at the lodge—but I didn't know if you were going back there or home or what. I can bring it day after tomorrow if you want." She waits for him to answer but he doesn't and she says, "Sorry, you don't have to decide right this second," and then after another pause puts a sudden hand to her face. "Goodness, you don't even know what happened, do you?"

"I went fishing."

She smiles a new smile, admonishing. "You tried to sink the boat with your head."

He touches lightly his forehead and the bandage there and his fingers follow it around the circumference of his head as his eyes appeal to her. "Why would I do that?"

"Dale hit another boat."

He closes his eyes a moment, trying to see it, but cannot. "What happened?"

"He was coming out of a channel into the lagoon when another boat went by." She studies his face for glimmers of memory and adds, "Says he was trying to avoid a manatee. But that he hit it and that's what caused it. If you can believe that."

Reese watches her frowning but knows no reason to believe or disbelieve. "Then what?"

"Then you went to the bottom."

"Who got me up?"

"Dale did."

"Anyone else hurt?"

"Just the manatee, I suppose. There were two guys in the other boat but your boat—Dale's boat—hit their engine so they were alright."

"What about Mafius?"

"I don't think he was there."

"For some reason I thought he was."

"Well, not in the story I got."

"Don't you believe it?"

She looks over at the man with the covered eyes. "I don't believe half of what Dale says."

179

"You don't like him, do you?"

"No, I don't like him."

"I didn't think you had a bad word for anybody."

She almost laughs. "Being Peace Corps doesn't make me a saint. But I don't think Dale gives a hoot about Laguna Vaca. It's just a good place to fish, a good place to play cowboy for yahoos. He's not part of the community."

"But he does employ some local people."

"Oh yeah, he's teaching a few people something about exploitation. Who do you think's getting the better deal?"

"You just told me the man saved my life."

"No, I just told you a reckless jerk nearly killed you and that a dead fisherman is no good for business."

Reese suffers a coughing fit and then they sit quietly for a few minutes, until Heather suggests some fresh air and they go down the staircase to a long first-floor porch facing the sea, where on wooden benches a teenage girl in a hospital gown giggles with two friends and a nurse sits beside an old, silent man at the far end, and in the morning breeze and screen-strained light they take their seats before a barren beach held by thirty or forty black vultures standing on the sand at the water like burned and ruffled shrubs under a raving sun.

"I get the feeling you tend to associate me with Dale," he says.

"I do that with every guest at the lodge. The thing is, I'm not prone to get very involved with someone who comes down for a week or two to fish and buys me cashew wine."

"I was just being friendly."

"Yeah, I know. There aren't so many women in Laguna Vaca and the occasional lodge beauty is usually with her husband."

At the water a plastic bag is torn open and a flapping tussle occurs between birds over the contents; one lifts off, sweeps away over the sand, joined in seconds by half a dozen more who follow closely its swift dips and rises, its sharp turns, screeching at the sight of the dangling prize in its gray beak, pursuing this selfish scavenger while their stationary brethren stand in onerous boredom.

"Thanks for coming anyway," he says. "We're not very well acquainted, I know."

She is watching the birds, not smiling, and after a few moments turns to face him. "The truth is, I was coming to see a friend of mine and I decided to drop in on you too."

A larger, more skillful and persistent bird overtakes its weary adversary on the ground, steals and swallows the reward, and stands alone while one by one the stray fliers return to the group. Reese smiles sourly. "I appreciate the honesty."

"Like I said, I'll bring your things up. Or if you want to go back there you can ride with us."

"What's wrong with your friend?"

"She's just had some tests done."

"What's the verdict?"

"They don't have a clue."

She fidgets in the heat of the porch while he arrives at the conclusion that he must begin to decide things again, and then does so by saying, "I'll go with you."

This she didn't expect. "Don't you need to get back to your landscaping?"

"I need to recuperate."

"I'll bet that means fishing."

"It means anything that helps."

She is ready to leave then, standing in the doorway, and asks if he'd like her to pick up something, if he needs anything right now, and he tells her no but thanks anyway, sitting and sweating against the wall in cross-hatched light and renewed pain, smelling the stale breath of the sea and watching the listless birds. "Why do you want to help me?"

She gives him a little smile. "Don't you need it?"

Alone and prostrate in his corner he sees men with knives

181

over green turtles flipped; their livers huge, smooth slabs in slippery stacks and their soft bottom shells cut to strips that will cook like jelly; flakes and scales and bins of fish; slick piles of baby shark, small, supple, gray bodies foot-long and finned and grinning in miniature ferocity; a tabletop jewfish head, monstrous mouth and thick gristle lips gaping a fixed and rigid complaint—market memories flooding vivid and dominant in these odd waking spells.

He follows himself past dark bottles of shark oil to a chart of herbs, dried remedies mounted to a cardboard human body, past bananas and tomatoes and melons to sunlight and fringe vendors alongside the shed with towels spread in quick displays of coral jewelry, black and spindly, of shark spine bracelets, white-linked, thin and delicate, of single chunk necklaces like piano keys on string, polished bone bored and grooved in bare design. He handles a smooth piece the squatting seller calls ivory. *You mean like tusk, like elephant? No, mahn, like sea cow, like manatee. They're hunted for their bones? Some folks eat dem, but dese pieces come from de boneyard, juss collected like stones from de river. Which river?* Big smile for the curious and a shake of the head. *Graveyard under water, mahn. De place dey go to die.*

They will travel by dory. Heather has arranged their passage with a man from Laguna Vaca who makes the trip twice weekly—each leg over two hours on flat water—and as they leave the hospital, walking to the river, raindrops begin to fall. Heather carries her friend's overnight bag and Reese, in his fishing shorts and blood-stained shirt, helps steady the woman, Barbara, and feels on his neck the heat in her arm. She wears a loose dress and a yellow headscarf and her skin holds the heat like dark paint in the summer; she lifts her face to the cool drops and attempts to carry herself as normally as possible but is short of breath and tells them her heart is swaying. She can't lie down or stay here any longer or travel in a hot and jumpy bus. "I would transport myself by my own feet," she tells them, "but I'm afraid my head could crack open on the long road."

"It's a contest of headaches," Reese mutters, and they are silent to the river.

Out of the brown mouth into a slanted easterly rain they head south along the shore, pushed toward it on a light chop, all but the pilot huddling under plastic sheeting that covers lumber, nails, window casings and plantains—the women sharing a seat, Reese behind them and the boatman behind him in a narrow-running balance. The land retreats as the dory crosses a wide bight toward the next point, rising and dropping on larger waves while a seaside village of thatch and palm passes thin and blurry in the drizzled distance. Two miles later another village appears, much the same but longer along the curve and then, past the point, the coast is tangled in mangrove, grass and sea grape. The passengers peer out of the plastic at a rain-erased horizon as the dory slices and slows in equal measure and the boatman bails with a cut jug the rolling puddle at his feet.

Barbara sings softly and shivers, leaning into the other woman; Heather cradles her friend's head and arms, and twists around to see Reese, whose eyes are closed and whose wet, hooded face looks hard as stone. Ahead of them they see dimly the edge of rain, a sheer, dissolving curtain hanging in their way that, in its movement to sea, leaves the sky opening inland to a far blue view of rising pines and smoky hills.

In the third hour they bask and dry in breeze and sun, spirits lifting, seating positions shifting out of stationary soreness as the dory roars over rippled water toward the hook of land hiding the huge lagoon from their northern approach. Beyond the hook and across a sandy inlet sits the two-story Tarpon Creek Lodge, prominently perched on the opposite point where lagoon and sea meet at the end of a thin peninsula that holds along its muddy cusp the small, weathered dwellings of Laguna Vaca.

Hundreds of ibis preen and glow at a distance like oblong blossoms grown in profusion on their green and freshly watered island. The lagoon is vast and flat, its far sides foliated, steamy and dense, its water saline but reddish from rain-run channels and the flooded creek weaving into its southern end. The dory rounds the point, the throttle is dropped, and they coast up slow to the end of the long lodge dock. The boatman grasps a plank until Reese has landed and then pushes the rocking craft off again. Barbara gives a little wave and Heather says over the idle, "Drop by sometime," and points down the peninsula in the direction they are then motoring.

The lodge is quiet. Dale's truck and two cars sit in the yard and both Whalers and the skiff are out. Reese finds the office locked, his former room taken; the girl, Julie, lets him into another room upstairs but does not know the whereabouts of his belongings so he sits on the railing of the wide porch overlooking lagoon and sea until their reflective surfaces hurt his eyes and head, and then he takes refuge in the hammock there, and sleeps.

Out on the flats, Mafius has the skiff and a couple from Baton Rouge; he poles and points from his platform, a black, near-naked sentry as quiet and rippled as the patterned sand over which they glide. The woman has fought and boated a twenty-four-pound permit but her husband misses his every chance at their target fish and settles instead for several seatrout, all of which they intend to have cooked for the evening lodge party.

Up the creek, Dale and three Montana men spend the afternoon trolling for backcountry snook, a pair fishing shoreline and a pair outboard—the captain easily managing all tasks—as they slow-motor along mangrove banks, enticing with diving plugs the jut-jawed fighters, taking the boat midstream to drift during each battle and releasing for its fine sporting effort every sleek and beaten fish.

Returning with pleased men who caught good fish, Dale gives them a joyride—skimming across the great lagoon with the sun dropping behind it, the craft bears down hard on its course for home, swinging around sticks and hyacinths and warning ripples—the fishermen drinking beer and yelling to one another over the bawl of the outboard while the lanky Texan drives one-handed, throttle open wide, scanning the glassy surface for imperfections and spitting tobacco juice into a bottle brought casually to his pursed lips for each sharp black squirt.

"Lordy," Dale proclaims as Reese crosses the yard to the dock, his bandage like a flag in the dusk, "a fisherman back from the dead. He ain't skipped out on his bill after all." He clasps the man's hand firmly and claps him on the back firmer still. "Good to see you up and around. How you feeling, hoss?"

"Like my dinghy's come loose."

"I expect so. I'd wager it's still in sight though." He gestures at the men gathering their gear. "These boys are from Montana. Did good but decided they would not cook a snook."

The men nod. A hand is raised at the injured sportsman.

Reese says, "They're good eating."

"From what the captain tells us," one of them says, "we won't be going hungry."

"Now, I did say my man Mafius would put food on the table. And I happen to know there are some fine delectables in our near futures." He spits a dark stream off the dock.

"He got the menu over the radio," one of the men says.

"But I didn't say that was the whole story," Dale says.

They hear the skiff making its turn at the inlet. The cook, Estella, has appeared in the kitchen doorway; floodlights brighten the yard and dock lights blink on. Dale expels the remainder of his plug into the water and takes Reese by the shoulder. "Let's get us a couple cold ones and go on up to the office."

He steps into the kitchen for the beers and comes back out, then leans to the screen and says, "Stella, let's put them puppies on the grill first, darlin," before he leads Reese up the stairs at the side of the building.

A boy boatman, a guide in the making, cleans the vessels while Mafius slits the fish; the barrel grill glows, loaded with coals outside the kitchen. From the dining room bar next door loud murmurs and laughs leak to the floor above, where Dale has retrieved a duffel bag and two tackle cases from a closet and Reese stands staring at the huge, worn and hookless deep-sea lures attached to room keys hanging along a row of wooden wall pegs.

"Second from the right," Dale says, sitting on the edge of his desk as Reese with his key turns to face him. "How you feeling, sports fan?"

"Okay, I guess." He stands at the desk, lifts one of the beer bottles there, takes a swig and winces. He takes another drink, amazed and dismayed by the unpleasant taste yet unable to recall anything similar. He is tempted to ask if the beer is bad but does not. He says, "Not that great really."

"How so?"

"I don't know. Kind of weak, kind of slow. Out of touch. Like being below the surface of things, you know?"

"Yeah, sure, of course. Hell of a thing. What you need to do is get back on the horse, hoss. Get out on the water, catch some fish."

"I'd like to do just that."

"Good, good. I'll send them boys out with Mafius tomorrow and we can go out just the two of us. Get us a silver king or three." He stands and finishes his beer, sets the bottle on the desk. "I guess you'll want to clean up a bit. Then come on down and eat, get some protein in that rattled brain of yours," he says, going to the door.

There is a weathered registry on the desk, a black rotary telephone and a white carving of a crocodile, curling back on itself in a circle, that could fill a small skillet. Reese puts his bottle down and picks up the piece—open jaws, clawed feet, etched hide, notch-ridged tail—and says, "I need to call my partner, bring him up to date."

"Go right ahead."

"Collect," Reese says, and then, "Where'd this come from?"

186

"Oh, Mafius made it. Pretty good, huh? Bone. He used to do that before he started guiding."

"Ivory, I think they call it," Reese says.

"I reckon they do."

"Hey, listen, Dale, thanks for getting me out of that mess."

"Shit, hoss, I'm sorry it happened. Let's put it behind us, alright? I'm picking up the boat on Saturday—fucking hull got cracked—and that'll be the end of it."

"I don't remember the impact."

"Let me get on out to these folks. I'll tell you all about it tomorrow."

A few men from the village, part-time lodge workers and their friends, have wandered into the compound and stand near the grill passing a bottle of rum. Estella turns sizzling strips of young barracuda and coats them with her special sauce as the guests spill out of the screened bar to investigate her aromatic efforts. Behind the edge of flooded light a gathering of children dances to music pouring over the yard and they are momentarily flashed in quicksilver movement from some vague distance over or beyond the black lagoon where heat lightning skips and sizzles like loose circuitry.

The festive occasion is marked ostensibly by the morning departure of the Louisiana people who are thanked by Dale for their patronage and who in turn promise to be seen again. To the woman he suggests, "Get yourself a piece of your permit, but be sure not to miss these little pups here."

"What is that, dogfish?" She laughs with several others.

"That there is barbequed cuda."

"Aren't they toxic?"

"No, ma'am, the babies ain't."

He eats a piece and she lifts a strip and bites it in half and nods as she chews, and says, "Nice sauce. I thought you guys fished snook."

"That we did. These little tidbits were collected as you

187

slept by that hardworking savage right there. Take a bow, son."

Mafius sitting on a cooler dips his head, barely, and keeps eating. When next he looks up Reese is coming down the stairs, his bandage almost covered by a bandana.

He takes a plate of rice and pumpkin and fish and Mafius joins him at the grill. "You okay now, mahn?"

"Yes, fine. How are you, Mafius?"

"Same thing."

Everyone with their first or second plates moves to the tables inside and Dale joins the locals for rum at one while the guests occupy another. By now the other fisherfolk have heard something of Reese's misadventure and the opportunity for inquiry cannot be passed up, though to him nearly every answer appears obvious, every question unanswerable. Could it have been prevented? Does bad luck happen to anybody? Is there such a thing as an accident? Did you think you were a goner?

"What did you see?"

"Pardon?"

The woman sits across from him, her arm moving slowly through the space between them. "What did you see?"

"See when?"

"As you were dying."

Her arm floats like a turtle, hawksbill bracelet at the forearm. He looks at her face but notices only her earrings, three-inch tusks aimed at her shoulders, like teeth hanging outside her mouth. He says, "I was unconscious."

"But didn't you see your life? Or even a bright light?"

"I saw an animal."

"An animal? What kind?"

"I may have dreamed it."

"What, a fish?"

"It was big. Huge."

"Wait a minute! They said you hit a manatee. Was it a manatee? You saw it? You saw the manatee?"

He only shrugs and Dale interjects, "If he did it was

bleeding to death. But I'll tell you what, the man was in no shape to be seeing much of anything."

"He may have had a vision," the woman's husband says. "They say ancient sailors mistook manatees for mermaids."

"Oh shit, I love that one," Dale says. "You couldn't stay at sea long enough to get that romantic. Or maybe they didn't expect a whole hell of a lot from their mermaids. 'Cause them sumbitches are ugly. Ugly with a capital U."

"I don't know," a Montana man says, "they're starting to look pretty good to me."

The rum drinkers laugh and push each other and one says, "Plenty out dere, all fat."

Dale speaks over the mirth. "Hell yes. Why you think they call it Cow Lagoon? Not for the longhorns, is it? You can't hardly spit without hitting one."

"Sorta like aquatic speed bumps," a man says.

"Goddamn hazards is what they are," Dale says.

"Well," the woman says, "they're mammals. Just big, gentle vegetarians. They don't do any harm."

"Don't do any good either. Basically useless as tits on a boar hog. I mean, if they all died off tomorrow, who'd care?"

"Some people would. I hear there are plans to make this place a sanctuary for them."

"Good god, yes, let's protect the fat bastards so we can walk across the pond on their backs. Make a lardbag bridge."

"What'd they ever do to you? It's a big lagoon. Can't you just coexist?"

He smiles at Mafius and looks around the room. Everyone is waiting. The woman finds him, just now, on her final night, somewhat alarming.

He looks down at the table a moment and when he lifts his face he is staring at the woman. "I'll tell you what they did to me. A couple years ago I married a woman—a girl, really—from this village. We were in love and she got pregnant right away. So she has the baby and we're coming back from the hospital in my boat. And right out here we hit a fucking sea cow. And no, I wasn't going too fast. But she and the baby get thrown out." He stops talking, looks around at everyone there, then resumes this telling eye to eye with the one he knows will gain the most from it. "Well, she went nuts, hanging onto the boat and screaming bloody murder while I dove for that baby for half an hour, until some other people came out and took her away. But I kept searching, going down into that mud for another hour, Mafius too, but we could not find him. We could not find that baby anywhere. So I gave up, thinking a fish had got him, maybe a shark, 'cause he sure was little. He was a little Dale, he was, my son. His poor mother, well, she still ain't right."

The woman cannot immediately speak, but finally whispers, "How very sad."

Dale suddenly stands. "I don't know what's got into me," he says. "Not a good topic for the occasion, is it? Your last night and all." He steps away, swings open the screen door, bends down to the cooler, catches the door with his foot, rummages through the ice for a bottom beer, stands holding it. "You folks enjoy yourselves," he says, and goes up the stairs.

After he is heard walking overhead, the woman looks over at the other table, at Mafius watching her, then across at Reese. "It wasn't the animal's fault," she says.

"Hardly ever is," Reese says.

TWO

In the caramel water blue crabs abound. Clinging to looped roots gnarled and bowed, to soft-silted sticks, they pick and parry and sift sideways and back like spiked and flattened puppets. In these estuarine shallows eggs by the cloudy billion convert in brackish oblivion to nurseries of large-headed and hungry larvae. Predator and prey, these transparent beings—insect, fish, mollusk, crustacean—feed and die in quick generations in a fuzzy bottom-world of consumption and growth and dire survival.

Tiny tarpon, silver minnows on a moon tide, awash in luck after long, harrowing larval journeys from deep-sea depths to shoreline shallows, arrive to rove and prowl the thin, murky creeks and stagnant back-bay ponds. Here the young kings bask and streak and gulp, moving out to the world of bigger bites and swifter foes—a risky place to grow up—dining on crab and eel, catfish and croaker, mullet and shrimp, as they too are taken in fast-snapping jaws or captured on sharp beaks plunging out of the light above. There is terror in the food chain but it is commonplace, not cruel. Size and speed are issues; weaponry and attitude count. Eat or be eaten. Lie low. Look before you leap. Develop; attain your best attributes, your perfect nature. Use your unique features to prevail. Be quick, be stealthy, be tough. Migrate. Cruise and spawn. Keep the drive alive. Navigate these rolling flows, these far inlets, these meandering maritime tentacles where fresh streams meet salty tides, where brown river mouths open into the shallow, tonic waters of a splendid, crystal sea.

A stork is fishing. Black and white, neck base red as a ring of flame. It strikes by touch and from the confluence of marsh and mangrove lifts off like a dead tree rising, a giant jabiru spread nine feet across, flapping up over the greenery to land and stand in its wide, gray nest, a platform of mingled sticks perched in a leafless tree. Ruffled barely by the breeze and more so by the sounds and movement on the distant creek, the bird is watchful and still, a white crab gripped in its great black bill, its black, naked head turned toward the boat and the two men standing in it.

The engine's howl dies away and a quiet heat closes around them as they float on the returning tide, moving with the dark surface as they fashion their gear. Dale picks a sluggish blue crab from the well, punctures its shell with the awl on his knife and works his hook into place while Reese files his barbs triangulate. In their tackle they have two reels apiece, all medium-weight spincasters, with twenty-pound test line and eighty-pound shock leader and each man uses seven-foot fast tip rods. They will begin with their few live offerings, then switch to artificial. Aside from each other, they will only compete with a single quarry—tarpon—stalking the silver sabalo in these dark channels and creeks, sight fishing, no matter the water's depth or clarity.

They must locate the fish. They do not cast aimlessly, flinging targets for bull shark, turtle or ray, anxious to hook and pull any manner of creature found below, but drift and turn and pole back to current and pass the time here in this wilderness with nothing to disturb their tacit pursuit. Only the creaking of the hull, the tickle and lick of water around the transom, the anhingas in low flight, their slow-passing flaps like a rustling of labored breaths in the heavy air. Floating open under a whitening sky, the men watch the water's filmy sheen, the bubbles and plops along the shaded shore, green herons under bent reeds, and hear the jungle close at hand, the croak and hiss and clatter all around.

The stream widens. A pair of river otters, stout and sleek, lie like elongated and earless dogs on a log at the bank, sunning sleepily, watching the white boat. Ahead of it a mullet jumps. A moment later a mouth appears at the surface, the fish takes air and rolls sideways, silver flank flashing, dorsal whip trailing, and disappears. Several more gulp and roll, a school on the lazy move, traveling toward the boat. A cast crab wobbles through the air, splashes ahead of the fish, sinks and bobs and swims as Reese at the bow winds its slow retrieval in the midst of their rolling path. A rising fish detours to movement, follows and eyes the bait, opens its wide mouth and inhales the crustacean whole. The man lets it go a second—the rod dips—then strikes fast at the armored mouth, setting the hook with a series of sharp jerks. In a shuddering blast of acrobatic panic the big fish bursts the surface, bending and shaking at a slackened line in a wild and powerful leap above water—a chaotic image of detonation and brilliance and bewilderment hangs in the torpid air for a sudden and inexplicable moment—and falls in a slapping crash as the animal turns and flees, running madly for the edge of the world.

With little drag, the line follows the tarpon downstream in its streaking search for depth—the impossible sea—around a bend to a bottom slot where the current cuts its outer curve. Dale races to start the engine and motor after it, Reese standing tight and already tired on the bow, reel singing, and he in tingling communion with this hard tarpon he has joined. While the swimming fish, some hundred yards away, pulls at this food fragment, this stubborn presence, this tugging pressure, an invisible force it cannot shake. And so it slows, shifting in annoyance near the dark bottom, alone now without its scattered school, gills flexing for oxygen and mouth working, instinct thinking at this odd problem it feels following.

Reese is taking in the line he gains, closing the gap and feeling the weight, knowing well the labor in store. His hands are tired—he woke tired—and his hurting head is all but standard. Dale is watching and spitting and they have so far spoken of little besides finding admittance to this arena now entered. Reese has his hookup and he's glad for it, though the thrill—fine at first contact—is missing, his taste for the fight faded, and so too his sense of taste all wrong, not lost but not keen either, he worries, wanting to land the fish merely for the sake of argument, with the sun bleeding through his hat, making it tight, heating his skull and distorting his senses, the smell of this brackish water like sewage in his nose. He is off—they both know it—and Dale figures him likely to fold before the fish.

Surging to the surface the fish jumps clear, thrashing its head in a silvery showering, smacks back to water, dives and jumps again, Reese leaning to each leap, surrendering the tension and then pumping against the dive. The tarpon returns, lifts its bulk upright, kicking its broad tail at the surface, and rages away from the boat in a standing backward run, metallic mouth open to the men, straining the man's biceps and dragging out his line in a staggering dance down the creek, and falls once more, heaving with fatigue, sinking to the cool bottom current while weary Reese fumbles and pumps, slow hand at the reel, arms like mud and his mind at this crucial time muddy too, in the light of day dwelling at some bottom place where he once lay.

"He gets rested he'll take your rod or pull you in." Dale spits over the gunnel. "Sumbitch may go a hundred or so."

"Cut the engine."

"You're gonna lose him, hoss."

"Then I'll lose him."

Silence in the vicinity. The rod is worked horizontally, low over the water, flexed again and again against this heavy fish, line stretching and leader wearing across abrasive jaws. The man sets his hook again for good measure; an hour has passed and his arms are trembling.

"Watch him heading for the roots."

"I see him."

To dissuade the fish, he draws back hard on the rod, adds to the drag with line squeezed between the cork grip and his grooved and burning finger. The tarpon tucks and turns, line scraping over its back, and runs parallel to shore, abruptly heads toward the boat and loops back on the slack, barreling toward the bank, a riverine engine jumping its track. Sweat shakes from Reese's face; the rod and his neck seem ready to shatter. He sees himself going overboard, down to darkness and liquid breathing, and he is holding his breath, not wanting to cough, giddy and hardly tugging any longer.

"You ain't tired him out."

Reese gasps for air, leaning too far back into the boat. "I got him."

"He's running," Dale says.

"I got him."

"That line breaks, you'll be falling back on your busted head, hoss."

In the shade of an overhang, the fish is still. Reese stands on the bow, sunlight clanging at his head, arms and legs disempowered, and stares at the place where line and water meet. Dale digs the pole in and they are moving to the place, Reese's left hand reeling automatically. When they are under the trees and over the spot he is looking down for the fish, begging this monster to quit so he can pull it up and see it and hold it and look in its eye and thank it for something and release it. He needs water on his banging brain, feels his body squid-like and sloppy at this fatigued degree, his ability and desire drying away like fluffs of beach foam. The taste in his mouth is rusted iron.

Bubbles rise, the fish blowing air to stay down, and under pressure the rod is hook-shaped, tip wiggling over the water like some erratic pointer. In this last tug-of-war Reese, beneath a hot, liquid coating and closed eyes, is without regard for fish or water or weather or angling any more, but has only the thought of inches lifting, these increments of sportsmanship an abstract accomplishment that keeps him with his peers in a school of singularity, and applies to them a relation across the vast territorial waters of history and science. Here the weight is lifting, the fish seen in the tannic gloom as a forged and silver prize delivered up, a live and wily missile rolling over to see these air-standing creatures, these surface tricksters.

"Gaff him," Reese pleads.

"He ain't up yet."

"Pull him up!"

"I can't reach the leader, hoss."

"He's right there. Take the line."

Leaning over the gunnel, short gaff in his right hand, Dale reaches for the line and takes it, watching a wide eye in the bright bucket head, the breadth of spreading gills, large scales like overlapping shells down its length, the blue back a stripe in contrast, and gently pulls, easing the big fish forward, and slips his hand down the line to get the leader. The tarpon turns away and with no apparent effort lunges and the line pops free of the hand.

Reese cups the spool hard, clamps the bail, the rod tip dips to the surface and vibrates—then whips straight up as he steps back to keep from falling, line whizzing loose to cut leaves above and dangle down the other side of the boat.

"Fuck it," he says, and Dale starts the engine.

They motor downriver to fish other waters, Reese hunkered sulking under his hat like some recreant undeserving, and tie up for lunch in a sliver of shade. He takes aspirin with a cold beer that makes him nearly nauseous and eats a bland sandwich and tries to determine the extent of what he now thinks of as his new variance.

"Not once did I feel I was going to land that fish," he says.

"Looked to me like you wanted to lose him."

"I love beer but this tastes wrong. What is that? Can you tell me what that means?"

"No, I can't."

"I don't think right now I could swim across this goddamn creek."

"That was one fish," Dale says. "One bad fight."

"What I'm saying is I don't feel right."

"What the fuck, hoss?" He finishes his beer and fishes another out of the cooler. "Experience is knowledge, right? That's all it is. You know how to catch these fish, I've seen you do it, and you cannot lose that. You're not somebody else. You're still yourself and that person is a fisherman. Let me put it another way. There's two kinds of people, those who fish and those who don't, or those who do what they like to do and those who don't, for whatever reason. I'm out here because I want to be and I've got myself in a position that allows me to do this almost anytime I want. To me, that's winning. Now, is there something else you'd like to be doing or somewhere else you'd rather be?"

"Right now, I couldn't really tell you."

"We can head back right now." Dale is pulling them by the bowline to the limb it's looped around.

"No. Hell no. We came to fish." Reese empties his beer over the side and takes up the bamboo pole.

Once they are adrift in the stream he puts the pole down and selects a lure from his box. "Going with a topwater plug," he says.

"Can't recommend it," Dale says. "I think we got a little lucky seeing that school. It's hotter now too. More likely to get 'em off the bottom."

"The plan was for sightfishing," Reese says.

"Well, that's fine on the skinny water, son, but in here

you're making it too hard on yourself. One hookup ain't much fishing. Tell you what though, I'm rigged for bottom so if we see any on top you got first shot at 'em."

They hang between tides, one man fishing with a precision unleashed, the other pushing the craft and scanning for snouts and dorsals breaking, keeping them creeping generally easterly in this labyrinthine land of lagoons and sloughs and streams, poling over holes and through pools on some dour and sundering quest. He loads his hat with ice, drapes a dripping bandana down the back of his neck and watches with polarized eyes the slow progression of heated greenery.

Dale hooks a snook, brings it in and nets it himself, removes the lure and lets it drop unrevived and Reese does not comment but moves onward, pushing himself through the day and resting in odd and solemn postures against the sloping pole.

He glimpses a sweeping tail and watches the pod grabbing air, this old-line species augmenting its oxygen at the surface like gigantic, prehistoric herring hoping for their descendants a life with lungs. Dale plays his bait perfectly and waits in their way but Reese miscasts badly, throws long and spooks the school, who move off alertly, uninterested and unseen again.

They see no more topsiding tarpon; Reese quits fishing and only poles, wearing himself out in a physical penance for another man's mistake. For his own loss. The thing missing, the thing he is seeking, his former self, or some peremptory perception of himself known at the sportive surface, seems sunken now, left behind on the muddy bottom, his soul waterlogged and lurking there still, he imagines, some alternate version of himself mutated in an evolutionary reversal, gills combing and absorbing molecules of oxygen from their hydrogen pairs. This vision he finds fairly disturbing, watching as Dale takes a strike, and then with the king running, the man on the line is asking for the motor.

The fisherman is hooked into a wild thing, into a battle he

feels traveling between them in a taut, thin line. He won't relinquish his hold or relieve the pressure he's applied to the animal. Though he will not eat this fish, he feeds on it all the same, takes from it what he needs in a natural world that must replenish itself. Amid the myriad hidden lives of this murky water, they grow closer, the endeavor as elemental as a clouding sky, as insects complicating the air, dark streams running to the sea, the tangled trees and the heat, the squawks and the calls and a man standing in the fundamental land.

Reese puts the point of the gaff into the gaping mouth and hooks it out under the thick bottom lip. With a good grip on the handle he holds its lanyard with the fingertips of his other hand—the floating fish rolls its belly up and lacks the strength to pull away—and lifts it halfway out of the water as Dale leans over the gunnel to inspect his catch.

"Name of the game, hoss," he says.

Like some primitive dentist he reaches with pliers the lure at the top of the throat and extracts it with a bony scraping. He lays his hand on the body below the gill, pats the animal, then pries up and plucks a single scale, a thin and silvery slug, from the pectoral area. Bent over the boat, Reese lowers the fish, holds it by the mouth and pushes the gaff out as Dale poles them toward the middle, trailing the torpid tarpon alongside and running water through its gills until it begins to swim again, then slips away dazed, worming in the turbid flow, with a chink in its armor and a couple of rough cuts in the hard cavity of its mouth.

Clouds are building in the west, over the land behind them, as they churn up puffs of mud in a shallow channel near the lagoon. Reese says over the chugging motor, "Mind if we have a look at that place?"

Dale spits in his bottle. "What place?"

"The crash site."

Dale squints at him, shifting the plug in his cheek. "You finish fishing?"

"I want you to show me what happened."

199

Along the rim of the lagoon they motor north, Dale looking across the wide body, plotting position from vague shoreline breaks and distant treeline heights, from cove and palm, from bottle-topped marker sticks that come and go, and from the island mound ahead, his primary reference point sitting on the water like a high green barge for birds. He notes far beyond it a stationary boat. Slows at the creek, turns into it, idles opposite the narrow joining channel and swings around, nosing off the bank with the pole and facing the way they came.

"We were coming out of there," he says, "and they came across us from the west as soon as we were out."

"Where was I?"

"Standing there, like you are now." They are drifting toward the creek's mouth, blinded at the sides by vegetation slightly higher than their heads. "As I came out I saw this manatee and swerved and then saw their boat speeding out to the pond and trying to avoid us but we would've collided so I tried to cut back and managed to catch their tail end anyway. Obviously it happened pretty fast."

The place looks new to Reese, though he scans the water, the channel, the shore, stares down from the bow at ripples and blank depth. "So I went flying up here somewhere."

"When I swerved you must've fallen away from the console and then gone forward. Hit the bow there, I guess, or the rail, and went over. Lucky the boat didn't run you over."

Reese looks back at the other man. "What happened to you?"

"Saw it coming, braced myself as much as I could, slammed into the wheel and whatnot." He lifts his shirt to his neck and shows discolored skin from stomach to ribs to chest, mottled yellow and green patches like diseased clouds in a jaundiced sky, bad weather bruises. "Swallowed my damn tobacco." He laughs. "Should've cured me but it didn't."

"Where was the manatee?"

"Right there at the junction, going which way, I don't

know. When I cut back and hit the thing, it slowed me down and we clipped the other boat."

"If it slowed you down, you could've missed the other boat."

"No, because once I hit that cow my turn wasn't as sharp."

They are idling in the lagoon and Reese is looking back up the creek. "What I can't figure is why you were going so fast out of a blind pass."

"Ain't you never run a stop sign on a country road?"

Reese is sitting on the bow watching the captain. "What occurs to me is that maybe you saw this cow in your sights and then sped up so you could hit it."

"That dog won't hunt, son."

"Why not?"

"'Cause you don't recollect what happened and I just told you the way it was."

"If I don't remember I have to look at what seems true."

"Even if it means calling me a liar."

"Nobody's ever said it wasn't an accident, have they?" Reese says.

"Not to my knowledge, they haven't. Aside from you and me, there's just the two fellows in the other boat. They've let it be known they expect some sort of recompense that hasn't been forthcoming. And likely won't be."

"What about Mafius?"

"He came when I called him so we could trade boats and I could get you the hell out of here."

"We went the whole way by water?"

"Actually not. An ambulance met us at Brophy Point."

They putter in the area while Reese stares into the water remembering the hospital and the nurses and wondering if Mafius saw an injured manatee. "You suppose you killed the animal?"

"I couldn't rightly say. You like to go down and have a

201

look-see for any remains?"

"If it wasn't dead where do you think it went?"

"What kind of a damn fool question is that?"

They are roaring toward the lodge, crossing the wide-open water when Dale abruptly throttles down, their trailing wake lifts the stern and Reese bangs into a corner of the console. Dale points west and brings the boat around to follow his finger. "Sorry, hoss. I didn't know if you'd seen any of our aquatic cattle yet."

Lolling on a bar across the front of a sheltered cove, two sea cows are half stacked on a sandy shelf, one rising above the other, from a distance resembling boulders born up from mud, gray and quaking in the afternoon light. Rotund and wrinkled fusiform, the male shivers and slides on his side, slips backward into deeper water and flukes forward belly to belly beside his mate, her flipper a paddle waving in the air, beckoning him on.

"First ones I've seen clearly."

"Like I said, they're around. Just pop up in front of you. No picnic to hit one either."

The men in the rumbling boat. A round head seems to look their way, a fleshy face and tiny eyes, the cleft and bristled lip quivers at the eastern breeze. Dale forms a pistol with his hand and takes aim. "Too easy," he says. "But how'd you like to hook one of them fat fuckers?"

"Never gave it a thought," Reese says. He gives it one now, trying to imagine such a ponderous and passive weight on the line. "What would you throw at them? A head of lettuce? A cabbage?"

"I don't believe you would." Dale spits a looping stream off the vessel. "You'd just fling your hook at 'em and hang on if it stuck."

The male slips back, the female rolls; their snouts sit at the surface like dirty bread, split and bloated loaves that sink from sight as the pair dives. Gray shapes fading away.

At the dock Dale says, "I reckon you won't be desiring a

trip out tomorrow."

"You reckon right."

THREE

In the dawn's brine mist two men cut across the cool, gray water, still and eerie out before the boat and in the widening split of its wake, rippled with fading waves and receding sound in this vague and early world. Pelicans appear out of the pewter light, seven spectral ships floating in low harmony above their waffling reflections. Mafius is at the wheel and in ten minutes they are north of the island and approaching two white jug buoys marking the night trap he's spread, his gill net surprise.

"Somethin heavy in dere," he says, studying the bobbing of one jug and the movement of water rippling out.

Dale sits at one side of the center seat drinking instant coffee from a thermos cup and looking away in the direction of town, his mind's eye wandering already over the activities he will undertake there.

On their port side a creek seeps like ink into the dark lake while the sky's fluid light spreads above all a pale canopy and illuminates the outline of the nearby shoreline, but for Mafius it sheds nothing on the contents of his net. Bent over, he peers into the water and hauls up one end line until a couple of net floats break the surface, then draws up some bottom line sinkers along with a crusted brake drum anchor. He plunks it down and begins to raise more of the mesh, pulling at the weight he feels below. He sees a shark, a four-foot blacktip, and near it another, smaller, neither moving as he draws them and the boat together, spilling the net onto the deck, a wooden club and a short-barrel speargun at his feet.

These sharks—flexible forms, tough and supple saplings—are flopped by their tails into the boat and Mafius removes his shirt and resumes his retrieval, clutching at the nylon fibers by the handful when he feels a flash occur underwater, some disturbance unseen, and as he gains more net the mystery is revealed. A fuzzy muzzle—a truffle mound whose twin nostril holes blow open for a rushed and noisy draw of air—pops up for a second and ducks below in a boil that leaves the other jug jumping at the surface. "Yah, yah," he says. "Found dat weight."

Dale glances over his shoulder but does not get up. "Some young cow hung up in your net, son?"

A red and fatty stain is noticeable now at the surface, yellowish traces hanging like chum over the discernable form of the submerged sea cow. Young mullet—translucent-looking prolate shapes swimming through drab swirls of silt stirred by the sunken mammal—move among the flecks sucking the color from a pallid spectrum. Mafius, leaning out over the gunnel, seeks the source of this bloodletting, and with the speargun holds his aim on the surface. Nothing moves but mullet. He tugs at the net, pulls the disturbance closer, and tugs again; a thrashing ensues. He sees a silver flash like a big blade turning, a barracuda caught close to its neighbor. The manatee rushes up to breathe, dragging the net's other anchor, and the rancorous fish, sensing a chance to bolt, lashes and bends. Mafius backs off a moment to let them settle down.

Taking up the net from its other end he is able to approach the fish alone, raises it slowly near the surface, shoots it through the head and pulls it by the spear's line to the boat. At the transom it is still moving and he takes up the club and cracks it across its razor face, breaks its teeth and beats its head, the face sustaining its sardonic smile the rest of the way to death. "Nasty fella," he says, working its body out of the net as the sea cow breathes.

He reloads and leans out over the water, holding the net in one hand, and waits for the mammal's next breath. Dale sits drinking another cup of coffee and says, "Well, the day's moving right along without us, ain't it?"

"Juss a few minutes, bossmahn."

"Then you gotta dress it."

"Juss wantin to seize de extra profit."

"Jesus, Joseph and Mary! These irregular activities should be on your time and your time only."

"One muss accommodate de tides of business, bossmahn. Your gas and my market day. No waste, juss cooperation."

"I applaud your hard work, sonny, but this is strictly fringe benefits. Let's not forget that."

Down for nearly five minutes, the young sirenian, an adolescent male, must breathe. He rises with the use of his tail, this fluke like a foot for a buoyant creature who needs only its nose to surface—and so feels somewhat invisible—but who is alarmed, bitten and bleeding in two places, one flipper tangled and twisted uncomfortably in this thing unseen he brings up with him. Seeing the darker shape of the silent boat, nothing more.

Mafius shoots it in the neck as it breathes, the steel point lodges deeply in the thick blubber, and the animal ducks back down rapidly, pulling away from a bloody pouring with squeaks and quick kicking, stirring the area to a desperate turbidity as it hits the cleated resistance of the steel's tight line and the well-held netting, and begins to turn the boat, then pull it by the stern, hampered by a hung forelimb and in shock, but with nowhere to go but up, breaks the surface for its last breath to drag streamlines of warm morning air down the dismayed lanes of its long lungs.

From the stern platform he clubs its head as Dale pulls the spear's line and holds the animal against the corner of the boat. Mafius climbs on the mammal's back and holds the spear for leverage and plunges his fillet knife through the upper chest where the heart lies. He holds himself against the bleeding body to catch his breath and then goes under the red water and cuts his net away from the animal's flipper. He drops the knife into the transom and hauls himself back aboard and pulls his net free from the manatee and the spear's taut line.

"I do believe you've dispatched this unlucky fucker, son," Dale says.

With the net gathered at the bow, Mafius tilts the engine and Dale fires it up and with the dead beast in tow they slowly motor to shallow water, one man watching the clearing bottom and the other standing at the burdened stern, his skin after this straining effort made to shine like grease in the light rising bright over the distant seaward rim of the huge lagoon.

Near the shore the boat runs up gently on a bar and Mafius releases the line and hops out in two feet of water and pulls and rolls the round body into the sandy shallows. He cuts the barb out of the animal's neck, drops the spear in the boat, then cuts a hole in the spatulate tail and threads the stern line through it. Straddling the mass of flesh he opens the abdomen, slits it down the middle—the knife sharp but the man working hard at this sawing of thick hide—and the animal is eviscerated there, with fish swarming all around the loose fat and snaking entrails of the large carcass.

The body is dragged apart from its mass of intestines, stomach, kidneys and lungs, and rolled onto its loose belly. In a rudimentary butchering, Mafius cuts a long center line from head to tail, cuts a cross line at the top, peels away as much skin as he can, and begins to cuts chunks and slick slabs from the muscle of the broad back.

"Neighbors will be passing us soon," Dale says, while Mafius continues his silent work, bent over the glutinous mass in water clouded and viscid and teeming with small fish and crabs. Shadow wings flutter and dip across the area, gulls circling above, their close revolutions noticed by nervous herons wading at the shore and by inquisitive terns floating high over the sparkling lake. He slices down along the ribcage, taking shoulder and side cuts dripping from the water, carves tenderloin, flank and then round steak out of the region where spine becomes tail, and wraps these pieces in plastic bags at the side of the boat and hands them up to Dale, who puts them on ice. "Good Christ Almighty," he says, looking at his watch. "You can't possibly get it all, boy."

The young man cleans his arms and chest in the water, foregoes the optimal removal of fluke and flippers—their vertebral center and skeletal arms too much bone for his knife and time—and wastes too the voluminous belly's fatty meat. He pushes the vessel backward into deeper water and hauls himself into it. When the engine has dragged the frayed and flapping carcass deep enough below the surface, he attaches a buoy to the stern line towing it, and drops it overboard. He sits aft watching the buoy and the adjacent shoreline until they have puttered perhaps a hundred yards, then drops his weighted net overboard and sprawls across the bow with a towel over his head as Dale puts them on plane and on course toward the northern reaches of the lake and the channel to the river.

At the Tarpon Creek Lodge, Reese lies at rest. Sleeping in, but awake now, under a fan, listening to his body's comments. Without plans, but at a crossroads, as if the one he just passed, that sunken junction between life and death, is still in sight, right behind him if he looks back. His head feels tight, seems to constrict upon itself at the most banal and commonplace of its owner's activities: thinking, standing, eating or drinking, even fishing. Only in sleep is he free of its pressing complaints. Only in repose, unconscious and uncaring. He cannot quite carry on in his normal manner but hopes in some trenchant moment to overcome what has happened.

Standing at the porch railing he gazes at the shimmering sea and believes he sees a jump—mackerel, marlin or manta?—but thinks then that he could not have seen something so far out, and possibly saw nothing at all. He thus starts the day in doubt, feeling a little drunk, and asks himself, What is reasonable?

Estella's in the kitchen and the other guests are gone. She brings him coffee but doesn't ask why he's remained. He sips the bitter drink out of habit and thinks of calling his ex-wife for perhaps the same reason, or to expiate further the person he was when he began this trip. But his eardrums itch, feel like thin scales scratched with a straight pin; he turns his head trying to alleviate the sensation but it makes no difference.

When Estella returns, he asks, "Is there no one around?"

"All gone to town," she says.

Back in the kitchen she is boiling green mangoes. The corrosive smell soon drives him away.

He leaves the compound and walks down the lone road in this peninsular village, past raised houses and a store and a new dock on the lagoon side, and stops in the shade of a mango tree across from a blue house, the pale sky-blue of the local boats, that in the bright sun begins in his eyes to turn the lavender of morning glory. A front window is open and a motion there catches his eye—white lace through a sunlit portal, a pattern like leaves weaving, a curvature of undergarment over dark skin, some section of a body rocking, it appears—but he cannot determine what is taking place. Cannot tell if what he sees is shoulder, back, hip or buttock. But it's a window on white lace and human skin. Not a curtain, he assures himself, but someone ironing or cleaning or writhing, and he stands watching this smooth movement in awe.

People are coming along the track. He moves on, nearly

limping with the stiffness between his legs, aroused more by mystery than desire, this condition common since his hospital time and resulting often from situations not at all sensual in his mind, or for no reason whatsoever other than the fact that his head and body seem disengaged, working on divergent courses whose intersections are unpredictable.

There is a tapping; he looks back at the blue house, at the side windows, as he hears again a sound like fingers rapping on glass. He sees a kingbird hovering, flapping in place at the top of a window, bang bang banging with its beak. Curtains part, the bird whisks away over the roof, and Reese turns to go as a boy passes him on a creaking bicycle.

"Hey!" someone calls behind him.

He stops and looks back. Her hair in the sun a cascade of flaxen ringlets bouncing at her shoulders, Heather stands waving from the front steps, and Reese finds himself heading drunkenly there to meet her.

They come to town from the west, entering the city by its artery creek, passing under the airport bridge, meandering through the green outskirts, past the tumbledown waterside hovels of squatters, the slanted catwalk shacks quilted with tarps and signboard scraps. An Indian market, temporary stalls of plastic sheeting and identical wares, the bright shirts and patchwork bags and woven bands, tiddlywinks of toiletry and grooming. Warehouses and river industry, an icehouse and the adjoining Baymen Boatyard where the other Whaler waits afloat.

They dock at the pumps and Dale steps out with an old leather knapsack. "Good trip home," he says, "and you might save me a piece of that fat vaca for Sunday dinner."

He steps through puddles of watery gas, passes the attendant and inside picks up spark plugs, oil, hooks, rubber jigs and overpriced line, and asks about his repairs while Mafius fills the tank and watches the traffic and the riverside bedlam. Up front, the street is full of horns and radios and squealing belts.

Trucks and taxis sit tight and the area shouts with the sounds of saws, drills and hammering; shoots of re-bar sprout from roofs and pillars. He shoves off as other boats arrive and motors downstream under the gridlock on the swivel bridge to the market at the mouth of the river.

Gulls bob with trash and fruit among the boats stacked in rows along the river wall. He ties up against an outer boat and with his sharks and cuda held by their tails he crosses the adjacent deck and lays his fish down at the end of the long concrete counter where they are seen by the prospective buyers standing at their bins with all manner of sea creature, whole or already parted. And from the rivers: the slim, bluish bodies of long crayfish and the hard-shelled hicatee turtles, black as mud, half as big as hawksbills. Holding a tin scale pan, dented and stained, a man scrapes out fish bits with a knife and in passing, Mafius says to him, "Sea beef," and goes on into the markethouse.

In the huge room odors mingle and mix with the crowd. Warm meats and yellow-skinned poultry hang in eye-level perimeters around their bordering zones. Food booths, mostly vacant now between breakfast and lunch, line one entire wall and give off an air of fried pork, egg, rice and spices. There are rows of stalls with vegetables and fruits, boxes of color in the light thrown through tall, roll-up doors; and muted versions in dusty orange, greens and tans: the gourds and odd squashes. Herbs and barks and roots in tied bundles, small labeled bags of sprigs and leaves, potions and oils in reused liquor bottles. Eggs and onions, carrots and cabbage. Knives, graters and plastic bowls. Out front, squeezed into the shade along the building and filling the space to the street, are piles of clothing, bags and hats, toys and jewelry.

In the throng Mafius locates a man with carvings, a bone and coral seller squatting at his blanket while two white women fondle his pieces. The seller stands to speak with the wholesaler and they engage in a brief conference as the customers decide, one of them selecting an ivory letter—a D for Donna—on a black cord that she hangs from her lovely neck.

Back at the waterside he sells his fish to an obese woman wrapped in folds of tangerine cloth, a matching piece tied high in her hair, then brings from his well some special packages, and she bends over to inspect this merchandise, her upper arm shaking like gelatin as she reaches into a bag. She purses her thick lips in thought as he speaks of freshness and rarity and wholesale price. After a few moments she motions to a boy sitting on a dock cleat and he takes a stack of bags from Mafius and carries them to a section of the counter and plops them down while the woman counts damp bills off a roll extracted from her enormous bosom.

He leaves the market, walking with another wrapping of meat, crosses the bridge and makes a kitchen delivery to a restaurant owned by his cousin. In the dining room he eats a Creole chicken dinner with rice and beans and salad and bread pudding, sips coffee and flirts with the waitress. Afterward he visits some friends, drinks rum, and returns to the market, where he trades meat for a shirt and fresh vegetables, and then departs for the icehouse and home.

Tea is poured for Reese. Heather sits down across from him, her arms sticking to the plastic sheet that covers the table. A breeze blows between front door and back, main room and kitchen, sea and lagoon, in a corridor through the middle of the house and they sit, sweating, at the wall in the front room. "We can move the table," she says.

"It's okay to sweat." He is looking at the green walls, the photographs of some family not living here; a political sticker for the blue party. From the front bedroom they can hear the sound of Barbara's breathing, short and shallow like a pump about to break. "Maybe it's hepatitis," he says.

"They said it wasn't."

At the side window, the rapping begins again and Reese sees the kingbird clearly now, gray with a yellow breast, and sees too the white moth fluttering inside the curtain at the top of the window, bumping the glass as the bird's long beak bangs at it every few seconds. Heather doesn't seem to notice.

"Is she sleeping?" he asks.

She shakes her head. "Just lying there." Lowering her voice she says, "She tells me she feels too heavy to move," and makes a pained expression of confusion and helplessness. "But she's not overweight and not what I'd call weak." She pulls her hair back through an elastic band and lifts the bundle off her neck and shakes it and lets it drop. "I don't know what to do to help her."

"I guess you're doing it," he says.

She stands and goes to the bedroom door and looks in the crack a moment and then stands in the breeze at the front door and returns to the table. "What about you?" she says. "How's your condition?"

"About the same."

"Aren't you supposed to see the doctor again?"

He shrugs. "To take out stitches? I'll do it myself."

"Can I see?" She lifts his bandana and the edge of the bandage underneath. "This should be changed," she says, and studies the knotted wound. "Looks okay, though. I can take those out for you."

"Whenever you're ready," he says, looking at the damp blond down of her cheek.

"Let's wait a day or two more." She pulls the bandage back into place and meets his eyes and smiles. "Now I have two patients." She takes her seat at the other side of the table. "But since you're not fishing you must be leaving."

He smiles too but it barely shows on his face. "I don't know what I'm doing."

"Is that a recent manifestation or the way you always are?"

A single bubble of laughter escapes and he says, "Well, it's always, but it's worse now."

"Why? Headaches? Nausea?"

"Not just that. It's everything. I mean, this tea, no

213

offense, tastes like wet dirt. And I feel like I'm hungover all the time."

"Maybe you'll be better off," she says.

"Why do you say that?"

"I don't know. You seem—more vulnerable now, not so forceful, I guess."

"What, more like a woman?"

"Well, yes."

"I'm in worse shape than I thought."

"Not really," she says.

He stands suddenly, moves into the central breezeway and looks around. "Is there a bathroom, a latrine?"

She stands too, points through the back door. "Down at the water there's an outhouse." When he's on the steps she says, "Or you can pee in the yard, if you like."

She takes another peek at Barbara—eyes closed and body now quiet as a warm corpse—and goes out the back to a bench under a tamarind tree and sits facing the house as Reese comes up the path from the water. He joins her on the bench and they sit in the shade in the buzz of an insect-filled humidity. A neighbor moves across the dirt of her shaded yard, sweeping, and they can see her occasionally through the leaves and smoke and they can smell the woodsmoke coming from there.

He says, "You live a pretty rustic life here."

"I'm used to it. Doesn't bother me at all."

A yellow-striped fly, the size of a housefly, lands on his arm; he is watching its brown wings become still as it settles down and Heather slaps it dead. "That's a doctor fly," she says. "They're stealthy and painful. They bother Barb when she's sleeping but the fan seems to bother her more."

He wonders how she is able to work and also contend with the sick woman's needs. "What is it you do here?"

"I have a few projects going," she says. "Community projects. I'm an organizer, really."

"I heard about this sanctuary thing."

214

"Yeah, that's one idea. We think people will come to study these animals, or just to see them—and the birds, of course—and stay here. So we need places to put people up and places to eat besides the lodge. You know, accommodations that will help more of the whole village."

"I saw two yesterday."

"Did you? In the lagoon?"

"Mating."

"How wonderful. It must have been thrilling to see."

"It was something."

"People say they've always lived here. Probably the most docile animals alive. We need to protect them."

"Dale thinks they're a nuisance."

"That fool. Look how he drives. And I'm real sorry about his wife and child but look what happened to you. There's no excuse for that."

"They're bound to get hit once in a while, don't you think?"

"Last week one was found dead, washed up back here with a bullet hole in it. You think that was an accident?"

"Maybe someone was hunting and it got away."

"People don't hunt those any more."

"Someone still might."

She stares at him a moment. "Yeah, someone might."

A doctor fly jabs him like a needle in the neck. He slaps at it and stands dizzily in the grass. "I think it's time for my nap." He looks down at her beautiful face. "Thanks for the tea."

She smiles. "Barb will be sorry she missed you."

"She will?"

"Come for dinner. She's usually better in the evening and it'd be nice for her to have some company. Besides me."

In the northwestern region of Laguna Vaca Mafius inspects the hole in his gill net and repositions it unrepaired. He finds his solitary buoy above the mutilated manatee and from a midday lake devoid of visible traffic tows this load backward into a near creek. In water deep enough that under power the head lifts and falls, the heavy assemblage of flesh and bone trails awkwardly, its turning paddle arms dragging and digging at the bottom like the wings of some clumsy dredging device, dislodging old shells and lifting sediment in long brown clouds behind the laboring boat.

Reese floats, asleep in a sable stream. He dreams and breathes, swimming through a languid, waving swale. Turtle grass in a blurry world. A shadow passes above, a boat blocking the light. No, not a boat—a silent and evanescent shape he cannot read. He swims on, looking to follow, reaching for this looming balloon that is gone. He chases it without haste along a muddy trough, reaching into reddish swirls to clear his sight. He stays down, following a trail like foggy flare smoke. Over stones and pearly bones. A fish creature he cannot find. He breathes below his own world, hands on the bottom, on the edges of oyster shells. He is lost, following a stain in the sea. Blinded by blood.

He wakes hungry and showers and goes downstairs to find Estella, who makes him a plate of rice and fish. He is eating to the growing sound of a boat approaching and sees it through the sunny screen. Mafius arriving at the dock.

He sprays down the boat and himself with the dock hose, carries his bags to the kitchen and speaks with Estella, and stands outside dripping and drinking a beer. He notices the other man sitting inside.

"Afternoon, Reese," he says.

"Mafius. How was town?"

He pulls open the door and enters. "Same crazy place."

"Dale get the other Whaler?"

"Yah, but he stay de night. Got a girlfriend dere and no fishing people here."

"Didn't you want to stay?"

"Oh, we can't both be away. Suppose someone come to

fish? Suppose you need a trip yourself in de mornin? Me, I find a little girl down de road here for a Saturday night."

"Is it Saturday?"

"Dat it is." He finishes his beer and goes to the door, pushes it open and looks back. "You need a drink, mahn?"

"I'll take a beer, thanks," Reese says.

Mafius brings two bottles from the boat, sits across from Reese and takes a long, cold slug and watches the other man drink. And feels there is something coming.

Reese puts his bottle down, wipes his mouth. "Dale took me to where we had the accident and showed me what happened." He takes another sip and looks at the other man. "He told me how he hit the manatee and then the other boat and how he called you after that." He smiles. "The funny thing is, I find myself wondering if you might have seen this sea cow we hit." His mouth dry, he drinks, and feels a throbbing starting at his forehead.

Mafius waits politely, giving the other man time to state his real question, and then says, "No sign of dat manatee."

Reese presses lightly at his bandana. Eyes shut, circling the void in his memory. "But did you think this thing was still in the area?"

"Movin out in de lake, to deeper water."

"Did you look for it?"

Mafius cocks his head. "You tryin to know what happen to you, or dis manatee?"

"Both, I guess."

He takes a drink. "Meat is meat, mahn."

"So you tried to find it."

"If de animal dies, it is a very great waste."

"But you lost it."

"I never see him surface. No trail, no direction, too much space to see."

"But if it was badly wounded, dying, then where would it go?"

217

"What do you mean, mahn?"

"The place they go to die."

"You hear about a place? You think dat's real, mahn?"

"Is it?"

The other man laughs. "How can it help you to know dis?"

"I don't know. Maybe it can't but I'd like to see it." Pain and possibility mingle in his mind, conjure a proposal. "If you can guide me to it, then it's a day's fishing fee in your pocket. If not, then it's just a free boat ride for me."

Mafius sits holding his bottle and watching Reese and turning the idea over, looking for its purpose and potential ramifications. "If I show you dis boneyard, den what next?"

"Nothing. I can't explain it but I think it might help me in some way. Like a funeral, y'know? Putting an end to it."

Mafius is nodding at last. "You want some bones, right?"

"No, that's not it," Reese says. The thought had not occurred to him.

"You want a souvenir of dis crazy time, de time Reese almost die, but when another die in his place."

The idea shapes and completes itself. "Maybe one piece," Reese says.

"Yes, mahn. A bone for a life. A lucky one, after all."

Reese is looking at his palm, cupped as if it holds an object he has fashioned with meaning. "Just one piece," he says.

At dusk he picks up a bottle of cassava wine on the way to Heather's, regretting his late lunch and wanting to contribute, resolving to have a few drinks regardless of how the evening goes or how he feels physically. Throw caution to the wind, he's thinking, and it seems as though he's referring to someone he used to know.

Chickens browse in yards and under steps. A dog stands in the road looking behind as the village generator thumps on a quarter mile away and in both directions house lights blink into being. The front door is open and Reese walks up the steps and knocks and Heather leans back from behind the kitchen wall and motions him in. Barbara's bedroom door is closed but the table is set for three and soft music comes gently to him from somewhere in the small house.

"Great," she says when he presents his wine. "Good idea." Catfish is stewing on the stove, rice and beans beside it, and she is stirring potato salad in a bowl, her hands greasy. "The glasses are on that shelf," she tells him, pointing with her nose. "You can pour me a little."

He unscrews the bottle, pours two half glasses and hands her one. "Cheers," he says.

She clinks his glass. "Good health."

He finds it sweet, palatable, warm in his mouth. He stands at the back door looking out, a mosquito coil burning at the lip of a bottle at his feet, the night sky benign above the trees, everything harmless in this muffled dark, the close water unheard on either side, a kindness here in this kitchen, in this house of women. "Is Barbara able to join us?" he asks.

"Ply me with wine," she says.

He turns to see her empty glass held out, her eyes more nervous than playful. "I already tried that," he says, and neither of them laughs.

He fills her glass and then his while she stirs the pots. "Hope this'll be as good as Barb makes," she says, and then adds, shaking her head slightly, "or used to make." She gulps from her glass, sets it down. "You're not married."

"Divorced, no kids." He says it automatically.

"Was she a fishing widow?"

"No, she seemed to enjoy it herself."

"You're not sure?"

"We didn't know each other well enough."

She nods, thinking, there's no answer to that, and says, "Barb should be out in a minute." Then, "I'm sorry. Go ahead."

"No, that's okay. That's it, finito." He steps back so he

can see into the main room and sees Barbara standing there in a white lace slip swinging her arms slowly in small circles at her sides like she's moving the air around her or conducting in her own way the low music they hear playing.

"Evening," he says.

"So nice to see you again," she says, smiling broadly, eyes lively and feverish. "Warm night," she tells him, fanning her neck with both hands.

Heather passes him, saying with surprise, "I thought you were putting that dress on, Barb," and puts her arm around the woman's waist as she turns back to face the man. "But this is the tropics, after all, and nobody cares what anyone wears, do they?" She kisses Barbara on the cheek and moves her toward the table. "Everything's ready so let's all sit down and eat."

With Barbara seated in the middle chair, Reese pours her a swallow of wine and Heather brings the food. They begin eating. A fan sits unused beside the couch, moths flutter at the open door, the air through the house as soft as their wing beats. The three of them sit with faces glistening, the food warm and spicy, Barbara in her loose garment shifting in her chair, tasting a bit of each dish, ingesting the odors rising off her plate, scratching her arm with a fork. Heather asking for more wine, sighing often as she smiles, blithe on the surface. And Reese, satisfied with this company, this joy attenuated, feels his grins at these friends, all of them hovering in a spirited foreground, the feeling here calescent and swelling.

"Reese is in landscaping," Heather says. "A designer, didn't you say?"

"Flowers?" Barbara asks.

"Some," he says. "Trees, bushes, ferns, anything."

"You miss it?"

"No. I'm concerned about it, though. The business."

She sits looking at him, imbued with a wide-eyed luster, gleaning some importance from his words, imagining his life in some place she has not seen, with plants she does not know.

"Landscrape," she says. "Landscrape." She is looking through him. She whispers this word, "landscrape," over and over.

He looks at Heather and she is watching the ailing girl, placing her hand on the other's bare arm to soothe her in this mild trance, lifting a fallen strap to her shoulder, and he continues quietly along his train of thought. "I heard the fishing was good, so I came down. I didn't expect to be here this long but then I got hurt and everything changed. So I'm still here but instead of fishing, I'm asking myself, what is fishing?—crazy things like that—and feeling almost like I'm a different person who'll be back to normal any day now." He stops, feels he's been talking to himself, and pours wine for Heather and then himself, killing the bottle. There is food on every plate but no one is eating.

Heather slides her chair closer to Barbara and winks at Reese and he can see that she is tipsy, or drunk, and as she rubs the woman's wet neck her eyes close with a moist sadness and he sees Barbara's vacant eyes shut too, so that he, in his own sudden intoxication, witnessing a tenderness so sublime, cannot help but think he now sees more than some sly simulacrum of love. And sitting almost alone, he turns up his glass and drinks to these girls, drinks wondrously of this thick and sticky philter at his lips and in his mind.

"Landscraping," he says, and laughs.

Barbara opens her eyes, looking at him, and turns to Heather and says, "Going home."

Reese says, "Pretty soon."

She pushes away from the table and stands. "Going home."

She moves to the couch and sits, then jumps up and moves to the door and whirls around and says, "Moho."

"Moho," Reese says.

As in a game children might play, the word is bounced back and forth like a ball between the two: moho, moho, moho, moho, while Heather drinks her warm wine and watches mutely this uncommon display of energy and direction in her ailing friend. Until Reese stands to utter emphatically, "Mo-Ho," and Barbara hugs him mightily around his middle, prompting his questioning eyes to seek help, and Heather leaves her seat.

His body released, the woman staggers back—her smell left on him like smoke, like heated oil—but holds on to his hands, telling him a secret with steampipe eyes, holes open to her soul, as she pulls him into her dance. On the creaking floor he moves his feet, her heels alternating a beat, and he feels her zeal. Affirms it unknowingly as it is confirmed in her. "They are calling me," she tells him. "Surely, surely, I cannot deny." His hands gripped tightly, heat transferred as Heather intrudes, taking a hand of each to form a triad circle because she understands something of this excitement now, this possession yet without a cure. She holds them all together, grounding her restless friend—she moving from foot to foot as if over coals, drops flinging from her shaking face—and bonding this man to a duality she hopes he can accept.

When Barbara finally sinks, they haul her to the couch and she lies on her back motionless but for her breathing, which with her pained expression makes him think of pleurisy. He steps back to the table, drinks her untouched wine in a shot, and sits heavily, glancing over at her prostrate and rattling form.

Heather sits beside him. "This is getting worse."

He nods. "Who's calling her?"

"I think she means her ancestors."

He stares at her long enough to see she's serious. "And Moho is a place?"

"The village she's from. Moho Bight."

"I'll look in on you tomorrow," he says, ready to leave.

"Please do."

He stops at the door. "Are you alright?"

"I'm fine. She'll probably just sleep now."

"This place, Moho—" He stares off down the pale track.

"What about it?"

"Is it on the map?"

FOUR

Early morning. Reese is on his knees retching into the toilet, disgusted by his violent heaving but amazed that his head, within the context of its physical injury, is clear. For half an hour he is sick, incessantly urged to puke, while his reasoning mind remains above, disembodied and gloating as if it has no need for this hurting and twisted torso forewarned. Pay the price, it says.

There is a knocking at his door and the voice of Mafius. "You takin a Sunday trip, mahn?"

"Yeah," he calls. "Be right there."

He descends the stairs shaky and weak, glances out at the bright water—Mafius is rummaging in the boat—and finds a cup of hot coffee on the table. He manages a few sips before his stomach rebels and he heads for the dock.

Mafius looks him over. "Your gear, mahn."

"What?"

"What we are doin is undertakin a fishin expedition."

"Right." He turns back toward the building.

The expanse of water, a marine wind rushing, the motion and speed in this large and open world. Clouds of aerial stature, an eagle's formal soar. Sunlight flaring in bolts along the vessel's railing. Blossoms rising violet on stiff green stalks, bobbing together in clumps, makeshift islands. These things begin in him a restoration of vitality. Of some bearing. A pursuit or mirage he cannot yet fathom. His senses firing like loose cannons, blood running blue and cool. *Moho.*

They stop somewhere in the middle, engine idling. Aside from two boats far to the south, near the main creek, they are alone in a water field, needlefish and silversides scattering about. Reese is looking around. "What is it?"

"Wheer we goin is not known by others." He taps his chest. "Only I been dere." He bends closer to Reese's puzzled face. "I have never taken any person to see dis place."

"Well, thanks. I am truly honored."

"No, mahn. I can't be happy with another knowin de way."

Reese looks from the man to the channeled land spreading far and low toward the western hills. "I couldn't find my way in there. You know that."

"No chance if you doan see it. If we juss pull dis rag down over de eyes." His fingertips point at the blue bandana.

"Mafius, this isn't necessary. Who am I going to tell?"

"Sorry, mahn, but I muss insist de expedition have one condition. After you see de place you woan have any complaint about a short ride without eyes."

Shaking his head, Reese relents, accepts the guide's demand, and positions the folded cotton across his eyes, a blue stripe below the white gauze, his head double-banded, color-coded like some buoy above a slatted trap he pictures as he pictures himself sitting blindfolded in the boat. Hands gripping the seat and he leaning with the boat as it roars first in circles and then speeds off, his mind's eye activated, imagination heightened without sight. In the trap he waits like bait, like the caged divers in shark films, looking to capture rare knowledge for the same reason he might seek a rare stone at the bottom of a cold pool in a dark cave.

With deceleration, his body leans forward, a turn is made and he feels the sun on the back of his neck. A channel mouth. The drone of the engine drowning all other sound. Vibration he feels mostly in his queasy stomach and his feet. Mangroves are close, their life and decay in his nose, his eyes closed under the cloth. He listens for depth, the gurgling hollow below the boat. Feels the stitches in his head, in his brain, the propeller working the water, pushing them up a creek he may never see. Like a condemned man taken out for his last rites, his last wish to see a place he cannot believe exists, but which has lodged in him like an arrowhead. Now would be the time for the cigarette. Forget the meal.

"Hey, soldier, how about some water?"

He hears the ice rattled, the cooler lid snapped down, and a bottle touches his hand. Cold water he pours down his throat, down his chin to his shirt; he presses the wet spot, the coolness at his stomach from inside and out.

There is a turn south, then a slight right, subtle shifts as their path meanders and narrows. He hears branches scrape like fingernails on the hull and he sits still in his blind isolation, his aim to visit dead mammals, a congregation of air-breathers who live and die in water. Like cetaceans, but whose closest relatives are elephants. How odd, these links and unexpected directions. But then, we are all related. And what has he done to get himself here on this trail?

The boat grazes bottom. He is led forward to sit at the bow and is facing the pilot when leaves brush his arm and he jerks.

"Captain, we're not lost, are we?"

"No."

"Seems like a dead end."

225

"Juss a shallow."

"Tell me how a sick manatee would get through here."

"De water low right now."

"Then I guess they probably wait for high tide to die. Or the rainy season."

"Dere's another way but it runs longer."

The muttering engine takes them through and spreads its sound to growl along the sides of a wider space as they lift and glide in a burst and then throttle down again. A whiff of rot as he turns his head. The bush closing—walls to a tunnel grown, the guide with a quick hand directs the man's head down as prickly fingers claw from all sides at the wedging vessel and touch his hair, pulling at blindfold and bandage—to keep them out, their motor silenced suddenly, and the pole pushed crackling at the banks to get them inside. Reese with his head between his knees going backward into some backcountry corner he was never fated to find.

A languor of space as they slip free of branches. He sits up and turns toward the bow. "Are we there?"

"Take a look, mahn."

"Dramatic bastard," Reese says, and lifts the cloth.

A lagoon. His eyes, released, rise like birds to freedom, to an oval sky and five or six black scavengers flapping away from the tallest logwood tops. A theater in the round, the stage empty and flat as they glide across its surface, the guide poling in silence, Reese kneeling on the bow, the sun over the trees and shining down to matted leaves, the brown bottom, greenish hues and strands of light connecting and disconnecting in leaps and twists around the minimal motions of small, weaving fish. Quickening fish in numbers increasing. The boat's slow block of shadow.

Reese leans over the rail as they approach an oily stain, some spill of putrefactive essence from which he recoils. Then they are upon it, parting this surface slick over a barrel carcass buried below water, a blurred and mealy mass barely sunken and its attendant fish in retreat.

A stream enters an opening at the other end and it is toward this flow that they are moving, the depth somewhat shallower still, flies and lacewings abundant near the reedy shore. Reese stands now, seeing the pieces strewn here. Knuckles of vertebrae, loose stars of a skeletal anatomy, the links of a tapering tail. Ribs like fallen sticks, white on the drab bottom, the bleached staves of a collapsed cask. He slips down into the water in his shoes to stand in the oozy ground; bubbles rise at his feet, methane released, as he creeps into this uncommon array of bones, stirring up silt and the unmarked communal grave of these disassembled dead.

He stands silently under the sun in this warm and shallow hole—losing his pain, his stomach calming, the water lapping at his loins—and feels a welcome peace among the adamantine remains. The comfort of those passed, the gathered gone. They need not be human. What matters is this: the dead cannot be molested; nor can they molest the living. And they will all be free and equal in a state of particles.

With his vessel grounded and his legs dangling over the side, Mafius sits whittling on a corner of the stern, shaving chips of bone into the water. Reese wades near the stream in fresh water three feet deep where tendrils of aquatic grasses sweep out and point wiggling into the pond and where a spread of gray and beige and ivory bones lies clean in this light current. With the toe of his shoe he nudges different pieces, reaches under to feel their various shapes, brings them up for inspection in the air and holds them for their texture and weight. Arm bones—the inner flipper, humerus and radius—like short clubs, dense and unbreakable as petrified wood. A paddle-hand, complete with carpus and metacarpus, finger phalanges falling apart in his own two hands. Why are they here? he thinks, lifting a shoulder bone, an axe blade scapula, and heaving it away; it cleaves the surface in its splash and sinks like granite. He spies a headbone—always the head the hunter seeks—and goes down to get it, aware in this immersion of his own head's essential shape, its roundness in this

227

warm rinsing, and he feels his wet stitches as a mere wrinkle at his brow, only a pulled snag of knotted line, and thinks that he is passing his injury at last. And grabbing the jaw he lifts it gushing from orbits and throat and nasal cavity, not to take it from this place but to look upon it, this long-faced cranium, this thick bird-head oddity, and see the animal naked beneath the behemoth. Something strange, like a lizard, a dinosaur, an ichthyosaur from the Mesozoic, but not what he expected. He could not guess. He cannot readily recognize the skull of any species but the human.

Cradling the beaked thing to his chest, he pushes on a molar with his thumb but it does not pop out, and he returns the big bone gently to the bottom, setting it down like some holy stone accidently dislodged.

He moves to a standing ribcage, an armature upright and held whole by decomposing cartilage and tendinous shreds. He pushes the curved slats and they bend apart like stakes stuck in the ground; with both hands he twists one free. He squats and feels for pieces of spine, his head underwater, his hand roving over horns of angularity. The guide watches curiously from the boat, and neither of them quite understands why Reese is here. He stands up straight, holding a large vertebra in each hand, giant wingnuts from the tail, lifts them overhead to show Mafius, who after a moment nods and then waves the stick of bone he is holding. Reese stacks the pieces in one hand and reaches down, submerging himself again, and comes up gripping his chosen rib. A blunt and curved and marrowless weapon-stick. He stares at these three parts together, sculptural components. The wingnuts he flings, end over end in double-bladed spins cutting into the far thickets. He goes to his knees along the shore and putters in the muck with his rib, rakes the shallow bottom and uncovers other items: teeth, mandible, sternum, the whorls of empty snail shells. A funny nubbin he holds, turning it in his fingers, a puzzle part, some hound's tooth piece, like a crude canine with no bite, and discards it without knowing—this pelvic vestige, dropped free-floating from musculature, the last loose trace of a hind leg.

Bent over with his bone tool and digging at the floor of this remote wetland pool, he feels, in the physicality of the place—the opaline light caught in clear water, the trapped heat, the swamp wood smell, the algae, the leaves and the bone scraps—cannot help but feel a relief. But relief at what? At being here, at his sheer survival? His movement onward? As others dissolve and turn to mud. He feels sorry and pleased, skeptical and celebratory. Feels in his own presence here the abstraction of being. The unseen miasma.

And yet, as he moves out into the pond again, he cannot quit wondering about the injury to one specific animal and its possible passing. He halts suddenly, meeting the stench of a carcass, the one they first glided over.

"Hey!" He consults Mafius about a doubt, his arm waving out at the area of the pond. "No sizeable predators in here."

The guide glances around from his higher vantage as if he is making certain, and says, "Only we two."

Over the body a fetid film coats the surface and though he spreads it with his stick, the substance reforms itself and closes around him like coagulating blood, clinging to his arms and chest. He clears an opening to see the thing and witnesses its uneven surface shifting in undulation; he prods it with his rib and understands a rash of crabs is feeding and creeping completely around the curve of its sheltering bulk. The broad back, a long open wound of pink and gray and rib white, lies like some flayed terrain. The wide tail spaded into silt, the head downward, likewise snuggled in the mud. Somehow, he thinks, this attacked and dying mammal made its way back here.

A flipper angled outward at his feet; he attempts to turn it upward with the rib, stretching his arm down to reach it without putting his face in the water. Touches it, straining his arm and feeling the rubbery limb slip away; tries again and fails, the bone slipping off, the settled mass not buoyant, lying at rest and refusing to help. He uses his shoe, lifts the slippery limb and tilts the carcass, prods it sideways with his rib-stick, rolls the body as he reaches down to grasp the animal's hand.

The paddle presses at his palm and for moments he feels more than he sees, touches the rounded edge and squints at the trees across the lagoon. The crude hand in his, he feels the three hard nails at the rim, leftover toenails on a wide and flattened foot. Paired fins molded from hoofs, from the feet of some ungulate order like swine or bovine or rhino.

This thing, he thought, this species, whatever it was, crawled out of the sea and walked on land, lived on the earth like an elephant, and then, for some reason, returned to the sea, gave up its legs and grew flippers and a fluke.

Using the paddle and the rib and his leg as a brace against the damaged mass, he rolls it over and gazes into the water once again, the stink filling his nose and his eyes, and his prodding rib finding the loose flaps of belly, the open and empty abdominal cavity. In his surprise he nearly backs away involuntarily as crabs move to his leg, but then presses forward and examines the butchered belly, the sliced and ragged flesh around a sunken center, the exposed rib ends that look for a moment like the long teeth and rotten gums of some huge and horrible maw about to clamp down on further invasion. Now he leaves it, with the fish returning, and the beast settling upside down in its liquid grave.

Beside the boat he submerges to clean himself, rubs his scalp, face, neck and chest, comes up with the smell of decay, and gags, his previous relief tainted by falsity and turned to nausea. Mafius hands him a plastic bottle of dish soap and though their eyes meet, neither speaks, and he bathes his arms and head thoroughly and then cleans the bone he has taken.

At the bow he pushes; the boat slides back and he pulls himself aboard. They are drifting in the small lagoon and he is watching Mafius turn them with the pole.

"What's the deal, man? You brought that cut-up fucker in here, didn't you?"

"Caught and delivered."

"Yes, I see now. A real secret place."

"No, mahn, you doan see." He drives the pole straight down into the mud and they stop, his arms holding the boat against this vertical anchor. "Why you think I bring him here?"

"Secluded as hell, isn't it?"

"Quite so! Quite so! And de bones already here. Dat's de actual reason."

"Oh!" Reese holds up the rib in his fist. "You bring them here because they come here themselves."

"Dat's de true thing, de natural way. Dey respect dere own dead."

Reese is mystified, turning around on the bow and looking at the water, thinking of the one he collided with, imagining it dead elsewhere, at the bottom of Laguna Vaca, or traveling injured. He points with his stick. "Is that the only fresh one here?"

The man nods.

Nothing but bones and the sun overhead, both of them now irritated at Reese's entanglement. A snail kite swoops low over the trees as he's looking up and he remarks as they're leaving, "You could sure as hell find the place from the air."

"Maybe." The guide points at Reese and says, "Eyes covered."

"C'mon man, let's forget that now."

"Look, mahn, we have a simple arrangement. If you cannot complete dis thing, you could spend a long night hereabouts."

Without eyes, he cannot get comfortable this time. There is no talking and in the burning heat he meets the hammering return of his headache. Without a hat he sits under his shirt, a draping hood, and does not feel healed. He feels greasy and senseless, awaiting his executioner. Drifting blind on a bone tide.

With his gear under his arm and the bone inside his held shirt he notes the other Whaler repaired and steps from the dock to the yard. Dale shouts a greeting from the porch and he calls back and goes to his room and then joins the other man a few minutes later.

"Howdy." Dale has a stack of papers he's going through. "I didn't see any great quantity of fish unloaded."

"Yeah, well, no luck." Reese takes a chair against the wall.

"It ain't the guide so much as the man fishing."

"I'll probably just go back to a cane pole and worms."

Dale laughs, holds up a letter. "Got me some fly fishermen coming for two weeks."

"Good, very good. How'd the big city treat you?"

"Mighty kindly, son. Got drunk as a skunk and then fucked blind. I'm only just now able to read my mail."

"I can barely remember what that's like."

"And you won't likely cultivate any new memories here."

"I was over at Heather's for dinner."

Dale slaps his papers. "The rabble-rousing bitch."

"She speaks highly of you as well."

Dale leans back in his chair, raises his eyebrows. "You know, son, don't you, that she's of the lesbo persuasion."

"Is that a fact?"

He nods with a sympathetic smirk. "'Fraid so. Ain't nobody nailed her in the year she's here."

"That'd be hard to know and it means nothing anyway."

"Well, I reckon you sound pretty sweet on her."

"I like her. I like them both."

Dale laughs. "Whoa ho, wouldn't that be something, you squeezing in between. The man's dream come true." His hands do a drum roll on his thighs and then he looks serious. "I'd be careful, though. I hear the girlfriend is a mite sickly."

He sees the girls, the previous night, in his mind. "I'm sure they care a lot for each other. What's that prove?"

"Nothing, but five'll get you ten you could peek in their window tonight and see them two eating each other's pussy."

"It wouldn't matter if I did."

"Jesus wept, boy. I'm only trying to steer you straight."

"I appreciate your sound judgment," Reese says, "across the board." He stands. "I'll let you know if I see anything interesting over there."

"Would you, now?" Dale's lips purse as if he's about to spit. "I'd truly enjoy an eyewitness account."

Holding the open door, Reese looks back. "I'll be leaving soon," he says.

Dale with his feet up, eyes on his papers, says, "I kinda figured that."

Down the road at a small store Reese leans on the smooth wood of the counter drinking a cold soda while somewhere back in the house an argument is occurring between two women. In the shaded sand of the yard next door a boy sits on a stool and a man cuts his hair close with scissors and then takes it off at the scalp with a razor blade held between thumb and finger and angled carefully over the contours of the head. His other hand at the boy's neck and the boy motionless as other children run and holler across the sand among chickens and standing dogs.

He finds Heather behind her house washing clothes in a pair of buckets and hanging them out on a line in the sunny area between the building and the trees. As usual she's in a tee shirt and baggy shorts, her hair pulled back in a golden tail, her smile pleasant even under stress. "Hey, man."

"Hey, woman. How's your friend?"

"Sleeping, I hope. She was up most of the night." Heather is wringing a sheet, getting herself wet. "We both were," she adds, and she looks tired around the eyes.

Suddenly he notices a boy standing on the back steps, and realizes he has walked right through the house; he is watching them and holding a plastic basin at his waist. "Tabletas," he says in a quiet voice as soon as he is seen. Reese walks over.

They are under a cloth, brown squares of coconut and ginger shreds. Reese buys ten for a dollar and puts them on a plate in the kitchen; he eats one there and when he comes out with the plate the boy is in the next yard.

Heather wipes her hands on her shirt and takes a sticky piece and they sit on the steps to eat.

"Now you've upset my sweet tooth," she says, and when he doesn't respond she asks, "Been out fishing?"

"What? No, not really. Just exploring with Mafius."

"Ah, the warrior," she says, and he looks over at her. "That's how I think of him. I don't really know him, though. He'd been adopted by the lodge when I got here and so we were already on opposite sides. I hate to say it."

"Sounds like a battle."

"It isn't, really. People just have different ideas about what's best for a place. Sometimes I can see the future ready to pounce on us here and I want to tell people to get prepared because they're going to be affected one way or the other."

"There's no escape any more. It's difficult to get lost these days, even if you want to."

"Hmmm, I know. There's always the contact with people who remind you of yourself." She stretches her legs and arms and then stands. "Excuse me." She goes to the front bedroom and peeks in and returning to the kitchen pours water for them both and sits again. "That's a relief," she says. "Sleeping like a kitten."

"What're you going to do? How long can this go on?"

"I have to get her to Moho Bight." He hears the small catch in her voice and she starts to wring her hands and then quits. "I want her to get there as soon as possible but I don't think she can make the trip by herself."

"Why don't you take her?"

"I can't yet. I mean, after last night, I think she should go right away, tomorrow, but I have people coming this week." She is wringing her wet shirt roughly though no water escapes, and pulling at the wrinkles left. "Don't you think I would if I could? I've been trying to get these two government people to come down here and meet with us for months." She puts her face in her hands a second and shakes her head and looks directly at him.

234

"The thing about Moho is there's no road to it. She'd have to take a bus to Rio Perez and then a boat from there."

"So you think going home would help her."

"She does. I don't know what to think any more." She looks out into the yard as if the answer may lie somewhere in the trees or the grass. "I only want what's best for her. And now—this is the crazy part—she tells me if she doesn't go home, then—then she's going to die."

"If it's not a medical problem, then what is it? Is she homesick?" He whispers toward her ear. "Is it mental?"

She shrugs, throws up her hands. "There's no shortage of physical symptoms." When she looks at him now she worries that he'll become as scared as she is. But she says, "She's Garifuna."

"I'm not familiar—"

"That's her culture. Garifuna. It comes from a mixture of African and Indian tribes. They've kept their own beliefs going, and even the language is still alive. They believe in a collective unconscious that's inherited from ancestors. But she left that years ago, left the village. Those ways."

She is at a loss for more explanation and he doesn't quite know what to add. So they sit. And then she steps down to the ground and says, "I need to finish this laundry."

"Let me give you a hand."

He likes being around her, twisting a sheet together, watching her hang clothes in the sun. And in his attraction to her—with this sweet taste in his mouth, even with his recurrent headache and random erection and what he's been told of her problems and possible preferences—he wishes for a moment he were living here in this small blue house.

She is glad to share her burdens with him and does not want his friendship to be so temporary, has begun to cherish it perhaps because she feels it is so close to being gone. "What are your plans?" she asks.

"I'd like to get these stitches out," he says.

"Give me that bandana and I'll wash it too."

In the living room the afternoon light diffused through white curtains is still bright and reflects off the green walls like a balm in the house that settles over Reese as he lies waiting on the couch for this procedure of healing and listens to the sounds of its preparation. Heather has shut the front door and pulled a chair next to his head and sits rustling through her first aid kit selecting the items needed for this operation: cotton balls, rubbing alcohol, tweezers, sharp-pointed nail scissors.

And when she begins to work he is like a man behind a veil, the breath from her nose falling lightly on his face, the cool shock of the alcohol and the smell almost absinthian as she spreads it over his knotted brow. In the safety of his sightlessness he lets himself float and surrenders himself to her care and the sensations produced as she leans closer and he hears her concentrated breathing spinning a sphere around him in this room which nothing outside can penetrate or oppose. He feels the tweezers tug and his head wanting to lift, and then hears the thin snip of the scissors, and the thread pulled wiggling from his head is like a nerve running through his body that is not disconnected at all, but woven down into his stomach and into his limbs so that he twitches involuntarily and does not try to prevent these small spasms or deny himself this pleasure, or acknowledge any embarrassment projected. With each minute removal his attachment grows more profound and he hears a groan he dimly attributes to himself until she whispers, "She's dreaming in there," and he listens then to the sounds emanating from the other woman and in his mind allows her in her dreamy sleep to float close and her moans to merge with his own. As if an apparition is observing, her nether comments audible yet nonverbal, while his penis like a puppet moves to the strings pulled at his head, jerking and pushing at the fabric of his pants, nosing upward along his body and out of his control toward the pampering hands at work up there.

Making a pile of black thread on his white shirt, on his chest, she is aware of his condition, notices his breathing and his movements, his fingers restless at his side like the tail feathers of a nervous bird. She does not mean to incite his blood to riot or spur his growth in her direction; she would like to see him happy as she listens to Barbara and works the last stitch out of the flesh closed around it. In this position, with these two prone patients under her care, she feels her responsibility more keenly extended than ever, and though neither is lively or completely themselves, she feels too the ambrosial delight she sees on his face, some unity among them that may possibly impel their lives onward to rapture and plenty. And for a moment, while his eyes are still closed, she thinks of letting her hand stray down, not in some wanton or false display, not even to touch the man but only his clothes, to perform another simple humanitarian mission and in this clinical guise squeeze him to release. It is no more than a thought but she is not ashamed of it, only thinks it excessive; she is unsure of herself too, of her ability and his reaction, afraid of upsetting the scales, of swaying the situation toward collapse, afraid most of all of risking the health and well-being of her companion and whatever additional chance of recovery is inherent in their fragile alignment with this third party, this man whose judgment she has enlisted.

"All better," she tells him, "but still tender."

"Thank you," he says. "It's a big occasion for me."

"Very exciting," she says.

He sits up. "It's not like you think."

"I don't think anything. It's a natural reaction. I'm trying to be therapeutic because I can't help it. I'm not good at it but it's real. If I like someone then I open up to them. It gets me in trouble sometimes but I consider myself a helpful person. I always have."

"I like you too."

They are watching each other; she reaches out to pick the threads off his chest. "I need your help," she says quietly.

"I know you do," he says. There is no sound from the other room but they are both listening for one. "I'll take her."

She stands and bends, cups his chin and touches his hair, kisses the scar on his forehead, straightens and sighs. "I'm going to make some fruit cocktail in cream. It was supposed to be our dessert last night but we didn't get to it, did we. So we'll have it now. Barb might enjoy it if she ever wakes up."

But Barbara does not join them as they sit on the back steps again, eating from bowls in the shade of the house and shooing flies while she explains the schedules and methods of the transportation he will need to get to Moho Bight. And says she doesn't expect him to stay any longer than he wants—that Barbara will then be in the care of family members—and that she will arrive herself as soon as she is free to travel. He is spooning up the creamy syrup left in his bowl when a cry issues from the house and Heather jumps up to attend her friend. He wanders in the yard, anxious already at his task, finds his bandana dry on the line and puts it back on, covers the weakened place and thinks comically that he should have his head examined. His stomach nervous and cramping, full of milky fruit and coconut sweets, unsettled from the morning's rough upheaval, the remains of a strange wine. The memory nearly makes him sick; he doubles over to press the pain at his waist, and heads down the trail to the lagoon.

A short boardwalk out over the water, the outhouse door latched with a loop of string, and in the space between roof and wall a view across the great, flat lake to sun-struck hills gathered there and running higher to the south and beyond his sight. There is a roll of paper on a nail, a board seat and under it an angled sheet of tin hung vertically as a splash guard. Below its rusted edge the water and the catfish sweeping back and forth through the shadows and straw light, appearing or reappearing in identical but more numerous form like multiple images of themselves. These whiskered fish seem replicated by sound, their ghostly maneuvers brought into being with signals sent vibrating beneath the box, and his shot droppings are devoured in fluid pandemonium, an instantaneous chaos of thorough worms in whose gobble and flash no waste is wasted. They then are eaten and returned in excremental measure—a fisherman feeds the fish—and this base cycle consoles Reese inexplicably.

In a sense, he realizes, he has been feeding on himself, his injured self, since the accident, and in escorting this woman afflicted—on a terminal voyage or not he cannot say, cannot stop thinking of leukemia for instance—he imagines nothing more than a selfless action. No bargain, no reward. Somewhere in those minutes of his lost memory he lost some part of himself and he had thought he was staying—not going home—until he could get it back. But now, sitting alone in this water closet, with this besieged woman nearly in his charge, he knows he can never reclaim what is gone and does not need to and into that space he feels her moving with her visions and her needs, to afflict or inform him in some way he cannot define and does not understand, as these sea cows have, and so he reaches for a description of this unfilled hole, a name for this sepulchral place. And he calls it Moho.

FIVE

The bus arrives at seven about half full and departs, after the driver's breakfast, at seven-twenty, with another six passengers boarded for journeys south. In the open compartment beside him, the driver has his tickets and logbook and newspaper and cassettes, and a pistol wedged on top in plain view like an overly purposeful paperweight that, along with his brusque and authoritarian manner, and perhaps too the hour, seems to establish for a time a noncommunicative air within the moving vehicle. Hanging in the open doorway, the young second, already adopting the ways of his superior, watches the passengers and the roadside world alike with a shrewd and steely-eyed glare as they leave the village and the long road to it behind and turn out rumbling onto the highway.

A few miles inland and south through pines and alongside cultivated fields of mango, orange and lime, and bulldozed areas yet to be planted. A huge speaker in the front blasts soca down the aisle, the driver in his arrogance shutting himself off from the riders and subjecting them to his taste for volume. Reese and Barbara share a seat near the rear, she against the window and not looking out but looking along the plane of the glass or at the back of the seat in front of them and not speaking either, so that she seems, even to him, to be someone he just happened to sit next to.

She is febrile, weak from hunger, and cannot eat. Her feet scrape the gritty floor and she would walk the aisle if she could. All these folks are strangers except Reese and he keeps her pinned in her corner for her own good and holds her hot hand tightly in his. She has lost control of herself; she may piss or scream or pass out for good or explode in light. Like being trapped inside yourself with voices and distant sights and unable to move out into the world beyond this dream of yourself, sitting with pains of the skin and stomach and this relentless internal heat and without the energy to run or dance or fling oneself out of a horrible state. How can this be real? An illness, some say, but these tablets do nothing for her. A sickness of gaps, of missing spaces between waking dream and fitful sleep, an interior turnstile jammed between life and death that she stays within to keep from exiting the wrong way. Dear God, she keeps saying. I am so young. Am I sleeping? Am I being born? Am I dying? Have I not represented myself decently? I love my family, my people, my stillborn baby too. I'm sorry. There's something wrong with my body but I only want to better myself like anyone does. Heather, bless her soul, she speaks of specialists we cannot afford. Miami, New York, Boston, Vienna, Jesus, Abraham, Job. Dear God, I'm going home like they tell me. Is it you? Is it me? My heart, my heart, it cannot be so hard to stay alive, so difficult to die. I have done nothing wrong. I don't deserve this foul treatment. Take them away. Please.

They make forays down bumpy coastal roads to encounter travelers waiting in seaside savannah places, villages made to stand between silk grass plains and clear green streams.

Red Bank, Russell Creek, Bonefish Bay. In South Water, Reese watches from the idling bus the water falling like mercury blobs from a high tower pipe that overflows in spurts that drop tumbling down the air to burst in explosive sprays over the brown children squealing under there. He buys a cold soda through the window and offers it to Barbara; she shakes her head and after they are moving again he holds some coolness from the bottle in his palm and places it against her burning neck. She looks at him and rubs her forehead on his shoulder.

At Monkey Branch, the driver stops for lunch and most of the passengers get out too and stand in the shade of the place or relieve themselves or eat something. Reese buys a snapper sandwich and takes some aspirin with an orange soda and when he comes out he walks along the bus looking in the windows for Barbara and jumps aboard to see if she's down on the seat and then sees her at some distance down the dusty road. "What the hell," he says running, and he catches up to her, takes her by the arm and leads her around. She is pointing at her bare feet as they walk, and he says finally, "There's nothing wrong with your feet, Barb."

The driver is back in his seat and the engine is running as they return and he gives Barbara a disapproving look and tells Reese, "I won't hang up my route for anybody." And Reese looks at his eyes a moment and leans toward the man as if he might answer or even strike the fellow, and then turns away and with all eyes on them follows his shuffling friend back to their seat.

The highway is unpaved from here and the old yellow bus rattles along at a speed meant to best negotiate the washboard ripples and a known pattern of potholes that make up this ocher track driven through jungle terrain and alongside hacked out Kekchi homesteads and over rushing waters in rock-made ravines. The sky clouds quickly, coming over the trees like a streaked, gray drape and the rain descends in a great wash whose cleansing sweep and mountainous origins could be smelled only moments before its arrival. Windows slide up all around, the driver presses ahead on a slippery ribbon of mud and the only music now comes from sluicing tires and spattered steel and the metronomic squeaks of hardworking wipers.

Just as suddenly the shower passes and the road is slick under a bright sun and fresh steam rises from rock and puddle and metal roof alike as they descend to the coast and the town of Rio Perez. Rounding a bend on a slope to the river and the open sea again bursting into view after a long absence, the water in a muddy torrent beneath them as they cross the bridge, and the demarcation at the mouth a cleanly drawn line, a stark division of colors: brown river, blue sea. On this wet afternoon a simple and brilliant presentation of the world here in this southern district with its buildings squat and gleaming, antennas shining, and in the near distance a light aircraft lifting in a silver glimmer against the dark green humps of a pair of hills alone at the outskirts.

She carries her one small bag and Reese has his fishing gear and his duffel and they walk from the central plaza down to the waterfront and the empty market area and find no working boats present. This is not a market day and there is no regular traffic to Moho Bight and he knows they will have to find a fisherman or someone else to ferry them onward. From a vendor's cart he buys bananas and peanuts and they move down the road to the benches of a small park near a public outhouse built out over the water. A small girl soon approaches with a tray and Reese buys a brick of Creole bread and sits eating in the sun while Barbara stands nearby staring out to sea.

There are a few cars and some pedestrians occasionally passing and Indian women appear one at a time to stand before him silently with small white baskets and embroidered cloths and Reese declines them one after the other. After a while Barbara sits beside him and he believes he sees in her gaze some lucidity and he asks her if she is doing okay. And she at first nods and then shakes her head and he isn't able to tell if this is some little humor or simply the general confusion regarding her condition. He pats her leg and what he asks her is what he's wanted to ask all day. "Why are you going back?"

And she says almost immediately, as if she'd been talking all day, as if she had been just about to explain herself, as if they were just two neighbors passing the time, "A man came to me." She covers her mouth and coughs hard with her head down and when she looks up again she stares beyond him at the sparkling horizon. "A man came to me. I do not believe in spirits. A man came to me, a man like you are sitting there. He was the older brother of my grandmother, my mother's mother. He was drowned fishing many years before but he came to me and said to me: 'Little sister, what is it you are doing?' and he poked me with a stick, here at my belly and I tried to walk away but I could not walk properly, my feet were swollen and in the sand I could not move well. He continued to poke me, my belly, and then my back when I turned away. 'You are so thirsty,' he tells me. 'Why do you not drink? You can die of a thirst like that. Is it your wish to die?' This is while I am in hospital. The night is glowing too bright and I think it must be the streetlight outside, but only the black ocean is there. And in the glow are people standing near this man, people in loincloths and holding bowls. And the man pokes me again and I say: 'Stop it, stop it, they have drinks for us, take what they have.' But he says: 'Little sister, you must drink, we are both so thirsty, take this cassava beer and drink too.' I am too sick to drink is my reply and so he hits my legs and I fall to the sand screaming. The water pitcher is spilling on the floor and the night nurse is very angry with me. And that was the time I began to know I was going home. Because I am not well. I do not believe in spirits but they will not let me rest. They wish to harm me because I cannot help them. They are not well. Do you understand? I am not well but what I have told you is true. Do you understand?"

"Yes," he says. "When did you leave? How many years?"

She sighs, seemingly calm. "Ten, I think."

"How old are you?"

"Twenty-six." She is looking at him. "Yes, it was ten."

"Well, I'm sure they'll be glad to see you."

To this she has no answer.

By three o'clock they have moved to the shade behind the market building and sit on the steps there watching a lone dory coming in from the south, its single occupant paddling, taking a long time in his approach but angling toward the wharf before them. An old man in a dirty straw hat scooting into the shallow water along the side wall of the concrete wharf, a few small fish at his feet, and the man standing in his craft now and squinting up at Reese speaking above him.

"Afternoon," Reese says. "We need to get to Moho today. The girl's sick."

The man adjusts his hat. "Hospital here," he says.

"She wants to get home," Reese says.

The man cranes his neck upward but cannot see her from his position. "Wednesday," he says.

"We can't wait. We don't expect a free ride either."

The man bends down and begins to string his fish.

"If I could get an engine, would you take us?"

"No."

"Anybody else out there?"

"Coupla fellas."

"They have motors?"

"Bleve so."

Reese walks back and squats in front of Barbara, who has her face cupped in both hands, leaning forward. "Listen," he says, "this guy's no help. We passed a gas station on the way in. I'm going over there and you either have to come with me or stay right here. Okay? Stand up if you're coming."

"Tired," she says, her eyes half closed.

"Listen to me." He grips her wrist. "I'll be right back and I want to find you right here. Okay? I'm going to find us a boat and you have to stay with our things. You hear me? Barb! Okay? Answer me."

"Alright."

He stands. "Don't leave."

He runs down the waterfront street past restaurants and stores, a pool room, post office, police station, the office of the Minister of Agriculture and Fisheries, and on around a bend to the sight of the station, and then walks up behind it catching his breath. The man inside is a businessman and once he sees the money he sends a boy running with his message and sits Reese down with a cool drink and they wait. A radio is on with a commentary and in a lull he hears distinctly the public announcement: Cholera prevention is in your hands—wash them! In fifteen minutes the boy returns and says the man with the boat will be at the wharf in three quarters of an hour.

The run back pains his head; he rounds the corner of the building and startles a dog smelling his bag. The dog jerks sideways and Reese panics at the missing person, racing to the end of the wharf to look in the water and then running back to the street and looking up and down and trying to get air in his lungs, leaning over with his hands on his knees and his head pounding. He goes into the building and finds her laid out on a table like a body awaiting an autopsy, the odor of old meat and fish and blood and marrow in the air and in the stone and in her hair. He bends over and places his head on her chest and feels her heart beating in concert with the blood in his head. He hears the humming flies and smells the rancid scraps and shuts his eyes as he holds her hand.

The dory is beat and scuffed, peeling yellow outside and maroon on the inside, the same blue undercoat showing through on both. The engine is loud but not powerful and they are out several hundred yards on calm, greenish water, heading south with the shoreline. The man at the motor has said it will take them an hour and Reese turns around from the forward seat he shares with Barbara, and says, "Appreciate the lift."

"No problem. You got to get where you goin." He indicates the net piled between them. "She can lay out if she needs to."

"Alright," Reese says, and looks ahead again and she stays against him on the seat.

Flying fish skim the surface, racing ahead of the boat in long, startling runs that tend to vanish in an infinitesimal splash. All along the coast the jungle is uniform, dense and unwelcoming; there are no breaks, no camps or settlements in sight. There is water, then the trees. The land runs southwest and then east in a wide curve, becoming a series of hazy bands layered in the distance down there, the front edge a soft, rich blue and the lighter shades resting above that—the land ascending beyond the coast—and spread gently on top a long white range of clouds lifted in dollops like meringue on an earthen pie. Here and there the solitary fishing boats, a drifting dugout or just a mark drawing itself across the flat expanse or to the receding east some tiny bump like a peanut shell on the horizon. Reese tosses his hulls over as he eats and behind them floats the bobbing, shifting trail of their journey here on the Gulf of Honduras.

The coast a series of bights scalloped wide between points; stubby fingers of reaching land and each indentation passed a tangled place. Until Moho Bight. Amid its promontories a slight headland, a breach of grassy field and a tattered flag, palms in numbers legion, and the thatched dwellings set back from the beach and composed along the curve from which in its southernmost region the sylvan river itself emerges from low swamp like a snake out of the jungle rising behind it.

At the sound of the engine children gather on the dock and on the sand and in the long shadows of the field. The passengers disembark and with a shout to someone on the beach the boatman leaves under the remaining light of day. Her bag carried and she followed by a string of children, Barbara goes up a footpath with some urgency in her steps and Reese, with his own group of curious kids, moves along behind her. In among the houses, some raised greatly and some barely off the ground, she turns up another path and this unexpected passing continues to draw the residents to their doors and to the clearings of their yards to witness what is quickly known to be the return of a familiar stranger.

On the steps of a brown, unpainted house, a woman waits. She wears a plain white dress and a plaid headscarf and she grunts once at the sight of her daughter and hurries down the steps and takes the young woman in her arms as she collapses and brings her up off the ground like she would a sack of feathers and goes on up the steps into the house. Reese puts her bag in the doorway and waits there on the steps with the children sitting and watching him and fanning out across the path and under the edge of the house whispering.

There are several voices inside and after a while the woman comes out and tells the children to get away and they do, mostly, and she introduces herself as Sophie Flores, the girl's mother, and Reese tells her his name and says he just wanted to make sure she got home safely.

"How long she been this way?"

"A few weeks, I'd have to guess."

She studies him a moment, looks down at his bag and his gear. "I half expected her," she says, "but I didn't know who else to expect."

"We met leaving the hospital a few days ago and it began to seem urgent that she get here so I was able to travel with her today. Her friend Heather will come as soon as she can."

"The American girl."

"That's right."

Her face is smooth and her expression has not changed; she pushes a tuft of graying hair under the edge of her scarf. "You sick too?"

"I had an accident on a boat. I'm okay now."

She calls to a boy lurking nearby in the fading light and tells him to take their visitor to the community center and go get the key from Mr. Ramirez and then show the man where the water tank is and to make sure there is fuel in the lamp. As he turns to follow the boy she tells Reese, "You need somethin, you let me know."

The center is a concrete room with wooden, screenless windows, a few of which the boy throws open. He shakes a kerosene lantern and then lights it and Reese sees the room has several tables and rows of benches and nothing more. The boy leads him outside to the end of the building to a spigot at the base of a concrete reservoir and as Reese bends down to drink, the boy walks off into the night.

Later, after he has been sitting inside doing nothing for what seems a long while, he blows out his lamp, shuts the door and walks down the path behind his flashlight beam and wanders toward other light sources, passing the glow of houses and looking for any kind of public place, hearing the waves rolling down at the shore and the low talk from open windows or a burst of laughter or a shout and occasionally passing someone on the path, and when he looks up, seeing sections of a dense starfield behind the dark, dark clouds of a low-hanging, pregnant sky.

Not far from the water he hears the talk of men and finds a store open and the men sitting outside on blocks or stools in the sand where so little light is thrown that the men are just vocal shapes in the dark. Reese buys a beer, the bottle wet but not very cold, and steps out among the men. He sits on a palm stump stool low against the wall and the men grow quieter and then silent as he sits sipping his beer. There is a faint rumbling in the sky that moves closer and rolls over and over itself for a long time, a longer time than he has ever before heard the sound of continuous thunder. Like the stirrings and grumblings of some invisible beast whose frightening size can only be guessed at. He has almost finished his beer when a flash occurs and in the brief shock of light he meets the eyes of the man nearest him and sees an old man black as a cricket with a round cricket head and in the resuming darkness retains this image of the man and thinks of him as an ancient cricket man. Instead of a chirp there is a monumental crack above them like a board taken to rock that jolts him against the wall and he hears the man speaking even before the air has quit quivering.

"—get more rain here than most places."

He speaks to the old man's vague shape. "Might have to take shelter."

"Got time for a next one," the man says, "if you still feel a thirst."

Reese stands with his empty bottle. "What'll you have?"

"Stout."

He returns with another beer and a stout and hands the man his bottle and sits again and the other men have resumed their talk in low murmurs. A match flares and the old man lights a cigarette and Reese sees that he is shoeless; by the light held he is offered a smoke, not from a pack, but singly, held between two fingers. "No thanks," he says and the flame is shaken out. He sits breathing the smoke while they drink.

"You brought the Flores girl."

"I did."

"She is not well is what I hear."

"I don't know what's wrong with her. I was up at Laguna Vaca fishing and I just met her by accident."

"Fishin holidays."

"Yeah, that kind of thing." He sees momentarily the man's eyes in the orange glow of the cigarette's draw.

"Catch many?"

"Sure. Tarpon, snook."

"You eat 'em?"

Reese smiles in the dark. "No, I throw them back."

"Hmmm." Smoke exhaled. "You plannin to fish down here?"

"Maybe. How is it?"

"Oh, fine, fine. We got that great sea gulf out there."

"You fish?" Reese asks.

"Yes, man, I fish."

Another rumble and a sudden clap shakes the place and with its sharp breath of cool wind leaves a rattling at the doors.

Reese stands. "It's coming now. I'll see you around."

The orange spot drops and with a foot the old man covers it in the sand. "Yes, man. Goodnight, goodnight."

SIX

A night storm. Gusts and rain lashings punctuated with growls and crashes so loudly cataclysmic, so sharp and near in their vibrations to the heart of the place that those newly arrived, a man restless on a wooden table and a woman ill at ease in her old bed, are unable to sleep deeply and well. He has risen to close banging windows, spread his clothes in a layer and make his bag a pillow to soften his stay. And in his tiredness hears without hearing the violent night subside, the complaints and grumbles moving off to dissolve at sea before the light rimming its way around and into this wet village hits his dwelling and burns like wires in the cracks between the window boards.

When he emerges from his dark and stale room, shading his swollen eyes against the brightness, a boy waiting on a bench in the yard comes over and tells him he can have tea at six at the house of the neighbor across from Mrs. Flores.

"This evening?" he asks, squinting at the boy.

The boy nods.

"Okay, thanks," Reese says, recognizing him from the previous evening. "You care to show me around this place?"

"School," the boy says, and laughs.

Reese looks at his watch, the time, the date. "Oh yeah, school," he says, and steps back inside.

Narrow footpaths run like lanes between the homes and yard spaces and bushy areas unattended. There are no cars here, no noise to speak of save the distant cry or hoot issued from the trees, the general hum and twitter of the jungle, the low-level sounds of the perimeter region, a background pure and wild in its nature. Grackles whistle in hibiscus hedges, a pet parrot squawks, young mothers sweep their floors while babies stand in open doors, teenage girls draw well water for washing, and old women stir about in their darkened cooksheds, smoke seeping out into the shade and lost in the white morning light. On the beach several dories and pirogues sit unused, pulled up to the grass on palm logs; a few men can be seen out on the bay, working the waters alone, each in his own paddled craft.

At the store he visited the night before, Reese buys sardines and bread and toilet tissue and continues on his way. He has seen several concrete buildings but nearly all of the houses are wooden with steep, thatched roofs; many have garlic cloves over the door or on the steps or both to discourage spirits and snakes. A small white church stands locked and shuttered and both the police station and the health center appear unoccupied. There are no overhead wires, no phones, and few young adults and by now he has seen most of the village; he follows a westerly path past the school—a roan mare grazes in the yard—and turns south toward the river.

The river runs ragged and reddish, angry but appeased, fed from the night's rain, churning with earth but already calming, like a jungle god feared and loved and used and left alone. In the only clearing he can see, Reese stands above the torrent and watches the rusty river rushing by to bend ahead into trees overhanging, its thickly hidden banks opening to the gulf a couple hundred yards away, widening its swampy mouth over sandy flats to merge there with a green, salty sea.

He pees his own stream down the mudstone bank and studies a dugout canoe tugging at its root-tied rope, in its rainwater puddle a single frog floating. He sees no other way to cross, no bridge or ropes over this river, thirty yards to the opposite side, and wonders if the boat might be common property, at his disposal for a little fishing trip on calmer water. He must do it, he decides, since he's here. Fish the Moho. An upstream venture into the wilds and a slow drift back to sea. No other way to see it than by water, so far as he knows, not with this density, this jungle reaching up to cover and protect it. See the Moho from its own point of view, he tells himself, as he wades carefully into the cutting grasses, stamps down a patch and squats there to make his first deposit on this place, elbows on knees, watching ants on a stalk and overhead the sky between leaves. Among the stems a blur of blue that stops and looks down, an iridescent flitting, a mot-mot, its feathers more fantastically colored than any sapphire. The breathing forest. Here, the vines and creepers and trees so exotically profuse, they beckon the damaged man, harboring a world with names many of which he does not know. Mamey and fig, mahogany, ironwood, santa maria, cortez and quamwood. Crabboe, yemeri, banaka, salmwood, cypress and cedar. He hears a kingfisher crying on the wing, rattling down the water, and his mind returns to water, to his passage below its surface and his unbroken link to the denizens of the liquid world below.

He walks home hungry and hot, eats his lunch and goes about fashioning a life for himself at the center, borrowing a bucket and drawing well water, washing his dirty clothes and draping them to dry over the hedges as he's seen the women do, and then in his shorts bathing himself in the sunny yard. He drinks a liter of cool rainwater from the reservoir, pulls a bench outside from the center and places it in a trapezoid of shade against the wall there and rests himself, his healing head lightly beating and drifting backward in the afternoon haze to dream of a boyhood in clear water, the boy and his silver spear and his first fish, all joined below the boat. And when he wakes he remembers. Ten years old, somewhere off Cudjoe Key, his frantic shot straight through the gills of a Spanish hogfish.

Just before six he walks down to the Flores house and stands outside watching it for signs of activity but sees none and decides not to intrude. He crosses the lane to a green house with a small porch where an old woman is sitting; he lifts his hand, she waves him forward, he steps up and shakes her hand—Mrs. Mullins is her name—and then inquires about Barbara Flores. "Not yet well," she says, and leads him into the house. He sits alone at a corner table by a window while she serves him from the kitchen, bringing a plate of chicken, rice and beans, then some bread slices under a cloth, and a small pot of black tea. She stands for a moment fanning flies and surveying the table before she sets a tub of margarine beside the bread and returns to the porch. He hears voices and after he's eaten finds her husband leaning on the steps, the two of them talking quietly, and he thanks them and they invite him back and wish him a good night.

The men at the store seem arranged in the same manner as before, but though it is not yet dark Reese can only recognize one of them. The old cricket man sees him coming and says, "Here he is again."

"A regular customer," Reese says. "Will it be a stout for you, mister?"

"A stout for Simmons, yes, man."

They sit drinking on their stools as the light drains away, the other men conversing in earnest, some children inside at the counter waiting for measured orders or just curious, observing the stranger and listening to the elders. A brown and white spaniel mutt lies in the sand next to Simmons and after a while Reese says, "That your dog?"

"That's my dog. Name is Zino."

The dog lifts his head and listens purposefully for a minute, until he's satisfied he is only being spoken about, and then resumes his evening leisure.

Reese says, "He's unusual. Most of the dogs down here are shorthairs and look like they all have the same parents."

"This boy belonged to an American fella who stayed here a time and then left. The dog moved himself under my house."

"And now he's at home inside," Reese says.

Simmons nods. "Oh yeah."

It is then that Reese notices a hole in the old man's ankle, a hollow in raised flesh, crater-like, and in the open fistula a glint of a wet spot the width of a pencil. "What happened to your foot, Simmons?"

He lifts his foot and looks at the place as if he had forgotten it. "Ohhh, got hit by a stingray."

"That looks bad, man."

"Not too much now. Two months past it was like this." His hands make a shape the size of a volleyball. "I was thinkin I would have to lose this foot," he says, rubbing his heel in the sand. "Could not walk at all. Unusually painful."

"It happened right out here?"

"At the mouth." Embarrassed by his own foolhardiness, he looks away, pats his shirt front, feels behind his ears for a cigarette, looks down at the sand around him. "You drop it, you lost it. Same lesson again. Never set foot on a mud bottom you can't see."

Reese picks up their empty bottles. "I'll keep that in mind. Will you take a next one?"

"Oh yeah."

Inside, Reese gets two more bottles, says to the man, "A pack of those Milports too, and a box of matches."

He hands these last to Simmons and sets their wet bottles down in the sand. The old man opens the packet, knocks out two and puts the rest in his pocket; he offers one to Reese—who takes it—puts the other in his mouth and fires a match, extends it cupped to the other man, then lights his own.

Reese inhales deeply, pulls the smoke down, regarding the cigarette in his hand and to his amazement, feels no dizziness or guilt. He feels Simmons watching him and says, "I quit five years ago. Just to do it. I always liked it, though." He takes another long draw and when he speaks his voice comes out slightly different, muted, or clouded a bit. "Just now I felt like trying it again. I don't know why. Reminds me of my old self, I suppose. Just the way things go, isn't it? The way it is."

"The way it is," Simmons says, and in the darkness fallen he can sense the younger man smiling behind the smoke and he knows too that the man will stay longer than he imagines now.

A night air cool, the inland thunder a far-off warning, voices approach, at the door people come and go in the feeble lamplight, stand as silhouettes or move among those gathered in the dark. A man kneels in the sand, taps at Simmons' pocket and seconds later, with the sudden scratch of a flaring match, Reese sees around him the hunched shapes of a dozen men; their images, in the darkness rewrapping itself about them, seep into his mind and tell him where he is, show him how to be with them, sitting here at the end of the world.

Without rain, mosquitoes. Reese breathes under a shirt, dressed in long sleeves and pants, sweating, waiting for sleep. For rain that this night misses the Moho mark, finds one bight as good as another, moves off with distant remarks and leaves behind oppressive, empty clouds of deception like a night gas lingering low over those lying ill or expectant.

He dreams of Barbara, lying in the bottom of a boat while he stands, fishing, he thinks, without his gear, as they drift and he watches the water for his prey. He will not look at her for she is near death but instead scans the surface seeking a source of meat for the dying woman; he will feed her by hand. Rip her a meal with his bare hands, apparently. Why is he so ill-prepared? Why has he no tools for this work? Why must he alone save her? His

257

desperation increases as he sees a being, a gray form fleeing, and he kneels to paddle with his hands, stands again to track it, kneels and stands, kneels and cries out, stands ready to leap into the water, spots the thing and does leap, splashes under and pops up, treading water and now unable to see his quarry and when he looks, the boat farther away, floating away, and he cannot even see her there in the bottom as he treads between the two in a useless position. She is going to sea, the creature already gone, and he is in thick water, warm water like soup, and he must struggle to breathe, to stay afloat in no direction.

Dawn brings him great relief, though as he rambles down the path he wonders what will become of her. From the beach he sees the dories already departed and he waits there with his gear. Simmons comes along with his paddles and they drag his humble logboat into the shallows and shove off, the old man at the stern, rocking on a ripple chop into the breeze and the bearable glare of an ascending sun. Zino sits on the beach and watches them digging at the water. Diminishing on it.

With his paddle deep in the water and its base at his ear, Simmons listens to the bottom. They are quiet, a bobbing log in the great cradle of the gulf, essentially alone, though they can see the other boats scattered about and the village back behind them, just hints of thatch in a coastal clearing. They move on, stroking the ocean with wooden blades, hunting a lucky spot they cannot see in all this sameness. Again he listens, and motions for Reese to do the same, to hear the faint crackling at the bottom, like parrotfish pecking at coral or crustaceans roaming over a reef, what he calls a rock sound. The men are still but anchorless, water lapping at their craft. On the seat beside him Simmons cuts pieces from his bait fish. Three handlines lay at his feet; he baits one—double-hooked and weighted, the line is spooled around a piece of wood—and hands it across to Reese.

"I brought my rods too."

"Throwin that thing may upset the boat."

"I thought you might want to try it."

"Just drop the line to the bottom and snap it when he hits." He jerks his fist toward his chest to illustrate.

Reese shifts around in his seat and the low boat wobbles. "What's the matter, Simmons? You can swim, can't you?"

Simmons is unrolling his line into the water, studying its descent. "I prefer not to," he says solemnly.

"Alright," Reese says. "Let's put some fish in the boat."

Looped around fingers, the lines move through grooves in the gunnels to the bottom twenty feet or more down where the weights are bobbled, the baits jiggled, and the fish hit them one after another for a while. Red snapper, grunt and yellow drum, none large enough to keep in Reese's opinion, if he were alone, but all are food for Simmons, for the villagers. A baby blackfin shark. A bonefish for bait. But nothing big enough to fight or overturn an unstable vessel. The catfish Simmons handles carefully as he removes his hook, knocking its head afterward with a club against the lip of the boat, and then breaking the three sharp spines, one dorsal and two pectoral, before he drops it near his uncovered feet. His finger curled at his line as on a trigger, feeling for the play with quiet concentration, he is the more prolific, twice bringing up fish on each hook, like twins, inches apart.

The gulf grows calmer and warmer and the men sit like knots on a log, the old man under a straw hat and Reese in his ballcap with the bandana under it hanging about his neck, the sun blazing and the fish biting with less frequency. They pass the drinking water between them, unwrap the sandwiches Simmons brought, and as they eat, their lines still out, Reese relates his dream to the other man.

"I guess it means something about helplessness," he says, "like I want to help her, like I'm frustrated, but it's really with myself, I think, that I don't know what to do. I mean, I didn't have any ability to do anything."

The old man rubs his leathery throat. "We say this: Sea breeze blow de pelican where he wanna go."

"What, a dream means whatever you want it to mean? Or that it's fine wherever you end up."

"She may die, she may live."

"Look, Simmons, fishing used to be like a religion for me. It's not like that now."

Reese begins to take up his line; Simmons gets a strike but misses it, and must examine his bait. "You caught fish," he says, glancing at the slippery pile beneath the man's seat. "We eat some and trade the rest."

"I'm not talking about food. Sometimes I eat what I catch, but I was never there completely for that. It was the science of it, reading the water and the weather, the communion with the world, meeting an adversary, all that."

Simmons laughs. "Just to do it. And throw him back."

"Yes, like church, Simmons. You don't keep anything."

The air is hot, the water glassy, and Reese feels sleepy; he would like nothing more now than a cool dive to the bottom, a peaceful swim around the boat, but Simmons will have none of that, certain that Reese could not get back into the canoe without flipping everything else out. The old man wants to try another spot; Reese is satisfied with the catch. Other village boats are heading in and he sits gazing at the water. A blunt head breaks the surface nearby, blinking, blowing air. Simmons turns to see it; the turtle sees them and dives, and Reese stands slowly, carefully teetering, to see it go, a dark, stony oval in graceful flight, then gone. He takes his seat again and Simmons says, "Old mister loggerhead."

"Ever hunt those turtles, Simmons?"

The old man is taking up his line, pushing fish with his foot into the shade under him. "This village began with turtle fishin. Most every man was a turtler."

"You were born here, weren't you?"

"Born here, yes. Nineteen ten. Went overseas in thirty-four. England, Holland, France, a couple of years. After that, Jamaica, Trinidad, Honduras, other places. Then I returned."

They are paddling back, working harder now in the heat, pulling themselves through the water and over the water, so low on it that Reese's lower hand brushes the warm surface with every stoke. At first, to him, the village does not seem to be getting any closer, and he digs into his strokes even harder, increases the pace of his motions, to get back. To get back and what? he thinks. He has nothing to do, no schedule or meeting to keep. It makes no difference, so long as they have light and fair weather and their lives are not at stake. He is just living here with these people.

He says over his shoulder, "Simmons, I know this is a Garifuna village, but I don't know who you are or where you came from." His eyes refocus on the distant clearing.

They move slowly and in silence, Reese tired out and the old man laboring too, each pausing to rest when the other is not. They can see the flag and the people in the field.

Children wade out to greet the boat, looking inside at the yield and helping walk it in to the beach and up onto the logs. With strips of grass Simmons strings together bundles of fish, sells some to waiting women, gives away others to his grandchildren to deliver to his children to share with their mother, the old woman he no longer lives with.

"How many children?" Reese says.

"Eleven."

"Good God, man, I hope you're retired."

As they walk away, a grin grows in his round, old face. "She lets me visit when I'm burnin'," he says.

Afternoon at the river. Light through the leaves falling and floating on a silky run and downstream boys bathing on stones. Standing in the water Reese peers upstream into the tunnel of trees, feels the continuous force of the river brushing his legs, in the current some cadence of nature within his ken, in his sight the entrance to the deeper realms of this Moho world.

Beyond the empty school and the domiciles of the village he takes the inland track into a channel through grasses. Down a path to his right he sees an object and stops cold, bones on his mind. A cross. A clearing overgrown, its headstones and markers mostly fallen, half hidden or broken. He is brushing aside the webs of spiders when he sees someone else, a woman, kneeling across the way, pulling at weeds, and she turns her head to look at him as he approaches.

"Afternoon, Mrs. Flores. How are you?"

She has cleared the area around two gravestones, and also, he imagines, enough space for another beside them. "Afternoon, young man. Fine, up to now."

He hesitates, glancing at the graves, a sick-feeling smile on his face. "How is your daughter getting along?"

She stands, brushing at her knees, and faces him. "We have an understandin of the problem."

"You do? What might that be?"

"She herself is the problem. Fightin her ownself."

"I don't quite understand."

She looks around at the small, unkempt cemetery and down at the Flores markers she has tended. "Children of mine," she says. "A bad heart and a motorbike accident."

"I'm sorry to hear it."

"You know, I have always felt we should put this lesson on the stone, the reason for this death, not just the name. That way, when you see it, you will understand somethin of the people and somethin of the world together."

He nods. "Yes, I like that. Excellent. Something I'll request for my own passing, however it comes. Whenever."

She smiles politely, says she must be going along. He asks about visiting Barbara.

"You may be seein her soon," she says. "Hopefully."

Simmons lives alone in a yellow house with red windows—the only yellow house in Moho Bight. The windows are open when Reese arrives, Zino announcing him, the old man outside at his smoker box poking at rows of small snapper, woodsmoke creeping sweet through mahogany limbs and over the roof thatch into the tops of the royal palms behind and on over the jungle wall at the back of his small yard space. A faint humming in the air. Reese squatting and petting the dog who is watching the smoker speak.

"A ship ran aground in 1635. That is how we got started here. West African slaves being taken to the New World hit a storm and the reefs near St. Vincent. There the Caribs, the Carib Indians from South America, had been fightin for many years against any European that came to conquer them. Spanish, French, English. And since these Africans were lucky enough to escape and of course never wanted to be caught again and would fight against it, the Caribs let them live in the hills and forests of their island. Over the years there was a lot of mixin and fightin between the two peoples and many of the Carib ways were taken by the Africans who became known as Black Caribs. They both kept fightin the English soldiers who built forts by the sea and tried to rule them. Later, the Blacks, who called themselves Garifuna in their own language, tried to revolt against the English but they could not succeed and many were captured and taken away. This was in 1797. Two thousand of those Black Caribs were deported to the Bay Islands, to Roatan, and put out there, and left there. These people are my ancestors and some of them, not so long ago, put their dories on the sea and found new places to settle. Such is the way this place was started, like the way we came to shore by our paddles this same mornin with these fish we are eatin."

Zino cleans the plates, rice and all, gingerly eats the weak bones, the smoked heads, stretched out in the yard with his own head tilted as he chews through dusk. The men inside smoking in the stillness can hear the crunch and break of the animal's feeding, Reese sitting in the hammock and Simmons in his only chair, his bare feet rubbing the hard, earthen floor. On the table between them are cigarettes and matches, and a lamp which the old man lights only when darkness has totally encased them; he brings down from a shelf a jar of clear liquor and passes it to Reese. "Try some Style," he says.

Beside and below the windows two walls are lined with shelves, the shelves with books—histories, biographies, novels, field guides and old reference books, the small home a village library of sorts—and with rocks, rough chunks of jasper and oolite, and placed among these the delicate white skulls of reptiles, mammals and birds. Over the door to the bedroom a margay hide, its edges stiff and curled, its spots fading out like raindrops in sand from a darker and densely patterned center.

"I was wondering, Simmons, when we saw that loggerhead today, if you see many manatees around here."

"They come around." He knocks his ashes on the floor. "Not like before."

"Were they hunted out?"

"No, no, but they move about. To protect themselves. Got to be so you would only see them at night."

"You hunted them yourself."

"Of course, man." He drops his cigarette butt, stamps it out with his heel. "But I don't kill sea cow any more and I am the last of the sea hunters here."

"How long ago are we talking about?"

"Twenty years."

"I don't guess you shot them."

He laughs. "Lost bottom meat no good to anybody."

"Nets?"

"Harpoon, Reese." He crooks his finger, extends his arm towards the other man. "You got to hook him, and go where he go."

They sit quietly with this image, Simmons drifting in his memory, Reese standing in a boat in a daydream. He pulls out a cigarette and holds it. "When was the last time you saw one?"

Simmons rubs his stubbled cheek. "Probably a few weeks ago."

Reese strikes a match, lights his cigarette, inhales sharply.

"Are we fishing tomorrow?"

"I need to work my farm in the morning," Simmons says.

"Want some help?"

"Sure, man, come along."

Reese flicks his ash. "Why don't we go get a stout."

Simmons picks up the smokes and matches, blows out the lamp, shuts the door behind him, and they are walking then in the darkness of starlight, Zino trotting quietly between them.

Lying hot in dark and light, your own smell like death to you. Feet swollen, your brain in pain, one arm and one breast hurting. When you sleep vultures eat your fat feet. Hospital told you nothing and make you worse, robust girl. Which world you livin in? You don't find yourself in X-ray medicine. We must determine if there is identifiable sickness or spirit malevolence. You must agree to determine this, girl. That is the work of the medium, nothing bad, just stories from olden times. Tell me then what it is you think can be called civilized. Take your broth and moist cassava bread and then tell me who you think can cure you other than your kinsfolk. Yes, now you want cassava beer. We can satisfy these angry ancestors and they will leave you, child. You are ready, are you not? Yes, you are ready to feel better. You are not crazy.

Barbara will not need a coffin, you hear them say. Is this you? Out of the house and helped along the dark path to another house. A room of white candles and these women, your mother, and the man with the stick. Him! He is not so clear in this light, not like the aunts and neighbors, the rum and the holy water on the white sheet over the table. The obeah queen—you mustn't call her that, you are not a child any more. The medium with her cigar smoke—and Him, your great uncle right here too. She rubs the rum on your heart, your aching breast, the sweet smoke descends on you and the big lady rocks you like a doll, rocks and rocks and rocks and rocks and you rise and fly again. You see the lights of Rio Perez, the torches on the dark sea, the boats on their long journey from the past and you are there with them on the water and one of them is speaking. Holding a spear, speaking in words you do not know but understand:

You people I have seen for many years, ridden among you on the breeze, you children of mine, offspring of my origin. And yet you anger me with your ways, this playful life many are seeking. Look at Victoria, how she sends her handsome dance girls away to catch bad men who only laugh behind them. Why is that? You foolish migrants, your babies leave as they have always done in this place, you lizards in the sun, old Roy and the sugar men going north and so too his children. The chain of the weak goes far back to the call of mahogany gangs, the cry of money which is slavery again and makes me vomit in the sea and makes all gubida so angry we must make again this difficult trip. Must you be stricken down as this one? Look at her, look at her mother, Sophie, and her brothers lying in the earth and ask if you want your health. Ask yourselves this, ask Joulouca what you may do and you will be told. Make mali, bake bami. Are you laughing, Yolanda? Is that Jaydee falling asleep? Silly little girl. Are there not enough candles to keep her awake? She can sleep in the sun, can't she? Yet her skin is cool like a Wish Willie reptile in the shadow of her house. Can you feel your health failing yet? This is nothing but a serious talk. This has gone on long enough and now you are reminded that I am among you because I have found this one who sought to deny me with her new ways and so she has been ill and so she will die if you want to laugh and sleep and play games all day long. I want black chickens and white hogs. Do you hear me, Yolanda? This is no joke. You talk too much and have nothing to say. I see all of you. I know where you go and I can bring you back from any city, from America or any place. I can make any relative fall sick and frightened and crawl in the sand. Fatten the hogs in that pen like I told you. I want a room full of China pumpkins. I want rum and tobacco and good food, yams and fish and plenty cassava bread. And beer too. I am very hungry. We will have a dugu for all of us. Collect the animals. I have a good mind to ask for baboon or tiger or mountain cow. You think that is funny? Alright, give me sea cow. Don't find yourselves crying over this poor girl. You will discuss and plan and call the scattered, the lost ones, who will come also or find themselves crying too late over a boy or a girl dead in the ground. Everyone will cry. I will laugh. These are my words and now I am gone. I gone.

Shaking on the floor, her dress up to her waist, she accepts without embarrassment the placation that must occur; they have spoken through her and she will suffer for them all until this thing is accomplished, and perhaps die if the ritual is not worthy or soon enough. They lift and calm her, watching her wild eyes in the candlelight and fearing for themselves too, speaking among themselves in confirmation of these events, reverting to tradition and the course known to stave off perdition, the sky bellowing deeply as they leave, the light lambent in the near heavens as they hurry ahead of it—under the thunder crack they jump and cry in unison, the air sizzling like magnesium—and her rolling eyes spy behind a hedge a man scorched white in that light, the flash and the man still in her eyes and the falling drops like stars as she is carried on her journey, the man looking like some European vagabond who might possibly belong to this modest and pluvial place.

SEVEN

Simmons has already made coffee and Reese watches him over a cup's hot rim as he brings an old black bicycle out of his room and lifts it down the steps. He has a sack and two knives and is wearing his hat and rubber boots, ready to go. Zino scampers out behind him.

"Wait a second," Reese says. "Isn't your farm in walking distance?"

"Yes, man, it's in walking distance. So is Rio Perez if you got the time." He laughs his high-pitched sound: who who who who.

"You're hilarious, my funny fellowman," Reese says. He sets the cup on the windowsill and follows the dog.

Down the trail, Simmons stops and speaks into a window from his bike and then points under the house at a rusted red specimen that Reese drags out and hops on and pedals away creaking and clanking and weaving on low tires with spiders spinning off the spokes and hanging from the handlebars.

The inland track past the cemetery—Simmons says this road west finds a Kekchi village in ten miles—runs through shallow, muddy streams trickling out of forest, and they are soon riding beside hacked-out plots on either side where corn and rice, plantain and yam, sweet potato, pumpkin, cassava and common herbs are planted among cultivated trees—nutmeg, molly apple, mamey, cacao, plum, citrus and papaw. Zino is mud-covered and wild, leaping along the roadside, chasing after grasshoppers and butterflies, sometimes snapping them down but ever in pursuit of others, running with a boundless zeal ahead of the men on their bikes, the sun behind them, patches of steam still in the weeds, hawks floating over fallow bush fields.

The farm is no garden, the ground uneven and perilous, cut stalks like dangerous spikes, the food groups grown in a haphazard fusion instead of rows and Reese is in many cases unable to tell which vines are valuable and which are just there. Simmons shows him where to cut and pull, what is good and what is unwelcome, and he adds to a burn pile in the center. The old man collects papayas and plantains, chops down dead banana trunks and points out to his visitor the leafcutter ants working on his potato plants and Reese follows their clear-cut highway—a green-flagged path in perpetual motion—back to the edge of the jungle and then asks if there isn't some way to influence their direction. Simmons says he just has to lose a few. They sit on a log in the nutmeg shade, sweating through their shirts, weed burrs and pollen gathered on their arms. Reese looking across the road at the opposite trees. "The Moho can't be too far in there," he says.

"Maybe half mile," Simmons says. "It cuts south and loops back to the sea, snakin around all the way."

"I'd like to take a trip up there someday soon."

"Fishin?"

"Yeah. You wanna go? I need your boat."

"No, no. You take it. Just watch you don't cross a tiger

269

nappin in there."

"Well, I wouldn't want to startle one but I'd consider it phenomenal luck and a great honor to see a jaguar or any big cat in the wild."

Simmons stands and whistles sharply. "That tiger like to eat my dog," he says, and sits again. "But if you see him—" He stares the younger man in the face, pointing two fingers at his eyes. "—and you lock eyes with him, don't blink and don't look away first. Make him turn away. Stare him down, man."

"I will, Simmons, I will."

"And that wowla that drop in the boat, that wrap-around snake, bring him home. He's good meat."

"I think you'd probably eat most anything, wouldn't you?"

"Tiger tasty too."

"What about sea cow?"

"Delicious. And mountain cow is good under that tough skin, but sea cow has many kinds of taste. On that big thing are places like beef, like pork, like chicken and fish too."

Zino comes crashing through the underbrush and between the cornstalks matted and brambled, his fur stuck to his body in wet mop strings, and licks the young man's extended hand and shakes himself, happy in their presence. "You rat mutt," Reese says, "you stay clear of this man's upper food chain."

In a while they are jouncing along on the return trip, the sun too severe now for open work under its giant eye. Simmons is watching his way on the track, holding his lumpy bag on the crossbar. In the quiet heat Reese is just ahead, steering his cranky wheel and following the silent flight of the dog.

"Last night there was some kind of séance involving Barbara Flores," he says over his shoulder. "What's that all about?"

"There will be a ceremony."

"What kind of ceremony?"

270

"One to satisfy her ancestor and prevent her death."

Reese listens to his squealing wheel for fifty yards or so. "You think her dead relative is causing her illness?"

Simmons says, "Can the dead affect the living?"

"Yeah, do you think that's true?"

"If you believe it."

"Yes, but is it true?"

"It's true if you believe it, man."

Babies awaken. Women stir from hammocks as the shadows lengthen. Under houses men repair their nets, sharpen tools and begin to drink. Wood is collected, fires started, dough kneaded, while children play games in the field by the sea. The few small stores reopen, people on the pathways stop and talk and the smell of woodsmoke drifts on the air with the measured voices and punta tunes of radio programs. A simpleton weaving through yards hears the private murmurs, glimpses through the slats of a bath shed the well water splashing cool down the backs and arms, and from the thrown taunts and laughing admonitions he hurries away hunched over, his dirty shirt stretched full of small, feral pineapples. He stops at a bench where a stranger sits smoking and stands staring at him and picks out a particular fruit and sets it next to him. Reese hands him a cigarette and he grins and puts it in the gap of missing teeth uncovered there, and the pineapples go tumbling to the ground.

Birds are flocking to roost at dusk and Zino is playing a game. He lies in wait under the house as the neighboring chickens approach the midden in his domain, and seeing their scratching and pecking, he launches his attack, scatters the skinny, clucking fowl into the bush weeds from whence they will reappear before he can resume his casual position. Two men have dropped by with dried shark meat for Simmons and they sit with him on his steps, passing his jar of Style. A social call, though as an elder his opinion is being sought on a matter of importance and now he listens, looking at the cavity in his foot and the gnats congregated there like beasts around a waterhole.

"She wants to jump in," Duran says, "and ride the plans of Etienne. Is this right?"

The younger man, Clement, reaches for the jar. "So short a time. How can she not weaken the whole thing?"

"Etienne's boy has been sick a long time," Duran says, "his family patient, and suddenly this girl, this migrant who practices unnatural—well, she returns with no warnin after her scorn and name-callin and disrespect. I mean, people are askin: Is this fair? How can she still claim us now?"

Simmons tells them without hesitation, "Any mother will seize an opportunity to save her child. She will not care if people talk. This is her responsibility and if she can gather her family in the time remainin then she certainly must consider herself quite fortunate to have these events goin in her favor."

"And what about Etienne?" Clement says.

"If he agrees," Simmons says, "who can protest her?"

"A dugu will affect everyone. What if Flores fails?"

Simmons laughs softly. "Hardships will fall on those who bring them. But listen here, Clement. Since when are you so concerned with these old ways? The women are carryin the spirits now. We will go along and enjoy ourselves and watch our people gather together. We will eat and drink and say it is a good thing we are doin and when we are drunk we will talk to our ancestors too and then thank the old women for their hard work and they will be dancin for all of us, man."

He sits smoking alone in the gloom, the house dark as a cave behind him, a few dim yellow spots blinking on in the weeds across the yard and then, as in a staged concert of duplicitous design, they materialize in all directions, moving around him like sparks from a flameless fire, following the orange tip of his cigarette until they sense its falsity and go flowing into the night. Stars on the wing in a miniature universe, they fly at the sky and the myriad sparkles so far above. Out there he will examine these things; he will see these days, his life represented in the movements of his children and he will still be something around here. His passing will be like a sea crossing. Will there be fish or slaves or work or the measure of time? Won't the many ancestors, all the dead descendants, crowd him out? What if he doesn't feel well?

"Are you there, Simmons?"

"Just sittin here."

"Trying to know something about yourself?" This from one who hardly mentions his own past.

"Thinkin about eatin some shark meat."

They move inside and Simmons brings up his corner fire. Reese has brought warm bread and a can of peas. He cleans a pot by lamplight at the door. Zino is bushed and flat out on the earthen floor.

"I've been thinking about going to see Barbara." The fish is quite salty; he drops one hand and feeds the dog, who is not bothered. "She got me here but what am I doing now?"

"You have nothin to do and yet you always seem busy."

"I'll probably go fishing in the morning."

"Actually," Simmons says, "you are lucky to be here at this time."

"The big ritual."

"The dugu, yes. Not many strangers witness it."

"When will it be?"

"In about two weeks."

"When was the last one?"

He leans back, rubs his smooth head a moment. "I suppose it was, let me see, maybe three years. Several years."

Reese nods, sets his plate on the floor. "I'm not sure I can stick around so long." He takes a cigarette from the table, lights it and leans back in the hammock. "It's an opportunity, though, isn't it. Something different."

"People will come for this. We will have a few busy days." Simmons lights a cigarette too and they regard each other across the space of a wavering glow.

"It's not just for Barbara," Reese says.

"No."

With one foot on the floor, Reese is rocking gently, smoking and watching the pale light moving on the rafters, the grid in the black thatch changing its pattern. "How will it help her?" he asks.

"We have to drop some chickens."

He looks across at the old man. "Drop some chickens."

"Yes, man." He extends his arms and lets them fall.

Reese is hanging still with a picture in his mind. Fire, chanting and screams, Barbara screaming. "And then they'll be dead," he says.

"Oh yes, then they die."

In the dawn's blush Reese moves along the beach, sitting stiff in his craft, slipping over the shallows with the breeze at his port, past the dock and down the coast to the Moho's mangrove mouth. He swings into the smooth current there, digging in against the flow, a wind and the eager sun at his back, his hacking paddle lifting a bottom haze from the scooting flaps of mudding rays. A passage then from light into dark, the water darker yet, and long, arching roots like hoops emerging into trees, and down among them the jerking claws of fiddler crabs, a chorus of hand signals like tiny white flags raised flashing from swamp shadows. The bending course narrows, the trees taller, and at the surface branches caught between rocks, the disturbance of snags. With sufficient energy the canoe glides anywhere in here, a log floating through the family of trees. He approaches the unused dugout he saw tied below the clearing and holds it to rest; he listens but hears no human sounds.

He studies the water. There is nothing like a river trip. Moving up the entrails to the belly of the land. The vines and the trumpet flowers falling. He stays at the edge of midstream when he can, working his paddle hard and seeing what he can, watching the surface, the banks, the waterline under the leaves hanging there, looking for swirls and pushed water as the sun's rising light seeps down into the river. He wants a fat snook for Simmons and the water looks good for it. In a surface blur, hind feet splayed and slapping, a basilisk lizard crosses the water from one log to another and runs into the bank's thicket of grasses and armored palms.

Reese doesn't know how far to go. The good river is an artery to unknown targets but this is also traveling, pure and simple. Up ahead the water should get rougher, falling down the country toward the sea, weaving through a land of cats—jaguar, puma, margay and ocelot. In the rising warmth butterflies flutter over this waterscape, and he sees the bright feathers of trogons and tanagers among the branches. He hears a grunting high in the trees and strains his vision upward as he pauses for these low notes, the hollow hoots of black howlers, the baboons of local nomenclature. Wild game for Garifuna in times of tradition, as are all the mammals of the land, like coati, deer and paca. And Simmons told him an anteater will rip a dog to shreds. Or a careless man.

Turtles are piled like stones upon stones. There could be caimans and he's already seen water snakes. He finds a limb he can reach away from the bank and bends it down and secures his bowline and hangs there in the current assembling his rod and thinking he's in too far for snook. With nothing organic but shark oil for scent he hopes to avoid catfish, though at the bottom he might also find eels or a roving gar; he wants no mullet either but something in the cichlid family would be alright. From a sitting position and with a sidearm cast he sends a diving plug downstream toward the southern bank. His fourth fling brings a bite but he misses it, his mind like his hearing wandering in the jungle. Trying the same spot again he hooks a mud turtle that he is able to shake off, and then switches to a yellow jig.

Where the sun reaches the boat and cuts down beside it into the water in rusty shafts of visibility he finds himself leaning over and peering there as if into irregular windows and soon he has lifted off the seat and crouches as he holds his rod and retrieves his lure in surface jerks, all the while shifting his weight, moving his legs and hips to maintain a standing balance. From this position he straightens upright using the rod's length for stability like a rope walker's pole before him as he sways with the boat and the water running under him. And after he has stood for a time without raising his feet he begins to turn himself in a circle, his arms and the rod outstretched, the small boat tipping one way then the other with his little steps and he lets it go at its roll a bit and counteracts with subtle shifts until he has come around completely and begun to find its play. In this stance, knees in constant motion, he flips out a short cast and reels it right back in and repeats the action several times.

He squats rocking and selects a black, plastic worm, crimps on the line above it more weight and a cloth tag which he dips in his jar of odorous oil. Standing again he throws it long with a side-whipping motion and begins to take it up almost before it plops in the river. He throws over and over, refusing to let the bait sink but flinging it farther as he struggles to keep his center of buoyant gravity, and then thinks he needs a strike, the element of chance and unpredictability to test his good standing. And so he recoats his bait and pours a spreading stream into the current and lets his next cast sink and doesn't much care what hits it any more. Feeling its long pull in the stream he shuts his eyes and seems to smell the fragrant sediment with the loose rot and the trees and their saps and falling seeds. Feels the worm wiggling and bottom bumping from the line in his hands. As it lifts and dangles past quivering whiskers it is swallowed in a lunge and Reese braces with bent knees and working hands, using his arms and his body. He feels the fish thrashing deep but not running, and knowing he must have a nasty cat, he brings it up flopping at the surface and cuts it loose and stands with the empty rod watching the waves of the splash as long as they last and longer, the rod tip over the spot. He stands and looks and finally puts the tip in the water, running it in and out like a fencing foil and not fishing at all now but only holding the rod as he would a sword.

To fish here again he would consider going ashore to dig grubs and catch caterpillars. He would consider a set of tools and techniques more in keeping with the scale of living he presently practices. He would consider fishing by bow and arrow, standing at the surface and waiting over shafts of sunlight. He would need to consider various kinds of wood and their differing properties. He stands holding his paddle like a spear, chunky and pointless, motioning a throw without letting go. And even as he stands on the wavering water he considers riding to sea on his feet, mastering this skill before he can undertake another, in this manner learning the vessel's rightful pitch and out of that place of knowledge imagining what else he might accomplish from it.

He is reminded of his dugout dream—standing over Barbara and then losing her, but standing anyway—as he loosens his line and drifts away. The paddle is his rudder but he will go mainly where the current takes him. He laughs, picking up some speed and feeling like a surfer with one arm out and the other dipping and turning the blade to see how much it will affect his direction. But the dugout begins to turn in the current and without paddling he cannot prevent it; it's like a leaf or a stick floating aimlessly. He knew this would happen and yet here he is sideways, facing the bank. He kneels quickly and corrects the spin; he will have to get a longer paddle or bend over enough to make use of the one he's got. It seems stupid to stand but when he's got himself back in forward motion he gets to his feet again. With his eyes on the water just beyond the prow he wobbles and leans and musters his thin stability while the banks slide by in pageants of natural profusion. Going between stones he catches an eddy and slips in a slow rotation into the deeper stream and tries to continue around and right himself with his paddle, running backwards in a crouch and paddling likewise and wanting to look over his shoulder or sit down but doing neither. Blind to all but balance and the thought of falling he teeters and talks to himself and knows he must look foolish to any forest eyes watching a man reversed on the river and trying to summon skill from wishful thinking. But he gets himself sideways nonetheless and feels the craft coming around and now is grinning like a fool when he feels a jolt, the boat jumping a bump, and the moment is gone. Trying to see what he hit and flailing his arms as the vessel dips low on the downstream side, all accord is lost in alarm, and he holds his oar over his head like a club as he falls crashing below the surface kicking his feet and thrusting the paddle out before him. His eyes open wide in a filmy concern as he is seized then with the imperative task of recovering the boat. Head and paddle blade break the surface at once, he leaves the oar floating and goes after the drifting dugout, cutting through the water in a few swift strokes and grasping its side and waiting for the paddle to reach him, looking back upstream at the eye level surface for any movement he'd prefer to be aware of. He catches the oar and drops it into the boat and prepares to board. Kicking up too hard, his weight pushes the gunnel down, the boat rolls as his torso falls forward and the top of his head thuds against the opposite side. He rebounds and slips backward into the water and hangs there holding the lip of the boat, stunned and amazed and drifting with it by one hand and sinking his face into the cool river.

He watches his progress, kicking along, directing the pirogue toward the shore and the sandbar and the other dugout and the clearing above them, the bird calls like bells and the light striking deep around him. Feels his feet touch bottom and then staggers up on the mud dragging his craft forward. To the line of the other he ties his boat, steps into it and gripping both gunnels lifts his other leg in, and then turns and sits down on the paddle and the gear and lies back dizzy. Puts his arm across his eyes against the whiteness of the sky but removes this weight from his forehead and lies still with his eyes closed on the day. Far screams from the schoolyard in his head with an oscillating volume and an odd, occasional crackle like the sound of an old phonograph.

"Unfuckingbelievable," he says.

On his bench in the shade of the water tank he passes the heat sleeping and waking and dreaming and the voices of school children for a time flow through these states equally until as the afternoon grows quiet he settles deeper into invention and hears his ex-wife on the phone and himself talking to her. He is then leaving someplace in his pickup and driving home in the late sun and when he enters he sees her sitting at the kitchen table and Heather is there too with the sunlight streaming in on her. She smiles at him and he stands in the doorway and lights a cigarette and then goes over to her and she stands and they kiss on the lips and he tastes her warm tongue. She pulls back and her cheeks are red and they both look at the other woman who scolds him for smoking and so he takes another drag and puts it out in the sink. They all sit talking at the table as darkness falls though he is not really listening and they seem to be doing most of the talking. He gets up and takes a bottle of whiskey from the cabinet and when he turns around the women are kissing each other and his excitement is tangible. He reaches for the glasses and knocks one off the counter and it shatters and he jerks violently on his bench and wakes to see a little girl standing and looking at him with her belly poking out and he rolls against the wall to hide himself from her sight.

Before dark he walks over to Simmons' place but the man is not there and neither is his dog. Reese is thinking maybe he should try to buy some aspirin or some food or wait for his friend a little while and he stands in the yard touching his temples and looking at the ground. He decides to sit down and starts toward the house.

"Hello, my friend."

He jumps at the sound, the voice of a woman, a voice out of the air or the bush or the house but he looks up and sees her on the roof, a woman on her back on the roof. Barbara. Laid out on the thatched slope with her knees up and her head near the peak, her arms at her sides and her head turned to the side so she can look down at him without lifting her head and a kind of grin on her face that he thinks must come from the fact that she seems so casual up there and appears so absurd. She is wearing a dress that has ridden up nearly to her waist as her body has moved down and it looks to him as if her position on the incline is such that she could slide down and off the edge at any time.

"You scared me half to death," he says.

"I had to get out of the house."

"I don't blame you," he says. "How'd you get up there?"

"Flew."

"Nice evening for it. Why did you land there?"

"Are you looking up my dress?" Her white underwear is the brightest thing in sight.

"I can't help it."

"That's alright. You want to come up here too?"

"I'd rather you came down."

"Why, you want to marry me?"

"You can find a better choice," he says.

"Best one here."

"When you get well you can leave again," he says.

"Do you live here now?"

"I'm still just visiting."

"Are you going to help with the dugu?"

"I might contribute something."

"Look out. You could catch a spirit."

"I think I'm probably immune."

"Oh man, let me thank you in advance."

"That's not necessary. But listen. You should come down before Simmons gets home."

"I'd like to sit here and watch the stars. You know, I think God is looking for me."

"I'm sure someone is looking for you." He steps into the dark house, grabs the chair and carries it out into the yard and sits below her.

"You tired?" she asks.

"A little." He settles into the chair and stretches out his legs and lights a cigarette.

She is looking down at the flame shaken out. "I'm not," she says.

Against the darkening ground he is now a dim figure and she watches the tip of the cigarette floating near his voice.

"Are you hungry then?" he asks. The yellow house is fading away and when he looks up he sees part of her silhouette and the pale sliver of her panties like a moon among the first stars.

"No," she says. "Are you?"

"I could use a little something."

"You can eat me," she says.

He is not sure he heard correctly and so he sits smoking and watching the sky and finally says, "Why do you say that?"

"Why not?"

"Is that what you like?"

"I'm a human being," she says.

Words in the dark, like fireflies or moths. And he has an image of her as a patient on an office couch instead of a roof and he is then thrust into the opposite role in some makeshift session he is embarrassed to be a part of. "Shouldn't it be someone special?"

"You're special."

"No, I'm not."

"Yes, you are."

"You don't even know who I am."

In the long pause that follows he can nearly feel her struggling and he does not let even the glowing coal of his cigarette move. She says, "You're my savior."

He counsels himself against a severe contradiction in his reply. And so he says, "I don't have any experience at that, Barb."

Her laughter surprises him at first and as it goes on he feels relieved that she's laughing so hard, and glad for some catharsis she must badly need, but she lets out a cry amid her laughter and he stands and hears her on the thatch, the dry fronds crackling with her movement. He drops his cigarette and kicks the chair back and moves under the sound, her giggling and sliding in the rustling darkness above him as he shifts from side to side and squints to see her shape materializing, his arms up and his mind making her seen by her rising voice and the rush of motion sensed. Averting his face as her legs touch his hands, thighs and hips heavy as grain poured down, and slipping past his embrace, her chest at his head a cushion crushing him as he bends back and falls and they thump the ground in grunts and groans, his breath lost on impact and an aftershock like high voltage between them and on the ground around them that she feels in her ankles stinging.

She lies silently on her side; he drags himself upright to sit and collect his rasping wind. In the darkness he sees sporadic sprinkles of brightness that are not fireflies or any form of light but optical manifestations stemming from his own mind and which begin to dissipate as he regains his breathing. He says, "You're not dead, are you?"

She sits up beside him. "No."

"You hear that humming?" he says.

"No. Nothing."

They sit quietly while he listens. Then he says, "It doesn't seem like this is really happening. Does it to you?"

She doesn't answer and he gets to his feet and takes her wrist. "Can you stand?"

She pulls herself up with his help and smooths her dress down as she shifts from one tingling foot to the other. He puts her arm over his shoulders and his arm around her waist and she limps beside him as he leads her across the yard. There is starlight on the path and they move slowly toward the flickers of active houses. Rain scents the air without the sound of thunder and someone is running on the crossroad they are approaching. A boy shouts and there is more running and calls in answer and flashlight beams are directed toward them.

Reese says, "Sometimes lately I feel like I can't tell what's real, what really happens."

"I have a scratchy back," she says.

"That's probably real," he says, rubbing his hand there. "You understand me?"

She sighs and says, "Oh man, everything really happens."

EIGHT

A Saturday, one of the twice-weekly connections to the greater world—a number of people are crowded together at this early hour on the Moho dock, their goods bundled up in bags and baskets and luggage selected by shape and weight and one by one positioned in a careful and lengthy loading undertaken by each pilot to maximize passenger and cargo capacity in his slender and wood-built transport boat—a regular chance to engage in the contact and the commerce and the collective strangeness of life in international time, or the closest thing to it: the market in Rio Perez.

It seems almost as though the entire village has turned out to leave or see someone off and Simmons is there too for one reason or another. Reese doesn't bother but goes instead to the old man's place and makes fire and coffee and sits outside in the damp air with a piece of wood and a knife carving a crude wide-tooth comb. When the laden boats have all gone and the place is quiet again—like a ghost town for half a day—and Simmons and Zino have returned in the hot light of the morning, Reese draws a bucket of water and pulls the dog down in the warm grass of the yard. He cuts the worst tangles out of the animal's coat, gets nipped a few times, and bathes the dog, standing skinny and sheepish for this treatment, and combs his wet fur fairly smooth while Zino watches him with sidelong expressions of gracious annoyance.

Simmons is at his fire boiling medicinal concoctions and Reese hangs in the hammock, waiting. By now he has confessed his misfortune in Laguna Vaca, his hospital stay, yesterday's foolish river incident, and the reason Simmons found his chair overturned in the yard—all strange and seemingly unfounded in his mind—and looking back these events seem to be not of his waking life, but rather some pattern of dream fragments he's observed from his unconscious mind. He has not known travel such as this.

Simmons bends over to place a poultice across his forehead scar. "Very lucky you didn't split that thing open."

"Yeah, Simmons, I'm a lucky man with an accidental head."

The old man brings over a steaming cup. "Hold that there and drink some too."

Reese sits up. "What is this?"

"That's comfrey and cedar and yellow ginger."

"You'd think it'd be external or internal, one or the other, wouldn't you?"

"Inside and out, when they meet they heal a bruise." Simmons places his familiar jar on the floor by the other man. "Take some Style too, if you need it." He sits back in the chair, pinches the tip from a cigarette, moistens it in his mouth and pushes it into the hole in his foot. And sits smoking the remainder.

"Is that all you did for your sting?"

"That's not all. I used sage and papaw and cow-foot leaf

and scagineel. Maybe I took some rat root too, I forget."

From the hammock Reese follows the old man's upward gaze and sees his examination of the thatch roof, a search for cracks against the day's vertical light.

"I guess you'll find out when it rains," Reese says, though he does not see a leak. "I can't see any other way for her to get up there but if she did go from inside, you'd still see some sign of it. First of all it'd be quite a feat to pull off physically, even though I know she's strong. And no ladder outside. I'd say she had to have help but then that seems pretty remote unless she got that crazy guy to do something. But he'd probably be scared of her." He sips some Style and winces, then laughs. "Maybe he took the ladder away, or maybe she pole vaulted and then threw the pole in the bush." He laughs again and Simmons looks over at him. "Either that or she climbed one of those royal palms and took a superhuman leap off the trunk and still managed to stay on the roof when she landed. She did say she flew."

"A little unusual," the old man says.

"She was trying to shock me and she succeeded."

"She wanted to find you, man."

"That was part of it. She thinks I might save her."

"How would you do such a thing?"

"That's a good question, Simmons. I hope you'll tell me if something occurs to you. All I did was bring her home."

The boats return from two o'clock onward, a small and staggered flotilla of low-floating vessels laboring on a calm sea, their homeward dronings heard as they reach the northern point of the village's wide bight. From a great distance Reese believes he can see a white-faced visitor and when those in the boat are near enough to recognize individuals on the dock she waves at him and he waves back. And judging from what he hears around him, there are other visitors arriving as well. And many more yet to come.

She wears a cap and her usual loose outfit, her forearms glistening with sweat and her face radiant to him as the boat swings alongside the landing. "I can't believe you're still here," she says over all the talking.

"It hasn't been that long," he says. "And besides, I was waiting for you." He takes her backpack and then her hand and helps her up to the dock. They hug and he starts to move them away from the crowd and the disembarking passengers.

"Take me to your leader," she says, glancing ahead at the dwellings and behind her at the scene they are leaving.

"I don't think we have one," he says.

"Take me anyway," she says, and they both laugh and she slaps at his face, joking around as they move up the bustling path and turn to skirt the field.

"I tried to imagine the place," she says, lifting her blond ponytail off her neck, "but this is less than Laguna by quite a margin."

"That's how we like it. Less strangers too."

"Oh, is that right? Now you sound like the leader."

They turn again into the west, her face shaded by the cap as they walk between houses and hedges, chickens clucking across their path. She catches him looking at her and he says, "Speaking of which, how was your presentation?"

She smiles. "Not bad. Actually pretty good, I thought. I got some unexpected support and the more progressive residents are starting to believe that something like this can really happen, that they can all benefit. Now they want to convince the others. And now I have to really get things down on paper and get together a solid group and take it to the capital."

"Great," he says. "Good work."

"Yeah, I'm starting to get excited. We can do something positive with our situation, with what's already there. We can use those animals, the fact that they're there, to create some kind of economic progress for people who honestly need it. And without destroying the place in the process."

She suddenly pulls his arm and steps in front of him; a group of people are following far behind. "Look, I know you

287

would've told me already if anything was wrong. Barb is okay, right?"

Up ahead, more people from the boats are on a cross path and moving to intersect them. "She's hanging tough, Heather."

"Have you seen her today?"

"I saw her last night."

"And? Was she coherent?"

"We had a conversation."

"What did she say?"

"She said a lot of things, but the situation was stranger than what she said."

"What do you mean?"

"I mean she ran away from home and sought me out."

"Sought you out. Where?"

"I'm not even sure she did, but it seemed like it. At this house I've been visiting, my friend's place. I think she'd just been cooped up too long and needed to get out."

They arrive at the community center yard and people are already sitting on the benches there and men are inside moving the furniture and stowing belongings and looking for ways to string hammocks. "Are you thirsty?" he asks, and they join the others in line at the water tank spigot.

"Is this where you're staying?" she asks.

"Had the place to myself until now."

"All these people—"

"They're from other Garifuna towns," he says. "We're about to have a ceremony."

He goes inside to reclaim his table if necessary but he finds his clothes still on it and his bag against the wall as he left it and most of the activity occurring toward the other end of the room.

She sets her bag next to his. "You sleep on this table?"

"I have been," he says, "but I see myself moving to a hammock very soon. We'll keep this for you in case nothing else works out." He laughs at her disapproving look.

"I was hoping for something a little more domestic," she says, "like maybe a little corner at the Flores house."

"By the looks of it, I would imagine their relatives will be taking any available space." He sits on the table watching the organizational efforts unfold before him, the guests arranging their personal spaces, and glancing over at them, nodding or offering an occasional greeting or just wondering. All the windows are open and the room is hot. "Listen, Heather. There's a process underway here—" He pauses and she gives him her full attention. "—and Barb is not in a position to be your spokesperson or represent you in any way."

"I don't know what you mean."

"I mean she's the subject of certain events and not the orchestrator. She's along for the ride."

Heather looks at him a moment. "Can we go see her now?"

"We can try."

A teenage girl answers the door at the Flores home and soon after, Sophie comes to meet them. As Reese introduces the two women Sophie steps out and closes the door behind her. "A bad night," she says. "We are all trying to rest just now."

"I understand," Heather says. "I was hoping to see her a second, that's all."

Sophie stands above them on the steps looking down at their faces and past them at the ground. She rubs her eyes and folds her arms and looks at the sky. "I wish to avoid any kind of backstep. Yet she must continue to look toward the past."

Heather steadies herself on the railing and Reese thinks her hand may be shaking. "Mrs. Flores," she says, "I might not be family but I'm as close to her as anyone."

Her face a cool mask in the heat, Sophie replies, "I would be quite surprised to find you educated in our practices."

Overcoming the catch in her throat, Heather says, "Mrs. Flores, I mean no disrespect, but I hope you are educated enough to realize I bear no blame for her condition."

The eyes of the older woman fasten on the young visitor. "We are not lookin to blame," she says, "but only for the manner in which we can restore the health of my daughter."

"I'm sure we all have the same hopes for her health—" Heather looks at Reese for support and he says nothing. "—but I just don't think it's fair to her if you leave me out."

"When she is well again she will make her own decisions."

"That's not good enough. I came here—"

"I'm sorry you had to make such a journey."

"I didn't have to. I wanted to, Mrs. Flores." Heather shakes her head gently. "I'm afraid you may not understand the nature of our relationship."

"Oh, I believe I do, and I must ask you to respect my judgment," Sophie says. "I'm old enough to be your mother too."

Staring at each other, the older woman keeps her expression fierce and Heather softens under it. "Mrs. Flores, I'm asking you. Please."

"I need to go inside now."

"At least ask her what she wants," Heather says.

"Good day, miss." Sophie nods at Reese and opens the door.

"When she wakes up ask her who she'd like to see," Heather says.

The door closes behind Sophie and they are left there on the steps looking at each other like rejected beggars.

"That explains why she left home so young," Heather says as they walk.

"There were probably lots of reasons," he says. "Even from what little I know of her, I get the feeling she was a wild child."

She laughs. "I've only known her a year myself, but yeah, I'd have to agree. Definitely too wild for this place."

"And now, in some strange way, she's paying the price,"

he says.

"Who's she paying it to?"

"Herself, her mother, the family, the village."

"She doesn't owe anything."

"No, but everything costs something. A part of her wants to be taken back and this is the only way to do it."

"It's kind of like going back to childhood, isn't it?" she says.

"Her great uncle has a hold on her and he's dragging her back. The only thing is, he's dead. Long dead." He grins at her. "But what can you do? You have to take care of the guy, right? C'mon, I'll show you the river."

In this lazy stage of afternoon the Moho flows like a benign spirit of fresh necessity, running its gargling mouth without a care in the world, carrying clumps of upland plants and scattered sounds, the whistles and trills and rattling calls committed to its steady presence. Mottled and stippled by sun squeezed through the tops of trees and thrown rippling across a velvet surface and in its ceaseless course a wandering alchemy drawn along between its banks, under the water and over the water and in the moist air the flickering flight of striped bees moving through a gold and broken light.

She remarks on the beauty here and wonders aloud why the people don't live even closer and he tells her that rain will change the river's face. He says, "Let's take a little ride."

"Where to?"

"Just around to the beach." He starts down the bank. "I want to take the boat over there where it belongs."

"That what you go fishing in?"

"This is her. The little one."

She climbs down after him. "How is the fishing?"

"Puts food on the table," he says.

He unties the line and pulls the dugout against the bank and holds it still. "Careful," he says. "She's a bit wobbly."

She steps in and sits looking around as he picks up an oar

291

and takes his seat. "You been up the river yet?" she asks.

"I went up a little ways yesterday."

"Catch anything?"

"Not much. We fish on the bay, mainly."

She is looking upstream as he pushes off the shoal. "Must be hard to go very far without a motor."

"It is, but I wouldn't feel good about taking all that noise up there with me. I'd rather sneak up on 'em."

"On who?"

"On whoever's up there."

He steers them to the middle and lets the current work, seeing her back and her blond curls as she shakes them loose, peering around her for the rocks up ahead. She sits quietly, watching the water and looking into the trees, her hands in her lap, expecting to see monkeys or macaws or long-tailed lizards. In the black roots of the mangroves she sees the crabs waving and around the next bend the sea view opens like a bright movie beyond the riverbank walls. They jostle in the swifter run there and bump the bay's tidal waves and he swings them south out of the rippling mouth and then back east again, making his turn for home.

Coming around he watches a fishing boat motoring in from far out on the gulf and thinks he has seen it before. She is looking off the starboard as they turn. "Look!" she says, and points south toward the shore. He looks down the curve of the coast and all the way to the violet hills and the far layer of flattened clouds. "No," she says, "over there in the water."

He stands in the stern and looks back over his shoulder and scans the shallows, searching for a run of feeding fish in the darkening shade of the shore. "I don't see anything."

She grips both sides to keep herself steady as she cranes around to see him. "I think it was a manatee."

He takes another long look and then sits and paddles to resume their course. "Maybe it was," he says.

"It was just a glimpse, but it looked like an inner tube

rolling over and sinking. A brown tube." She is still looking back that way. "Don't you want to check it out?"

"I want to meet that boat and buy a fish if I can."

She looks out at the approaching vessel and then back at him with a disappointed face. "Buy a fish?"

He smiles. "It's good for the economy," he says, and hands her the other oar. "Do a little work now. We'll go out another time and see if we can't round up some cows."

In the other boat is a man-and-wife team who fish with nets and often travel farther and work longer hours than the other villagers who also ply these waters. There are people waiting on the dock but ahead of the landing Reese meets the couple and picks up a gray snapper from their harvest and goes on to beach his boat. "About eight pounds," he says, hefting the fish. "Damn good timing too. That catch will go pretty fast with all these extra people around." He grips her shoulder in his free hand and shakes it lightly. "Alright, woman, now I can invite you over for dinner."

Simmons sits smoking in the lamplight of his house as his guest makes his request and prepares his fish, smelling jars of herbs, cutting onion and bitter orange, poking the fire and stepping over to sample the Style the old man is holding.

"She may end up staying over there but I'd like to give her an option. All we have to do is hang another hammock next to mine. She's only here till Wednesday anyway, and I thought you might enjoy the company for a few days. After the dugu I'll be gone too and you'll be back to ordinary life, man."

A forlorn hooting carries through the new-moon dark, a distant discourse among monkeys that sounds like warnings, guttural and sustained messages from the northwest, disputes in the air that remind the Americans of Halloween tricks, and make Heather—alone on the path and feeling unwelcome here—think of pagan ceremonies and animal forms loose upon the forest night. Zino lifts his head and listens to this language, declamatory in his ears, and goes to the door and hears the approach of her feet on the ground; he growls with his mouth closed and then sits, and for the first time in his life, barks back and howls at the unseen baboons.

There is plenty of the sweet fish meat to go around; the dog too is given his due. Reese sits on the floor with a plate in his lap and the old man leans over his little table to eat. With Zino at her feet Heather sits in the hammock picking at the flaky white flesh with her fingers and talking about her village work and about how she wanted to be a nurse before she decided to see the world, or at least some of it. Now she has taken an interest in natural medicines and asks Simmons about blood purifiers and herbs for bronchitis and he tells her if she has time he might be able to show her some things growing nearby. In walking distance, he adds.

Reese excuses himself to buy more Style before the store closes. With the empty jar he steps outside and walks off into the dark as Zino watches him from the door.

"So, you think any medication is being given to Barbara?" Heather bends to put her plate on the floor.

Simmons puffs a cigarette over the lamp's chimney, draws smoke and leans back in his chair; his face in this light has the sheen and darkness of gunmetal. "Maybe somethin for fever or appetite," he says, and shrugs. "I have not been followin her treatment so close. I have not seen this girl since she was fifteen or sixteen."

"But you think she'll be fine after these proceedings?"

"This is what we believe."

They sit without talking awhile. She lets her shoes drop off and runs one foot back and forth along the dog's spine until he moves, lifts himself at the sound of Reese's return.

He holds a palm stool like a small barrel under one arm and says as he hands the Style to Simmons, "I have to replace it or bring it back tomorrow." He positions it on the floor and sits and smiles into the lamp. "You need the furniture, man."

Heather takes a sip from the jar and gasps and shakes her head and says, "This is not any kind of wine."

"C'mon girl," Reese says, taking it from her, "the stuff's already watered in half." He takes his turn and puts the jar on the table and picks up a cigarette and lights it.

"I didn't think you smoked," she says.

"Oh yeah," he says.

The old man chuckles. "We can find somethin in the bush to stop that," he says. "We can cure the man."

"You can't help someone with no desire to be helped," Reese says.

She watches him smoking and follows his statement back to her own concerns and the smoke itself up to a rafter and to a mouse skittering along, a soft scratching which the dog in his napping does not hear or care about within the greater texture of the cricket chirr and the creak and clink and slipsounds of the human movements so close. She says, "I have the fear that she won't leave this place again."

The old man doesn't answer and she looks to Reese and says, "That either she'll get better and stay, or that she won't recover and she'll stay. In the ground. I'm sorry. I don't want to be negative. It's just the fear I have."

"The ritual will work," Reese says. "Believe me."

"Why did she ever leave in the first place?" she asks.

"She did not understand how to live here," Simmons says. "She did not like her mother. She did not like herself. She felt too big for this world. Nothin unusual."

The jar is passed. The lamp flickers. The dog yawns.

"Do you speak the old language?" she asks him.

"I speak it."

"Could you teach me to say thank you?"

"Tanke-ne-bo." He accents the third syllable.

"Tankenebo," she says.

"That's right."

"It sounds African, doesn't it?"

"Maybe so. But our language is Arawak, with Carib and French mixed in. Some Spanish and English too."

She looks at the shelves around her and yawns. "Would it be alright if I came over tomorrow and borrowed a book?"

"Of course."

"Tankenebo," she says. "And goodnight."

"Goodnight, goodnight," he says.

Reese walks her out and along the path to the community center; in the yard a few people are about and inside a lamp still burns and there is the murmur of multiple voices. "You might be in for a long night," he says at the door.

"I'm not worried about it."

"He didn't say no, but if you want to pay your dues—"

"Reese, I can't leave without seeing Barb."

"I know. We'll try again." He takes her hand in his. "Now be a good girl. I'll see you after fishing."

"Sleep tight," she says. "Don't let the bedbugs bite."

Wind out of the southeast, down over the hills and the coastal plain and across the gulf to the adjacent land where the smoke plumes of an early village morning float westerly; these will join the ready heat as it rises into the day and rolls inland to smolder before a wet mountain wall, climbing and cooling and dropping in a thermal reversal that may gather low and sputter to combustion in a force unleashed by falling night. Electrical explosions and wild, driving rain. It is like living in a pocket of fire and water. The fishermen generally prefer their outings of a morning.

In the cooksheds, cassava—manioc root—is peeled and grated by hand, processed in the same ancient way the Caribs and their continental forebears used to remove the prussic acid and make their durable and staple bread. The slushy starch is packed into long tubes of woven palm bark, hung from rafters and with the pull of human weight the poisonous juice is forced from the mash, the coarse flour is left to dry, then sifted through a sieve and spread to bake on a round, iron plate placed over fire. The flour is flattened and smoothed, beaten with broom and spoon as it cooks, flipped and spun by hand as it hardens, its rough edges trimmed by knife and the whole stiff piece, like a white pie crust, scored into eighths to be eaten warm or stacked and stored for later occasions.

Heather is a volunteer, working in the company of women, being taught by two women she met at the center, learning the procedure, baking and preparing the flour for the next day's fire, and she wants to dig the roots too. She is soaking wet in the smoky shed and among the youngest there; her fair skin is smudged with ash and she's glad to be busy.

The opening of the river can be seen and Reese squints at it across the shimmering surface of the sea and on down to the south, looking for other openings or breaks in the coast. It seems an uninhabited land that way, down toward the deepest corner of the bay where maps show another river and the border and the next country beginning.

"That last manatee you saw, Simmons, was it south of the river?"

He wipes his shaded face with a rag. "It was right at the river."

"Was it late in the day?"

"Well, now," he says, casting an eye at the younger man, "it may have been. It may have been."

They are soon moving that way, changing their position in a most gradual manner, as if to a compass directed by the mere suggestion. From where they sit the sea seems stitched to the hem of the land and behind them it stretches like a thick and flawless fabric to the end of sight, seamless as the pale blue sky, the clouds between like white fiber slowly pulling apart.

"Back when you were hunting those animals, did you ever hit one and have it get away from you? Wounded but loose?"

The old man is baiting his hooks, a trifle annoyed. "On

occasion," he says. "Very seldom." Still, he cannot prevent his mind from jumping back. "There was a time when I was not huntin much any more but if I was out fishin and I saw one I might try to slide close enough and throw my harpoon."

"Yeah, so, if one got away, could you still follow it? You know, to try again." Reese rises into a crouch to better his view.

Simmons is used to fishing alone and quietly. "If it was possible to follow him then I might actually do so. Look here, what about this?"

Reese is looking away over the bright flatness, a hard, flat light off the water and in the air, the stillness of the summer's front edge. "What I'm getting to, Simmons, is did you ever come across their bones, a place like a graveyard? I mean a boneyard in the water, some place where they went to die."

"Sit down, man, sit down." He is motioning with one hand and jiggling his line with the other. "The weather," he says, tossing out his hand, "storm tides wash everything around."

"What about the bones from the hunt?"

"They sink, man. Now sit down." He shakes his head. "You some kind of scientist fella makin a study?" He watches the man ease down opposite. "Thank you, thank you. A man can't fish with you standin there like that. I never heard so much talkin on a boat." He is winding in his line and glancing around at the horizon and the shore. Boys on the dock. Not much fire smoke. The wind has died.

She wades upstream away from the clearing and along the cusp of the shoal looking for a private place to bathe, wet to the waist and her rubber thongs pulling at her feet. She has a bag with her soap and shampoo and towel and she stuffs it in the shore grass and removes her outer clothes. Bent over at the edge of the current she scrubs her dirty shorts and shirt underwater, glancing downstream from time to time, and then dips her hair in the water and scoops handfuls up the back of her neck. She lathers and rinses her long pile of hair, shakes and squeezes it as a bubble trail floats behind her, and moves with her soap down a few paces to a shallower area and begins to bathe her legs. Out in the sun and knee-deep now in the cool current, long-haired and lean and light-skinned in her sudsy underwear, she is like some kind of wicked river nymph to the three boys lying on taut bellies up on the bank, peering puerile and petrified through the tall grasses.

Her clothes dry as she walks, strolling around the vacant school in the bright sunlight, moving along deserted paths in the midday stillness with her damp hair starting to shine. She heads toward the Flores house, looking for other ways to approach it as she nears and trying to guess which window will show her to Barb. The windows are all open but white curtains obscure her view and as she passes she can hear voices inside. An old woman suddenly appears in the doorway of the cookshed adjacent and startles her, watches her as she goes on and she wants to scream with frustration. She's so easily noticed; she might as well be in a formal gown and neon tiara.

Outside Simmons' she finds Reese chopping and breaking firewood with a machete against the base of the mahogany tree. "Hey," he says, "how'd you sleep?"

"Badly, like you said."

"Why don't you go in and lie down awhile. I've got some things to do but I'll make coffee later."

"Okay," she says. "Where's Simmons?"

"I don't know. Don't worry about it."

In this hottest part of the afternoon he constructs his stool, a kind of stubby bench with four coconuts grouped as a base and the split trunk of a small tree sectioned into boards and placed on top, flat side up. In the old man's meager tool supply he has found a few old nails and a rusty hammer and he somehow renders a seating piece that will keep a person off the floor. He tests it in the yard and feels pleased enough.

After a rinse in the river he buys rice, sugar, coffee and kerosene. When he returns Heather is still sleeping with a book on her stomach, pictures of terra cotta pottery on the cover. He is boiling water as she awakens.

"Have you figured out how I'm going to see her yet?" she asks.

"Yeah," he says, "you'll have to get real lucky."

She sits up in the hammock and puts the book on the table. "I usually like to roll over when I sleep," she says, "but I was out like a light."

He brings two coffee cups over and sits in the chair and hands her one. "Rice and beans coming up," he says.

She sips her coffee sleepily and smiles. "Cute bench," she says. "What he needs now are some new clothes."

The dog leaps up into the house; Reese grabs the animal's head with both hands and ruffles its floppy ears. "Magazino," he cries. Simmons comes to the door and peeks his grinning head in, holding the doorframe for stability and keeping one hand behind his back. He seems at first unable to speak or move further, as if he is the intruder.

"Well, yes," he says, "so it seems. What you children doin in the library?" He sniffs at them. "Cookin a little."

"Right on time, mister," Reese says. "Come in, come in."

The old man steps up and staggers some as he whips around the bag he's been hiding and dangles it before them, full of shrimp, still warm and spicy-smelling. "Well, yes," he says.

The other two look at each other and at him standing and wavering between them and she blows him a kiss and Reese says, "A man can get mighty thirsty on a hot Sunday afternoon." He stands and takes the bag, offers the chair to Simmons, who looks in need of a seat, and sees him staring at the new item on the floor. "You see, Simmons, I'll just put it against the wall and sleep sitting up."

The old man looks at Reese and at Heather in the hammock, turns around and goes into his bedroom where they hear him rummaging and banging about until he emerges with his arms in front of him holding up an old hammock—frayed and gaping in too many places, no doubt the predecessor of the one now in use—which he drops and steps on as he heads for the chair.

Heather says, "I have some bread just made today."

"Bring it over," Reese says, "and bring your stuff too, before it gets dark." The dog stands against his leg to smell the bag of shrimp.

Simmons lights a cigarette and waves it in the air. "They say I get all the foreigners now, startin with my hairy dog."

Reese laughs, returning to the fire. "A hand-to-mouth haven for the abandoned, the unwelcome and the roustabout."

Soon after dinner Simmons is sleeping, gone to bed and snoring, and the wind is picking up, rattling fronds up in the royals with a sound like shuffled cards. Reese is hanging the holey hammock and Heather is cleaning up the kitchen area.

"She must be a prisoner over there," she says. "It's not fair, treating her like a total invalid. She's not."

He has set a temporary knot at one end and now he sits easily into the low middle to check its weighted height. "They must take her out sometime," he says. "For a walk, to keep the body moving. Probably at night."

"You think so?"

"Makes sense to me. I don't see what other chance you have unless you want to wait for the ceremony when she goes public. But even if you did see her tonight, what would you do in the dark, shine a light in her face?"

"No, I'd shine it in mine."

"Scary," he says, grimacing. She gives him a pronounced smirk and he stands in the chair and tightens the rope to the rafter. "There you are, darling," he says. "Twin beds."

They walk without a light, relying on a come-and-go moon in a fierce, rolling sky and the reference of houses, the scarce and feeble glow spots drawing the way. In the whistling wind they don't speak but look for signs of others moving along the thin paths. At the field by the sea they catch the glimmers of

301

whitecaps appearing here and there like ruptures in the flowing night, portents of breakage from above. As they retrace their steps the far flashes begin in the west, quiet indications of a darker darkness bearing down on the coast. At the juncture they turn toward the Flores home and are standing in sight of its lighted windows in a snapping wind, bushes and limbs bending and shaking, her hair lifting in flight. There they remain, straining their eyes for some miraculous sight of Barbara walking in this wild weather while the air temperature drops and the falling sky skulks about them. Until there are cracks in the black firmament, clapping reports and blinding bolts above the river. Until they are running and the first flung drops are hitting them like pellets fired from above.

An early exodus of men to the forest behind the farms. Cabbage palm cut and split; long, narrow boards bundled and shouldered home, walls for the longhouse—the temple needed for the dugu—to be built near the beach on the site of the old, the previous structure burned by lightning fire down to its packed and stamped ground some two years past. New holes are dug in the wet earth, mangrove poles placed for the frame. Upon that the rafters, then the roof—the layers of comfrey palm fronds being stacked to dry and brown—put on in overlapping bunches from eave to peak, bound with tee-tie vine ripped from the jungle, some of it already lying in loops and coils about the work site. After that, the walls of board.

Some days Barbara has the energy of an athlete and it does not seem possible that she can endure this time before the dugu. There are family members of every stripe to divert and console and entertain her: teenage, female cousins that sleep on her floor and giggle with her in the night, somber aunts and an old, creaking uncle taking every step of this community endeavor with care and veneration, and the two young boys, nephews, who have been given the task, in an effort to engage their active participation, of small protectors, lookouts and defenders of the home. They play under the house, drawing pictures in the dirt, making family figures with sticks and stones.

But today Barbara has a case of asthenia and she lies listless and uncertain in her bed, refusing meals and water too. Listening to birds and hearing voices in the other rooms and voices from her youth, the sounds of a long-gone father. There is a shout, a woman calling her name outside, some well-wisher, no doubt, or a dream she has risen from. More shouts and people making a fuss. In sickness and in health, her past and present joined in this room and the rest a whole new passage. Her mother enters and sits her up; she drinks her tea, billyweb and contribo, combination febrifuge and appetite stimulant. She has lost weight, listening for the footfalls of ancestors in the dark. She dreams of Heather, alive and dead.

Amid the activity—the longhouse hammering, the stream of working men and supplies around the project, the cooking and cleaning, the presence of visitors—Heather wanders like a lost soul. At the beach she wades into the saltwater to calm herself and swims in the warm shallows and contracts a seaweed rash. Red blotches at her waist and upper arms. She remembers aloe growing near the center and breaks a stalk there, coats her affected areas while she walks. She finds Reese at work in the yard—extending a paddle, affixing a length of cypress to its handle with tee-tie vine—and stops him for lunch.

"Baby jellyfish," he says of her rash. "Most likely."

She shrugs, disgruntled. "I just don't feel lucky here."

They have eggs, fry cakes and coffee and he says he wants to take her out in the boat later. She leaves him to his work.

The village is becoming a center of industry and communal preparation. Bread baking is nearly constant now and berries are boiled and stewed for jam, the juice strained and put up to make wine. Corncakes and banana porridge; coconut boil-up with dasheen and yam. Johnnycake fires are burning and last summer's sea grape wine is unstocked and sampled. Cohune nuts yielding oil for soap and from the palm itself fly brushes are constructed for ceremonial trappings and market crafts.

Dozing in the better hammock, Reese hears Simmons and Zino come in and feels the dog's nose at his side. The old man goes into the back and then sits in the chair across from him. He puts batteries in his old radio, clicks it on and skims his way through static and music to find a news broadcast where a voice delivers the afternoon bulletins. Some scandal in the government, corruption and bribery and a foreign man arrested for reef destruction; a fire in Brophy Point, four deaths; the dollar is down. And coming up next week, for all those who may have an interest or family calling: An ancestral observance in the village of Moho Bight, sponsored by the Etienne and Flores families. Reese says, "You'll have to build a hotel, Simmons."

"Only Garifuna will come," he says. "Even in this day we need some little notice for a journey."

Outside in a palm's high greenery, a flash of movement unfolds, its own strike sends a black rat snake falling from the fronds, a shock-eyed mouse in its coil; the ensemble hits the grass silently, the snake's head quickly raised and wary and ready for flight, the mouse still ensnared midway down its length and none to witness this event but a single chicken strutting quickly away from the yard. The reptile loops back to smell the furry head of its prey, flicking the air around it with a thin black tongue, and widens its mouth over the pointed nose and works expanding jaws around the mammal in gagless bites that soon engulf it whole and leave the snake bulging at the neck as it glides away, hairless tail hanging from its face.

Out beyond the mouth and creeping south, Reese stands at the stern and steers with his long paddle, maintaining their heading and distance from shore, slinging a line of water on Heather whenever his oar crosses the boat, and gaining little forward motion. His desires lie in keeping a balance and being with her, no further destination than here in mind.

The sun is just over the treeline and she wears her hat,

watching him work and sweat in his awkward position, gazing up at him against the clear sky. Her other lives left on land.

"Why do you like to stand up?"

He glances around to show her. "You can see better."

"Are you looking for something?"

"Always looking for something. Anything."

She smiles. "I knew that when I first met you."

"Oh yeah, you really sized me up, didn't you?"

"Well, I was a little distracted at the time."

"Defensive," he says. "I can understand that. Everyone is, one way or another." He is breathing hard.

"Sure," she says, noticing the river farther behind now. She puts her hand in the water. "Are you staying here because of this special ceremony? You can't tear yourself away?"

"I want to see it. And I want to see her pull through."

"But aren't you—and I don't mean this badly—aren't you being sort of irresponsible? About your business, I mean. About things at home."

"My course got changed," he says, "and I haven't tried to change it back. Maybe I won't. But I have a partner and I know he can manage." He glances down at her and she is just staring away someplace, dreamy-looking. "I did dream I was home once," he says. "You were there too and we kissed."

She looks up sharply but he is looking toward the shore. "What happened then?"

"Then you kissed my ex-wife."

"Oh really?" she says, laughing. "You can't say I wasn't fair. Was there any more?"

"I woke up."

"Too bad. Couldn't handle it, I guess."

He can see the bottom, the dark grass and the sandy mud, as small waves push them closer to shore and he keeps them parallel to it. A glimpse of bonefish feeding and he can hear the surge of water breaking over and through the rocks and roots off the starboard and the restless rustle of cormorants ready to vacate their perches. They drop one by one in a rush of sweeping noise right over the surface and with an ungainly effort of hard-working wings lift up and level out toward the boat, veering away to the south with honking alacrity and then settling again in nearby branches with a long display of disorderly wings and web-foot difficulties.

"I love this time of day," she says.

"Yeah, it's nice out here, isn't it," he says. "Get away from all that village congestion." They both laugh.

The sun has disappeared and the shadows of shore stretch toward them, the light in the treetop leaves yellowish and the sky behind a pallid orange that turns to powder blue above and deepens across the world to the east. The water calmer now, as if to find peace before the night's wild resurgence.

He sees a bump at the surface some distance to the south and thinks it's probably a turtle—up and down, a break in the sea. He stirs the paddle to keep himself straight and keeps his eyes cast upon the area. In a few minutes it's up again. And gone. Then again, moving in their direction. Points on a line north, a head taking air and it is not a turtle.

"Okay," he says, seeing the rim of the back now like some type of airship adapted to navigate below the surface. "Here's one of our bovine beauties coming this way."

She half stands and watches as it breaks for air, the round muzzle and the bloated body moving slowly through the water and then gone, swimming below. "Oh, it is," she says.

They are motionless and quiet as it passes some twenty yards away and begins to angle inward toward the river. "Just one," she whispers. "Do you see any more?"

"No," he says, "but it's getting hard to see."

They watch the big animal negotiating the flats, rolling and turning itself and kicking forward in the stream, finding the mouth's narrow channel, the hump of its spindle shape seen at dusk as a blimp taken by the river and lost from sight. Gone now completely in the darkness of the Moho.

"A night up the river," she says, settling in her seat.

He is nodding, staring after it. "Fresh water," he says.

"Oh yeah," she says, looking up at him now, "and we were just sitting here waiting for it to come along. Weren't we?"

"We had a hunch," he says, sitting down to paddle.

In the evening they are home alone, eating quietly in an amber light, she feeling she's pulled him away from the people here and he thinking he is unable to help her finally with her personal life and not knowing if he is filling in as a friend, the two of them together at the edge of an ancestral assembly. Brushing their teeth and spitting out the window with thunder like kettle drums rolling down the mountains, bedding down to hang side by side though the hour is not late, the lamp so low and Reese smoking with a hand behind his head, ashes going to the floor, a strange kind of safety in this house of thatch.

"Where's our old buddy?" she says.

He looks at his watch. "Probably out cattin around."

"That old guy?"

"Yeah, well, who knows? He takes some kind of root tonic to keep him going."

She wiggles to her side, faces him. "You think it works?"

"I don't know," he says, "but I took some myself."

She giggles. "Do you feel any different?"

He is looking into the rafters, smoking. "I haven't had a chance to put it to a test."

A pause and she says, "You have a bar of soap, don't you?"

He looks over at her. "Yeah, I have one," he says. "Might go down to the river with it tomorrow."

"What time? I might want to be hiding in the bushes."

"I'll tell you before I go, but if you want to watch, you can't hide. You can help if you want, but not hide."

She smiles and sighs and says, "Goodnight, man," and when the light drops away and darkness swoops, says, "Dream of me."

A large woman in a morning dress walks barefoot into the bay and wades out up to her chest to several sticks poking up above the surface while her daughter waits on her knees on the beach with a green gallon bucket. The woman goes under, draws up a crab trap's line as she surfaces, and with it the metal basket, and pulls out the blues around the bait bone, shreds of gray meat in their claws, and stuffs them in a plastic bag.

Fishermen heading out into the sun, other men clustered at the temple, Reese and Heather sitting on the dock drinking coffee, watching the day begin. They walk along the beach and inspect the crabs, bending over the bucket, a shifting mass of clicking, gripping shell; the big woman stands dripping on the sand, hands on her hips. Reese says, "How is your morning?"

"Fine," she says, "up to now."

She will make a big pot of roti soup, she tells them, and if they want a taste in the afternoon, she can offer direction to her house. We do, they say.

A man on horseback brings a pig from the Kekchi village ten miles inland, the white swine on a long tether and walking behind them on the muddy track. The tired animal is placed in a pen behind Duran's house and after drinking at the trough begins to gorge itself on the breadfruit tossed in.

They walk to Simmons' farm and find him digging there. He culls a few medicinal herbs at hand, then takes them into the woods to look for more, helping Heather cut bark strips and pick the proper leaves. Reese follows Zino in different explorations about the area, then waits at the edge of the forest, watching a flock of yellowtails assembling to roost in the next field, oropendolas screaming in from all directions to their high meeting tree. When the others return, he takes up the sack and the old man walks his bike beside them.

By nightfall thunder has come on the breeze. The sound travels alone, without the jagged light or slashing water it foretells, like the long-reaching track vibrations from some hurtling, invisible locomotive. They leave the old man and the dog and venture out into the village night, intent on taking what Heather fears could actually be her last chance, covert or otherwise, for contact with Barbara—recognition, words spoken, or just the plain sight of her. She lacks even still the simple comprehension of her friend's strange condition. She fears a death already occurred.

They approach the house from the rear and pause on the lookout for any movement in the vicinity or around the dark kitchen as they whisper in agreement, picking a window and watching the shapes and light on its fluttering curtain and they are timorous in their predicament, hearing voices inside from places they cannot specify.

Through an aura of light cast from the window they pass into the darkness under the edge of the house, the floor above creaking like a ship, the muffled resonance of conversations moving in the boards as from a crew on deck. Thunder rolling but not worsening. They stay nervous and still, waiting and crouching against each other like prisoners in a hold.

The light lessens before them, words are exchanged and footsteps groan away. The back door opens and from the steps there is a sound of slung water sprinkling the yard and then the door shutting. They move out to the side of the house and Heather steps into the cupped hands of Reese and stands, her palms going up the wall, her fingers finding the sill, her face lifting slowly into the window space. She sees Barbara in her white slip sitting up in bed staring at her, her hair plaited like a little girl's and her eyes in the low lamplight burning bright as a lemur's.

Barbara stiffens at the sight, the white face and golden hair showing between the waving curtains, the head of her lost Heather on the window ledge smiling at her like one come on a foreign wind, on a long journey through sleepless nights. "Oh my," she says, her hands lifting to her mouth and her voice rising. "Oh my, oh my dear, my dear, my dear." In her surprise and excitement her voice is too loud in the small room. "OH MY DEAR."

This disruption, then rapid movement in the small house. Heather hisses, "Shhhh," as the string beads of the doorway are parted and Reese tries to let her down while she still grips the windowsill, he hearing a skittering like rats under the house as a thump strikes his thigh and he grunts and turns his body to shield himself from this assault—a stone hits the corner post and another whistles past into bushes. He is holding Heather's legs as she slips down beneath Sophie's appearance, seeing as she goes the younger girls crowding through the door and Barbara standing on her bed crying.

She stumbles on the ground and Reese takes her hand and pulls her as the boys at their secret rock pile are throwing wildly in this night game of scary figures and upset adults. She is hit at the mouth and hollers like a shot dog and goes down on all fours and Reese lifts her to her feet and they are running while Sophie leans from the window and her silent stare follows them into the darkness and thunder.

Simmons is snoring. Zino sniffs at the blood she spits on the floor and Reese blots her split and swollen lip with a wet bandana and makes her rinse with Style, so that she cries at the stinging pain and the ugliness she feels in her face. Her tongue running over the area finds a sharp edge and he says, "A chipped incisor but I don't think you need stitches."

He finds some aspirin and tries to settle her down, ease her away from the guilt she feels, that last sight of Barbara blown up in her mind, both of them drinking the Style and with no ice for her mouth but only a cloth of cool rainwater, the sound of it falling on the fronds now like the sound of seeds shaken in a dry gourd, a sound of futility that makes her cry all the more and brings with it the fatigue she needs.

They aim for sleep, hanging in their hammocks without light and unable to talk as the rain increases, the thunder rumbling closer and closer until its cracking accents are just above the village, bursting with a volume and voltage immense even for a place with a proclivity for meteorologic intensity. In this air-splitting cavalcade of ferine weather, the savage and dazzling ruptures seem to touch the very roofs, blasting the fronds and the walls and the sleepless people shocked and scared in their simple structures. Zino is shaking under Reese, hiding from the jolting noise, bumping the man at each electric flash, cowering quietly and nuzzling the lowered hand. Like a descent of dynamite without destruction, or from hollow bombs these crashing strobes, in this ruthless pounding of threatening sound, there is the accepted danger of lightning, along with the greater fear of natural annihilation.

In white sky instants, in the brevity of light, they see each other wide awake across a narrow space; and in the times intervening, in the closure of night, a black chasm divides them. They hear Simmons; he coughs and clears his old throat between bolts, over the lashing rain. In mute, frozen moments they catch incandescent glimpses of themselves hanging curved in this room, slung low over the earthen floor, and he thinks she wants to speak. When the storm begins to relent, when its rapid cracks are going, its spectacular thunder diminishing in severity and frequency, Reese leaves his hammock, mindful of the dog, and kneels beside her.

"I couldn't hear you," he says at her face.

"I was wishing we had one big hammock tonight." Like a child learning her words, some consonants poorly pronounced.

His hands on the twine by her arm, he waits over her for the next flash, softly rocking her hammock, holding her this way. Mere grumbles tumbling earthward, light flaring through the room and he sees her eyes moist and her mouth puffed and pulled open slightly by its swelling, the red cut a line in her upper lip. "Are you alright?" he says.

In the ensuing dark they remain this close, in wordless conversation, the distant light not reaching them, nothing but themselves and the thought of Barbara reaching them. She says,

"We were just trying an experiment. It isn't a crime, is it?"

"Not to me, it isn't."

He bends and brushes her lips with his as gently as he can and she moans a little and he waits, breathing at her mouth, as her hands find the sides of his face and hold him there, bringing to bear as much pressure as she can take and her tongue in this makeshift kiss finding its passage to his.

"Like your dream," she reminds him.

"Better than that," he says, kissing places on her face, finding again her bruised and open mouth, his hand too on her face and moving to the warmth of her neck and over the light cover of her clothes and him breathing like a runner. Kneeling and kissing her with his hand snug between her legs and moving her there, pushing the hammock off its axis as he leans and she is held tight in a string web, suspended under his touch.

"I don't know if this thing can handle us both, or if we could even move," he whispers. "What about this smooth floor?"

"I don't want to move," she says, holding his hand down and breathing in sharp spurts. "Put your fingers in me."

With his hand pushing her open, fingers moving inside, she kisses him harder, squirming on her back with the hammock swaying and creaking at its knots and he strokes her onward, her mouth bleeding as she finishes, his head resting on the rise and fall of her beating breast.

He climbs naked into his hammock and the dog shifts its position as she takes hers on her knees beside the man. She wets his bandana and blots her lip and whispers, "Fair play," in his ear and kisses him, her hand cool on his stomach and trailing down to grip him tight, his convulsions imminent and with her fist moving there she catches his eruption in cloth.

They lie apart, released in the dead of night and lightly sleeping, the sky quiet, the trees dripping the soft remains. Nearby a rooster crows, and is answered down the lane; his heightened reply is abruptly met and the strident exchange is soon a serious invasion of slumber for those unaccustomed.

"Sounds like he's right outside the door," she says.

"What's wrong with their inner clocks?" he says. "Don't the sons of bitches know it's two-thirty in the morning?"

He rises and spreads his sheet on the floor and stands sipping Style beside her until she senses his stiffness and reaches for him in the dark and takes his hand and pulls herself up and stretches out down on the solid earth. He whispers, "Heather, you sweet angel," and then lowers himself and mounts her on the hard housed ground.

Simmons wakes them at six. He stands boiling water in the corner and says, "That boat leaves at six-thirty." She gets out of her hammock in her sheet, slips on shirt and shorts and goes to the outhouse. When she returns Reese is sitting over coffee; she takes a few sips from his cup, collects her things and says goodbye to the old man. He suggests a remedy for her cut lip and wishes her well, and the dog leaves with them.

At the dock, bags of coconuts loaded and people boarding. She feels like crying but smiles instead. "You come see me," she says, hugging him. "Let me know how this works out."

"I plan to," he says. And he waves sadly, and stays there alone but for the dog, until the boat rounds the point.

NINE

In a cove a few miles south of the Moho a mating herd is breaking up. The female is no longer in estrus and she moves out alone into the bay, grazing along the bottom on turtle grass. Sometime later another cow moves into her vicinity and they greet each other and continue their feeding and dozing in the warm tropical water. In the afternoon they encounter a lactating cow and her calf and spend several minutes touching—rubbing against the mother's barnacled back and nuzzling the nursing infant with their bristly lips—as they click and squeak among themselves. The youngster suckles at the axillary gland under its mother's flipper while she feeds, swims at her flank as she rises to breathe, finds her other side when they rest; the calf is barely seventy pounds, the cow over nine hundred. It is said that their name—manatee—originates from a Carib word meaning woman's breast.

The courting bulls, five of them, have slowly dispersed,

and rove singly about the area of the cove and the mouth of a creek nearby, rolling in fresh water, munching on shoal grass and mangrove leaves, sleeping on the bottom, following the sounds of their kind. One of them, the eldest of this loose group, moves north in his forage. He is about eleven feet long and the expanse of his gray-brown back is blotched with the lighter and greenish hues of algal powders, etched and pitted and lined by whitish cuts and yellow scratches, a mottled and growing record of forty years of his life and travels in these rivers, lagoons and coastal seas. He carries one distinguished scar from a very old puncture wound and were he to be given a moniker by humans it would likely be Starback.

With forked poles the men on the ground lift bunches of brown fronds, six in a load, to the rafter men thatching the roof of the ancestor house, closing up from both slopes the open peak alongside the ridgepole. All pause to pass a bottle around, joking and discussing aspects of the impending ritual. Reese is there too, one of the lifters, in his dirty fishing shorts and bandana and nothing more and known to all these men as well as they know the American mutt Zino trotting along the beach and nosing in the nearby weeds as they work. One old man has taken too much of a bottle and he sputters around telling stories and showing when he laughs the two or three teeth left in his mouth, and lifting a bunch of fronds lets black ants fall on his head and down his shirt and then hollers and hops around and rubs his back against a corner post and provides an amusement he did not intend.

By the next day the walls have been erected and there are window spaces in all four sides and doorways in three; the area inside is one large room but for a section walled off at the doorless end—a private chamber with its entrance cloaked by hanging fabric. This room houses the altar and its window is shielded from outside view by a reed screen. The other end of the building is open to the sea and a porch is added there, a flat-roof extension with benches on either side and no walls. On the beach at the edge of the sea stands an archway of palm leaves to welcome the spirits, to welcome the gubida home.

White altar, white cloth, white candles, white rum—a brightness condensed and potent and all else dark in the night compared to this place with its private light playing and its airy visitors liable to invade at any time, to float like gas threads inspecting the orchestrations of the shaman—she who awaits their voices—and witness her interview with this late sponsor. Sophie crosses the floor of the outer room and parts the curtain and enters the small, flickering space with her own candles and her drink. With a willingness to fight for herself in this discussion of timing, propriety and money. She is the eldest female relative of the focal spirit and she begins to state her case with this fact. The wizened old shaman tells her, "Etienne has prepared for three months."

"Since he is my cousin, I am lucky for my chance to contribute," Sophie says, lighting her candles. "His father, my uncle, who raised me like a father, has accepted this offer from me too, even so late as it comes. My daughter, God bless her, she had the dreams for a long time and I did not know because she never talked to me. She turned her back on her people and the ancestors and she went any place like the smoke in the wind, livin as a wastrel and a mischief-maker, as I have been informed, and ignorin all of these dreams."

"Circumstances are one thing, but people may see you as an opportunistic person," the shaman says.

"They only wish to step on my luck."

"Yes, sister, but time is short now. You will not care to hear that people are callin you stingy."

"I cannot stop this wickedness out of nothin. My brother has gone to buy five gallons of strong rum and we are cookin all the time and I have many friends helpin me to prepare. I will be generous and honest and I will still be criticized but I am only tryin to protect my child. Even the American man, the one who brought my daughter home, even he came to me and said he would try to put some weight in my corner. This is what he said, as if he knows of these demands placed upon me."

The shaman looks away from the other woman and glances about the room and down at the floor and through the lively light and the dusty flutter of white moths at the wall and she appears to be listening more than seeing. With Sophie waiting, nervously rearranging the small glasses of rum on the altar and then just sitting with her hands in her lap. Finally, the shaman nods and says, "Your hog is too thin."

Sophie is startled. "I am very sorry," she says, "but he is still a hog, and I will pay the drummers myself."

The older woman is rocking on her stool, her hands at the sides of her head, and she smiles. "He is gettin happy," she says, "for this occasion to come from the other side to enjoy the company and the gratitude of the livin. To dance and eat again with the old friends."

To all those there, Sophie vows, "No one will go hungry."

Reese has brought home a lifting pole he intends with some help to transform, and he needs to get the knowledge of his fellowman. Simmons wants to know if he's hunted.

"I shot doves when I was a kid," he says, "and I grew up spearfishing before I ever wet a hook."

"Not the same."

"I know it's not the same. I learn things by doing them."

The old man puts some scraps down for the dog, saying, "You don't have anything for the points, man," and when he turns around Reese is digging through his duffel, producing the rib he has carried here. He takes it over and hands it to Simmons. The old man holds the bone by one end and swings it side to side in the air like a scythe and then slaps it in his other palm and rubs it there, feeling its basic traits, his rough thumb running smooth over the ivory, and when he looks up Reese can see that they have reached an understanding.

On Saturday more celebrants arrive and the animation and general enthusiasm of the villagers grow appropriately except at Simmons' quiet corner-edge, where there is no appreciable difference shown. Each morning the two men leave early to fish or travel to the farm, the old man amassing food for the cooks and Reese along to collect anything useful that might spill from the old man's mind. In the afternoons Reese works on his weapons; Simmons has drawn the shape of a two-barbed point in the dirt on the road to the fields and Reese saws his rib in half and begins to shape the blunt pieces with a file. For several days the rains abate. He sits on the steps with a knife and a whetstone and his fingers tire and grow weak. In the late light he takes to the river, filling his pockets with stones from the shallows. He floats down to the mouth and out of its flow and stands to scan the surface toward the south. Then works back up the river past his embarkation point into the whistling dusk to stand and steer the craft and listen for sounds below the high-pitched realm of birdcalls. Working the surface and the current, coasting and turning and tossing his stones, his legs braced wide to the sides, the long paddle in his left hand for balance as he throws at whatever he chooses—a bush, a log, a leaf floating by—aiming without force but waggling unsteadily aboard the moving canoe. Afterward he bathes in the dark at the landing and then from the bank looks down on the passing night water with a low-powered flashlight.

"If you make your strike standin," Simmons says, "you may throw yourself out of the boat. Then you lost your next strike." He laughs, rubbing his stubbled chin. "Maybe better if you kneel down, paddle up close, you know, then strike him hard."

"You want a stout?"

"Yes, man, I want a stout."

Under a rain-free sky, in the clear moonlight on the path,

the old man says, "Take a good aim. Hit him in his lung." He squats and whistles and Zino comes to him and he places one hand over the dog's spine and pokes the index finger of his other hand at a spot on the dog just outside his thumb. "You got to miss the backbone," he says, and the dog pulls away and runs ahead. "And when he runs, you go with him." And after the running dog Reese hurls his imaginary spear.

As they sit bobbing on the bay, their lines in the water, Simmons says, "First you understand him and how he lives. When you can't see clear you look for bubbles—these fellas make a lot of gas—and you might see the water move when they pass, their wake. You got to pay attention, you got to look for shit too because it always floats up top." He jerks his line, pulls up a flopping goatfish. "Tell him you have a good reason, that you must regrettably take him to your side but you will use him well. Tell him you will return his bones, most of them.

"Many people would be fed. We fried the meat in its fat and we kept it a long time. We made oil for cookin and the skin was very strong, good for straps and such. Even shoes. I made shoes for myself, long ago. I wore them a long time too."

Reese is just listening; his bait is gone but he sits hearing the old man while he wishes to speak like this and the old man is fishing and dreaming and floating in his mind.

"Look at this place," Simmons says, but keeps his eyes at the water. "The young people go away and we must have a feast for the dead to get them back, to remember the old ways, to keep us together in this world." A sorrow seems to come across the water like a breeze off the land, the water riffled and the air rife with human odors and memories and stories of life on land, a scent that brings to Reese a taste like rust, a smell of decline, some vague feeling of leaving. He has seen the sadness too, not the obvious poverty or the slow wither of a small culture, but a kind of necrosis, the inexorable nature of a spiraling force—life by man. What the humans do.

Dizzy in these thoughts, he hears Simmons again. "We spoke of ourselves as men of the sand beach. This was our name and our proper life. We always hunted from the sea."

Reese in his confusion says, "It's not simply food on the table. I want her to pull through." In his mind he's bumping over descriptions, thinking it a worthy task, an event needed to overcome his modern misgivings, to fuse this murky journey with his native inclinations, to bridge any division between he the man and his natural world. But he cannot find purchase among his reasons; the sun and heat disrupt his concentration and he utters, "Barbara," in explanation and feels the faint throb of a trauma almost forgotten, and a sound moving upon him like hoofbeats across a distant plain.

To the men in the boat the sound comes and goes on the breeze as a rhythm of faraway thumps—bom bom, bom bom, bom bom—that vanishes into the swimming heat of the air, into the sea and the sky from which it seems initially to emanate, and returns to touch them internally and feels to be their own inaudible heartbeats. Drums across the water.

Warm-up riffs and pauses, interruptions at the temple and shifts in the wind, patterns of a simple song drifting to its outer ranges, an announcement made. Reese is gazing back at the land. "It's starting up," he says. "We are underway."

The old man is listening, his head cocked. "Oh yeah."

"Let's go in, Simmons."

A casual crowd around the ancestor house; folks strolling in for a look; children lurking near the doors or hanging back at a distance as the drums beat on. Women bring basins held on their scarfed heads, tubs of covered food placed up on boards running across the rafters. Three men sit inside pounding deep notes from heavy instruments, the sturdy wooden drums clutched upright between their legs, strong hands striking tiger hide.

A goatfish meal and Reese sits smoking on the steps in a slot of frond shade, his tools and boneworks about him as the rhythms resume, beating their way to every path and dwelling, into the bay and up the river and even to the nearest farms. Like a life force revived, the pulsing of spirits, an impetus to movement and appeasement. He uses the sound, measures his filing strokes to match the meter of the drums, scraping the raw material, turning its graceful curve to a dangerous shape.

His hands sore, his mind tired with heat and headache, he takes to the hammock and falls asleep to the beating—in the air and in his ears, in his breath and pumping organs—one steady sound all around. He drifts in and out as the drums cease and start anew and his mind's eye cannot quite rest, opening and closing, attuned already to the presence of the solemn rhythms—part of the ritual plan, he's thinking—organic and mythic at once. Like a riverine boneyard.

The current in the river is troublesome but he likes the confinement, the limited space between the banks; he's picked out a couple of spots and he practices late in the day at one of them. Tied fast in the stream, he mans his craft diligently and waits with his throwing stick, holds it at the ready even though it does not yet have its bone point. But he handles it well, becoming familiar with its heft and range.

The river carries more noise than the open bay, in its motion and in its surroundings, and many more insects too, the mosquitoes driving home this point as he waits, quietly bitten, without repellant or any extraneous smell but his own, as much a part of this riverscape as he can be, waiting for his prey, hoping for a sighting and at the same time not wishing to waste one; he's trying to see the elements of the act and he must be here to do it. Insects are singing over the water as dusk comes on and the river itself drowns the sounds within it. So he has chosen the place and he can see himself in this light. Hunting on the Moho.

At seven in the morning the fishing boats are departing for the ceremonial journey to the cays—two old pirogues each outfitted with sails and a crew of four, men and women both aboard but no engines—to gather from the sea the offerings required. With blessings and incantations the priestess leads them from the temple to their launching, the people gathering along the shore with shouts of encouragement and good fortune as the fishermen row out, followed by the somber and hopeful tones of the beating drums. After two nights away they are expected to return at dawn, accompanied by the ancestral spirits, this event signaling the start of the ritual dugu.

The drums comfort Barbara, bring to her over-pounding heart a steady rhythm and a solace immeasurable; when they stop she cannot remain in bed but moves about the house and yard in heated agitation. She lives on cassava beer and it calms her and makes her want to dance, which she does under the house with her little cousins laughing and clapping and joining her in the fast and scrappy motions. She feels agile again, neither her feet nor back nor breast hurting any more and only the fever in her mind and the wildness of her heart to plague her now. She sweats profusely sitting on a bench in the house with her relatives eating and talking around her as if she were not there. She falls asleep among them and dreams crazy: Reese is washing her feet in the warm sea, sponging off her muddy thighs when a turtle surfaces and speaks to them in a tongue they do not understand; she sees her ancestors waving and calling behind watery curtains; she sees strangers sucking her breasts; she dreams a dugout is approaching a night shore, the flaming torch is Heather with her hair afire. She dreams a mound of fresh dirt and kneels to vomit her jumping heart.

Among the moist leaves and tangled grasses of the muddy riverside a coral snake threads a slender path, nosing through layers of soft debris for hidden lizards and pausing now to taste the ripe morning air, its small head lifting into the sunny grass, the black and yellow and red bands of its body making a starkly painted stalk. Nearby a woodcreeper poking under bark pulls forth a spider and suddenly freezes at some disturbing sound, then flits away into the forest gloom with its catch still in its beak.

The snake freezes also, feeling vibrations too near, the bank shuddering and grass bending to the water as the reptile tries to flee, the grasses and roots beneath it ripping away and pulling it within this bunch over the edge. The manatee slides down into the water dragging a mass of grass with it, pendulous yet dexterous lips working the succulent sedges into its mouth, pushing the vegetation back between grinding molars as the snake wriggles loose into the water and swims free of the feasting behemoth and an accidental death.

Floating and munching at the surface, the manatee moves along the bank perusing the plants, flexible flippers moving fresh growth to his face for closer inspection. He nibbles first on hanging strands and then strains upward for more; he settles his buoyant bulk low in the water and heaves himself forward, wide tail pushing in a huge kick, flippers and face grabbing at the bushy bank. Some distance downstream a young female follows the same bank, snagging freed pieces that float her way and generally feeding in a less particular manner than the other. She is recently pregnant, her gestation still over a year, and though this scarred male was one of her partners, he pays her little mind now and she does not get very close to him. They are both grazing upstream, however, and if the food is found to be sufficient, may remain in the river for several days.

Out of a rib, chipped and cut and caressed, the bonehooks have emerged. Two sharp charms. They are half a foot in length and he has planed the curves down to sharp, straight points, each with a short thorn carved in its stem, a secondary tooth to grip far inside the hide, to lodge and counter like a raptor's back talon. At the base of the stem a hole is bored and a nylon line tied through it and wound several times around and the piece then fitted like a peg into a hole reamed in the flat end of the staff, pushed snugly into place on the end of the pole but made to pull free of it when enough force is applied. This smooth harpoon with a detachable head, an eight-foot spear meant to carry and install its point and then separate from it, the bone piece connected to its own line. A long brown spear with a white, hooked head. He admires the pieces in their unused beauty, tests each point's fitting and holds them one in each hand like ivory daggers. Crude tools, he thinks, these strange and shapely objects whittled from bone. Utilitarian but artistic. Make someone a nice souvenir. An artifact for an unaccountable future. But he's honing his bones for a single task. And they are more valuable than pottery, hardwood or precious stones.

The points he keeps in his pockets; he cannot risk their damage on practice runs. He carries his stick on the path to the river. People greet him and he responds, but he doesn't explain his actions or feel a need to. Not here. Not in Moho, where only the lone simpleton might not guess his intentions.

At the places he has chosen—bends in the river where the course widens and slows—he takes his throws. The closer place he calls the Bulge, the farther one the Bend, as it is sharper and narrower in its turn. He has two targets there, loops of tee-tie vine floating on a stringer, and from a position across the stream he heaves his blunt spear in a flattened arc over the water and in his follow-through goes down to grip the gunnels and stabilize the dugout. He kneels and retrieves the staff by its line, reels it in, and stands for another shot. Hits and misses, plunging deep in the water, a game of ring toss reversed. His lines are not very long, but they're strong, and to succeed he knows he must be close to his target. He throws for an hour and then rests his shoulder, cradles his heavy arm, and watches the passing surface and the birds undisturbed by his primitive and unhidden presence. A man standing on the open river, waiting but not stalking. He does not smoke here. Not even against the bugs or the nervousness in the air.

All day long a trail of women like ants to a nest. Platters and basins of food for the ancestor house, with no queen there, but only the old ministrant sitting transfixed yet observant while the rafters fill with offerings. At dusk a boat arrives from the east and searching for family these pilgrims blend into the citizenry moving about the temple and are fed there and invited to rest in hammocks while the night passes in murmurs and lamp-lit movements and tired shadows that seem in the early hours to be harbingers of the dead awaited. Before dawn has fully broken a sail is sighted offshore, a cry goes up and the drums begin to talk among themselves, a low, conversational interplay of beats, the muttering of wandering spirits that rises into rolling bursts like admonitions or laughs or shouts of pure excitement. The village called to witness the small sails catching the sun's rising fire and burning bright in their momentous approach.

A procession to the beach, the shaman and the drummers and women with prayers of welcome, welcome, you have all come home. The pirogues running into the shallows and then dragged up onto the sand and the rewards seen, the hot light cutting across the bent figures scooping their harvest onto sailcloth and then hoisting these ragtag slings out of the vessels and carrying the catch up the bank and beside the longhouse to be washed in basins of sweetwater, to be cooked there over a pit fire and made ready for ritual use, the priestess proclaiming this bounty to all those gathered and with her rattles raised before the seaside arch she hails the arriving ancestors and sings them songs of salutation.

Lobster and conch, crab and cuda and shark, spadefish and jack and cero mackerel, snapper and sheepshead, cobia, seabass and tripletail and a bucket of shrimp caught running through the moon-soaked nights. A reasonable haul and the fishermen look haggard for it; some of them go home to clean themselves and others take straightaway to hammocks in the longhouse and lie resting amid the din of drumming and the swirl of ceremony getting underway. The shaman in her chamber now and a ring of people circling the house, small crowds pressing at windows and doors as inside the cadre of women assembles itself for dancing and prayer and singing.

Etienne stands by the table beside the drummers; he is tall and gaunt in gray slacks and white shirt and one of the few men of the village taking a role in the proceedings. The shaman brings him a bowl of rum and he moves about the room sprinkling drops through the windows and doors—the people at each backing away as he does—to attract the spirits, and then sprinkling the dancers waiting in the middle area, and the drummers too, and the drums and the floor under the drums. The women—twenty or more of them, all barefoot and uniformly dressed in headwrap, blouse and gathered skirt—begin their dance in unison, in a kind of formation, hopping slowly from one foot to the other, each holding a strip of white cloth that is shaken downward on the same beat as they all dip together in a circle, moving methodically around the room.

The shaman in her sanctuary bathes her rattles in rum. Her assistants kneel on mats, rows and rows of bottles set before them, rum and wine and soda like cylinders of colored glass and candles burning in bright lines glimpsed when the curtain is parted. The old woman weaves her way between the dancers and takes up the beat with her gourds, the two shaken in one hand and her arm outstretched as she shuffles in their midst and inquires aloud, speaks her phrases in the old tongue and receives replies in song by the chorus hopping around her. She invokes and they respond, questions and comebacks chanted and sung. The drummers pounding all the while, heartbeat of the tribe, and those along the walls on benches and hammocks, the elderly and the weak, the ailing and the needy, seekers of ancestral advice. Etienne's sick boy lies in one hammock, ten years old and rigidly alert. Barbara hangs next to him, quite still too, but bored or sleepy-looking. Reese is watching her from a window but her eyes have closed. Her mother is dancing.

"Not too near," Simmons whispers to him, and they step away from the building.

Hanging from the center beam are several items: a carved boat, a headless doll-like figure with a thick torso and cloth pants, a shred of fishnet, a couple of lanterns. In front of the drummers a sandy mound that resembles a bare grave. From this house issue the rhythms of ritual—the chanting of the medium, the chorus in alto and soprano harmony, the deep and rolling drums interwoven—in patterns mesmerizing, African-sounding, a tribal singing that dances on its own, grabbing the dancers and the spectators and reaching out to the other side of life for spirits called by name. Sophie sings for Uncle Thunder, the guest of honor who is Etienne's father, and others call for their relatives in the hope that they will arrive too, brought along on Thunder's journey—a plethora of pleas and praises both fluid and powerful, a sound to grip the organs and souls of those inclined and lift them from what they know toward the state they believe will follow.

People come and go; the day wears on, the drums starting and stopping. For some, there is always the work to be done. Reese is resting in the heat, leaning back against a palm and smoking with his eyes shut. Simmons comes over and squats next to him. Reese can hear the dog sniffing around the other side of the tree and he feels the ivory in his pockets pressing into his thighs. He says, "Beautiful music, man."

The old man lights a cigarette, draws in and gradually lets his breath out. "Spirits slow to appear."

Reese opens his eyes. "Aren't they here?"

"Oh yeah," he says. "Most probably down by the beach."

Reese looks over that way too. "Are they standoffish?"

"They came from St. Vincent," the old man says, "but they must also come from the earth." He points his cigarette at the temple. "From the dirt of this new homeland."

"I'm not sure I follow. They come from two places?"

"From both," Simmons says.

"You have to coax the old-timers out of retirement, don't you? After they bitch and moan and make trouble and you invite them back and they accept, they still play games. They're just as fickle as the living. Isn't that what you're telling me?"

327

Simmons stands, looking at the sea, and blows smoke into the dead air. He squats again, the pit in his ankle like a dry bullet hole. His feet flat in the dirt, dusty dark on top, the thick, calloused soles almost orange, feet like slabs of aging clay, cracked and lighter along the edges. He is not looking at Reese. "Probably in the nighttime," he says.

Reese takes his harpoon staff out of hiding, slips it down the bank into the mud. He lays it aboard and stands cooling down in the current, coming out of his lethargy, holding the canoe by its line. He heads upstream paddling easily with long, smooth strokes, drumbeats again in the air and in his head and in his muscles, as if he's dreaming a gentle dream of himself on a river trip, moving sleepily despite the urgency he feels.

Though he does not ignore the green banks, the land, the life in the trees, the possibility of surprise—delight or danger—from either side, he concentrates almost totally on the water. The sky is clear, the air hot and still, the drums a faint thumping through the jungle enclosure. Killifish and tetras hit the speckled surface under strands of grass as he passes and everywhere along the shore the dimple and pock of insects in motion, the wrigglers and swimmers, the aerial skippers and dragonfly dodgers. He looks ahead and behind for bigger breaks, for round snouts popping up and blowing open; he watches the plants floating by, afraid he may miss his only chance, his weapon fitted and ready, sharp white head sticking out over the stern, pointing the way home, water visibility good without a recent rainwash even as the sun moves into the treeline. But what he's thinking, aside from the uncertainty of finding even one of these shy giants, aside from the fact that Heather is working on plans for conservation—sanctuary as economic incentive—and aside from the fact that the animal is venerated by many as a peaceable oddity—what he's wondering now is how he'd get the thing back without a motor. Butcher it on the beach, Simmons says, but it must be towed there. Or at least to the Moho shoal where he began.

Beside the temple the cookfire is burning, the flames seen through windows and doors, and from where Reese watches on the opposite side, the firelight leaps among the dancers, blurring their movements and casting dim shadows across the walls while under the pale lamps their bodies throw shorter shapes over the floor, an effect of actions multiplied in a room made larger and fuller than daylight will allow.

Behind him the old man says, "You come late, man."

"Sorry, Simmons. Overslept."

A placation dance is in progress, the shaman shuffling around to face the drummers, shaking her rattles at them as the middle drummer—the heart drummer—is taking up the rhythm of the dancers while they chant in time with him. The shaman swaying and the dancers in motion, their singing woven into the thumping of the single drum, providing together the musical balance, the highs and lows of a luxuriant voice. And then abruptly the drumming stops, the music ceases and the old medium bends over the sandy mound, shakes her gourds at the ground as the man tilts his drum forward, then raises her rattles toward the roof with a shivering sound of seeds and shells and sweeps her solid arms down again, the brittle instruments hissing at the earth and then lifting upward in gestures aimed with a frightening intensity, directing her demands and calling expressly for a shifting of the spirits.

The dance resumes, the women hopping in their formation around the room, moving a little faster as the percussionists pick up the tempo, the two groups soon driving each other to a higher pitch, the volume rising in chants with the dancers in a swaying circle and some of them exuberant now in their vocals and their motions. The drums speak of life but none will be cured without the spirits. A woman breaks from the unit and begins to dance independently, her elbows out, her arms snapping from side to side, her eyes closed and then fluttering, her mouth open but without words and stepping away from the group, her hips swinging in time with her arms, drum-driven but not as before. The other women stand back to watch this free-form dancing and even the children squeezing into the doorways can see that the woman has caught a spirit, that the gubida are here at last.

The audience now is rapt, wondering who she harbors and hoping for a word or a sign of some kind. When she staggers, two women rush to support her, taking her under the arms and helping her move about the room dancing as she wants and doing what she will, her face showing a complete absence, reflecting a removal from consciousness while her body is being used and the energy seen is the drive of the ancestor. She will have no memory of this state. Nor any other place. It is as if she has gone yet still remains. When she swoons the women ease her to the floor and the ministrant brings a soda beverage and some rum from her sanctuary and the woman sips at each and her face is wiped clear of perspiration while she sits staring ahead.

During the breaks the men outside stand together in small groups talking softly and drinking. Simmons and Reese are in front of the temple passing a bottle with several others. Over the sea a round moon rises higher before the stars and the air off the water seems cooler than usual. Down on the beach young boys normally asleep by now are seen running along the surf. An atmosphere of friendly unity prevails and here and there laughter burbles into the night. The fire can be heard and smelled and Reese is reminded of a family reunion. There is a sense of plenty and the feeling that the harsh and difficult aspects of life will be dispelled by the spirits and that if they remain pleased the afflicted will heal and satisfaction, if not prosperity, will come upon all these descendants.

Throughout the night possession occurs. The spirits are summoned from the center of the room or from the mound by the drummers. At times there are two or three individuals dancing apart, crying out or laughing in a manner they are not known to exhibit. An elderly woman in black-framed glasses, moderate and dignified in her carriage, leaves her place at the wall and joins the chorus, breaking away soon after to thrust her hips wildly, dancing this way for a lengthy period but never seeming exhausted, simply stopping to stand distracted for a spell, still harboring, and beginning again as she feels the desire. Another enters her trance dance so deeply she finally faints fully and appears apoplectic in her helplessness. Often the ones possessed visit the ones afflicted—the boy and the young woman—and stand working over them, passing hands over their bodies, sprinkling rum over their faces and chests and bending to blow on these same areas, letting them feel the ancestral presence and the power of tradition.

Outside the people sway or dance as the spirits appear; they drink and laugh and cry and kiss, calling out to those they love. Wanting to know things, to be blessed and cured of any trouble or pain. Recognizing in a particular possession the words or habits of an ancestor and sharing their joy with the living relatives convened for this wondrous occasion. All by this hour eager to make the temple a feast hall too. Fish searing over the fire and inside the long table at the rear being dressed with food from the basins brought down.

The drumming has ceased. Reese is nodding off, half drunk against his tree, chin at his chest. Simmons nudges him with his foot. "Come see the fowls, man," he says, and Reese lifts his head and gets up and takes the flask offered. He lights a cigarette and they walk over to the porch entrance together.

A hush has fallen over the ancestor house. Babies asleep on benches and the lazy crackling of the cookfire and the wind rustling the ends of the roof fronds and the grasses and trees nearby. From the sea, silence, its breeze pushing the woodland sounds toward the mountains. And running quick across the cool moon, high scraps of clouds like lost agents late for a rain.

The ministrant is moving around the room, the area inside her perimeter empty, as if she is clearing space, keeping the people back at the hammocks, the walls and windows. When she nears an entrance the children there back away fearfully and Reese moves forward to the edge of the doorway. One of the drummers brings a concrete block and places it in the middle of the floor; the other two stand at the rear holding chickens by their feet, the birds alive and upside down, wings flopped out and feathers fluffed, an occasional flap or shudder given, but all of them quiet in this darkened arena. On the ground beside Reese a man drops a small black pot of fire; he squats behind it with a bowl of water and with his fingers splashes the hissing contents until smoke streams forth. The first drummer brings a bird to the center and stands with the shaman in some silent conference beside the block, then circles it slowly several times, dangling the chicken at his side and dipping into a little rhythm. He swings the bird up behind him in an easy arc and brings it down fast in front, slamming its head on the edge of the block, and steps back as the chicken is twitching and brings it down again and then again and after that there is no jerking seen nor blood visible but only a few feathers floating to the floor. Beside Reese the firekeeper is adding fuel and tamping it down, turning the pot and stoking the burn, containing the flame with water and with his quick and attentive motions making smoke flow. The next man follows with two birds used in the same way, dropping them four times each and then making way for the last drummer and his pair, the second of which he throws directly at the floor, releasing it as he does and then scooping it up as it flops sideways over the dirt and with focused force delivering the fatal blow. The five dead cocks are taken out to the cooking shelter and a woman there begins to pluck them at once. Reese is squatting with the man and watching his sputtering pot, the movements within taking form as he studies them, the tunneled wood pieces of a burning termite nest, thin flues of pouring smoke and the solid discharge the milky insects themselves running out to perish in the heat.

The possessed eat first, served by relatives of the

honorees and feeding these spirits through their bodies, Sophie and her sisters and Etienne's wife making certain that the spirit women get all they need. The table is piled with stacks of cassava bread, plantains, tamales, sweet potato pudding, fruits and cakes and coconut candies. Plenty of wine and rum and soda pop, and out by the fire hot pots of pumpkin and rice and platters of fish and crab. Banana leaves are used for plates, or the stiff pieces of cassava, people standing or sitting anywhere for the feasting. The afflicted are shaken in their hammocks and made to rise and eat and the spirits are said to be enjoying themselves. The shaman smokes a cigar in her chamber and directs the lesser ministrants in the preparation of food to be tossed in the sea, this for the wandering souls of the sand beach, those who will not enter the house. In this quiet community of the ceremonial, the tired sleep where they lay, or go home for a while. Much of the food is divided between the fishermen, the dancers and the drummers and a good portion is left out in the temple for the remainder of the night. Reese eats alone on the beach and sits sleepily smoking, the surf sound and the settlement all winding down.

He wakes to see Simmons squatting beside him. He sits up and takes the warm bowl in both hands, sips a salty broth and with his fingers picks out a sliver of meat. Chicken soup. "Tankenebo," he says, and lies back down on the sand.

When he wakes again the moon is gone and he is chilled, the dawn he feels not far off, and he trudges up the bank. A few candles are flickering in the house and still bodies lie about the ground. The lamps are down as he passes but inside he can see an old man in motion, dancing in a drumless void.

Three miles up the river in a shallow slough a pair of manatees lie resting side by side in the dark, flipper tips in soft mud, both backs at the surface like long, leather shields. Alone in the Moho for days, the young, pregnant cow chanced to meet another single female the day before and they have spent much of the night grazing together on weeds and hyacinths in a rich vegetable bed farther upriver. They are touching each other already as the younger one stirs; her companion bumps her back and a friendly game of jostling and pushing ensues, their tremendous weight and perfect buoyancy translating in this contact to a kind of harmless water wrestling wherein no one is pinned and no one wins but the immediate area is kicked and stirred to a swirling sandiness and first one and then the other scoots out into the depth of the moving stream. Hanging there in the dark they breathe and sink, touching the bottom and each other and then beginning to drift with the current, floating like islands of tissue and air toward the sea.

He has gone directly there. And now he sees materializing trees, the light seeping from the sky into the reaching leaves and skimming the river's dark surface, his tired eyes burning, his strategy to coincide with a morning high tide, when the mouth and the bay more deeply meet. A good time to exit. Or maybe they already left—yesterday, last night or last week. Maybe they're miles ahead, or going under him right now. He doesn't know why but he feels they are still here. One, two, a dozen perhaps. He reaches down and cups the cool river up to his face, rubs it in his weary eyes and keeps paddling, stroking hard to come alive, to send blood rushing to the muscle systems and to his cloudy brain. He knows his prey is here; he's taking himself to it, putting himself in position.

The birds of the morning squelch all other sounds. Trills and peeps and every register of whistle. He is covered in a sheen of sweat and the flies are finding him; he shakes them off his face and lets them have the rest. It seems he can feel the dent of scar like a fish hook in the skin of his forehead.

He pauses at the Bulge, standing to hold a limb with his arm overhead, studying the passive flow, checking the eddies, rubbing his eyes. Webs on his head, a thin-bodied green spider on his arm. Glances at his weapon. Wonders about waiting here or going on. No coffee and no tobacco. No sleeping in the boat. He goes on. Mind over matter. Keep a method in your madness.

Standing, looking ahead, glancing behind. Would he chase one to the sea? He looks down into the cut water of his oar stroke and he cannot yet see below the surface. Bits of waterweed cling to his paddle. Strands of plants uprooted. And this clue lodges in his predator head.

Shirtless now, no bandana, no hat, no food, no water. He swings into the main current and kneels around his throwing stick and drinks straight from the source, slurping pure Moho to slake his after-Style thirst while his eyes scan the coming stream even as it is turning him, wanting to push him away.

The two cows are traveling downstream, basking in patches of surface sunlight, not feeding now but frolicking as they go, nudging and rolling, the older one now and again diving and shooting ahead in a burst of speed with the other following right behind, chasing the tail ahead of her and catching it, biting the fluke playfully or grasping at its base with her flippers and resting her face on her companion's back as if she only wants an affectionate ride.

Secured in the shade at the edge of the Bend, he sees them coming, two of them together in the middle of the stream. He takes up his spear and spreads his feet and stands waiting, his body shifting and swaying with the motions of the boat, his hands gripping the smooth wood of the staff while he watches them enter the broad, sunny heart of this place. Barely below the surface and still upstream they appear quite round, as spheroid as blown-up bags dumped in the river, benign and bloated targets just floating by. As they approach they seem to lengthen, becoming more streamlined, huge and tubular and tapering at both ends, small heads downward, tails spatulate and rounded like a beaver's. Together and slowly passing ten yards away they are in his eyes a great unmissable mass. With his throwing arm cocking and his other gently lifting in front he is balanced and ready and thinking: When they breathe their vision shifts upward to the surface world. Throw it now.

The harpoon in its flat arc flies from the dugout as he

staggers and crouches and sits heavily in the bottom and tries to see his shot. A shot thrown so well at the entire target that its point descends between the two, rakes down the far side of the nearest and gouges into the belly of the farthest, tearing superficially through the skin and outer fat and sinking still, the shaft slipping down and the lines over the back of the near cow as they both explode into motion, diving and kicking in opposite directions, the water roiling above their maneuvers and turmoil as they plow about the area in panic, running back upstream and then down, acting independently but finding each other again in bursts along the bottom, squealing some and swimming as rapidly and deeply and as far without air as they are able. Reese holds his weapon's line and stares after them and knows they are gone.

The sun rises well over the treeline and spreads across the water's surface to the dugout's stern. The man continues to wait and hope, staring upriver despondent and confused, damning his luck and doubting his motives. Hot and hungry and thinking of recharging down there in the cool current but needing to stay up here, aboard and alert. He cannot get them out of his mind or divide himself from them. His obsession amounts to an odd apotheosis, the animal's image having become something like a deity floating inside his mind. Killing one would be a massive act and an accomplishment, capturing the fat of the land—what once moved on land—to present to the citizens of his temporary home, this adopted place where he thinks he could be coming to a new self. A gift of flesh and bone for Barbara and Simmons and Uncle Thunder. And for himself, what, an inverted and perverse resurrection?

The shadow of a fish hawk skims across the prow and the shaft of the weapon, running flat over the water and up into green in a disintegrating instant. A trail of bubbles down the channel and dissecting the water plane into which the man is staring, slow-blinking like a stricken turtle, and turning his head to follow the trail upriver where a long and faint broken line is floating out. He stands to look, glances down into the boat; the staff line is tied to the forward seat board, the spearhead line is tied to the bow line above its carved hole. He squats and picks up the harpoon. Searching the length of the surface trail he spots an object among the bubbles and leaning over the gunnel waits for its arrival. Greenish brown like a spoiled sausage or a water-logged dog biscuit and he sees several more of these solids coming down the line.

Up around the bend the star-scarred bull is lolling at the bottom, well-fed and heartbeat slowed, resting on his travels after days of river gorging. Rubbing his back on a sunken log and hearing nothing much but his own rumblings. Excrement expelled and methane rising. He rights himself and lifts without effort, floating up like an airship, gaseous and dun-colored. His nostrils bust the surface with a loud chuffing sound.

To Reese the noise is like a canister popped open under pressure. In another minute he sees the beast coming into his view, a dark shape under the sunlight, bigger than the others, like a long brown balloon threatening to rise into the air.

The force of the throw sinks the ivory deep into the animal's upper back and sends the man wobbling to his knees, hands gripping both gunnels for balance. The animal turns crosscurrent at the sharp impact and flukes away with powerful strokes, shocked and frightened and heading back the way it came. Reese is watching the long stick waggling from its back as the manatee gains speed and reaches the extent of one line and hardly pauses as the staff is jerked loose. Feeling the hook snag and the stress mounting in the delirium of its flight, the animal surges ahead and the boat is pulled forward as the hook line slides up the bowline and that line begins to slide and rip down the length of its tree limb, shredding leaves into the water.

He realizes his mistake, his depending on the bow line's tree limb anchor against the manatee's power, and now he imagines the limb breaking and the line ripping free, its weakened knot sliding to meet the next knot and failing under pressure.

Down below, the barb has torn into lung and holds the

membrane. The bull feels the internal pulling and slows in surprise against the resistance. The pressure relents and he must breathe now, his heart pumping hard as he rises for air, chuffs loudly, and drops to the bottom again, squeaking in agitation, blood flowing from his back wound.

The triangulated point of the stretched bow line goes slack, and Reese waits for a moment, then leans forward and tugs the line, pulls the boat toward the point of attachment with the harpoon line. He means to seize this chance to attach the line directly to the boat. The knot draws closer and then he has it in his hands as he glances at the calm surface—at the spot where his line disappears—for any movement this tugging may trigger. He struggles with the lines but his constrictor knot is too tight now to loosen by hand. He withdraws his knife and cuts the harpoon line at the base of the knot, drops the knife in the boat, quickly ties the line in a half hitch around his wrist as a temporary hold, and moves his hands to the bow hole to make space to reattach it there.

As Reese bends forward, the confused animal comes up beside the dugout, bumps it with a flipper; the vessel rocks toward the shore and the man pitches sideways. He tries to right himself in the other direction, his hand pushes down on the gunnel, and his momentum sends him overboard, one hand grabbing the side of the boat as he splashes into the river. His knife and the other bone point tumble out of the tipping boat and vanish below him.

The startled manatee flukes toward the center current as Reese gets both hands on the gunnel. His left hand jumps off abruptly, violently straightening his arm and wrenching his shoulder. He slides by the other hand to the bow point with the dugout moving too.

A line from manatee to man as his hand eases down the turning boat to the stern and he sees the bow line taut to the tree limb. A sequence of links and one must break, the hook freeing or a line snapping or his trembling arm out of its socket. The frightened animal pulls toward freedom, separates the man from the boat and tows this lesser resistance behind a steady red stream leaking from its punctured organ.

Fleeing in chaotic fear, the animal swims relentlessly and hits the bottom frequently, leaving silt clouds in its silent wake, heartbeat accelerating and shock like a cancer spreading. Reese in his own panic dragged under by his torn shoulder and constricted wrist, struggles to the surface and catches his air whenever the manatee turns and slows in its course, not knowing where he is headed and scared that he will be pulled out to sea, the thought of being trolled across the bay an unnatural horror. With one arm thrashing he tries to move toward shore to snag his line. Needing air too quickly in this rush of water and going against the current he suddenly realizes his true and upriver Moho journey, thinking one solution on top of another, how if he rides it out the thing will stop and the river will return him no matter how far he goes and he will swim back with one arm. Shedding its blood the animal must sometime die. It drags him backward by the hand and his other strains for the knot. Just a second of slackness and he can pull it loose.

As his fingertips reach out a submerged branch jabs into his neck and snaps off and he feels the piece there and the blood flowing under his jawbone and his mouth working and swallowing and taking in a wet breath. He goes under for a final sounding, down in the darker flow of his sirenian steward and his mind plays a flickering image of a girl while his strength seeps away and his oxygen is coughed out and the current turns a grainy gray, then white, and some kind of sonic texture runs through his nerves and darkness becomes the portal into which he can breathe. A mind of sounds, not words, like notes from a screaming box of strings, guitars growling electric and pure distortion, all harmony gone and vision static ceasing.

TEN

The sky is in halves over the bay, the lower side an eastern storm reaching for the village, thick gray swirls leading a slate-blue mass and its upper edge a clean line above which a far, fair blue firmament seems the very dome of space. An early darkness falling and a change of drummers, another three of the nine are starting their shift, keeping the rhythms strong.

Simmons walks down to the beach and stands watching the sky and the water and then moves along to the dock and goes out to the end looking south toward the mouth of the Moho. He takes the westerly path past the school and veers over to the river, Zino following close behind. He stands on the bank listening and waiting while the dog peers cautiously into the tall grasses beside the trail, his head out of sight. The old man lights a cigarette and with it held in his mouth lowers himself by the roots down the bank and walks out on the shoal and the dog scampers down and into the water also. Simmons cups the cigarette behind his back, squinting upriver. "Zino," he says, and the dog glances up at him. "Is that boy comin home?" The dog is staring into the darkness upstream. "You can't smell him, can you?" the man says. "You don't hear him."

The rain washes over the land in hard, windswept sheets and some of the spectators take shelter in homes and the rest crowd together in the ancestor house until the system has left the sea and the coast and gone shuddering westward. The fire is restarted with kerosene and the dancing resumes with all its dramatic intent and the celebration soon resembles quite closely the one of the previous evening.

Barbara leaves her hammock and stands among the people watching; she makes her way slowly to the table in front of the drummers and pours herself a glass of rum and smiles at the men while their pounding jumps at her skin and thumps all around her racing heart, the drums in perfect time, all hands flying like pistons, the eyes of the men closing in the music and the work and the sweat soaking through their headscarves and falling from their faces. She downs the glass and pours another and doesn't care who frowns; her pains are departing, the intervals between bouts grown longer and longer until now she feels her next life beginning. Her fifth, she reckons. A childhood, a lunatic youth, a settling, a sickness, and now this one. She wants to dance but fears she might pick up a spirit. After one more drink she goes ahead, joining the group moving around the room. A man says as she passes, "Catch one, girl," and she says, "I got my own," hopping and dipping and following the path of the dance, passing the doors and windows and those lining the walls, the faces at the edge of the light and those beyond it. Several times around she goes, shaking and stepping with the drums, examining the people.

"My friend," she says at a side window, "have you seen my friend?" And as the woman in front of her leaves the circle, she leaves too, not possessed but just walking and talking, asking people, "Where is my friend? Have you seen Reese?"

She moves outside through the crowd gathered there and encounters Simmons and asks him these same questions. When he does not answer she takes the bottle from his hand and drinks. A woman nearby tells her to go back inside and she says, "Nobody rules me," and Simmons takes his bottle from her and points into the temple and she goes back inside.

The woman dancing free-form is the younger sister of Etienne; she beckons to Barbara and says, "Be still, little sister," in a voice not her own, but one known at once to belong to the guest of honor, Thunder, her dead father. "You are not crazy," the voice says. "Come in here and be humble, my willful niece." And when she steps forward to face her contorting cousin, the dancing ceases and only one drum delivers its calm heartbeat.

"Listen to your elders," he says, as his messenger moves back into the center, her eyes closed and her arms held close and crossed over her chest and the message she carries for all to hear. "Be generous, my friends. Do not go about trickin your neighbors. Do not deceive the family." His laugh is harsh and cruel-sounding. "Oh, you must be attentive to us, the dead ones. You do not want to invite trouble and see my bad side." He laughs again. "Look at Sophie," he says, and she bows her head. "Look at my own son. They tried to forget me but now they think of me more often." There is silence in the temple and only the fire popping and the whispering voice of the sea can be heard. "Keep the memories of our people." The messenger stamps her foot toward the entrance. "Don't be so sexy, you children," and a few titters are heard out there. "Read your books," he tells them, "but keep the traditional cures. Draw close on the occasions of death. The ancestors can keep you together." He sighs; she shudders. "Be decent." And after a long pause, "Bring me rum and rock candy."

The signs are good, the night clear. There is much more dancing and drum-song-singing and from time to time a spirit speaking, the speeches warm and witty, reproving or amusing. Late in the night the two hogs are sacrificed, stunned with a club and cut—the shaman catches the blood in a bowl as it falls from the throat—and butchered beyond the fire. With this the feasting begins. Chicken and fish and beans, bread and eggs and tomatoes and pork. Hog blood boiled with water and lard-fried with salt, onion and pepper to make a pudding treat for the spirits. People blessing each other, laughing and crying and eating as one. Simmons with his children and grandchildren, all of them hugging and his old wife kissing him hotly. All bitterness abated, the offerings accepted and the ancestors pleased and a great happiness real and binding among these members of a far-flung community.

In the morning Simmons returns to the dock searching and then to the river and after bailing the dugout there sets off upstream, paddling through a hovering mist with Zino at the bow, front paws up and leaning like a mascot into the hazy air ahead. The water somewhat swift to the old man, its current slightly swollen and opaque, and he is the one panting, unable to recall his last trip this way and feeling his age and his personal solitude, even as the final day of the dugu is starting.

In the lifting mist he sees his own canoe appearing and then the shaft floating out behind it in the stream. With the dog growling he slides alongside and holds the other boat to examine its contents, the long paddle, the shirt wadded in the bottom water. He sits for a few minutes looking upriver while the dog sniffs at the abandoned boat, then shoves off and continues onward.

He travels inland for nearly an hour more but does not find anything that might make him anxious to go farther, and so he swings around and returns easily in the current, dipping his oar for direction and resting as he goes. He pauses in the shade where his old boat is held, stands with his knife and examines the section of stripped limb, the hard knot, then cuts the bow line below it; he sits drifting, tying the line to his stern, and then straightens the canoes and strokes for home.

Three days later most of the visitors have gone and the village is as quiet and small as usual. Under the afternoon's cloudy sky a ceremony is occurring in the unkempt cemetery. There is a shallow hole in the ground and several items piled next to it, and Zino is sniffing at the smells remaining. The attendees each offer acts of remembrance, Barbara kneeling and hooking together a necklace of lures, placing the folded bandana at the bottom of the hole and a ring of feathery jigs and shiny spoons and painted plugs on top of it. "We can only bury the baits," she says, and with her hands pushes the dirt into this small semblance of a grave and pats it down firmly. Sophie squats beside her and plants an oval chunk of jasper upright into the spot, and seeing her daughter's tears, begins to cry herself. Simmons is holding a flat white stone, reading the inscription he has scratched into it, and he squats between them and presses this marker into the soft earth.

"A man takin a long trip will get thirsty," he says, and tipping his bottle sprinkles Style over the dirt and the markers, and then stands and drinks some himself. The women stand too and the bottle is passed around and they all remain a moment over the grave.

Fellowman Reese
1961-1992
Drowned Moho River

As the women are moving away, Simmons squats again and says, "I'll be comin around for a next one." He stands and walks and the dog comes crashing out of the weeds.

About seven miles inland a Kekchi man and his eldest son are on a jungle trail near the river, checking their snares and collecting herbs and bark as they travel toward home. The boy carries an armadillo by its tail and the man has a pouch woven of grass hanging at his back. He is not much bigger than the boy and together they move like fleet shadows through the forest familiar. The boy follows a set of paca tracks to the riverbank and stands above the flow, as still and watchful as a snake. Downstream a pool is seen and something in it, and he edges along the slope to better his view. He whistles his call and the man comes to stand behind him. They see below the surface what looks to be man and manatee and the boy wants to descend. His father waits and watches, with the rain and the natural thunder beginning then, and nothing more troubling to be seen.

About the Author

Michael Jarvis is the author of the novel *Field of Vision*.
He lives in Miami, Florida, scouting locations for various film projects and writing fiction.

www.michaeljarvis.net